I0847262

THE NEW KING

Also by Nathan Shore

The Blue Flame

NATHAN SHORE

THE NEW KING

BARQUE
POINT PRESS

Published 2026

ISBN: 979-8-9868807-5-4 (Hardcover)
         979-8-9868807-6-1 (Paperback)
         979-8-9868807-7-8 (e-Book)

Library of Congress Control Number: 2025926303

Book jacket design by Onur Burc

Printed in the United States of America

Barque Point Press, LLC
Saint Paul, Minnesota
c/o Nathan Shore
nathan@barquepointpress.com

www.barquepointpress.com

Prologue

The crack of a rifle shot shattered the stillness of a Michigan summer night. A young woman stumbled at the roar, collapsing headfirst into the forest floor. Cowering against a dense bed of rotting leaves and fallen pine needles coating the ground, she bit her hand to keep from screaming. Overhead, tall stands of white cedar, red maple, and quaking aspen trees sheltered her from the moonlight bathing the island in a silver radiance. She raised her head and wiped away a greasy layer of slime coating her mouth with the back of her hand. The girl inched upwards on her elbows, focusing on her surroundings. A faint rumble of lapping waves in the distance offered her a chance at salvation.

She stood and ran blind across the uneven ground towards the crashing surf. Fallen twigs and sharp stones bit into her bare soles, but she refused to let the pain slow her progress. Her hands clutched the sole object she'd managed to seize before her escape—a twin-sized bedsheet that offered her bruised figure the faintest protection against the chill of the night.

A second shot rang out, pulverizing the brittle remnants of a dead birch branch suspended overhead. Splinters of wood rained over the girl as she again lost her footing and slipped sideways down a narrow ravine. She tumbled end over end until a boulder at the base of the hill arrested her fall. A twisted ankle sent spasms of electric pain coursing through her body. She had no time to tend the injury; they were close behind her. Through a clearing ahead, the silhouette of a narrow dock jutting into the dark water hovered beyond. The lunar glow overhead illuminated her path forward.

The girl scrambled to her feet, losing her grip on the stark-white bedsheet and its scant protection against the elements. It caught the wind, billowing upward and shimmering in the moonlight until a high-velocity slug pierced the fabric. The sheet wrapped itself around a cedar branch and hung useless a dozen feet overhead. Naked, the girl limped towards the water's edge as her blonde hair streamed behind her. She heaved with winded breath from the half-mile dash away from the compound as she alighted on the dock, her footsteps producing hollow thuds as she traversed the weathered decking. She halted midway across, unsure which way to turn. Far across the pitch-black water, a rotating radio-tower beacon flickered on the mainland.

"It didn't have to be this way, BreAnn!" a hoarse male voice shouted from within the cloak of the darkened woods.

"You can come on back. We'll forget all this ever happened," a second voice, that of a woman, echoed.

BreAnn knew they were lying. She'd made the mistake of trusting them once already. The girl looked straight ahead, filled her lungs with air, and hobbled towards the dock's terminus. She pushed off the edge with her uninjured leg, extended her arms overhead, and broke the water's surface in a shallow dive that plunged her into the dark water.

The chill of Lake Michigan knocked the breath out of her. Rising to the surface, BreAnn gasped in lungfuls of fresh air to clear her head. The renewed sight of the beacon in the distance oriented her towards her goal. She commenced a vigorous breaststroke as a pair of bullets entered the water on either side of her. The slugs produced spumes of water that crested in the night. BreAnn glided forward as the stocky figure on the dock gripped a bolt-action hunting rifle while sizing her up for another shot. A ponytailed woman in a fleece vest stood beside him. A third figure—tall, thin, and loose—wearing camouflage trousers approached the pair from behind. A lit Marlboro clamped between his lips glowed orange in the darkness.

"Hand your weapon over, private," the approaching figure hissed through his teeth.

"The waves mess with your aim," the stocky man said as he flipped the safety on the Remington 700 rifle and turned it over to their companion.

"Let me show you how it's done, Clint," the rangy man said. He discharged an empty shell from the ejection port and chambered a fresh 7mm round. Cradling the cigarette between the ring and middle fingers of his left hand, he stepped forward, disengaged the safety, and raised the rifle to his shoulder. An ear-splitting boom filled the air, drowning out the scream from the waters beyond. The man returned the Marlboro to his lips and hoisted the rifle over his left shoulder.

"This is your mess, you clean it up," the woman said to Clint as she turned her back to the water and headed towards shore.

Clint wiped away the sweat plastering his brow with a hand. "You didn't say nothing about killing anyone, Lisa."

Lisa stopped. "There's loads I've never told you about this life. You sure you want to know?"

"Nah," Clint said and spat on the dock.

"Then get the boat. I'm going back to bed."

A hundred yards beyond, the girl dangled in the current.

The rotating red beacon beckoned in the distance. She glued her eyes to its pulsing crimson glow until the water and air mingled as one as she lapsed into unconsciousness.

PART I

Chapter 1

BEN HIRSCH SAW NO END in sight to their demands. A new notice of a payment deadline on a past-due account surfaced each day, threatening to send him to collections. Hirsch scrolled through the stream of emails cluttering his inbox as the service-station pump in Shingleton ran up an ever-increasing tally of funds he didn't have.

Nine hundred dollars to the Escanaba auto glass shop that replaced the shot-out windows of his 2006 Toyota Tacoma.

Fifteen hundred dollars to a Sault Ste. Marie dental clinic for a crown to cap a cracked molar that sent piercing spasms of agony through his jaw with every sip of cold water.

One thousand dollars to a local plumber to repair a burst water line in his basement. Naturally, the corroded iron pipe gave way on a holiday weekend resulting in a double charge for the plumber's after-hours services.

A late-payment reminder from Bank of America warning him the monthly minimum payment on his six-thousand-dollar credit card bill was three weeks overdue and threatening to cancel his last credit card if he didn't pay up immediately.

The latest insult was an eight-hundred-dollar bill from Michigan's attorney disciplinary board asserting that Hirsch still owed costs and fees related to his disbarment from the practice of law earlier that year. Those bastards had already taken him for ten large—now they were coming after the scraps. His $14.50-an-hour job inspecting gas lines for the utility company barely covered his basic living expenses. That gig would end in a few short months when the snow hit. He fought the urge to fling his phone onto the highway and let a passing eighteen-wheeler pulverize it.

Hirsch had no time to worry about creditors nipping at his heels. He was running late for an important meeting. He pocketed his phone, returned the nozzle to the pump, and hopped into his battered truck to finish the drive to Marquette along Michigan Highway 28. Lake Superior emerged as a blue ribbon along the horizon as Hirsch entered downtown Munising. Motorhomes piloted by preoccupied tourists clotted the roadway, rendering the standard forty-five-minute drive from Manistique into a nerve-taxing hour-long odyssey. Impatient to reach his destination another forty-odd miles beyond, Hirsch cruised through downtown Munising at ten miles over the speed limit. He risked a hefty fine but feared delaying his 9:30 A.M. rendezvous with Catherine Winslow—Marquette's wealthiest woman.

His upcoming meeting filled him with trepidation. Hirsch's entanglement weeks earlier with Catherine's brothers, Lionel and Marcus Shaw, had led to one's death while the other recovered from a crushed spinal cord in a Green Bay hospital under the watchful eye of a sheriff's deputy stationed outside his door. Catherine Winslow was the last person Hirsch had expected to hear from—at least to request his assistance.

The seemingly limitless inland sea, known as *Gichigami-ing* by Hirsch's maternal Ojibwa ancestors, remained his starboard-side companion for much of the remaining journey. He'd left Manistique after a frenzied forty-eight hours during which he'd begged for yet another leave from his gas-company job; reconciled with his on-again, off-again girlfriend, Lauren; and spent the early hours of the morning balanced on a wooden ladder while reattaching an aluminum gutter that had been ripped free from his decaying Victorian home by an overnight storm.

At five minutes to 9:30, he roared into the outskirts of Marquette and headed for the high bluffs overlooking the lake. He passed through downtown along Front Street, hardly glancing at the historic ore dock with its patina of rust jutting out into harbor or the limestone-clad Landmark Hotel, to which he'd promised to take Lauren for a weekend respite from their mundane jobs. He turned right on Ridge Street and slowed to twenty-five. The staid residential neighborhood of historic homes demanded a modicum of restraint.

The Winslows and their peers had spent decades plundering the U.P.'s natural resources and exploiting the immigrants, Natives, and desperate jobseekers who labored for a pittance under their yoke. Most robber barons had long since absconded to warmer climes further south with scant consideration for the environmental destruction and human suffering left in their wake. In contrast, the Winslow family—descended from patriarch and copper mining baron C. F. Winslow—remained in Marquette and continued to manage the family's ample timber and land holdings from their ancestral home. Hirsch parked alongside the curb fronting the three-story, Georgian brick mansion built by C. F. Winslow in the 1890s and passed down from one generation of Winslow overlords to another. Its present owners were C.F.'s great-grandson, Herbert Milford Winslow, and his wife, Catherine.

Hirsch stepped out of his truck into the cool morning. A soft, easterly breeze wafting off Lake Superior bathed the neighborhood. A gray-haired matron wearing a tweed skirt and leading a Pekinese on a leash walked by, glowering with disdain at the interloper whose scratched and dented vehicle featured Peninsula Energy Company decals on either door. Hirsch regretted not parking the mess down the block and concealing it from the prying eyes of the patrician neighbors. As Hirsch ignored the matron's icy stare and walked towards the Winslows' front door, the vibration of his phone in his trouser pocket alerted him to a text message. He paused to retrieve it, and his heart jumped into his throat as he opened a message from Lauren featuring a mirror selfie of her clad only in a powder-blue thong and white knee-high socks with her ass pointing towards the mirror. Below the picture were the words: "Come home quick bby. I'll be waiting for u."

Hirsch swallowed hard and returned the phone to his pocket, doing his utmost to focus on the mission at hand. As a concession to his hosts' standing in the community, he wore a white dress shirt, a light-gray Banana Republic summer-weight sport coat, and a dark-green tie that complemented the broad maple leaves sheltering the Winslows immaculately maintained lawn. Hirsch owned a closetful of suits and dress clothes from his years spent practicing law in Lansing, but he rarely found an opportunity to wear them in the U.P.'s relaxed atmosphere.

He pressed the doorbell, and the chime echoed through the house. A man in his early fifties, clad in a linen suit, two-toned saddle shoes, and a narrow red tie decorated with miniature hummingbirds opened the door. A graying flop of blond hair fell across the close-shaved sides of his head, giving him a boyish quality despite his age.

"You must be Mr. Hirsch," the man said, squinting at the visitor through round, white horn-rimmed glasses. Hirsch's interlocutor looked more suited to an art gallery opening than a Midwest city on the fringes of American civilization. "Follow me, please. Mrs. Winslow is expecting you." He stood aside for Hirsch to enter.

Hirsch stepped inside the cavernous vestibule. Its vault extended three stories above to the ornamental plaster ceiling overhead. A crystal chandelier retrofitted with electric bulbs dangled from a wire.

"This way." The man beckoned him though another set of doors and into a wood-paneled hallway, leaving Hirsch little time to admire the trappings of the Winslows' home. The footfalls of Hirsch's leather-soled oxfords echoed across the gleaming black-and-white marble floor before they turned towards a salon decorated with ample plush seating and fringed with antique furniture likely worth more than all of Hirsch's worldly possessions combined. The décor was fussy but undeniably tasteful.

A woman with ramrod straight posture occupied a Louis XIV chair and was reading from a leatherbound book. She sported a coral-hued skirt with matching blazer and wore her dark blonde hair loose so it fell about her shoulder in soft curls. Though a dozen years Hirsch's senior, Catherine Winslow appeared younger than him.

"Mr. Hirsch, ma'am," the man said as they paused inside the salon's threshold.

"Thank you, Winston," she said while closing the volume with delicate, manicured hands and setting it aside on a table adjacent to her chair. *Collected Poems of Stéphane Mallarmé* the gilt-lettering on the spine read. "Would you kindly give us the room. I'll ring if we need anything."

"Certainly, ma'am," Winston said, executing a comically stiff bow before drawing together two pocket doors to close off the salon.

"Thank you for coming, Mr. Hirsch," Catherine said as she stood and offered him a downturned hand. Hirsch wasn't sure if she expected him to kiss her hand, but he decided against it.

"It's nothing. Sorry I ran a few minutes late," he said

while shaking her hand.

"Don't give it another thought," she said and moved towards a long wooden sideboard. "I was lost in my poems, as usual, and hardly noticed the time pass. I studied French literature in college and adore it to this day. Thank heavens I had the sense to attend Ann Arbor for my MBA, though. Who knows where I might be otherwise. *Lisez-vous le francais, Monsieur Hirsch?*"

"Er . . . *non*," he replied, shaking his head. "My dad's parents came from Montreal and spoke it, but they quit after immigrating to America. The usual story, I suppose."

"A shame. It's a gorgeous language. I find I can express myself in a freer manner." Catherine selected a cut-crystal double-old-fashioned glass from atop the sideboard and uncorked a green-labeled bottle of Michter's Straight Rye. "I'm told you prefer whiskey, Mr. Hirsch. Any ice?"

"Well, it's a little early yet for me, and—"

"Here," she said, pouring two fingers into the glass and handing it to him. Hirsch's relationship with alcohol had caused him no shortage of trouble. He strove—with mixed results—to place guardrails on it whenever possible. Day drinking didn't help.

"Please sit," Catherine said, motioning towards a red-velvet Louis Philippe sofa on the other side of the room stationed beneath a series of oversized sash windows that offered expansive views of Lake Superior.

They sat, and Hirsch sipped the whiskey out of politeness. The amber liquor was of higher quality than his usual blue-collar Canadian whiskey. The smooth, satisfying burn as it slid down his throat warmed his body. He placed the glass atop a ceramic coaster resting on a Chippendale coffee table polished to a mirror-like finish.

"I imagine you're surprised I reached out to you," she said.

"Well . . . yes. I mean, it's just with everything that happened and all—"

"Let's not beat around the bush, Mr. Hirsch."

"It's Ben. You can call me Ben if you like." Catherine's penchant for referring to him by his last name evoked his days in law practice, resurrecting unpleasant memories of being dressed down by cranky judges.

"Very well, then, Ben it is. As I was saying, we both know very well what happened. I know you killed Marcus at his cabin. Mind you, I can't prove you did it and neither can the authorities—believe me, I inquired. But what's done is done. Let's face it, Marc made poor choices in life, cooking meth the least of them. He was my baby brother, and though I can't forgive you for what you did to him, I see little purpose in persecuting you either. Now, as for Lionel, good grief, what really can we say? He's the most vengeful of us siblings, and he must bear the consequences for his actions, I'm afraid. Does that about sum up where we stand, Mr. Hirsch?"

"Ben, please, Mrs. Winslow. No offense, but I still don't know why I'm here."

Catherine folded her hands in her lap before replying. "Yes, well, as I said on the phone, I need your help."

"With . . ."

"Our daughter, Alexandra. She's fallen in with the wrong sort, it seems."

"Drugs?"

Catherine sighed. "If only it were that simple. There are any number of clinics we could send her to for treatment. I'm afraid it's more serious than that." She leaned towards him and fixed her steely-blue eyes on his. Lowering her voice, she continued, "Alex started college at Stanford University last fall. While I preferred that she attend my alma mater in Ann Arbor, she wanted to do her own thing. Mind you, Alex is smart as a whip, and headstrong too. Once she had it in her mind to go to California, well, we couldn't refuse her. Besides, Alex struggled to make friends here. We hoped a change of scenery might help.

"All seemed to be going according to plan. She made decent grades her first semester and got on well with her classmates. The problems began when she returned to school after winter break. You see, there was this group. She got involved with them and matters went downhill in a hurry."

"What type of group?"

"Ben, does the name James Strang mean anything to you?"

"King Strang?" Hirsch replied, referencing the nineteenth-century leader of a breakaway Mormon sect who established a kingdom of sorts on Lake Michigan's Beaver Island. Hirsch was vaguely aware of Strang's murder and the forceful eviction of his followers from the island.

"The same," Catherine said. "I confess I wasn't all that familiar with James Strang before these troubles with Alex began, but what I've learned deeply concerns me."

"I'm sorry, ma'am, but what exactly does some crackpot who lived two centuries ago have to do with your daughter?"

"It seems the ringleader of this group, a university professor, fancies himself Strang's successor. He's recruited around fifty followers already, Alex included."

"Is your daughter still in California?" Hirsch asked. With it being early August, school had been out for nearly three months.

"No, that's the rub, you see. A month before she was set to finish spring semester, the university informed us that Alex had withdrawn from all her courses and vacated the dorm. She abandoned nearly everything she owned. They wanted us to come clean it out. We've learned that she and several others followed their leader to Beaver Island. That was over two months ago—it's the last we heard of her."

"Is Alexandra religious?"

"Not exactly. She experienced what Herb and I called her 'God moment' as a junior in high school. It mostly involved her reading the Bible and leading bake sales at the Episcopalian church. Harmless, really. We thought she'd grown out of it by the time she graduated. Seems we were wrong."

"So who's this guy claiming to be James Strang's successor?"

Catherine crossed her legs and leaned into the sofa with steepled fingers. "He calls himself King Strang the Second, but his real name is Jonathan Teller. He's around forty-five and taught mathematics at Stanford before resigning at the end of fall semester. Brillant, undoubtedly, but delusional."

"What does the LDS church think of all this?"

"It's quite simple—they regard him as a crank and an embarrassment, no different than how the church's founders viewed James·Strang after the schism."

"But even cranks can be dangerous," Hirsch said.

"Precisely. They're quite active on campuses around the country, not only at Stanford. From what I've gathered, the Strangites are even recruiting right here in Michigan."

"What, exactly, are this Teller and his followers doing on Beaver Island?" Catherine's story piqued Hirsch's interest, and he sipped from the glass of rye.

"Why, they have every intention of reestablishing the kingdom of God on Beaver Island," Catherine replied, as if the notion were the most obvious thing in the world.

"And just how do they plan on achieving that?"

"Teller owns close to three hundred acres of land on the island. He and his followers have set up camp and are developing the compound as we speak."

"It sounds like you've done your research on this already. Have you hired a PI or something?" Hirsch asked.

"No, we haven't, but Winston—the gentleman who

showed you in—he's quite adept at research. He's hit a brick wall, unfortunately. That's where you come in, Mr. Hirsch."

"I'm not sure I follow . . ."

Catherine smiled. "My husband and I would like you to go to Beaver Island and locate Alex. Bring her home if it's in your power."

"Why not call the county sheriff and request a wellness check? They do that all the time."

"The police can't promise discretion or confidentiality. We'd as soon keep the Winslow name out of the papers, Ben. Your imbroglio with Lionel and Marcus was enough as it is."

Hirsch exhaled, retrieved the cut-crystal glass, and sucked down about half the remaining rye.

"Any chance she followed a boyfriend or someone close there?"

"No, no boyfriend that we know of. But I really can't think of anyone else she'd follow—apart from this so-called prophet."

"How old is Alexandra, Mrs. Winslow?"

"She turned nineteen three months ago."

"Well, she's an adult now. I'm sure you already know this, but unless she's a danger to herself or others, no one can force her to do anything. Not legally, anyway."

Catherine pressed her palms together and looked out the window. The blue expanse of Lake Superior shimmered beneath the late-morning sun. "Ben, it shouldn't come as a surprise that we vetted you before I called. It's no secret you ran into trouble with the bar for an indiscretion with one of your clients. Setting that aside, it's undisputed that you were an exceptionally talented attorney, outstanding even. I'm told you had a way of convincing even the most skeptical jury to find in your favor. What I mean is—if anyone can convince Alex to come to her senses, leave that dreadful man's little island, and get her life back on track, it's you."

Hirsch blanched at Catherine's allusion to the events that led to his disbarment. Hardly a day passed that he didn't shudder at the personal failures that had resulted in his one-off dalliance with his then-client, Alice Martens. Every calamity that had befallen him since—his divorce, the disbarment, and his entanglement with Catherine's sociopathic brothers—flowed from that singular moment of weakness. His face burned, and he swallowed another slug of rye to mask the shame, leaving the glass empty.

"Okay—but first I'd have to find Alex," Hirsch said. "You know I'm not a detective or a private investigator, right?" he continued, uttering this phrase for the second time in fewer than six months.

"We don't need a PI," Catherine said as she reached towards the coffee table and snatched up Hirsch's empty glass. She refilled it with another couple fingers of Michter's from the sideboard. Hirsch's eyes widened in horror at the prospect of drinking that as well. The last thing he needed was a DUI or worse on his drive home. He leaned back on the plush sofa and ran his fingers through his thick, dark hair. *How the hell do I keep getting myself in these situations?* he wondered.

"Here," Catherine said, handing him the glass. "As I was saying, we have a good idea where Alex is. All Herb and I are asking is that you visit the island and see if you can talk some sense into our girl. I'd say it's the least you can do for our family."

"What makes you think I can waltz right into a cult compound and start asking questions about a follower? I can't imagine a nosey outsider will go over well." Hirsch sipped from the fresh glass of rye. This second dose was already going down easier than it should.

"Prophet Teller's building a movement—a new-world utopia, I've even heard it described. I think it's all foolish nonsense, of course, but you try telling that to the true believers.

Any movement needs new adherents to carry the vision forward, especially a handsome gentleman like yourself who's good with his hands." Catherine took Hirsch's left hand into her grasp and traced the ball of her thumb across his knuckles. Hirsch flushed at Catherine's attention, reluctant to offend her by pulling away.

"It . . . wouldn't be the first time I've pretended to be someone I'm not. The thing is, I work for the gas company. I've already been away most of the past week; I doubt they'd look kindly on my missing more work."

Catherine dropped his hand. "If the issue is money, Herb and I intend to compensate you for your time. Would ten thousand be worth your trouble?" she asked with pursed lips.

Ten thousand dollars was life changing. Ten thousand dollars meant correcting the extensive damage to Hirsch's truck from his run-in with Lionel Shaw. It meant a new air conditioner for his house to combat the summer heat and humidity that left him coated in sweat most nights. It meant getting square with the Michigan Bar. It meant finally getting ahead for once instead of living paycheck-to-paycheck on the paltry gas company compensation.

"Ten thousand dollars?"

"That's right, by check."

"Well, yes . . . yes, I think that would work," he stammered.

"Good," Catherine replied, smiling. "I thought it might whet your appetite. Oh, and as for the gas company, you can leave for Beaver Island this weekend if it suits your work schedule."

Great, another fucking island, Hirsch thought, recalling his ham-fisted attempt to reconnoiter Marcus Shaw's cabin on Big Summer Island with his friend, Edgar Trehearne, and their subsequent night spent in a dilapidated lighthouse on neighboring Poverty Island. Why couldn't these Shaws and

Winslows stick to solid ground?

"I can manage this weekend. I'll have to leave Friday evening to catch the Saturday morning ferry, though."

"Don't be silly, Mr. Hirsch," Catherine said, standing and smoothing out the front of her skirt. Hirsch stood as well, taking the cue that their meeting was concluding. "Our pilot will fly you there. Chris can meet you at 8:00 A.M. sharp at the Manistique airport. Don't be late. You'll have to find your way from the Beaver Island airfield to Teller's land, I'm afraid. It should be easy enough to hitch a ride, though."

"One more question," Hirsch said. "Do you have a picture of Alex I can bring with me? Something recent without a bunch of filters on it."

"Of course. One moment." Catherine paced across the salon to a side table littered with framed family portraits and returned with a formal photograph. "It's Alex's senior photo."

Hirsch accepted the silver-framed image that depicted a young woman from her shoulders up in a third-quarter profile and wearing a yellow top. Alex was smiling with her lips slightly parted. Wavy blonde hair matching her mother's fell around her shoulders, and she regarded the camera with chocolate-brown eyes. A silver nose ring glinted in the sunlight.

"I have a conference call with the university board of trustees in five minutes." Catherine glanced at Hirsch's half-full glass. "Now finish that up. It's far too early for me, but I loathe seeing premium liquor go to waste."

Navigating the Winslows' house would already be a challenge. Nonetheless, Hirsch swallowed his pride and drained the remaining contents before passing the empty tumbler to Catherine, who returned it to the sideboard.

"Winston will escort you to the door," Catherine said and pressed a brass call button on the wall above the sideboard. "I do appreciate your taking the time to come see me today. I know it was unexpected, but if anyone can help us, it's you." She grasped Hirsch's hands and looked into his eyes. "Please bring our daughter home, Ben."

"I'll do my damned best to find her. I don't know if I can convince her to leave, but I'll try."

"Thank you. Our family's well-being is in your hands."

Hirsch didn't have the foggiest clue how to persuade a college dropout to listen to her parents, but he figured little harm could come from trying. Besides, the money was too generous to refuse.

Winston's approaching footsteps clicked against the marble hallway floor. He parted the sliding doors and poked his blond head inside.

"Ma'am?" he asked.

"Winston, would you be so kind as to escort our guest to the entrance? Good day, Mr. Hirsch," Catherine said as she released his hands.

"Follow me," Winston said with a click of his tongue and a jerk of his head.

Hirsch swerved as he trailed Winston's trim figure clipping down the hall in his two-tone shoes.

"You worked for the Winslows long?" Hirsch asked.

"If you consider fifteen years long, then yes, I suppose so."

"They treat you well?"

"I couldn't work anywhere else."

"That good of a job, eh?"

"You'll see what I mean soon enough."

"One more question," Hirsch said as he paused midway down the hall. "Did you ever meet Catherine's brothers?"

"We had our encounters, yes," Winston replied, adjusting the knot of his tie in discomfort.

"Did you ever wonder how on earth she's related to them?"

"It crossed my mind. She's not like them—for the most part."

"For the most part?"

"That's right. Don't underestimate her, you hear me?" Winston said.

"Thanks for the warning." They navigated the marble-floored hallway, where the softest footfalls nonetheless echoed throughout the solemn space.

"Here," Winston said, reaching into his linen suit jacket. He handed Hirsch a check. "This will cover what you and Catherine discussed as your fee."

Hirsch whistled as he examined the figure. He folded the check and slipped it into his pants pocket.

"Come this way. I'll show you out," Winston said, leading the way back to the entrance. He opened the towering wooden door, revealing the Winslows' immaculately kept lawn dotted with maple and chestnut trees. "Here's my card. Please call me if you have any questions or run into any difficulties with your assignment. We won't disturb Mr. or Mrs. Winslow unless absolutely necessary."

Hirsch accepted the cream-colored business card and read the inscription lettered in royal-blue cursive—Winston Maki, Executive Assistant—followed by a phone number and email address. Hirsch fumbled for his wallet and added the card to the empty billfold.

"That's my cell number, and you can reach me any time, day or night—though I'd prefer you not disturb my sleep unless it's a genuine emergency. As Mrs. Winslow said, our pilot, Chris Foster, will meet you at the Schoolcraft County Airport this Saturday at 8:00 A.M. You'll be on Beaver Island within an hour. Here's a map and some information about the island that might be of use," Winston said, handing Hirsch a manila envelope stuffed a half-inch thick. "Also, leave your personal cellphone and ID at home. The less anyone but Alex knows about you and your employers, the better. Take this instead," Winston said, drawing a flip phone from his pocket and offering it to Hirsch. "I've known Alex since she was three years old. She's like a daughter to me. Please save her from these creeps."

Hirsch nodded.

"Good. Best of luck, Mr. Hirsch," Winston said as Hirsch navigated the steps of the Winslows' imposing portico one at a time. He stopped and turned as Winston was midway through shutting the door.

"Is it always this intense working for them?" Hirsch asked.

Winston laughed. "You don't know the half of it," he said, then slammed the door shut.

Chapter 2

THE TWO TUMBLERS OF RYE left Hirsch unsteady on his feet by the time he stumbled away from the Winslows' front door. The humid morning air clung like a damp rag, and he reached for his collar and yanked his tie loose as he trampled towards his truck. An unpleasant sheen of sweat nonetheless spread across his forehead, and he hurried to fire up his truck's air conditioner and blast his face with a jet of cool, dry air.

By the time Hirsch turned left on Front Street, it was obvious he was in no condition to drive. He parked in front of the Peter White Library and ditched his sport coat on the passenger seat. A stroll through town to clear his head was in order. He walked south, dodging pockets of tourists and hoping no one smelled the booze emanating from his pores. A call to the police reporting a drunk native was the last thing he needed. Upon reaching Father Marquette Park, he crossed the street and returned up Front. A solid meal would aid his recovery, and he dove into the Vierling Restaurant. Hirsch polished off a bowl of Whitefish chowder before gobbling an order of beer-battered shrimp with French fries, all washed down with a pitcher of fresh iced tea. While he longed for an extended nap, he had a mid-afternoon date with Lauren at her place in Gladstone. Showing up sweat-drenched and reeking of whiskey wasn't the impression he wanted to leave.

Hirsch returned to his truck and headed home to Manistique. He fed a Merle Haggard CD into the Toyota's stereo and cranked up the volume to stay awake and keep his truck out of the ditch. He lowered the windows, thumped the steering wheel, and sang along to "Sing Me Back Home" and "Silver Wings" as he tore through the Hiawatha National Forest. A hot shower and a fifteen-minute snooze on his couch restored his mood and appearance, and he threw on jeans and an untucked collared shirt before making the forty-five-minute drive to Lauren's one-bedroom Craftsman home in her quiet neighborhood in Gladstone. Lauren taught mathematics at the local high school, but she still spent several evenings a week pulling pints and running orders of grease-laden, mediocre pub fare at Lily's Tavern—a run-down watering hole in Garden Corners established by her grandparents in better times. Its low-life clientele generally annoyed Hirsch, and he limited his visits to when Lauren could use a supportive face.

Lauren answered the door wearing a light-orange sundress. A gold-bar necklace hung a couple inches above her visible cleavage. She wore her dark-blonde hair in a ponytail, exposing her delicate ears—a favorite feature of his.

"Come here, you big fool," she said, grabbing his shirt and pulling him close to her. She devoured him with hungry kisses while tracing her slender fingers through his hair. Hirsch responded with equal vigor and wrapped one hand around her waist while the other caressed the firm flesh of Lauren's rear through the thin fabric of her dress.

"I've been here bored and horny, waiting for you all morning," she purred in his ear.

Hirsch wasted no time rushing her inside the door and closing it with a kick of his heel. They didn't even make it to the bedroom as Lauren clung to him with frenzied scratches at his back while he looped his fingers on her hips and lowered her panties to the ground.

"I want you right here," she said as she undid his pants and laid a hand on his chest, nudging him backwards.

Hirsch lay supine against an oriental rug spread across the hardwood floor while Lauren straddled him and guided him inside her. She rode him, her tempo mirroring the growing intensity of her moans. Hirsch freed her breasts from the top of her sundress and cupped them firm in his palms. An orgasm like a white-hot pulse ripped through him, cleansing his mind of the accumulated worries and tension in his life. She ground against him in concupiscent gyrations until climaxing herself. Lauren rolled off and curled aside him on the rug, their hands joined as they gasped for air and came down from sheer ecstasy. The ceiling fan humming away overhead offered relief from the heat of passion.

"That's exactly what I needed," she said, panting.

"Why can't we do that more often?"

Lauren raised herself on one elbow towards him and smiled. "It'll just make this weekend all the more special when I come over after my shift."

Hirsch had entirely forgotten about their weekend plans when he agreed to the Winslows' mission. "Okay, so I know we talked about maybe driving up to Munising and hiking the Pictured Rocks this weekend . . . There's been a change of plans."

"Why? You get a better offer or something?"

Hirsch laughed. "Hardly, but I got asked to do a job. It'll take me out of town a few days."

"The gas company wants you working weekends now? Assholes."

"It's not them this time. Look, remember that asshole from the bar the first night we met?" Hirsch asked.

Lauren rolled onto her stomach and regarded Hirsch

with a critical gaze.

"You mean the one whose meth lab you burned down and whose brother tried to murder you with his truck?" Hirsch wasn't convinced Lauren had forgiven him for his initial deception in their early days of dating.

"Yeah, so, they have this sister, Catherine, in Marquette who married into the Winslow family. She called a few days ago asking me to meet with her. I didn't know what it was all about, but I met her. Long story short, her daughter's gone missing. She's a college kid but quit school and left campus. Catherine wants me to talk some sense into her and convince her to come home—or try, anyway." Hirsch eschewed the details of being asked to travel to a remote island, infiltrate a cult, and extract a wayward college student from the clutches of its charismatic leader.

"And they asked you? Why? . . . It sounds weird, Ben." Lauren rested her face on her palm.

"I guess Catherine was impressed with how I handled her brothers. I mean, Marcus and Lionel were a royal pain in the ass for who knows how many years. Honestly, that's the only reason I can think of."

"Ben, are you bullshitting me?" Lauren was sitting up now and fitting the top of her sundress back over her shoulders. "If this is some kind of joke or another lie, you might as well grab your shit, get out of here, and never bother me again."

Hirsch raised his hands towards her. "I'm dead serious here, babe. Look, I know it sounds crazy. I should've told them to fuck off and gone on my merry way. I guess I feel like I owe them one after what happened to Catherine's brothers. Besides," Hirsch said, pulling the Winslows' check out of his wallet and holding it up for Lauren, "they're giving me this for my efforts."

Lauren's eyes widened at the amount printed on the

check. "Wow, that's more money than I've ever seen at one time. You'd better not get yourself hurt," she said, tapping his shoulder with a closed fist.

"I know, I know," Hirsch said as he returned the check to his wallet. "Look, I didn't ask for any of this. I never wanted anything to do with the Shaws in the first place. Coming home to the U.P. was the best decision I've made because I met you. But it's been one mess after another since I set foot in town."

Lauren had lain down again alongside Hirsch and stared up at the white beadboard ceiling of her living room.

"Okay, so where are you headed, anyway? I mean—if you can tell me and all."

"It's probably good someone else knows. I'll be on Beaver Island. It's not far from Traverse City. I should only be gone a few days."

"Should I call the police or something if I don't hear from you in a week?"

"That's not going to happen. I'll go, try and convince the kid to leave, and get back home. We'll put all this shit behind us and then I'm finished with these Shaws and their family. Okay?"

"Fine, but this better be the end of it, Ben. Look, you're an amazing guy and I'm really glad I met you, but I don't need more weird crap in my life. I've had about enough to last me a lifetime already. If you spent half your evenings in a place like Lily's having to deal with drunks, abusers, and criminals, you'd know what I mean."

"It's over after I find her, I promise," Hirsch said. He punctuated his statement with a long kiss. Lauren snuggled closer to him. Her fingers massaged his groin as he hardened in her grasp.

"Okay," she said, breaking the kiss. "Now you'd better take care of me again before I have to get ready for work. I'll need something to last me the week."

HIRSCH HAD TO WALK THE GAS lines the following two days, and he devoted long hours in atonement for his recent absences at work. His boss didn't chew him out for neglecting his duties, but Hirsch was an independent contractor; the gas company could drop him without explanation if management's patience wore thin. He rose before 6:00 A.M. both days, drove to Escanaba, and traced his way up and down the residential streets of Delta County until nightfall, leak detector in hand, doing his part to prevent a catastrophic explosion.

He caught a break on Friday and called it a day around two in the afternoon so he could devote a few hours to preparing for his upcoming mission. Hirsch started with the New Strangite's webpage. Despite Jonathan Teller's exemplary academic credentials, the website had all the panache of an early-2000s GeoCities page, complete with cheesy graphics and animation. It featured the usual blend of doomsday prophecy, theological psychobabble, and the story of how Teller assumed the mantle of King Strang's legacy. The website's most modern feature was the donation box—ubiquitous on every subpage and able to accept offerings through multiple payment sources. Hirsch declined the opportunity to contribute.

A link to the prophet's YouTube page was more illuminating. Hirsch clicked on the most recent video—a two-week-old clip entitled "Prophet Strang explains universality and channeling your inner light through intentional living." A computer-generated logo depicting a stylized capital "M" surrounded by a dozen miniature pine trees arranged in a circle filled the screen. An ethereal New Age pan flute solo played in the background. The music faded and the logo dissolved into the image of a man seated cross-legged on a Persian rug in the middle of the room. The room's walls were clad in honey-hued vertical wooden slats, unadorned by any artwork save for a single banner bearing the logo from the video's introduction. Hirsch got his first look at the new king—Prophet Jonathan Teller.

Teller was draped in a long-sleeved, linen V-neck caftan. In his mid-forties, Prophet Teller had shaggy golden hair that fell over his ears, and he reached up to brush a fallen lock away from his gold-rimmed granny glasses. Hirsch bit his lip to suppress an involuntary wave of laughter upon realizing the so-called "King of Beaver Island" resembled a cross between John Denver and an acid casualty from the psychedelic era. The camera zoomed in on the man's face and upper shoulders as he commenced speaking. Hirsch increased the volume on his laptop to listen.

"Greetings, disciples and friends old and new, and welcome to this month's installment of prophecy journeys with King Strang the Second, coming to you live from our ancient and secret retreat of Manitou in the kingdom of God. For those of you new to our journey, I welcome you as we explore how you can harness the human potential inherent within each of you and banish past and future transgressions to allow God's light of truth to cleanse your soul and leverage the power of prophecy to deliver you to a higher plane of existence with an unshackled conscience.

"Building on last month's lecture, today we explore how communal living through a shared intentionality can liberate you from the ego of individual desire and help you shed the negative exigencies imprinted by a lifetime of alienation in a society predicated on hiding the truth and distracting you through the spiritual futility of libidinal and appetitive distractions of the flesh. God's revelation through his divine presence, our martyred King Strang the First, inextricably reveals to us the folly of our ignoring the one and true light— the light which is all around us, the light which is inside you right now. Have you felt dead inside lately? Do you suffer from anguish that your day-to-day existence in the rat-race we call modern society is leading you astray from the real you—the you that was born a perfect and pure being but was corrupted at the hands of a depraved, destructive society; the you that recognizes your true calling in dreams and fleeting shadows of enlightenment; the you that's tried to break away from the evil but has been drawn back in by your so-called family, friends, and colleagues; the you that yearns every moment like a dull ache you can't put your finger on but haunts you through that whispered voice at the back of your head? Yes, I'm talking about the *real* you, the manifestation of God's shining light that inhabits every one of us and can be unshackled by channeling the Lord's divine spirit.

"See, my friends," the prophet paused and gazed into the camera with a knowing nod of his head and half smile, "I know all this because I was one of you as well. A year ago, I spent my days going to work, 'educating' my students, and coming home to a house full of worldly goods but devoid of any meaning. I'd wake the next morning only to repeat the whole process in a pattern of insanity that most of us feel we are doomed and destined to replicate. But I'm here to tell you that doesn't have to be the case. Our Lord, through the spirit of King Strang chose me to receive continued divine revelation. That revelation brought me here to my ancestral homeland on Lake Michigan to pick up where his divine eminence left off and rebuild God's kingdom.

"Ours is a life that doesn't discriminate or judge. It doesn't matter what your past is, or your present, no matter how far you've been led astray in life. Your one path to true salvation resides within each of you if you can only reject the corrupted seduction of false idols that present themselves as glittering distractions from the path. You see, the seven epochs of human existence have been successively demolished atop the false idols of greed, avarice, and vanity. The first epoch of the

Assyrian triumvirate—"

Hirsch hit pause five minutes into King Strang's forty-five-minute monologue. If the prophet was half this tedious in person, the coming weekend promised to be an excruciating exercise in monotony. Hirsch failed to see how anyone could be seduced by this torpor-inducing New Age word salad, but he figured there were people out there desperate or lonely enough to give it a spin. Clearly even someone of a privileged background like Alexandra Winslow could fall prey to the charlatan's seductions.

He'd heard enough from the so-called prophet for the time being but needed a primer on the original King Strang. Despite growing up in northern Michigan, Hirsch remained woefully ignorant about Strang's story. The name meant about as much to him as the names William Bonifas, Henry Schoolcraft, or Russell Alger did. It was beyond time for Hirsch to get educated. He called his friend Edgar Trehearne, a retired gas company employee and lifelong Yooper.

"Hiya, Ben! I was wondering when I might be hearing your voice again," Edgar bellowed.

"Hey Edgar. How's the arm holding up?" Edgar and Hirsch's confrontation with Marcus Shaw months earlier on Summer Island had left Edgar with a serious gunshot wound to the shoulder. It was touch-and-go for several days at the hospital, but Edgar had pulled through and resumed his usual antics about town, albeit with his arm in a sling.

"Oh, it still hurts like the dickens when it rains but seems to be healing a little more every day. I should be sore at you for ruining fishing season for me, ya know. Hard to reel in the big ones with one good arm."

"Yeah, I made a mighty fine mess of that, I suppose. I'll make it up to you next summer," Hirsch replied. "Say, can I run something by you, Ed?"

"Sure, what can I help you with, son?"

"You know much about any cults around these parts?"

"Cults, eh? Ben, I've been around these parts for going on eighty years now. If I had a dime for every group of kooks running around these woods chanting and hollering about divine revelation—well, I could buy some fishing bait, I'll tell you that much. Don't even get me started on the hippies. A group of them once set up camp on the Whitefish River. They had their neighbors so pissed off with their nude bathing and 'free love' that the state police ran them off clear to Wisconsin. Right in Schoolcraft County a hundred-odd years ago you had a bona fide colony. Called themselves the Hiawatha Village Association. They weren't a cult so to speak, but they lived together and tried to make a go of it."

"What happened to them?"

"The powers that be put an end to it all. You'd know this if you'd paid a lick of attention in school, but the Chicago Lumbering Company dominated Manistique and Schoolcraft County for fifty-plus years. They owned the housing, doled out most jobs, controlled the railroads, and ran near every store in town. If you needed groceries, you bought them from the Company. If you needed a keg of nails, the Company supplied them. So if Abijah Weston and his cronies didn't like the way someone was living, the Company would squash him like a bug. See, the colony grew crops and did a decent job of it, all things considered. Potatoes and onions, mostly. Problem was, when it came time to bring them to market, the Company had a countywide monopoly on freight prices and retail. They didn't care for these utopian newcomers meddling with their business. They refused to buy a single goddamn potato from these poor idealists. Nine thousand bushels rotted under the sun. Sickening when you think about it, Ben. As you might expect, with no money the whole enterprise petered out quick. A few years later, all the timber was gone and the Chicago Lumbering Company cashed out and left a lot of people jobless."

"You know anything about King Strang and the Mormons over on Beaver Island back in the 1800s?"

Edgar chuckled. "They were before my time—even an old codger like me—but sure, I know about them. James Strang was a remarkable man. Say what you will about his beliefs, he built a real community. Why, what do you want to know?"

"Why were they on Beaver Island in the first place?"

"From what I understand, Strang was one of Joe Smith's disciples back east in New York a hundred-and-fifty years ago or so. After old Smith's murder, Strang tussled with Brigham Young over leadership of the Mormon church. Seems Brigham won out and led his flock to Utah, but Strang still had followers. Way I understand it, Strang wore out his welcome in Illinois and ended up on Beaver Island of all places with a couple thousand disciples in tow. Strang was a wily young man and got himself elected to the state legislature, if I recall correctly. Anyway, Strang declared himself king of his people after they set up shop on Beaver Island."

"Sounds like he did pretty well for himself."

"I suppose so—but he rubbed a lot of people the wrong way too. He was a fanatic, a true believer. Hated booze like you wouldn't believe. Some of his own followers couldn't handle the strict lifestyle. The island's locals wanted him out, and plenty others had issues with his multiple wives and pooh-poohing liquor. Lo and behold, a couple of them took matters into their own hands and shot Strang in the back. That ended the reign of ol' King Strang."

"What happened to all his followers?" Hirsch asked.

"Ya see, they might've gone on with their lives on the island, but Strang and his kind pissed people off something royally. Once the king wasn't around to protect his people, they were at the mercy of the locals. About a month after he died, a mob from Mackinac Island invaded Beaver Island and evicted near every one of the Strangites. Took their land and stole everything they could get their hands on. I'm ashamed to admit this, but some of my ancestors helped with the dirty work. They believed they were doing the right thing, but the whole mess seems shameful nowadays."

"What happened with the Strangites after they were forced off the island?"

Edgar paused. "Beats the hell out of me. I suppose most drifted away and went on with their lives. Maybe some rejoined Brigham out in Utah. They sure aren't on Beaver Island anymore. Say—why are you so interested in this, anyway?"

"Oh, just curious, really. I read about Strang the other day and realized I didn't know much about the history. Figured I'd ask you since you know as much about the U.P. as anyone."

"That right, eh?" Edgar said. "I feel like you're not telling me something. Anything you're leaving out, Ben?" Edgar's suspicion was well justified given their entanglement with the Shaw brothers.

"Nah, just curious, is all. You still getting together with the guys at the coffeeshop next week like usual?" Hirsch asked, changing the subject.

"Yeah, Thursday around 9:00. I'll be there. Maybe we'll be seeing ya."

"Thanks, Edgar. I'll try to make it," Hirsch said before ending the call. It wasn't much, but Edgar's insights gave him a scintilla of background for his weekend mission.

Hirsch woke early Saturday morning to ensure he wouldn't miss his rendezvous with the Winslows' pilot at the Manistique airfield. He took Winston's advice and packed light. He left his wallet at home, pocketing eighty dollars in cash, a Swiss Army knife, and the burner phone. He slipped Catherine's picture of Alex Winslow into the breast pocket of his well-worn flannel work shirt. Before leaving his house, Hirsch strapped on the sturdy walking boots he used to reconnoiter the gas lines.

Hirsch drove three miles east on Highway 2 to the Schoolcraft County Airport and parked his Toyota in the airport's near-empty lot. The airport sported a five-thousand-foot asphalt runway with a crosswind strip. Having arrived fifteen minutes early, Hirsch grabbed his overnight bag and headed for a weathered wooden bench facing the runway. Thin cirrus clouds dappled the sky at a high altitude, and a modest breeze blew from the west. The airfield was silent save for the clicking of grasshoppers in the fields and the rustle of distant maple and aspen leaves trembling in the wind.

At five minutes to eight, a black speck manifested on the horizon from the northeast. It grew larger as the low-pitched hum of a piston-driven engine drowned out the sounds of nature. The aircraft descended and entered its final approach before touching down on the main runway. The yellow-and-orange Cessna 182 turned the corner onto the crosswind strip and taxied towards the apron. Fifteen feet from where Hirsch sat, the pilot killed the engine and popped the door. A woman in her mid-forties wearing jeans, tennis shoes, and a light-red windbreaker alighted on the apron. She wore her dark hair in a long ponytail draped across her right shoulder. An oversized pair of reflective aviator glasses obscured her eyes.

"You Ben Hirsch?" she asked the only other person in sight at the airfield.

"Yeah, that's me," Hirsch said. He stood and picked up his bag.

"I'm Chris Foster, the Winslows' pilot. We have a quick trip to Beaver Island this morning, but I'll see to it you get there in one piece. Should have you on the ground in twenty minutes. Hand over your bag," she said and snatched it from his hand before he could reply. Chris popped open a small rectangular door behind the main cockpit door and shoved his bag inside. She latched the cargo door shut and turned to him.

"You ever flown in a small plane before, Hirsch?"

"Does an Embraer to Escanaba count?" he asked, recalling the handful of times he'd travelled home from law school or work aboard the noisy twin-engine commuter plane that ferried passengers from the Upper Peninsula to the outside world.

Chris shook her head. "First time for everything. Climb in and buckle up," she said as she hopped into the pilot's seat with a series of effortless moves.

Hirsch walked around the nose of the Cessna and made a ham-fisted effort at climbing inside. In the process, he managed to kick multiple control surfaces, poke himself in the eye with the headset dangling overhead, and bang his knee against the instrument panel. Chris stared at him with a tight smile, heightening Hirsch's self-consciousness.

"Here, strap yourself in like this," she said, taking pity on her novice passenger and demonstrating how the seatbelt and shoulder straps connected. She reached across his lap to grasp a loose end of the seatbelt strap and cinched it tight around his waist. "There, that should keep you from running off too far. Now, grab that headset you keep bumping into and put it over your ears." A pale-green David Clark headset dangled from a hook to the right of Hirsch's head. Striving to redeem himself, he slipped on the headset and adjusted the microphone so it rested in front of his lips.

"Twist the knob on the right earmuff and we'll be able to talk while the engine's running," Chris directed.

Hirsch turned the small black dial, which issued a dull click as it activated. In place of the dull, muffled sounds created by the earmuffs, a crisp buzz filled his ears.

"That better?" Chris asked in a tinny voice that was none-theless clear as a bell."

"Roger."

"Okay, let's get you to Beaver Island. Sit there, enjoy the ride, and don't touch a damn thing unless I tell you to."

Hirsch nodded and folded his hands in his lap. He had every confidence Chris could—and would—eject him out the door midflight across the lake if he managed to fuck up his limited role as passenger.

"Clear!" Chris shouted after popping open the window of her door. She cranked the ignition key, and the matte-black propeller turned over twice with a low whine before roaring to life. The propeller became a blur, and Hirsch breathed deep as the unique aroma of Avgas, exhaust, and Naugahyde upholstery filled his nostrils. Chris released the brakes, and the plane crawled across the apron and onto the main runway. She executed a hard left-hand turn to bring the Cessna about-face so they looked west towards Manistique. The array of gauges, instruments, knobs, and levers baffled Hirsch, but Chris's hands darted across the menagerie as if the movements were second nature.

"Ready?" she asked.

Hirsch nodded, red-faced with shame. She shook her head after observing his death-grip on the armrest and seat cushion.

"Just relax," Chris said, then depressed a black button affixed to the control wheel. "Schoolcraft County traffic, this is Cessna Seven-One-Six-Three-Romeo on Runway Two-Eight for westbound takeoff, over," she said.

Chris advanced the throttle. The Cessna gathered speed as it rolled across the runway's weathered concrete. Within seconds, the pilot inched the yoke back and they lifted off the ground. Hirsch was plastered against the seat but reminded himself to breathe deep as the plane gathered altitude.

Five hundred feet off the ground, Chris banked left, offering Hirsch a bird's-eye view of Manistique spread before him. He quickly picked out landmarks—the obloid forest-green water tower, the spire of St. Francis de Sales Catholic Church, and the ribbon of commercial businesses lining Cedar Street. Using those reference points, he located his neighborhood and childhood home.

"Not so bad, is it?" Chris said, having observed her passenger's fascination with the newfound vantage point.

"I've never seen it like this—the town, I mean."

"Some folks get hooked their first time in a small plane. I grew up outside Ironwood and my dad owned a Super Cub. It hooked me from a young age, and I never looked back. Careful, or you'll end up going broke on flight lessons and Avgas." Chris grinned broadly, revealing a row of white teeth.

Chris angled southeast and leveled the plane over Lake Michigan. Hirsch had spent countless hours on the water's surface as a youth while fishing, but the perspective from two-thousand feet above ground gave him a distinct appreciation for the lake's vast expanse and menace. A green smudge on the horizon caught his attention.

"Is that where we're headed?" Hirsch asked.

"Yeah, that's Beaver Island. About thirty nautical miles from where we left—not too far a trip at all. Ever been there?"

Hirsch shook his head. While Beaver Island was close to home as the crow flies, his father's sixteen-foot Lund was no match for the deep waters of Lake Michigan. They kept to the shallows around the Garden Peninsula and the chain of islands extending south to Wisconsin's Door Peninsula. The nearest ferry required a lengthy drive across the Mackinac Bridge and south to Charlevoix by car.

Hirsch relaxed for the flight's remaining minutes. The silver-capped waves generated by the wind rippling over the lake enchanted him, and he hardly realized their journey was near-finished when Chris reduced the throttle. The Cessna descended north of Beaver Island.

"Beaver Island traffic, this is Cessna Seven-One-Six-Three-Romeo in-bound for a left-based turn for final approach and landing on Runway Two-Seven," Chris said over the radio.

The Beaver Island Airport sat near the island's midpoint. They crossed over the village on the northern tip before Chris lined them up with the asphalt runway. They touched down a handful of feet beyond the numbers with a faint squeal of rubber tires against the pavement.

"This is the end of the road," Chris said as they taxied and stopped near the airfield's gravel parking lot. "You're on your own now. When it's time to come home, call Winston. I'll meet you here. Now, try to get out without damaging my plane, and don't forget your bag before you go." Chris slipped off her aviator sunglasses. With deep-blue eyes and high cheekbones, she made for one hot pilot. In another time and place, Hirsch wouldn't mind spending more time with his newfound companion.

"Thanks for the lift," he said.

He returned his headset to its hook and extracted himself from the passenger seat with far greater grace than his haphazard entry. Hirsch recovered his small travel bag from the cargo bin, then walked towards the gravel parking lot. Chris raised two slender fingers at him before engaging the throttle and turning towards the runway. Minutes later, the Cessna returned to the air with a throaty whine of the six-cylinder Continental engine that drowned out all other sounds.

Hirsch stood alone at the airfield. This was his mission now, and it was time for him to take charge. He walked along the rutted gravel road that led away from the airport, the gravel crunching beneath his feet. Bird calls from a row of balsam firs echoed around him. A calm western breeze off the lake lent the air a pleasant chill. Upon reaching the main road, Hirsch stuck out his thumb at passing traffic for his first attempt at hitchhiking in his life. Experience taught him that most motorists hesitated to stop for single men who looked even vaguely Indian. Over ten minutes passed before a beat-up Ford Lariat pickup with generous patches of rust fanning out from its wheel wells slowed to a crawl and halted beside him.

A bald man wearing a pair of scratched-up glasses held together at the bridge with Scotch-tape leaned across and rolled down the passenger window. "Where you headed?" he asked.

"I'm looking for a camp a couple miles south of here. Supposed to be off East Side Drive near Lake Geneserath."

"I know the place. Get in."

Thus began Hirsch's journey into the world of the new King Strang.

Chapter 3

"You one of them?" the bald man asked with his eyes glued to the two-lane road.

"One of who?"

"Those New Age Mormons or whatever they call themselves. You're headed to their camp, right?"

"Yeah . . . how'd you know?" Hirsch asked.

"Not a whole lot else out there, truth be told. I've seen a few young people from their colony about town. What's your interest?"

"Nothing to lose, I guess. I lost my job last week. I've heard good things about the prophet. Figured I'd see what they have to offer."

"None of my damn business. These days, it's live and let live on this island, but sometimes you wonder."

"You from here?" Hirsch asked as they turned southbound along a narrow two-lane asphalt road.

"Born and raised. Spent a couple years in the Navy, but came home as soon as I could. I don't plan on leaving."

"What do you know about the colony?"

"Not a whole lot—and I'd just as soon keep it that way. The land's been in the same family for generations. You can see all the way to the mainland from the beach. It'd make one helluva resort, not that anyone here has a pot to piss in. Pretty quiet until last year. Before you know it, trucks are coming and going all hours of the day and trees falling every which way. Lots of strange-looking young people too. Brings to mind my grandfather's stories about the old-time logging camps. They'd spring up overnight and you'd have a hundred-odd men living in the forest. These guys aren't foresters, that's for sure."

"You know any of them?"

The man turned quiet, contemplating the road ahead. "Not personally, no. Thing is, Beaver Island's got a history with this sort of business. King Strang and all his followers, if you know the story. Long as they're not diddling children or sacrificing animals, it's no skin off my ass. Well, here we are," the man said as he halted the Lariat alongside a weed-clogged irrigation ditch.

"Here . . . really?" Hirsch asked. The area was empty save for the asphalt road stretching ahead. Tall stands of red pine and cedar trees with hardwoods lined the roadsides.

"No—the entrance is another thousand feet or so ahead, but this is as far as I go. Like I said, I don't have a beef with whatever it is they're up to, but I damned sure don't want a thing to do with it myself."

Hirsch popped the door and exited the cab, dragging his bag off the seat. The man extended a calloused hand, and Hirsch leaned back in to accept it.

"Thanks for the ride," Hirsch said.

"Take care, buddy. And don't get in over your head."

"I'll do my best."

The truck made a U-turn and rumbled north towards the village. The airport was a good ten-mile walk away. If Hirsch needed to escape, he'd have to hoof it.

Hirsch ambled along the road towards his destination.

Glimpses of Lake Michigan emerged between the trees on his left. He had the road to himself, and the fall of his footsteps atop the broken asphalt competed with the shrill cries of three crows circling overhead in slow-paced gyres. Hirsch slapped at a stray mosquito buzzing in his ear, a harbinger of the swarms of insects that had only recently begun to dissipate before winter's onslaught.

True to the man's word, the entrance to Teller's encampment stood around a thousand feet down the road. The rutted dirt driveway and rusted metal gate spraypainted with chipped and faded dayglo-orange paint looked like most other approaches in rural Michigan. What wasn't normal was the pair of three-by-five-foot signs affixed to the gate. The first bore the following message in bold-faced capital letters:

WARNING: YOU ARE ENTERING MANITOU –
THE KINGDOM OF GOD.
THE RIGHTEOUS ARE WELCOME.
ALL OTHERS WILL BE SHOT.

Manitou—the great spirit of the Anishinaabe people. Yet another fine example of white people appropriating the cultural heritage of his mother's people, Hirsch lamented. The second sign reproduced the logo from the prophet's YouTube channel—a dozen white pine trees arranged in a circle surrounded the capital letter "M" against a dark-blue background.

No sentry guarded the gate. However, a small camera atop a stainless-steel pole pointed at where Hirsch stood. In the compound beyond, a vigilant watchman undoubtedly observed his every motion. Having come this far and unwilling to renege on his promises to the Winslows, Hirsch stepped around the gate and continued along the driveway.

A two-hundred-foot walk released him into a clearing. On his left, a low-profile, single-story building constructed from logs with board-and-batten siding painted a rich chocolate brown stretched along the ground. A ribbon of clerestory windows unfurled beneath a gable roof surfaced with hunter-green asphalt shingles. Windowless doors stood at either end of the structure. The building evoked the many summer camps Hirsch had visited as a child while a member of the Manistique troop of Boy Scouts.

A smaller structure sat opposite, on Hirsch's right. Built in the same style as the dormitory, the gambrel-roofed building faced the clearing. A screened-in porch with wooden steps anchored its front. A variety of structures in half-finished states of construction competed with the mutilated remnants of conifers, shrubs, and tree stumps dotting the landscape. With no one in sight, Hirsch resumed walking. As he passed the smaller structure to his right, the screen door burst open. A squat, wrecking ball of a man barreled towards him. His laced-up, black utility boots thundered against the wooden steps, which bowed and sagged beneath the man's heft.

"You're new here—I don't recognize you," the man said in a gruff bass voice as he stopped inches away from Hirsch. While he stood a good five inches shorter than Hirsch's five-foot-ten frame, his melon of a head sat atop a set of muscular shoulders that strained against the rolled-up sleeves of his blue denim work shirt. A tattoo decorated his lower left arm—a golden dagger spearing a blue-and-gold rose superimposed on an eight-point sun. A pair of denim cargo shorts revealed calves knotted like twin cantaloupes above his leather boots. While his scalp shined in the morning sun through short-clipped hair, he wore a mustache-less ink-black beard a good two inches in length.

"What brings you to our little corner of heaven?" he asked, his narrow eyes scrutinizing Hirsch through squared-off glasses.

"Consider me a lost soul in search of salvation. I've heard

Prophet Strang's message about finding your inner light, and I've come here to find mine." Hirsch was pouring it on thick but didn't know what else to offer. Given his father's Jewish heritage and mother's Ojibwa brand of lapsed Catholicism, Hirsch's main point of reference for the Protestant lexicon was the unavoidable hellfire-and-brimstone rhetoric of the demented preachers on fringe radio stations throughout the U.P.

"The only salvation here is through the virtue of hard work. If you're only here to laze around, eat our food, and bed down for the night, you'd best turn around and walk right back down that driveway," the man said while extending a bratwurst-like index finger towards the county road. "Any number of churches and retreats will take pity on you. That's not how we do things around here. If you want to work your ass off, listen to what the King—our prophet—has to say, and help build the kingdom of God, then maybe there's a place for you." The man punctuated each of these phrases with a firm poke of his meaty finger into Hirsch's chest.

"That's exactly what I'm looking for. I'm no stranger to hard work, I can assure you," Hirsch replied.

"Who are you, anyway? How'd you even find us?"

"Name's Mike Hackett," Hirsch replied. His last attempt at undercover work had ended with him beaten and left for dead in a drainage ditch on the Garden Peninsula at the hands of Catherine Winslow's miscreant brothers. He had scant desire to repeat that experience. "I heard about the prophet on the campus where I worked. Once I watched his videos, I knew this was the place for me."

"I'm Elder Clint, King Strang's righthand man. No one enters Manitou or leaves without my knowledge. And I can't let every random person share our bounty and exalt in the glory of God's mystery."

"I don't have much in the way of money," Hirsch said.

He wasn't lying. He'd already pledged Catherine's payment to the autobody shop in Escanaba and made a dent in the remaining fees he still owed to the state disciplinary board. Other creditors would have to wait.

"There are other ways to contribute, Mike. Every person here was called for one reason or another. Besides, if you prove yourself, you can help us earn money."

"Where is everyone, anyway?"

"It's the middle of the day and they're hard at work, same as I'd be if I weren't here talking to a newcomer. Most prospects have the sense to tell us they're coming. We may exalt the virtue of physical labor, but we're not luddites. If you found our website, you could've reached out ahead of time. People showing up unannounced makes us nervous. It won't surprise you that Prophet Teller's made a few enemies along the way."

"I'm not here to cause any trouble, believe me," Hirsch said. "The apostles were called by the teachings and spirit of Jesus, not the other way around."

Clint drew within a couple inches of Hirsch's face. "Look, if you *really* want to join us and help build the kingdom of God, then we need to see you can work. We have jobs for people of all ages and abilities. The strength of young men like us can't go to waste."

Clint referring to him as a young, strong person pleased Hirsch, considering his age and the gray hair infiltrating his head.

"Drop your bag and follow me," Clint said. Hirsch abandoned the satchel and followed his muscle-bound interlocutor as Clint navigated through the series of outbuildings and a dense cluster of verdant maple trees. Their green leaves rustled and shimmered beneath the morning sun amidst a gentle lake-cooled breeze. Clint led Hirsch into another clearing dotted with fresh-cut tree stumps and strewn with macerated brush. A half-finished trench stretched twenty feet wide by three feet deep. A square-edged shovel sat alongside the edge. Clint stopped at the trench's edge with arms akimbo on his sides.

"This is the site of our future tabernacle. In a couple months' time, it'll be too cold to meet outside. Thing is, we can't pour a foundation without a twenty-by-twenty hole, three feet deep and level. You said you're no stranger to hard work—prove it," Clint said as he seized the shovel and pointed the handle towards Hirsch.

"Kinda small for a tabernacle, eh?" Hirsch said.

"Are you a wiseass?"

"No."

"'Cause you sure as hell sound like one. We don't need that shit here."

"I'm not. Sorry."

"You'd better be sorry. Questioning the prophet's vision is a surefire way to wear out your welcome here. Lunch is in three hours," Clint continued. "You'll hear the ring of the dinner bell. When you do, join us at the picnic tables behind the dormitory."

"I guess I'd better get started," Hirsch said, accepting the shovel. "Say, you got any work gloves you could spare?"

Clint snorted and held out his bear-paw hands for Hirsch to observe. Calloused and lined with dirt-stained cracks, his hands told of countless hours of physical labor.

"You see these, Hackett? I wasn't born like this. My second week in Afghanistan our C.O. ordered me and two other soldiers to dig a twenty-five-foot latrine trench at our combat outpost near Kandahar. A few hours in, my hands were bleeding, and I pointed it out to our sergeant. He told me to quit whining unless I wanted an extra shift of guard duty. I earned these hands working out here same as everyone else. Do your damn job and you'll earn yours too, in time. I'll leave you to it."

Clint slapped Hirsch on the shoulder and walked away from the clearing. Twigs and dead leaves snapped and rustled beneath his heavy boots as he departed. Hirsch stood alone with a shovel facing the half-finished pit. He had to hand to it Manitou's leadership—within fifteen minutes of his arrival, they'd already manipulated him into doing their dirty work. Finding Alexandra Winslow would have to wait.

He seized the shovel and drove the blade into the ground, loosening the first spadeful of soil and tossing it aside. Rocks large and small littered the work area, impeding his progress as he probed and removed them one at a time. Fierce temperatures in recent weeks had baked the soil, rendering the desiccated crust resistant to the blade's bite. Hirsch longed for the comfort of the ten- to fifteen-mile walks normally required by the gas company. At least they paid him for his troubles.

Hirsch's father, Murray, was fond of reminding his children that hard work was its own reward, but the three hours Hirsch spent laboring with the shovel felt like abject punishment. Thirty minutes in, sweat had soaked his flannel shirt. He unbuttoned it and draped it atop the fleece jacket he'd shed at the project's start, taking care to avoid bending the photograph of Alexandra Winslow buttoned in his shirt's breast pocket. The August sun, at its apex, hammered the clearing, raising the temperature to over eighty degrees. Hirsch spent the next two hours shirtless with sweat streaming down his brow, his tanned skin glistening in the fierce sunlight.

The bright clang of the dinner bell announced the lunch break. Hirsch dropped the shovel to the ground, where it clattered against the stones embedded in the hard-packed earth. He rested his hands on his thighs, his back screaming from the exertion and promising a night of sheer agony. Years of office work had rendered him in no shape for this shit. Red welts traversed the palms of his hands where he'd gripped the rough wood of the shovel handle. Hirsch dripped with sweat, and the stench emanating from his body filled him with disgust. He recovered his shirt and slipped it over his shoulders before approaching the main camp and the promise of lunch. The morning's labor had left him ravenous, and he looked forward to whatever the colony had to offer by way of a meal.

A row of rough-hewn wooden picnic benches sat end-to-end behind the dormitory. Around thirty individuals clad in the colony uniform of jeans and long-sleeved denim work shirts had found their seats. They patiently waited with hands folded atop the table and placid expressions on their faces. Most were middle-aged and male, supplemented with a handful of women. Stragglers advanced towards the dining area to secure the remaining places.

A quick scan revealed a young woman with dark blonde hair pulled into a ponytail seated at a table. Like the others, she had her hands folded in front of her. She tugged at the rough denim collar around her neck. Hirsch made a bee line for the empty place opposite the girl and swung his leg over the bench seat. Each place setting included a tin plate, silverware, and a jelly jar pre-filled with spring water. Ribbons of gray meat surrounded by globules of fat suspended in glistening juice awaited on a platter at the table's center. Beside the platter rested a bowl filled with flaccid steamed vegetables accompanied by store-bought sliced bread days past its prime. No one joined a cult for the food, Hirsch realized. Despite the hunger gnawing at his stomach, he knew better than to reach out and fill his plate before others did the same.

"What's your name?" Hirsch asked the young woman opposite him. Silent, she regarded Hirsch with a mixture of bemusement and distrust. She matched the photo of Alexandra Winslow, even clad in cult wear and sans nose ring and makeup. "I'm Mike. I just got here this morning," Hirsch continued.

"We don't talk at the supper table!" a woman approaching Hirsch from behind hissed. Slender but rawboned with fair, freckled skin, she hurriedly sat alongside Hirsch. She wore her long hair in a braid and glared at him through ice-blue eyes. She had a good six inches in height on him. While not exactly pretty, her stern handsomeness nonetheless grabbed his attention.

"Sorry, I'm new here. No one explained the rules yet."

"You're Mike Hackett, right? Elder Clint warned me you needed instruction."

"I'm here to learn."

"Elder Lisa," she introduced herself. "Only the king is allowed to talk during meals," she whispered. "You'd best shut your trap and listen if you know what's good for you. If you want to chit-chat, find another time and place to do it. Consider this your first lesson."

Cowed by Lisa's fierce rebuke, Hirsch slouched and stared at his hands for want of anything else to do. He snuck a glance at Alex. She maintained a stone-faced expression opposite him. After an interminable length of silence, the congregants rose to their feet. Hirsch followed their lead. A swishing sound heralded the approach of a man sauntering across the grass shod in open-toed Birkenstocks. Prophet Teller's ankle-length caftan swished with each step. He reached the head of the row of tables and raised his hands. A pair of brass bangles clinked as they slid along his right forearm. The assembled flock bowed their heads with hands clasped.

"Be seated and accept the fruits of our bounty as recompense for the hard work laboring in the cause of our Lord," Teller commanded. The prophet took his chair as well, with Clint seated at his right.

The congregants ate in silence. The dry, stringy meat had

the texture of microwaved beef jerky, but Hirsch choked down three slices for sustenance and swallowed a half-plate full of the vegetables. The mélange of boiled Brussels sprouts, sliced carrots, and okra had the consistency of a watery mush, robbed of any nutritional value. Their mealy cores had liquified into a fetid mucilage that required conscious effort to avoid gagging. Hirsch drained the jelly jar of tepid water in a single gulp and pined for a pitcher of ice water to quench his thirst.

With the meal finished, Prophet Teller stood to dismiss the congregation.

"Go now and return to your labors. Always bear in mind the Lord's mission and the part each of you plays in that plan. Our community of Manitou, this new Jerusalem of the north, belongs to us all. Take care that your endeavors reflect the heavy burden our Lord and I, your prophet, have entrusted in you. Tonight we gather at the theatre to revel in song and receive the divine prophecy."

Alex was among the first congregants to depart the dining area, before Hirsch could address her. However, Prophet Teller had paused facing the woods beyond with his hands clasped behind his back. Hirsch leapt into action and approached him. His flight caught Clint's attention, and the strongman rushed to head Hirsch off.

"Prophet Teller!" Hirsch cried out before Clint could intercept him.

Teller stopped and turned at the sound of Hirsch's voice. "Mike, welcome to Manitou," he said and covered his heart with his hand. "I'm told you joined our community this morning."

"Prospect Mike here's excavating the foundation for the new tabernacle," Clint said, grabbing Hirsch by the upper arm. "He'd best get back to work now that lunch is over."

"Is the hole going anywhere?" Teller asked.

"Well, no, but—"

"Then give us fifteen minutes' grace, Elder Clint. I like to get to know our new adherents. Come, walk with me, Mike."

They moved away from the clearing inland towards Lake Geneserath. Prophet Teller ambled with his hands still clasped behind his back and peered at a Northern Goshawk perched midway up a white pine. The keen-eyed bird surveyed the forest through alert yellow eyes. The hawk alighted from the branch as the two men passed beneath the pine and flapped its gray-and-white-streaked wings as it soared west towards the lake.

"Amazing the freedom some creatures have," Teller said.

"I've always thought the birds have it best. Able to fly halfway across the world twice a year and not get lost," Hirsch replied as they picked their way through the forest.

"What brought you here, Mike?"

Hirsch paused, summoning the cover story he'd concocted. It could've been the tale of any number of his Manistique High School classmates who fell off the rails early on and never found their way back. "I've had my share of troubles, I guess. I got into booze and drugs in high school and just kept at it. I wasn't a great student anyway. I spent most of my life in the U.P. working odd jobs. Earlier this year, I did ninety days at the Marquette Branch Prison for possession. When I got out, I caught on with a landscaping crew on the Northern Michigan campus. I hated the work and didn't expect much out of it, but it's how I learned about you. I found this flyer crumpled up next to a trashcan. I planned to toss it like all the other junk I picked up, but something about the promise of building, like, heaven on earth right here on Beaver Island caught my attention.

"The flyer had a link to your YouTube page on it, so I checked it out. That talk about finding your inner light and being part of something bigger opened my eyes. Your whole aura and sense of inner peace really clicked with me. From that day forward, I didn't feel the need to take drugs or touch another drop of alcohol. I quit my job and came here as soon as I could."

"The kingdom of God welcomes all who seek the truth and wish to liberate themselves from suffering," Teller said.

The unimproved pathway they trod led the men to the shore of Lake Geneserath. A grove of cedar and aspen trees terminated near the water's edge. Sunlight dappled the lake's placid, green water. A pair of ospreys alighted from their nest. Midway across the lake, a muskrat churned along the water, leaving an S-shaped wake. The two men stood in awe at the lake's picturesque beauty.

"I heard this is your land, but I didn't know what to expect. It's . . . it's fucking incredible," Hirsch said with legitimate awe. Teller chuckled and gave Hirsch the side eye. "Sorry. How'd you find it, anyway?"

"The land's been in my family for years. My great-great-great grandparents, Josiah and Ellen Teller, settled here in the 1850s. They were devout followers of King Strang but avoided eviction, unlike most of his congregation. The family's passed the land from one generation to another—going on one hundred seventy-five years now. My dad died last year and it became mine. It really belongs to nature, though, and I plan to keep it that way. I never imagined living out here, but . . ." Teller drifted into silence.

"But what changed?"

"I had a vision."

"What kind of vision?"

"A vision of order for a world gone mad. A community living in harmony with nature. The trees, the birds, the water—all fostering a new era of tranquility in this sacred corner of our blessed world. This land survived nearly two centuries in our family unmolested—that was no accident. God meant for me to heed the call and continue King Strang's work. And here I am today doing just that with the help of followers like you. We gather in joyous celebration every evening and express our vision through song. Men and women who've never handled a trowel or felt the soil between their fingers are growing their own food now."

Maybe they'll learn how to cook next, Hirsch thought.

"What made you give up the life you had before? I heard you taught math or something," Hirsch said.

"It's true. I was a professor of mathematics at Stanford University specializing in algebraic topology, Riemannian manifolds, and knot theory."

"Ah, yeah, knot theory," Hirsch said, feigning comprehension. "I wasn't much for math in school."

Teller grunted. "You and most others, it seems."

"And you just, like, walked away from it?"

"I recognized both the limits of my field and my own constraints relative to advancing our understanding of the subject matter. Articulating the limits of comprehension through non-Euclidean, four-dimensional space wouldn't bring me any closer to saving our world. My path isn't unique. Alexander Grothendieck retreated from academia and, eventually, society at large when he recognized the inherent contradiction between the pragmatic outcomes of his work and his devout pacifism. He tried communal living at first, then withdrew into absolute seclusion for the last twenty-five years of his life. Kurt Gödel spent copious mental capital reconciling the cool, rational realm of logic with his theological outlook on the world and his devout belief in an afterlife. For all Gödel's brilliance, his waking existence became a parallax view of epistemological torture. In the end, paranoia drove him to madness and self-starvation. If you want a more recent example, the most brilliant mathematician of our time, Grigori Perelman, proved the elusive Poincaré conjecture before walking away from mathematics in its entirety—at least publicly. The absence of ethics amongst mathematicians even of his caliber disgusted him."

"Perelman . . . heavy," Hirsch said. He had zero clue who Grothendieck, Gödel, or Perelman were.

"Mike, I'm seeking here at Manitou the harmony and order I couldn't find in mathematics. And I've discovered it through God's grace as transmitted through his late prophet, James Strang. And like Strang, I await our Lord's revelation and will share it with you and all our adherents."

"Still—it's quite the change going from being a professor to, well, this," Hirsch said, gesturing at the untamed forest around them.

"I'm not sure I see it that way," Teller replied. "After all, King Strang himself was an atheist and libertine until a chance encounter with Joseph Smith at Nauvoo. He saw the path to a kingdom of God in heaven and on earth and never looked back."

Hirsch looked Teller in the eyes. "And are you Strang's true successor? Are you the new King Strang?"

Teller rested his hand on Hirsch's shoulder and smiled. "That's for you alone to decide, Mike. Maybe this makes me a poor prophet, but it's for each person here to find. Think about what you want to believe. Now, you'd best get back to work or Clint will go ballistic."

Teller and Hirsch gave the lake one final look, then turned with reluctance and headed back towards the camp. They paused at the edge of the clearing between the dormitory and the open tables.

"One more question, Prophet," Hirsch asked as he spotted his musclebound enforcer out of the corner of his eye. "Are Clint and Lisa part of your vision of order?"

Teller sighed. "Those who also receive our Lord's call are a varied group, Mike. Elder Clint and Ms. Dykman are enthusiastic, I'll say that much. All I can do is lead by example and protect my flock from the evils of the outside world."

Clint rumbled towards them, denying Hirsch the opportunity to follow up. "I need to speak with you, Prophet. Excuse us, Hackett, and get back to work. The day's not getting any longer."

The last thing Hirsch needed was getting crosswise with this ogre. He nodded and headed towards his workstation. He glanced over his shoulder and caught a fleeting glimpse of Clint guiding the prophet away with a meaty paw clasped around Teller's upper arm. As Hirsch headed towards his pit of misery, he encountered Alexandra Winslow crouched in a garden bed, alone and weeding a furrow row of carrots. The bright-green strands of leaves extended in a neat line parallel to a row of onion stalks.

"Nice-looking veggies," Hirsch said as he approached and crouched alongside her.

"Thanks," she said, glancing up at Hirsch while plucking weeds from the ground with dirt-streaked hands. "Another week and they'll be ready to take to the farmer's market in town."

"You sell them?"

"Some, yeah. You're new here, right?"

Hirsch nodded.

"I thought so. We keep what we need for food, but we sell or barter the rest. There's still a lot we can't grow here yet. Give it another year, and we'll have our own wheat and corn. I can't wait to mill it and learn to bake our own bread."

"I need to talk with you, Alex."

"Umm . . . how do you know who I am?"

"My name's Mike. Well, actually it's Ben, but please call me Mike while I'm here." Hirsch mimicked her by weeding the next furrow.

"What do you want from me?" Alex stood and backed

away from him.

"I'll get right to the point—your parents are worried about you, Alex. They asked me to check on you."

"Wait—*my parents* sent you here? For real?" Alex looked at him with her mouth agape.

"I know, I know. I'd be pissed too if my parents sent someone after me. Seriously, though, Herb and Catherine think you're in trouble with these crazies. They don't want anything bad happening to you."

"I came here because I *want* to be here, because I like it here. They're just pissed I didn't want to stay in school and spend my life doing boring shit like them all day. I mean, look around—no one's forcing me to stay. I could scream right now, you know. Clint and Lisa would be hella pissed if they knew why you were here. I don't even know who you are." Alex crossed her arms, glancing around her.

"Please don't scream," Hirsch said. He stood facing her with his palms out. "My name is Ben Hirsch. I'm from the U.P. and used to be a lawyer. I swear I'm only here to help."

"Look, you could help me by going home and telling my parents I'm fine and don't need them to send some lawyer or whatever to look after me. Actually, tell them I'm happy here with dirt under my fingernails and living with nature. The prophet's a sweet guy anyway—they don't need to worry about me."

"I get it. I really do," Hirsch said. Beaver Island and Manitou were, admittedly, unabashedly beautiful. "I suppose there's nothing I can say to get you to change your mind and come back to Marquette with me."

Alex shook her head. "Seriously, I'm fine here. I'm sorry you had to come all this way, but tell them I'm happy. My mom especially is used to getting what she wants, but they need to, like, just drop it and leave me alone. I'm *nineteen*. I can take care of myself, okay? Now let me get back to work."

"Fine. I should too, or Clint will have my balls in a vise. Can we talk later?"

Before Alex could answer, Lisa emerged from behind a building and made a beeline towards them.

"You," she said, pointing to Hirsch. "What do you think you're doing? I thought Clint told you to get back to work. Why are you bothering Sister Alex?"

"I was trying to get the lay of the land; learn more about the garden. She's helping me figure out what I'm supposed to do the rest of the afternoon. Right, Alex?" Hirsch said.

"Uh, sure," Alex said.

"Well, Elder Clint already explained what you're supposed to be doing—finishing the foundation trench so we can erect a new tabernacle. I don't know how Alex was supposed to help you with that. If you came here to flirt with girls, you've got the wrong idea, Hackett. Sister Alex is here for one thing only—building Manitou. I suggest you do the same."

"Yeah, well, I'm getting back to that right now," Hirsch said as he wiped a line of sweat from his brow and faced the clearing where his assignment waited.

"Good, that's more like it. Alex, I'd like a word with you." Lisa dismissed Hirsch with a curt wave of her hand. She waited until Hirsch had moved away before grasping Alex by the shirt and getting in her face. Hirsch couldn't hear a word she shared.

Hirsch returned to his labors. He grabbed the shovel and reentered the growing pit. By mid-afternoon, angry blisters had replaced the tender red welts lining his palms. The fluid-filled sacs burst and the skin stripped away, revealing patches of raw flesh that sent spasms of agony radiating through Hirsch's body with each thrust of the shovel blade. The trees had cast long shadows across the clearing by the time he completed excavation of the hole. With the last shovelful of earth removed from the twenty-foot-square pit, Hirsch crawled out with trembling legs and labored breath. Enervated by the day's labor, he collapsed onto a nearby patch of grass. Within seconds, utter exhaustion propelled him into a dreamless sleep of abject fatigue.

The clang of the dinner bell came all too soon. Hirsch glanced at his watch—he'd only been asleep twenty minutes. Rising to his feet proved to be the hardest task of all. He rolled onto his stomach and pressed his elbows into the ground, doing his utmost to keep any dirt and grime from the open sores on his palms. Once on his knees, it was another minute before he could rise to his full height and advance one step at a time towards the communal supper table.

Hirsch was the last straggler, and he drew glares from both Lisa and Clint as he found an empty seat away from the Strangites. His body and clothes reeked of sweat, and he didn't dare give one more reason to piss people off. The meal passed in a blur of exhaustion and hunger. The searing pain in his hands couldn't keep him from gripping his fork and shoveling forkfuls of dry pork, black beans, and undercooked wild rice and carrots into his mouth.

His bleeding hands and disheveled appearance drew glances of concern and disdain from his fellow diners, but Hirsch was too hungry and exhausted to care. While he'd hoped to crawl into bed and sleep for twelve hours, the Strangites moved *en masse* to a natural bowl on the edge of the clearing. Prophet Teller sat at the base, tuning a guitar, while a handful of young women, Alex included, sat beside him. Hirsch settled towards the back, hoping to lie down, only to hear the prophet's voice. A lit bonfire separated the performers from the congregation.

"Friends, we have a newcomer who joined us today," Teller said as he plucked the D string of his Gibson acoustic guitar and adjusted the tuning peg. "Mike, will you do us the honor of coming forward and sitting up front?"

Hirsch groaned but rose to his feet with shaking knees and moved to sit at Prophet Teller's left near his groupies. Clint hovered nearby as well, glaring at Hirsch. What followed was the most mind-numbingly dull two hours of Hirsch's life.

Prophet Teller strummed a series of chords on his guitar while Alex and another girl rattled tambourines at regular intervals. After a minute's instrumental lead-in, Prophet Teller began to sing.

You gotta find the inner light inside
Insiiide, the girls harmonized in unison.
You need to discover how to believe
Belieeeve
You need to wake up your mind
Your miiind
'Cause the truth is there to receive
Receiiive

The song had no chorus to speak of but went on for ten minutes, punctuated by extended pan flute solos played by a long-haired, barefoot girl a foot taller than Alex. When the song at last ceased and the congregation burst into furious applause, Hirsch prayed it was the end. Nine more "songs" of a similar style followed.

An open-air sermon ensued. While Hirsch expected a hellfire-and-brimstone sermon, Teller spoke like the university professor he was. His subject matter veered from Cartesian geometry to Aristotelean ethics to the health benefits of an organic diet and communal eating. After what felt like an eternity sitting on the hard ground, Elder Clint dismissed the congregation for the evening. Hirsch followed the other men towards the dormitory, where a few hours of relief from the skull-crushing drudgery awaited.

Upon entering the dorm, Hirsch spotted his bag sitting atop a narrow twin bed. He pawed through it for a fresh change of clothes. He undid his shoelaces with trembling fingers and slipped his aching feet from his boots. His sweat-soaked socks had to be peeled from his feet, and he balled them up and shoved them deep inside his boots to mask the stench. Seated on an adjacent bed was a man in his early twenties. Dressed like the others, he had his hair shorn close to the sides of his scalp, mimicking Clint's appearance.

"You know where I can wash up and change?" Hirsch asked the youth.

"Sure thing, man. Showers are at the end of the hall," he said, jerking his thumb towards the back.

"You been here long?" Hirsch asked his dormmate.

"Nah, only like a month or something."

"How'd you find out about this place, anyway?"

"Um, college, I guess."

"Which college?"

"Eastern." His answer fit the pattern. Eastern Michigan University was in Ypsilanti, a college town tailormade to recruit young idealists.

"So what happened? Fall semester should be starting any day now."

"Uh, well, college and me just weren't a good match. Like, I tried to go to class and all, but me and my roomie bowled up every morning. I was flunking most of my classes spring semester. Anyway, I met this girl there in, like, April and we sorta hooked up. She told me about this cool place up north. Said there was plenty of work, I could swim in the lake, and they were cool with smoking weed. My parents were crazy pissed at me, but it wasn't like Eastern wanted me back for fall semester. So I decided—fuck it, I'll come too. Took me a while, but I made it here."

"What about the girl? Did she show up?"

"Nah, man, she ghosted me. Haven't seen her since I left Ypsilanti. Not like we could've fooled around—they make guys and girls sleep separately. And no weed either. Pretty lame, but I dig what Prophet Teller has to say."

"Are there many girls here?"

"I mean, a few, but they mostly like to rehearse with the prophet and work. Some are on the boat."

"What boat?"

"Like, something to do with Elder Lisa's family. Spreading the prophet's word and stuff, I guess."

"How's that?" Hirsch asked.

The kid shrugged. "Dunno, man. Like, I just work in the garden, you know."

"I'm Mike. Thanks for showing me the ropes here."

"Liam," he said and fist-bumped Hirsch. "It's lights out in, like, fifteen minutes. You may want to hit the showers now."

"Thanks," Hirsch replied. Liam's eyes followed Hirsch as he walked away.

He stumbled towards the washroom. A handful of converts stood within, but all ignored Hirsch's pathetic spectacle. He gathered his experience was a rite of passage for anyone entering Manitou's hallowed grounds. A communal shower not unlike what he remembered from his high school locker room beckoned. He peeled off his sweat-soaked clothes and twisted the faucet open to unleash a narrow jet of ice-cold water. The water stung the open sores extending in twin lines across both palms but cleansed him of the day's accumulated filth. He dried off with a threadbare towel borrowed from a stack near the entrance and slipped into a fresh change of clothes. Too tired to do anything but collapse onto the rock-hard mattress and lie sideways with his hands extended over the bed's edge, he fell fast asleep to the dronelike murmur of prayer from his dormmates.

Chapter 4

Two sets of hands gripped Hirsch and ripped him out of the narrow bed. A towel dropped over his head and knotted tight in the back enveloped him in a cloak of blackness. Awake in an instant, Hirsch broke out in a cold sweat of terror.

"Don't say a fucking word or I'll bust your skull open right here," the unmistakable gravelly drawl of Elder Clint hissed in his ear. "Now walk."

They hurried him out of the dormitory and into the sharp chill of the Michigan summer night. With his boots and socks left next to his bed, the tender soles of Hirsch's unshod feet experienced every twig, rock, and stone littering the ground. Hirsch did his best to keep pace with his captors lest he stumble and collapse against the uneven, stone-strewn ground. His shins banged against wooden steps as they dragged him up a flight of stairs, eliciting a howl of pain. They entered a damp building. Even with the towel knotted tight around his head, the stench of mildew and soap scum invaded his nostrils. His knees slammed against a rough plank floor as the goons shoved him downward. Clint ripped the towel from Hirsch's head. His eyes adjusted to a shadowy room illuminated by an unshaded light bulb dangling from a black wire.

It was the compound's laundry room. A row of wash-ing machines lined one wall while a variety of drying racks strung with denim clothing and stark-white bedsheets stood opposite. A knee-high tin basin filled three-quarters full of water rested inches from where Hirsch kneeled. He turned his head to examine his captors, but a firm swat from Clint's hand caught Hirsch's ear. He cried out as Clint's signet ring sliced open a gash. Blood trickled and pooled in his ear canal, and he tilted his head to drain it. Lisa walked around the basin and crouched opposite Hirsch. Having abandoned her cult uniform, she sported jeans and a puffy yellow vest zipped up over a long-sleeved shirt. He shivered as her ice-blue eyes scrutinized his face.

"Why are you here, Mike Hackett?" she asked.

"What the hell is your problem? I mean, what's this all about?" Hirsch said.

"Mind your own business and answer her," Clint replied, delivering a sharp kick to the small of Hirsch's back. He lurched over as pain shot down his legs.

"Jesus, man, is this how you treat all newcomers?"

"Answer her fucking question, dickhead!" Clint kneed him in the ribs and Hirsch went down on his side, stunned by the dual assaults. Lisa crouched impassively opposite him until Hirsch recovered sufficiently to rise to his knees.

"Who are you and why are you here?" she asked.

"I've been out of work and struggling with a bit of a drug problem," Hirsch said, maintaining his cover story. "I heard about Prophet Teller. I'm trying to get my life back together; this sounded like the place to do it."

"Who told you about Manitou?" Lisa continued. She rose to her feet and paced in front of the basin.

"I worked on a landscaping crew at the Northern Michi-gan campus. I found this crumpled-up flyer on the ground. It led me to the prophet's website."

"A flyer, eh?" Lisa said. She gave Clint a curt nod.

A hand clamped firm across the back of Hirsch's head and shoved him face first into the basin of ice-cold water. Hirsch struggled and thrashed, but Clint's leg, pressed against his back, made escape all but impossible. Seconds ticked by and his oxygen-deprived brain went into panic overdrive. Thirty seconds beneath the water's surface passed before Clint yanked him out. Hirsch gasped for air as frigid water dribbled down his face and soaked his T-shirt.

Lisa shook her head. "Stop lying to me, Hackett." She gave her conspirator the cue to repeat the treatment. Hirsch's head plunged into the drink once again. Clint submerged him for well over a minute this time, and his lungs ached as though they would burst any moment. The agony nearly overwhelmed him by the time Clint relaxed his grip.

"We found this in your shirt," Lisa said as she displayed the photograph of Alexandra Winslow in front of him. "Why the hell were you talking with Sister Alex earlier?"

"She's . . . she's a family friend. I hadn't seen her for a while and wanted to visit," Hirsch said.

Lisa sighed. "The towel, Clint."

The towel once again wrapped around his head, erasing the room from view. Clint shoved him backwards, slamming the back of his skull onto the wooden floorboards. Rough hands pinned him to the ground as a stream of water splashed across his covered face. *Jesus, waterboarding,* Hirsch realized, as the full horror of his predicament came into focus. It felt as though they'd shoved a faucet into his mouth, pinched his nose shut, and opened the tap full blast. Unrelenting panic chased any rational thought from his brain. The dread-inducing sensation of drowning far exceeded the discomfort of having his head below the water's surface. Death was but moments away, and—in a perverse way—he longed for the permanent relief it would bring. He lapsed into unconsciousness as the flow of water ceased and Clint ripped the towel away. Hirsch trembled, afraid to move or breathe lest they repeat the treatment.

"Who are you working for, Hackett? Why are you here? I suggest you talk unless you want another dose," Lisa said.

The jig was up. No amount of the Winslows' money was worth the indescribable agony of torture by waterboarding—or worse.

"Okay, okay. Alex's parents hired me to find her," Hirsch sputtered between gasps of air as he coughed to expel water from his mouth. "She quit college a few months ago and came here. They're worried about her."

"Who are they?" Lisa asked as she paced the room and crossed her arms against the cold. "Don't lie to me again, I'm warning you."

"Their names are Herbert and Catherine Winslow. They're from Marquette on the U.P. Seriously, all they wanted me to do was visit, check and make sure she's okay, and try to convince her to come home. I tried; she refused."

"Listen, Hackett, anyone here has joined of their own free will and volition. We don't appreciate interlopers weaseling their way in and messing with Manitou. You seem stupid enough to do this; I hope whatever they're paying you was worth it."

Hirsch nodded in resignation.

"What should we do with him?" Clint asked Lisa.

"I'd like to think Mr. Hackett's learned his lesson. He's going to tell this young woman's parents the truth—that she's fine and doesn't want to leave." She turned to Hirsch. "I'm warning you, if we ever see you here again, Clint here will put a bullet through your head. He's an expert marksman—you won't be the first person he's shot."

Hirsch nodded. His mission was an abject failure, and they'd shamed him beyond his imagination, but he'd walk away with his life intact.

"Let me take care of him, Lisa," Clint said. He approached a corner of the washroom and grabbed a 7mm bolt-action rifle tilted against the wall.

"As you wish," Lisa said as she headed towards the door. She paused and waved Winston's flip phone at Hirsch. "We found this too. I didn't even know they still made pieces of crap like this. I don't think you'll be needing it anymore." She lobbed the phone towards the tin basin. It sent forth a splash of water as the device sank to the bottom. Lisa departed the washroom.

"Get on your fucking feet," Clint said as he pointed the rifle at Hirsch's midsection and motioned him out the door. "Here, tie this over your head like before," he continued, tossing Hirsch the soaked towel. The latter did as instructed. "Now walk."

In his blindness, Hirsch strained to leverage his other senses and gather his bearings. Fallen leaves and branches crunched and snapped beneath his bare feet. They walked amidst the forest with the dark canopy spread above them.

"Stop," Clint said after they'd walked for five minutes. He reached forward and yanked Hirsch's blindfold off with one hand. The faintest hint of dawn illuminated the sky to the east. Clint jabbed Hirsch in the back with a sharp thrust of the rifle barrel. Hirsch fell to his knees, slamming his mangled hands against the forest floor. He howled as jagged rocks dug into the bleeding wounds.

"In Afghanistan, we'd march traitors like you naked to the edge of the canyon and let them run for their lives. My C.O., Captain Nygren, wouldn't let me shoot until they had a two-hundred-yard head start. Once in a while, they made it. I never much liked that."

"The Winslows—they know I'm here."

"Then I guess you'd best run like hell."

Hirsch trembled.

"Now get the fuck to your feet," Clint said, raising the rifle to his shoulder and squaring Hirsch's head in the center of its iron sights a mere five feet from where he stood. "I'm giving you ten seconds to get the hell out of here before I open fire. If you survive, don't even think about coming back, you hear me?"

Hirsch nodded as he dragged himself off the ground. The dense mass of trees beyond represented his sole salvation.

"On my count: one, two, three, go!" Clint shouted.

Hirsch tore away at a breakneck pace, his legs flying and chest pounding as the forest swallowed him. His ten-count head start felt like a nanosecond as a seven-millimeter round whizzed by his right ear with a deafening roar that left his ears ringing. Hirsch screamed as he zigzagged between the trees. Intoxicated by fear, he didn't even feel the detritus of the forest floor slicing his tender feet to ribbons. A second shot pulverized the trunk of a sugar maple a couple feet in front of him. Hirsch dove and rolled along the ground. Dirt and rotting leaves coated his soaked shirt and pants. Clint cackled in the distance as Hirsch stumbled to his feet and resumed his race through Manitou's woods.

A third shot from Clint's rifle never materialized. After several minutes, Hirsch reached a weed-covered embankment leading to the asphalt strip of the county road. He ground to a halt, resting his balled-up hands on his knees. He sucked in oxygen with greedy breaths that couldn't keep up with the metronymic pounding inside his chest. He'd reached the road and a modicum of safety from the malevolent lunatics running Teller's sanctuary.

Dehydrated, sheathed in a veneer of sweat and grime, bleeding from his ruined hands and feet, and starving, Hirsch made the long walk up the highway towards Beaver Island's village. The driver of a single vehicle took one look at his be-draggled, shoeless figure and sped past him, likely taking him for a drunk at this early Sunday morning hour. He longed for the comfort of his own bed across the waters of Lake Michigan. Home felt like a million miles away.

By the time Hirsch staggered into the village's outskirts, dawn had ushered in another glorious August morning. While too early for any stores or restaurants to be open, a water spigot alongside a shuttered rustic home-décor store caught his attention. Hirsch fell to his knees before it, his mouth parched and tongue raw from his ten-mile hike. He cranked open the spigot and a jet of frigid water splashed against his filth-streaked jeans. Abandoning any remaining pride, he stuck his face beneath the spigot and drank deep from the streaming water. He swallowed mouthfuls, pausing only to catch his breath. Satiated, Hirsch collapsed against the store's yellow-hued clapboard wall. He looked for all intents and purposes like a common lush coming off a night-long bender after losing an epic bar fight. The lines of the song "Sunday Morning Coming Down" came back to him, and he belted out an acapella version for the birds and whomever might be around to listen.

It was another half-hour before the first businesses opened for the day, and Hirsch took the opportunity to bathe his wounds and cleanse the accumulated grit and grime from his macerated feet. The water felt like pouring alcohol on his cuts, but losing his feet to infection sounded worse. Shortly after 7:00 A.M., he wandered towards a bakery that had just opened for the day. The owner, a slender redhead wearing a dark-blue apron dusted with flour, recoiled after taking one look at his soiled clothes and bare feet.

"Sir, we serve food here. You can't come in barefoot," she said while clutching a baguette with both hands as if to defend herself with it.

"Do you have a phone I can use?" he asked. The suspicion and reluctance on her face compelled him to add, "It's an emergency."

"If I give you my phone, will you go outside?"

"Yeah, sure. Anything."

She tossed her phone across the glass display case filled with pastries, decorated cookies, and an assortment of frosted and caramelized sweet rolls. He bobbled the phone but caught it before it clattered to the ground.

"Thanks," he said as he took it outside and stood on the empty sidewalk.

He'd committed Winston's number to memory and tapped the digits with his cold, sore index finger. Winston answered the call after a couple rings.

"This is Ben."

"Mr. Hirsch. I trust your mission is going according to plan."

"Winston—get me the fuck out of here."

Chapter 5

Hirsch woke in fright the night after returning home from Beaver Island and the horrors of Manitou. He'd drifted into exhausted sleep only to feel Clint's rough hands dunking his head into a vat of frigid water while Lisa observed. The sharp yelp of his own scream awoke him from the vile sensation of drowning at 6:00 A.M. He rolled out of bed, crashing against the weathered hardwood floor. Entangled in sweat-soaked sheets, he twisted free and came to rest against the bedframe. He clenched his face in both hands and massaged his head into semi-coherence.

Hirsch crawled across the bedroom floor and slid open the bottom drawer of his dresser with trembling fingers. Relief lay concealed beneath a pile of old T-shirts and back issues of the *Pioneer-Tribune*. He'd largely banished alcohol from his house following an ill-fated bender earlier that year when he'd drunk dialed his ex-wife, Allison, and made a total ass of himself. The half-pint of Seagram's VO was his emergency stash. Hirsch cracked open the cap and drank a long pull off the bottle. The uncut spirits hitting his lips brought instant solace, and he welcomed a second sip before replacing the cap and returning the bottle to its hiding place.

Fortified by the Seagram's, Hirsch staggered down the hallway into the bathroom. He parked himself under a jet of steaming-hot water for a full half-hour, holding his hands aloft to keep the open sores lining his palms dry. He'd lost weight in recent weeks of penury, and his ribs stuck out beneath the taut skin of his torso. Revived by the shower and restored to bitter reality, Hirsch scrounged through his laundry basket for a pair of wrinkled Levi's and a faded forest-green Northern Michigan sweatshirt. He smeared ointment on his oozing blisters and rebandaged them with fresh gauze before going downstairs to the kitchen.

Hirsch's fridge offered little in the way of fresh food. He cobbled together a meal comprising three fried eggs drenched in Tabasco sauce, stale sourdough toast smeared with Lingonberry preserves, and an overripe orange, all washed down with a pot of strong black coffee. With the rest of the day earmarked for walking a section of gas lines between Negaunee and Ishpeming and a meeting with Winston to debrief on his expedition to Manitou, he needed to get his shit together.

He'd had it with the Winslows and their naïve daughter. What business was it of his to worry about Alexandra's life choices? For better or worse, she was an adult. If she wanted to piss her youth away serving a bunch of humorless assholes, so be it.

The Tigers were hosting the Twins for the first of a three-game series in Detroit that evening. Hirsch wanted nothing more than to order a large sausage-and-mushroom pizza, collapse on his couch, and watch the game without having to think about any goddamn cults or rich-people problems.

But that wasn't to be. He faced a two-hour drive to Negaunee that morning. Traffic would only deteriorate the longer he waited. He poured a to-go cup of coffee, slipped into his regulation-issue Peninsula Energy blue vest, and grabbed his leak detector. Unraveling the world's theological problems took a back seat to keeping the U.P. safe from exploding gas lines.

WINSTON MAKI WAITED OUTSIDE the Winslows' front door as Hirsch arrived later that afternoon. Winston wore a blue-and-white-striped seersucker suit, white suede shoes, and a powder-blue shirt paired with a canary-yellow bowtie. Once again, Hirsch felt woefully underdressed in his gas-company work clothes.

"Welcome back," Winston said as he pumped Hirsch's bandaged hand. The latter winced as fiery pain shot through his forearm. "I trust your drive was uneventful. It's just the two of us today. I'll show you to my office down the hall."

"Where are Catherine and Herb?"

"*Mrs. Winslow* has a university board of trustees meeting in Lansing the next couple of days. *Mr. Winslow* accompanied her to fly fish the Grand River. In here," Winston said as he directed Hirsch through a door off the mansion's main hallway and into his office. The office's stark minimalism emphasized Winston's no-nonsense approach. An impressionist oil painting of the Pictured Rocks—undoubtedly from the Winslows' personal collection—adorned the cream-toned walls, along with a framed University of Chicago degree awarding Winston Maki a Master of Science in electrical engineering.

"Sit," Winston said as he gestured to a Steelcase armchair in front of his desk. Winston shut the office door and sat in his high-backed burgundy leather office chair. He uncapped a rosewood fountain pen and poised it over a yellow legal pad atop the desk.

"Well, you were Chris's only passenger Sunday, so I'm assuming Alex is still on the island. Was the Winslows' money well spent?"

"I found Alex and talked with her. She's fine but doesn't want to come home. She told me she's an adult and can make her own life decisions. She didn't appreciate her parents sending me there, either."

"Well, what did you tell her?"

"Exactly what Catherine—I mean, Mrs. Winslow told me—: that they were worried about her and wanted her back home."

"Did it seem like she was in any danger?" Winston asked.

"Not really. I mean, the place is weird as fuck and all, but I came across her weeding a garden by herself. She's really into organic gardening and all that hippie stuff. We only had a few minutes before the prophet's goons chased me away."

"So what else?"

Hirsch crossed his legs and scratched behind his ear, searching for adequate words to describe his experience at Manitou without making it sound made-up.

"Look, something really fucked up is happening on Beaver Island. Forgive my language, but I don't know how else to describe it."

"Fucked up? It's a cult—that's their nature. Mrs. Winslow wouldn't have forked over ten grand if that's all we wanted to find out. Can you tell us something we don't already know?"

"No, I mean, I get it's a cult and all, but I don't think this Jonathan Teller guy is calling all the shots."

"You mean the so-called 'king' isn't in charge?" Winston asked.

"The dude seems harmless to me. We visited for several minutes alone. He was calm, placid even. I spent most of the evening listening to him sing these god-awful folk songs around the campfire. He talked a big game about order and harmony, but he's not what comes to mind when I think of some charismatic cult leader ordering people around and governing with an iron fist. He has these two sidekicks—Clint and Lisa—who run the show. Like, from the minute I arrived, Clint was busting my balls. He had me digging a foundation pit for some tabernacle. I sat across from Alex at lunch and tried to talk to her then, but the woman—Lisa—shut that down quick."

"Tell me more about Clint."

"Really nasty fellow. Beard but no mustache. Not tall but built like a brick shithouse. He's ex-military and mentioned serving in Afghanistan. I have no clue how he ended up with Teller. He has this tattoo here that looked like an upside-down sword with a flower," Hirsch said, indicating the location of Clint's tattoo on his forearm.

"Did you ask Alex about Clint and Lisa? Maybe they're controlling her and pressured her to lie to you."

"Well, I'd planned to, but they decided to waterboard me during the night."

"Hold up. Excuse me—they what? Who?"

"Clint and Lisa hauled me out of bed around four or five the next morning. They dragged me into another building and repeatedly dunked my head into a tub of water and asked me who the fuck I was and what I wanted with one of their converts. They swiped the photo of Alex and your flip phone."

"Don't worry about the phone—it was a cheap piece of Walmart crap. We never intended that to happen to you, Mr. Hirsch."

"Yeah, well, chalk it up as a new life experience, I guess."

"I hate to ask, but what did you share with them?"

"They don't know my real name, but they know I was there on the Winslows' behalf. Law school never covered resisting enhanced interrogation techniques. Once they found out I was just some guy looking for a missing college girl, they ran me off at gunpoint."

"Is there anything else that might help the Winslows convince their daughter to come home?"

Hirsch steepled his fingers. "There is one more thing. A

kid I talked with that evening mentioned a boat. He said some girls from the camp worked on the boat and that it was connected with Lisa's family. The kid was a bit of a dumbass quite frankly, so who knows if it's true. The prophet mentioned her name was Dikeman or Dike-straw. Something like that."

"Interesting." Winston scrawled on his legal pad. "I'll see what I can dig up." He softened his expression. "I'm sorry if I came off as rude. You did more than most would and have the battle scars to prove it," he said, gesturing at Hirsch's gauze-wrapped palms. "The Winslows' money includes a presumption of confidentiality on your part. I'm the only person aside from Mr. and Mrs. Winslow you discuss this with, understood?"

Hirsch nodded.

"Will you excuse me for a moment while I make a call? You can wait outside."

Hirsch took the cue and stepped out of Winston's office, shutting the door behind him. The solid-core door clicked shut, and Hirsch ambled along the marble-floored hallway while examining the Winslows' collection of Upper Peninsula paintings executed in rich oils. He leaned forward to scrutinize the brushstrokes of a piece depicting an Ojibwa Indian camp on the shores of nineteenth-century Mackinac Island when Winston's office door opened. He paused alongside Hirsch in front of the painting.

"You recognize the artist?" Winston asked.

"No, who is it?"

"Seth Eastman. He was a nineteenth-century Army officer but devoted the better part of his career to documenting the lives of Native Americans in the Great Lakes before their way of life vanished."

"No small part thanks to his employer."

"Yes, well, I can't argue with you there. I spoke with Mrs. Winslow. While disappointed, she recognized they might not get their daughter home after a single intervention. She's even more concerned after I shared the details of your experience and is terrified Alex might be in more danger than she realizes. We're square moneywise, but if you want more work, I have authorization to offer it to you. We'll even double the fee considering the—erm—hazards of the job."

Hirsch considered the money and all he could do to reconstruct his life with the Winslows' continued backing. But he glanced at his bandaged hands and recalled the sheer horror of having his head shoved into a trough of water until his lungs nearly burst from the strain. No amount of money was worth reliving that experience. He'd pay down his debts one paycheck at a time, walking the gas lines and earning it the old-fashioned way. If he had to flip burgers at Clyde's, so be it.

Hirsch shook his head. "I've done what I can, Winston. I'm out."

"As you wish, Mr. Hirsch. I'll show you to the door." Winston led the way towards the entrance to the Winslows' manse.

"Help me understand something, will you," Hirsch asked as they walked together.

"I can try."

"How does a guy with an engineering degree from an elite school end up as a fixer for people like Catherine and Herb?"

Winston paused at the threshold. "The Winslows offered me a lifeline during an incredibly dark place and time. It's the least I can do to repay them. If you repeat this to anyone, I'll deny having said it, but Catherine has a sixth sense for desperation.

"Remember," Winston said as he opened the door, "their offer is still on the table. Should you change your mind, I'll be a phone call away."

Chapter 6

HAVING PUT THE WINSLOWS and their problems in his rearview mirror, Hirsch turned to his neglected relationship with his family. It was his Aunt Margie's seventieth birthday the Saturday following his meeting with Winston. He'd never hear the end of it if he was a no-show. After a hurried lunch of a steaming-hot pasty drizzled in thick ketchup at Lehto's in St. Ignace, Hirsch continued up I-75 to Sault Ste. Marie, known to the locals as the Soo. Fifteen miles out, he called his mother, Justine Archambault Hirsch, to tell her he was on his way.

Justine resided in a sixties-era, single-story hotel converted to condominiums on the Soo's southern edge. Though the structure's weathered gray façade needed a fresh coat of paint and the parking lot could use fresh blacktop, the units featured balconies, modern appliances, and a host of other features his mother could never have afforded in a newer establishment. As Hirsch drove up, he found her waiting outside her unit. She looked frailer than the last time he'd seen her. Her pale-yellow sleeveless dress revealed the birdlike thinness of her upper arms. Her once dark and full head of hair was now entirely gray save for a few strands of jet black, but she wore it loose like he remembered her doing since his childhood.

"You're lucky I wasn't already at Aunt Margie's when you called—or maybe you were hoping I'd be," she said as Hirsch exited his truck and walked towards her.

"Ma, I came here to see you both," he said, kissing her on the cheek.

"It's okay. Uncle Henry's on his way over. We'll ride with him if it's all the same to you."

"Fine by me. Will his wife be joining us?" Henry's second wife was thirty years his junior. She worked at a lounge in the downtown Soo before Henry married her and appointed her manager of his restaurant in Kincheloe near the state prison. Catering to locals, it performed well year-round, something many businesses struggled with in the tourist-dependent U.P.

"Your aunt Nicole," Justine said, with a grimace at the words coming out of her mouth, "is working today. It'll just be the three of us."

"That's a shame. I was looking forward to finally meeting her," Hirsch said.

"You and every other man in this family. Last time we all got together for Cousin Bill's memorial service, she wore a black miniskirt that showed off way too much leg. Aunt Margie near had a heart attack. What do you expect from a former cocktail waitress, I told her."

"As long as Uncle Henry's happy, I suppose."

"He'd better be. Say, Benny, you have anyone special in your life these days? I know you miss Allison, but I hate to see you alone," Justine said as she led him inside her condo. She instinctively fastened the chain and security bar left over from her unit's motel days.

Hirsch blushed. "I'm seeing this girl from Gladstone. She works part-time in Garden Corners. We get together a few times a week."

"What's she do there?"

"Um, well, she tends bar—"

"Not Lily's, right?" Justine said with a grimace of revulsion evoked by memories of that disreputable dive from her years in Manistique.

Hirsch sighed. "Yes, at Lily's—but in her defense, it's her grandparents' bar and she teaches math at Gladstone High School full-time."

"Well at least she's well-rounded, then. Is she Anishinaabe?"

"No, Ma, she's not," Hirsch replied, having expected the question.

"A shame," Justine said with a shake of her head as she tottered towards the kitchen.

"Like you're one to talk," Hirsch muttered.

Justine stopped in her tracks. "Your father was a second-generation French-Canadian Jew. He understood . . ." She let her words trail off with a hand in the air.

"I know, I know, Ma. Sorry to disappoint you *again*."

"You're not a disappointment. You never have been. Forgive me too. Tell you what—come in here and help me finish this potato salad before Uncle Henry shows up."

Hirsch followed his mother into the kitchen. She pointed at a colander laden with boiled Michigan red potatoes. "Chop those for me, will you. Knives are in the drawer. Leave the skins on."

Hirsch diced the cooling potatoes into bite-sized cubes with a razor-sharp chef's knife, then dumped the cubes into a yellow ceramic mixing bowl that had been in the family as long as he could recall. Justine took over and added diced red onion, sliced celery, and three chopped hard-boiled eggs to the bowl. She then slathered the contents with a mixture of yellow mustard and mayonnaise.

"Stir that for me," she directed, handing him a long-handled wooden spoon. As Hirsch churned the contents, Justine ground salt and pepper over the salad before dusting it with smoked paprika. "That should just about do it," she said.

"I'd better test it and make sure it's not poison," Hirsch said as he scooped a generous forkful and brought it to his mouth.

"One bite and that's it." Justine hunted for a box of plastic wrap in a kitchen drawer. "Well?"

"Delicious. Can't tell you how much I've missed this."

"If you came over to visit more often, that wouldn't be a problem."

"Ma!"

"Just saying . . ." she replied as she sealed the bowl with plastic wrap.

As they put the finishing touches on Justine's contribution to her sister's birthday party, Henry Archambault's maroon 1976 Buick LeSabre hardtop sedan roared into the parking lot outside Justine's condo complex. The Buick's blown muffler announced its presence from down the street, and Hirsch headed to the door to greet his larger-than-life uncle.

Despite being in his mid-seventies, Uncle Henry leapt from the car and moved with the energy and sense of purpose of a man half his age. Formerly chairman of the Michilimackinac Band of Chippewa Indians in the 1980s, he'd lost everything and rebuilt his life from the ground up more times than Hirsch could count. At present, in addition to being a successful restauranteur, Uncle Henry was an elder statesman of the tribe and served on its board of directors. Several of Hirsch's cousins owed their jobs to Uncle Henry's influence. That job security was a double-edged sword, as those cousins understood he could call upon them for a favor at a moment's notice with little option to turn him down, no matter how uncomfortable the assignment.

"Still driving that boat, I see," Hirsch said as Uncle Henry approached. His six-foot-three bear of an uncle wore jeans, a blue linen shirt, and a dark-gray tweed sport coat with leather patches on the elbows rubbed to a glossy sheen. A pair of aviator sunglasses with yellow-tinted lenses had been Henry's signature eyewear as long as Hirsch could remember. His full head of hair was well-streaked with gray and fell across his forehead in a deep part to the right.

"Benny, if you can find me a vehicle with three-hundred-plus horsepower that's like riding in butter, I'll trade her in. You won't, though. Besides, the ladies can't resist when they see me cruising through town behind the wheel of this beauty."

"I thought you were married, Uncle Henry."

"How do you think I met your aunt Nicole? You should've seen the look on her face when I rolled up to the Ojibway in this beauty."

"I can only imagine," Hirsch said.

"Will one of you give me a hand with this?" Justine said as she emerged from her kitchen bearing the enormous ceramic bowl of potato salad. Hirsch rushed across the room and relieved her of it.

"Thank you, Benny. Well, I can already hear Aunt Margie's complaining about our not being there yet. Shall we?"

Uncle Henry led the way to his Buick and held the passenger door for his sister while Hirsch climbed into the back seat and wedged the bowl between his knees. Forty-plus years of salt-treated winter roads had decorated the Buick's undercarriage with wide swaths of rust and had even eaten a ragged hole clear through the floorboard between Hirsch's feet. The gold-colored upholstery, however, was in fine shape, and for all the grief he gave Uncle Henry about his vehicle, it was undeniably comfortable. Hirsch sank deep into the plush seat and shut his eyes as he reclined against the headrest.

Aunt Margie lived fifteen minutes south of town off Riverside Drive in a pale-blue doublewide trailer she'd purchased with her late husband in the early nineties. A former social worker for the Michilimackinac Tribe, Margie struggled with diabetes and relished in haranguing her sister about her children and grandchildren's various woes. For all that, Hirsch made a point of visiting her whenever he was in the Soo, as he had fond childhood memories of weekends spent with her and Uncle Alvin. Her fridge never failed to have an ample stockpile of popsicles, and no one minded if he and his cousins spent hours out behind the trailer plinking at aluminum cans with BB guns.

They pulled into her yard, and Uncle Henry parked alongside a dozen other vehicles scattered across the front lawn. Hirsch exited the Buick and walked into Aunt Margie's backyard, where a plastic folding table supported a variety of potluck dishes. He added the salad bowl to the mix.

"Ben!" his Aunt Margie said as she advanced towards him. The adjustable cane in her left hand clicked with each step, and she clutched a sweating can of Diet Coke in her right hand.

"Happy birthday, Aunt Margie," Hirsch said as he leaned in to give her a hug.

"Your ma wasn't sure you'd make it. I'm glad to see you did. I don't know how many of these I have left." A bulky medical boot encased the lower part of her right leg. Despite being Justine's younger sister, Aunt Margie appeared the older of the two as the ravages of diabetes had taken their toll. "Ah, I see Justine made her potato salad," she continued, eyeing the bowl with ravenous attention.

"Only a couple bites for you, sis," Justine admonished as she joined the two. "I don't want your doctor blaming me for your blood sugar going haywire."

"We'll see about that," Aunt Margie replied.

"I'll be coming by more often now that I'm back in the U.P.," Hirsch said.

"That's good to hear, Ben. Now come say hi to your cousins." Aunt Margie led Hirsch at a snail's pace towards relatives gathered in groups around the yard. There were several he hadn't seen in years, and he took the opportunity over the next hour to bring himself up to speed on their goings-on. Midway through his cousin Lester's BSing about his fishing exploits on Lake Superior, Hirsch excused himself to grab a drink from an ice-filled cooler adjacent to the picnic table. Uncle Henry approached as Hirsch fished through the cooler for something other than cheap light beer.

"Let's take a walk," Uncle Henry said as his huge palm came to rest on Hirsch's shoulder. "I want to run something by you."

Aunt Margie's backyard gave way to a wooded area and unkempt clearing that rolled downhill and terminated in the St. Marys River. Hirsch had played there with his cousins as a child, enjoying the collection of rusted-out equipment and collapsed outbuildings that dotted the former farm.

"Your ma tells me you're working for the gas company these days. Is that right?"

"I am, but it'll wrap up in the next month or so. Once winter hits, we can't walk the lines no more," Hirsch said. "I did some part-time investigative work on the side, but I'm done with that now."

"Since when are you an investigator?"

"Since I lost my law license and needed to earn money," Hirsch said. "Really, though, it's not all that different from my lawyering days. Just dealing with even more lowlifes, if that were somehow possible."

"I read about that bit of trouble with those brothers over Delta County way. Tell me this isn't the same mess."

"It was different this time. These were legit businesspeople—the Winslows of Marquette."

Uncle Henry shook his head. "What'd I always tell you

about getting involved with rich folk? I made that same mistake when I was young. I ran a frozen-custard shop in St. Ignace and wanted to open another here in the Soo. These two businessmen from Saginaw came up this way. Told me they wanted to put money in the business, help it grow. Silent partners, they called themselves. Sounded great at the time, but within six months, they'd locked me out of my own business, and I was flat broke again. The St. Ignace shop's still there, and I curse the name of those long-dead assholes every time I drive by. My point being, even if they pretend to be your friend, you're not one of them. Never forget they're using you."

"I know, I know. Like I said, I'm done with all that. I need to find a regular job if I'm going to keep the lights on at the house. Can I ask you something, Uncle Henry?"

"Go right ahead."

"Running an ice-cream parlor's one thing. How'd you stay out of trouble with the casino business?"

"Well, it isn't easy, I tell you," Uncle Henry said while lowering himself into the cast-iron seat of a broken-down International Harvester tractor. He toyed with the steering wheel, its action stiff with rust. Hirsch leaned against the rusted hood and listened. "When the tribe got into gaming thirty years ago with one casino outside St. Ignace, no one gave us more than a year. Every bank but one laughed us out of their loan offices. The one that said yes required near all the tribe's assets as collateral on the construction loan. No one imagined that someday we'd operate seven of them across the U.P. What landed us in hot water was trying to expand south of the bridge. The powers that be didn't look kindly on a bunch of Indians from up north nosing their way in." Uncle Henry paused. "They still give me trouble now and then."

"What kind of trouble?"

"Downstate trouble."

"Who downstate?"

"Look—organized crime never abandoned Michigan. Not after Hoffa vanished, not after Indian gaming went legit. It's different now, but certain characters out of Detroit love to shake us down and make our lives as difficult as possible whenever they can."

"I'm sorry—what would Detroit want with a bunch of U.P. Indian casinos?"

"Money. And politics . . . always politics," Uncle Henry said with a shrug.

"Meaning?"

"Just that, politics. What it's always been up here and what it always will be."

"Jesus, getting involved with the mafia sounds like the last thing we need right now."

"Don't worry about me, Ben, okay? I wanted to talk about you. Whatever you've got yourself into in Manistique, it's not a good life for you. You belong here with your people. You're an enrolled member of the tribe. With your education, you shouldn't have any problem finding work at the casino or with the tribal government itself. Besides, if the disbarment's a problem, there's always a place for you at the restaurant. Say, you know how to handle a gun?"

"Unfortunately," Hirsch said, recalling his showdown with Marcus Shaw on Summer Island. "Why do you ask?"

"Because we need someone who can help keep the peace at the casinos. I've had three employees quit in the last two weeks saying they're sick of the abuse. Unruly customers mostly. I'm not saying it'll be easy, but you can make a difference here."

"I'll give it some thought, Uncle Henry. Thing is, I don't know where I'd live. I can't afford to commute from Manistique, and Mom's place is too small; I'm not sleeping on her couch."

"There's a little apartment over the restaurant. It's not much, but it'd be a roof over your head. I'd let it to you at a reasonable cost."

"Tempting."

"Come home and join us."

"Lemme think about it, okay?"

"Good, I can live with that. Now, let's go find your mom and see what kind of trouble we can get ourselves into," Uncle Henry said as he patted Hirsch on the arm.

Henry stood and brushed loose dirt off the seat of his wool trousers. They made their way across the clearing towards Aunt Margie's place. A half-dozen small children splashed in an inflatable pool set up in the backyard while a handful of adults surrounded a propane-gas grill, chatting and sipping from cans of light beer.

"Think fast, Ben!" Hirsch's cousin Neil said as he flung a can of Busch Light dripping with water and chunks of ice at Hirsch's head. Hirsch bobbled and caught it a split-second before the can demolished his nose.

"Jesus, small wonder no one could hit your fastball," Hirsch said as he cracked the beer. Neil laughed and approached. Still lean and sinewy from his ballplayer days, he wore his long, dark hair pulled back into a ponytail.

"I remember you sure as hell couldn't." Neil was Aunt Margie's son by her first marriage and, being a year Hirsch's senior, was both a friend and a tormenter growing up.

"You still play much?"

"Nah, not really. Pitched for the Soo's league team for a few years but gave all that up. Too worn out from work these days." What Neil left unspoken was that most evenings, he'd drained three or four beers by the time 7:00 rolled around. Neil was an all-star pitcher in high school but flamed out after a couple years of junior college in Bay City. He'd bounced around various rust belt cities in Michigan and Indiana for several years, living with girlfriends and working dead-end jobs, before landing a position with Chippewa County's road maintenance division—courtesy of Uncle Henry's influence.

"You've still got the arm," Hirsch said.

"Yeah, well, this arm spends most of the day spreading asphalt. Besides, I got three kids now and can't be running around in the evening playing ball."

"I might be joining you on the road crew, the way things are going."

Neil scoffed. "Benjamin J. Hirsch, Esquire, laying asphalt. That's a good one."

"Easy now. I worked on a road crew during college, remember?"

"And hated every minute of it, I'll bet," Neil muttered.

"I'm learning to appreciate the working life now."

"Spoken like someone who doesn't know what it means to work. At least I never pissed away a lawyer's pay for pussy. Enjoy your beer and don't patronize me, you downstate fuck."

Neil stomped off to visit with his kids playing around the pool, bumping his shoulder hard against his cousin and leaving Hirsch slack-jawed at Neil's sudden burst of rancor. He glanced down at the beer in disdain, reminded of what had contributed to his downfall in the first place. He abandoned the can on a makeshift table fashioned out of a weathered cable spool turned on its side. He wandered into Aunt Margie's house and found the bathroom unoccupied. He relieved himself, then rinsed his hands in the iron-streaked sink basin and dried them on a threadbare cloth hanging from a hook on the wall. As he went to leave, he paused and flipped open the door of the medicine cabinet. He flicked through the contents before finding a dust-coated prescription bottle at the back. Hirsch inspected the label—half-milligram tablets of clonazepam, three-years expired.

I doubt anyone will miss these, Hirsch reasoned as he popped the lid and shook two tablets onto the palm of his hand. He swallowed them with a gulp of the ferrous tap water and slipped the bottle into his hip pocket before returning to the gathering on the back lawn.

Tamed by the sedatives, he reconnected with family, and the afternoon flew by. Hirsch declined multiple opportunities to couch surf in his relatives' homes and returned to Manistique that evening as the sun set in the west. Swallowing another clonazepam to keep the nightmares at bay, he lay down that evening in his decaying bedroom. As the pill worked its magic and his vision grew fuzzy, he wondered if following Uncle Henry's advice and coming home wasn't the best outcome for all.

A HIGH-PITCHED SQUEAL INTERRUPTED a dream in which Hirsch was back in Lansing. He'd come home from a twelve-hour day of depositions in a civil case. His ex-wife, Allison, greeted him at the door wearing a sleeveless top and skinny jeans that hugged her slender legs. At the moment the racket eviscerated his sleep, Hirsch had her in his arms, stroking one hand through her auburn mane with the other wedged down the back of her jeans. Awake in an instant, he levitated out of bed and raced down the stairs clad in a T-shirt and boxer shorts. The worn and bowed white oak steps groaned as he clambered down them two at a time until reaching the ground floor. The squeal intensified as he crept along the hallway towards the kitchen. As he feared, the noise originated from the basement. An ear-splitting screech greeted him upon opening the basement door.

Hirsch had next to zero mechanical aptitude, but the cacophony screamed loud and clear that his steam boiler was royally fucked. He managed to locate the main steam valve and slowly twisted the rusty valve closed. He then shut the boiler itself down. The screech dissipated to a throaty whine before gurgling to a stop. As silence fell across the damp basement, Hirsch cursed and kicked at the boiler—yet another expense he could scarcely afford.

Later that afternoon, a local plumber, Vern Sigurdsson, responded to Hirsch's frantic call for assistance with his latest catastrophe.

"Yep, your boiler's definitely on the fritz, Ben," Sigurdsson pronounced after a ten-minute inspection. Hirsch stood at a distance with hands clasped in front of his waist, afraid to ask how bad it was. Vern turned to him, wearing a blue-and-white-striped pair of coveralls with "Vern" embroidered in red thread across his left breast. Running a hand through his salt-and-pepper hair, he looked at Hirsch with what the latter interpreted as amusement at his predicament.

"You got cracks in the tank itself *and* in the main steam line. That's what was making the awful racket you told me about. Your feed water pump's just about shot as well." Sigurdsson turned back to the boiler, shaking his head and clucking at the misfortune.

"Okay, so what'll it cost to fix this?"

"Fix it? There's no fixing this mess. You're looking at a total replacement, Ben. I can install a brand-new unit for seven thousand five hundred, parts and labor included."

"Can't we just patch the cracks or something?" Hirsch asked, desperate for any alternative to shelling out a ransom far outstripping his meager savings.

"Oh, I'd say we're well past that point. This here boiler's a good fifty years old. I'm surprised it lasted this long. These usually give out around the thirty-year mark. You're lucky in a way."

Lucky was the last thing Hirsch felt, trapped in his parents' basement with a licensed-and-bonded extortionist. There was no deferring this repair far into the future. As it was late August, he might have a month or two until cold weather descended on the U.P. The lack of a reliable heating system would render the house uninhabitable. He'd have an even bigger mess on his hands if the pipes froze and burst.

"Can I call you next week once I figure out a plan?" Hirsch asked.

"Oh, sure you can. I'll be a phone call away. I can have a new system here in three to five days once you say the word. Should only take me a day to install the thing. Until then, you might want a space heater or two if it gets chilly at night, you know."

Hirsch dismissed Sigurdsson with a handshake and a pledge to contact him once he scrounged up sufficient funds. He collapsed into a chair at his kitchen table, burying his head in his hands and at a loss for a way out of this latest debacle. At most, he had another couple months left walking the lines before the gas company suspended operations for the season. At his fourteen-fifty-an-hour rate of pay, even a month's worth of work wouldn't come close to covering Sigurdsson's repair bill. As was all too common in the past year of his life, he faced a desperate conspiracy of circumstances. He picked up his phone.

"Hey, Winston. Is that offer still open?"

"The Winslows would greatly appreciate your continued assistance," Winston replied.

"Then count me in."

"Very good, Mr. Hirsch. Welcome back to the fold."

PART II

Chapter 7

THE BRIGHT CHIME OF HIRSCH'S cellphone woke him from a deep sleep. He'd walked fifteen miles the previous day through rain-sodden neighborhoods of Munising in search of gas leaks. He plucked the phone off the floor while rubbing the sleep from his eyes.

"Hello," Hirsch groaned.

"I hope I didn't wake you, Mr. Hirsch," Winston said.

"Nah, well, yeah, but I needed to wake up anyway."

"Okay, good. Listen, I have background on Prophet Teller's two associates. The information you gathered proved helpful. I'm a half-hour away from Manistique. Would it trouble you if I dropped by?"

"No, that's fine," Hirsch said while rising to his feet. He pawed through his dresser for a change of clothes. "I'm not going anywhere."

He gave Winston his address and hung up. He showered and donned chocolate-brown corduroy trousers and a dark-green Merino-wool sweater, then walked to the kitchen and brewed a pot of strong black coffee. The aroma flooded the house, and Hirsch washed down a microwaved pasty with two generous cups. A nip of medicinal whiskey in each gave him the necessary fortitude to renew his association with the Winslows.

Winston arrived around 7:30 a.m., parking his dark-blue Acura MDX behind Hirsch's beater pickup truck. Even Winston's casual wear was a model of professionalism. His gabardine trousers featured a sharp crease, and he wore a light raincoat zipped up to his neck. His right hand gripped a cognac-hued leather attaché case embossed in gold with the logo of Swaine Adeney Brigg of London.

"So this is where you call home," Winston said after Hirsch answered the door. Winston's eyes darted around the living room. A collection of fast-food containers, empty bottles, and crumpled papers littered Hirsch's coffee table. "You're not one for heat, I see," he continued and tightened his coat.

"Not by choice. Come on in." Hirsch hurried Winston through the living room and into the kitchen. "Sit anywhere you like," he said, gesturing at the kitchen table. "You want any coffee?"

"No, thank you. I never drink any this late in the day," Winston said he as placed the attaché case on the table and popped open the brass fasteners. Hirsch shrugged, wondering when his visitor rested. He sat opposite Winston.

"What have we learned?" Hirsch asked.

"I haven't found much on Clint, but the woman you met is another story. Is this her?" Winston asked as he removed a glossy 8x10 photograph from a manila envelope and slid it across the table. Hirsch examined the professional headshot of a well-dressed woman in her early thirties. She wore her straw-colored hair parted down the middle and loose about her shoulders. In lieu of the Strangites' denim uniform, Lisa wore a dark-gray business suit over a light-pink collared blouse, open at the neck to reveal a pearl necklace. The image was one of an up-and-coming businesswoman rather than a cult enforcer.

"She looks . . . different, but yeah, that's her," Hirsch replied.

"Good. Her full name is Lisa Dykman-Van Raalte."

"That's a mouthful. What's her deal?"

"She belongs to a well-off family out of Grand Rapids. Downstaters like to joke about the Dutch mafia in western Michigan, but the Dykmans are as close to the real deal as you'll find. Your tip about girls working on a boat may have legs. Turns out the Dykmans' holdings include a fleet of fishing vessels and pleasure cruises out of Muskegon and Traverse City. They've long been suspected of drug smuggling all over Lake Michigan. The authorities have busted a handful of crews hauling oxycontin to the U.P. and Wisconsin but never managed to flip the low-level guys and build a case against the Dykmans themselves. The seafaring arm of their business goes by the name of 3D Fishing and Cruises."

"Why 3D?" Hirsch interrupted.

"Because three immigrant brothers from the old country founded the outfit years ago. They were commercial fishermen and sold wholesale all around the region. All three are long dead, but the middle brother's son and his wife now run the enterprise. They took a humble fishing business and added the pleasure cruise aspect—not to mention moving drugs all over Lake Michigan. The latest twist is they've branched out into running an exclusive escort service aboard the pleasure cruises."

"You think girls from Manitou are working the boats?" Hirsch asked, unfazed by the tawdry allegations.

"That's our suspicion, yes."

"Could Alex be one of them?"

"Hard to say, but Catherine and Herb are terrified she's involved."

"So how does Lisa Dykman-whatever fit into this?"

"Dykman-Van Raalte. She's the daughter of the current heads of the family business. She holds a BA from Vanderbilt University and studied applied mathematics at Stanford. She's 3D's chief operating officer, but the company's website claims she's on a leave of absence. Her husband's name is Braden Van Raatle. His LinkedIn profile says he's involved with the company."

"Wait—you said she went to Stanford, right? That's where Prophet Teller taught mathematics," Hirsch said.

"It is. From what I can tell, Lisa never graduated. She attended for a year and a half but dropped out before her fourth semester. The university wasn't forthcoming with details on her attendance and coursework, but Teller did teach graduate-level classes her last semester."

"You think Teller recruited Lisa for his cult?"

Winston removed his glasses and rubbed the bridge of his nose. "Seems reasonable enough, but I have no way of knowing for sure. They both stood to benefit from this arrangement. Who the hell knows what this so-called prophet's MO is, but the Dykmans are known troublemakers. My suspicion is they're using Teller's compound to distribute drugs and recruit girls for their escort service. Maybe they saw an opportunity to enrich themselves and hatched a scheme to team up."

"I take it this is more than just getting Alex home safe and sound?" Hirsch said.

"I'm afraid so. If drugs and prostitution are involved, Alex might be in danger. Others too."

"I mean, I get why they want to bring their daughter home and all, but this seems like a criminal matter. Why not call the Charlevoix County Sheriff and launch an investigation? Surely Catherine and Herb have that clout."

"You're entirely right—it should be, and Mr. and Mrs. Winslow tried. The police refused to do anything given Alexandra's an adult and there's no evidence she was kidnapped. As for the drugs and prostitution rumors, normally the Winslows would have the leverage to put an end to it. I'm afraid the Dykmans have similar power. It's a classic stalemate, in other words. The only solution is getting someone on the inside who can put an end to this madness."

"Catherine didn't seem that concerned about the crime ring her brothers were running right here in the U.P."

Winston groaned. "I see your point, Mr. Hirsch, but that was family. Believe it or not, the Winslows have a vested interest in keeping our Great Lakes homeland free of organized crime. Small timers are one matter, but widescale organized crime can't be tolerated. 'Chicago and Detroit, we ain't,' Herb said to me. The Winslows run a legitimate business. They want to keep it that way. And need I again mention their daughter is in grave danger?"

"Do the Winslows have any contact with the Dykman family? I imagine they move in similar circles."

"Hardly. Different class."

"Meaning?"

"The Winslows are old money. The Dykmans, well, their actions speak for themselves. Does that answer your question?"

Hirsch nodded and drummed his fingers on the Formica table. "What do you want me to do?"

"We can't send you back to Beaver Island, obviously. Clint or Lisa would beat the shit out of you—or worse. We'd rather put you on one of 3D's pleasure boats out of Traverse City and see what happens. Rumor has it they offer girls and drugs to well-paying clientele on sunset charter cruises. Take a ride and see what happens."

"Hold on—how on earth do you even learn about this?" Hirsch asked, puzzled by how the Dykmans could run a hooker and drug ring without the authorities knowing.

"People of the Winslows' social standing have access to services and information the likes of you or I never would. It's an ugly world out there, as I'm sure you're well aware by now."

"And if my cover's blown and they tie me to the anchor and throw it overboard?"

"There's a risk," Winston acknowledged, "but Herb and Catherine want to make it worth your while. Twenty-five thousand dollars, plus whatever's leftover from the action money on the cruise."

"They'd pay me twenty-five grand to get on a boat, try to get laid, and see if they offer me coke?" Hirsch asked.

"Twenty-five thousand dollars is a pittance if the authorities revoke the Dykmans' charter license or file criminal charges. Not to mention leverage to see their daughter returned home. Even if she's a true believer, she'll have to leave if Prophet Teller's arrested and Manitou is shut down. You've written your share of affidavits in practice. Learn as much as you can and write it up. Help us bring this outfit down, and it's one fewer scumbag crime ring ruining people's lives."

Hirsch knew when he'd called Winston that he'd say yes to almost anything. The Winslows' money would replace his boiler and leave enough to cover most of his remaining debts. Besides, he'd gladly stick it to Clint and Lisa after his experience on Beaver Island. In for a penny, in for a pound, he reasoned.

"Tell me the plan," he said.

"A young businessmen's charter cruise is scheduled for next Wednesday out of Traverse City. We'll book your passage under a fictitious name. Chris will pick you up in Manistique around 3:00 and fly you to the Traverse City airport. The ship departs at 5:30. A Dodge Charger will be waiting with the keys in the glove compartment. You'll find a wallet inside with a fake ID and four grand in cash. Don't spend it all in one place. Or do, if need be."

"Isn't that illegal?"

"Isn't what illegal, Mr. Hirsch?"

"Running around with a fake ID. What if I get stopped?"

"Then you'd better damn well drive safe, I guess. We can't figure out everything for you. Look, I'd do it myself, but they're not going to buy a middle-aged gay man masquerading as a horny bro trying to score some college-girl tail. I mean, really."

"I see your point."

"One more thing—you're a well-off pharmaceutical rep from Kalamazoo looking to blow off some steam. Dress the part, okay?"

"I can manage that."

"Don't screw this up. You may not think highly of the Winslows, but they mean well. Let me know when the job is finished; we'll arrange a time to meet." Winston stood and gathered his materials into his briefcase. "I'd best be returning to Marquette—I'm taking the minutes at a foundation meeting in two hours. One more thing—stand against that wall and face me," he continued while gesturing at the kitchen wall opposite them. Hirsch walked over and straightened his back against the wall as Winston snapped a picture with his phone. "I'll need that for your fake ID."

"You could've warned me first," Hirsch said, wishing he'd shaved. He walked Winston to the door.

"Good luck, Ben," Winston said, shaking Hirsch's hand. "I'll keep you in mind."

Hirsch stepped onto his front porch and watched as Winston entered his Acura. A zinc-colored band of clouds hung low over the skyline, and muddy puddles dotted the street in front of Hirsch's home. The rain and wind blown by a Lake Superior storm had chilled the house to its core, and Hirsch already longed for a new boiler. The breeze carried the mellow tang of fresh pine. At this early hour, Manistique's east-side was otherwise deserted—save for Hirsch's elderly neighbor, Dale Cromley, across the street.

Cromley was a retired journalist and elevated being the town's busy body to a virtuoso artform. He had a cigarette clasped between his lips and his quaking left hand shoved into the pocket of the soiled bathrobe he wore around the clock. His eyes followed the spotless Acura as it pulled away. While Hirsch generally avoided his cantankerous neighbor, Cromley was one of the few people who could help him better understand his latest nemesis. Hirsch waved as he crossed the dirt road towards Cromley's dilapidated 1940s cottage.

"If it isn't Ben Hirsch," Cromley said after removing the smoldering Winston Light from his mouth and tapping a long chain of ash against his porch rail. "Fancy company you're keeping."

"He works for my employer—one of them, anyway," Hirsch replied as he stopped alongside his neighbor.

Cromley grunted. "I wondered when I'd get another visit from the mystery man of Manistique."

"Yeah, sorry about that. Work's kept me on my toes lately."

"I figured as much from the looks of your front yard."

Hirsch surveyed the weeds and brambles overtaking his property. He'd fallen behind in recent weeks after a concerted effort to rehabilitate the place when he'd moved home months earlier.

"I'll add it to my list," Hirsch said and sighed.

"A bit early, isn't it?" Cromley wrinkled his nose after catching a lingering whiff of whiskey on Hirsch's breath.

"I had one hell of a week. Say, mind if I ask you something?"

"I suppose not. Not like anyone else comes by these days," Cromley replied. His wife had passed away several years earlier and both their kids had long fled south. Cromley was also notorious for his ostentation of peafowl, which occupied an impressive aviary behind his otherwise derelict house. The shrill birds haunted Hirsch's childhood, having never let him traverse Steuben Street without a cacophony of screeches memorializing his journey. Their strident calls were the bane of the neighborhood, but few residents challenged Dale Cromley's passion given his connections in town and knowledge of how to make people's lives even more miserable.

"You ever heard of a Dykman family of Grand Rapids?" Hirsch asked. "Businesspeople into commercial fishing and pleasure cruises."

Cromley started to respond but lapsed into a coughing fit that left the crank clutching his chest and fighting for air. His half-finished cigarette loosened from his grip and fell to the porch floor, where it smoldered atop the rotting wood.

"Shit, that was a good one too. Oh well." Cromley extracted a replacement from his robe pocket. He placed it with trembling fingers between his blue-tinged lips and lit it with a flick of a stainless-steel Zippo. "Grand Rapids wasn't really my stomping grounds, but oddly enough, yeah, I know of them. When I freelanced for the Traverse City paper, the Coast Guard busted a fishing boat on Lake Michigan carrying ten kilos of cocaine with a street value between three- and four-hundred thousand. It didn't seem like a big deal at first. I mean, ten kilos is a lot of blow, but we've had bigger busts on the lake. But it was a slow news week, and the editor gave me the go-ahead to write up an article.

"The crew members charged weren't all that interesting—two undocumented Nicaraguans and a captain from Benton Harbor with a pair of drug convictions to his name. I was trying to find anything to give the story a shred of interest, so I looked up the ship's registration with the state. I figured it'd be the captain's boat or some rental, but the owner turned out to be a company."

"3D Fishing and Charters?" Hirsch said.

"Exactly. I discovered they owned eight boats. Six were fishing rigs, but two were larger, charter-type vessels you'd associate with hosting parties out on the lake. One was based out of Traverse City and the other out of Muskegon. They advertised regular evening sightseeing cruises on the lake, as well as charter sailings for private parties and weddings. It seemed odd that an organization running a legit business would stoop to drug trafficking. I knew I had a compelling angle for the story, but common sense dictated this 3D Fishing and Charters would have a reasonable explanation for the bust."

"Did they?"

"I'm getting to that. It took me a couple of days digging through the Secretary of State's records. There wasn't much online at the time, but a few well-placed phone calls revealed a man named Piet Dykman was the principal owner and manager of 3D Fishing. Piet turned out to be something of a big man around town in Grand Rapids—a Lions Club member and Rotarian who served on multiple community and charity boards. I wanted to speak first-hand with Piet, so I contacted his office in Grand Rapids and asked for an interview. I pitched it as a straightforward businessperson profile, and I don't think it was even on their radar that anyone had connected him with the drug bust. Piet's assistant set up a meeting for the following week in Grand Rapids.

"So there I was, sitting in a conference room in Grand Rapids, when Piet Dykman burst through the door. He was in his mid-fifties at the time and a big man with huge hands. It seemed like his entire face was flushed dark red, which only made the white of the hair around the sides of his head stand out. Piet was all smiles and handshakes at first, thanking me for driving all the way to Grand Rapids to take time for a simple Christian businessman.

"My first few questions were softballs about his community service. Then I got down to brass tacks and asked him about his fishing and charter business. From the tightening around his eyes, I could tell it made him uncomfortable, but he answered my questions until I brought up the drug bust earlier in the month. At that point, he froze and glared like he wanted to leap across the desk and jam my pen into my throat. He hissed that the interview was over and all but hovered over me until one of his lackeys could escort me outside."

"That must've raised your curiosity," Hirsch said.

"Tell me about it. Once I got the runaround from Piet, I set out to interview anyone I could find about the company and its employees. I was convinced it wasn't an isolated incident and that the Dykmans had to be either aware of the activity or one hundred percent behind it. I tried to interview the county prosecutor, the detectives who led the investigation, and the county sheriff. Most of the time they're eager to talk since they have ambitions for higher office and want to highlight successful cases and wins. Not this time. They stonewalled me at every turn and referred to the county public relations officers—who were of zero help whatsoever. They got to my editor and killed any story. I never got another freelance job from that paper again."

"Sounds like they have little patience for anyone interfering with their schemes."

"I can't argue with you there. What's your deal with the Dykmans anyway?"

"I'm doing a little freelance work of my own. It started with trying to locate the missing daughter of a wealthy couple up in Marquette. One thing led to another, and now I'm knee deep with these assholes."

Cromley snorted and ran a hand over his nicotine-stained mustache. "If there's one thing I learned in the reporting business—it's all about the money. Either someone's out to make a buck by hook or crook or he's trying to stop another person from enjoying theirs. Don't ever forget that. And take care of yourself, Ben. The Dykmans could've ruined my life if they wanted to. People like them will stop at nothing if that's what it takes."

"I appreciate the insights, sir."

Cromley glanced at the cracked glass of his digital Casio watch. "Sorry to cut this short, but I need to head inside. *The Price Is Right* starts in a minute. Unless you want to come in and join me."

"I'm good, but thanks for the offer, Mr. Cromley." The thought of spending an hour cooped up in Dale Cromley's smoke-saturated home watching an insipid gameshow made digging a trench on Beaver Island sound appealing.

Cromley opened the door to his house and shuffled across the threshold. An unholy stench of stale smoke, rotting food, and sour sweat emanating from Cromley's living room assaulted Hirsch's nostrils. He held his breath while waiting for Cromley to shut the door, but the old man paused and turned towards him.

"Now remember, if you pick up a good story around town, you'd damn well better tell me so I can run it and get back in the game. Have a good one, Ben."

Cromley shut the door, sparing Hirsch further exposure to the house's corrosive odor.

Chapter 8

By the time the Cessna was midway across Lake Michigan, Hirsch had learned to relax and enjoy the subtle pleasure of flying five thousand feet above the water in a light aircraft. The lake stretched in every direction, with the Lower Peninsula's landmass a mere ribbon of texture along the horizon ahead. Hirsch craned his neck for a better view out the windshield.

"You see why we do it now, right?" Chris said. Hirsch nodded at her with a smile before returning his gaze to the undulating blue water of Lake Michigan highlighted by the sun behind them to the west.

Their flight path bisected the channel between South Fox Island and the smaller North Fox Island. They made for the tip of the Leelanau Peninsula before banking right to parallel the length of Grand Traverse Bay. Chris reduced the throttle and initiated their descent into Traverse City's Cherry Capital Airport. The city unfolded below them as they crossed town and began the final approach over Boardman Lake. Seconds later, the Cessna touched down on the runway and they taxied to the airport's general aviation section. Parked alongside a hangar was the cherry-red Dodge Charger promised by

Winston.

"You're on your own from here," Chris said as she brought the Cessna within ten feet of the car. "Fork over your wallet and phone."

"Is that necessary?"

"I'll give them back tomorrow. You'll find another wallet and phone in the Charger's glove box."

Hirsch handed them over and Chris slid them into a pouch on the left-hand door.

"I'll be here at 8:30 tomorrow morning. The Winslows booked you a room for the night at the Park Place Hotel downtown. Return the car to this same spot. The code for the airport gate is written on a sticky note on the dash—don't lose it."

"Wish me luck," Hirsch said as he crawled out of the plane with greater grace than his previous attempt. He grabbed his overnight bag and fastened the door.

Chris was already headed for the runway by the time he reached the Charger. He checked the glove compartment and found the promised cellphone and leather wallet. A fat wad of greenbacks swelled the latter. Hirsch's new identification bore the name "Roger Sampson" above a Kalamazoo address. The photograph was the headshot Winston had taken during his visit to Manistique.

"Roger Sampson, Roger Sampson, Roger Sampson," Hirsch repeated as he flipped the wallet shut and shoved it into a trouser pocket. He recovered the key fob from the glove compartment as well and pressed the ignition. The 370-horsepower Hemi V8 engine roared to life and settled into a satisfying purr as Hirsch donned his sunglasses and put the car into gear.

He felt like a colossal douchebag behind the wheel of an American muscle car headed for the lakeshore marina. Taking Winston's guidance to heart about looking the part, he wore lightweight black trousers, black leather ankle boots, and a stark white dress shirt. His rolled-up sleeves showed off a gaudy, oversized silver watch on his left wrist. A pair of wrap-around reflective sunglasses completed the ensemble. All he needed was a Michelob Ultra in one hand and a vape box in the other to fit right in with the happy-hour bros at a Lansing cocktail bar. In his years of practice there, he'd encountered their type on a regular basis and made it his mission to avoid becoming one. For one night, he could swallow his pride and act the part.

Hirsch parked the Charger at the marina and approached the gangway of the *Wanderlust*, the Dykmans' booze-cruise vessel. Sporting a royal-blue hull with a white stripe from bow to stern, the ship was ready to host a gathering of pleasure seekers for the evening. From the main deck, a set of stairs led to an elevated sundeck occupied by a smattering of young partygoers with drinks in hand. The temperature sat in the upper sixties with light winds out of the west. The faintest wisp of cirrus clouds streaked across what was an otherwise flawless evening sky. Conditions were perfect for a twilight journey along the bay.

A woman with curly strawberry-blonde hair and wearing a navy-blue pleated skirt with a short-sleeved white blouse cradled a tablet in her hands and smiled as Hirsch approached the gangway.

"Good evening, sir. Are you sailing with us tonight?" she greeted him.

"Yes, Be—Roger Sampson," he said, already flubbing his first minutes as a new man.

"Welcome, Mr. Sampson. I see you on our list for this evening's sunset cruise. You're welcome to board and make yourself comfortable. We'll depart in fifteen minutes."

Hirsch thanked the hostess with a twenty-dollar tip and climbed the gangway. As Hirsch stepped aboard the *Wan-*

derlust, a waiter bearing a tray of bubbling champagne flutes thrust the tray towards him and said, "Prosecco, sir?"

"Don't mind if I do," Hirsch said as he lifted a glass by its thin stem and brought it to his lips for an initial sip. While he wasn't much of a sparkling-wine drinker, the tart sweetness and the delicate play of the bubbles on his tongue made for a congenial start to the evening.

Nurse this baby over the next hour, he told himself. *You need to stay sharp.*

Hirsch explored the *Wanderlust's* open deck, getting the lay of the land and evaluating his fellow passengers. Near the bow, a gaggle of millennial tech bros stood in a circle drinking from bottles of Heineken. They cackled as one regaled the others with a story about the number of college coeds he'd banged on a recent work trip to Austin. A man with spiky hair and a silver chain around his neck caught Hirsch's eye and motioned him over.

"What's up, man?" the spiky-haired bro said as he fist-bumped Hirsch. "You ready to party?"

"Goddamn right I am!" Hirsch replied. "A buddy of mine in Kalamazoo raved about this cruise. I figured I'd see it for myself."

"Oh man, I remember my first cruise," a second man in designer jeans and a cashmere pullover sweater said. "Cost me a month's pay but worth every penny."

"That good of a time, eh?" Hirsch said.

"It always is if you know the right people," the first bro said.

"And who's the right person to know around here?"

"McKenzie," said the man Hirsch had christened as Spike.

"Nah, Ariana," cashmere-sweater man chimed in.

"How about Addison?" another bro commented.

"Oh, fuck, man, I totally spaced on her. Good call," Spike replied.

Cashmere-sweater man laughed and started to reply, but a third member of the group interrupted. "Seriously, though, Jerry the bartender is the best friend a young man looking for a good time can have—if you take care of him in return."

"We take care of our friends, right?"

"Damn straight, bro," Spike said and fist-bumped him again.

The conversation devolved into comparing nightlife and bars in their respective hometowns. After feigning knowledge of the mysteries of Kalamazoo, Hirsch drained his remaining prosecco. "Excuse me, boys. I'm going after a refill—maybe something stronger."

Hirsch left the gaggle in search of his procurer. Midway along the starboard side deck, he located the open bar.

"Evening!" Hirsch said as he raised his glass towards the middle-aged, mustachioed bartender whose nametag read "Jerry."

"Welcome aboard, sir. This is your first time on the *Wanderlust*, I take it."

"Yeah . . . how could you tell?" Hirsch clearly had "newbie" written on his face.

"Always can with new folks. I've had my eye on you. Most regulars already know what they're looking for and don't wander the decks as much. Can I get you another of those?" he asked gesturing towards Hirsch's empty champagne flute. The silky booze went down easy, and his brain and tongue already felt its influence.

"Nah, but I'll take a club soda with lime," Hirsch said as he deposited the empty flute on the varnished bar.

"You got it, boss," Jerry said as he filled a highball glass with crushed ice, sprayed it with soda water from a dispenser, and jammed a lime wedge over the rim.

"You know how a guy can have a good time here?" Hirsch said as he slid a hundred-dollar bill across the counter.

"Booze is included, and these sunsets can't be beat," Jerry said as he glanced at Hirsch while deftly sweeping the c-note off the counter and into his pocket. "But it depends what kind of a good time you're looking for."

"Let's say a *real* good time." Hirsch added two hundred dollars to the counter.

"I'm liking you more and more, sir. Tell you what, once the ship gets underway, stick around deck. I'll see what I can do for you." Jerry stroked his mustache and smiled.

"Appreciate it," Hirsch said as he took his drink and ambled towards the stern. He rested his forearms against the deck rail. Within minutes, the ship's horn blew, its plangent moan echoing across the bay. The vessel eased out of port to begin their two-and-a-half-hour cruise along Grand Traverse Bay. The marina and city skyline faded into the distance as the engines churned forth a white, frothy wake.

"I heard you needed company, Mr. Sampson." A delicate hand came to rest on Hirsch's shoulder.

Hirsch turned to find a young woman beside him. Standing around five foot two with long sandy blonde hair falling a few inches past her shoulders, she wore a variation of the hostess's uniform—a navy-blue skirt reaching only mid-thigh on her toned legs with a white sleeveless blouse. She accented the blouse with a scarlet handkerchief loosely knotted around her collar, and she gave off a delicate aroma of rose mixed with a sweet fragrance Hirsch couldn't place. Looking like a college student, she was far too young for Hirsch's taste. Her eyes made the biggest impression on him. While large and blue, they lacked even the slightest luster. Her pupils were constricted to tight pinholes. They looked straight at him, seemingly without seeing him.

"I could use a friend," Hirsch said, wishing he could whisk the girl off the ship and away from whatever mess she'd got herself into. "What's your name?"

"I'm Candy," she said while tracing her fingers along Hirsch's left arm and drawing herself closer to him. Her voice had the faintest slur to it. "Jerry said you were lonely and might need some cheering up."

Hirsch smiled. "Sounds like Jerry knows how to take care of his friends. Tell me—what would it take to get to know a girl like you better?"

"Well . . ." she said while leaning in and nibbling on his earlobe, "if you have a thousand dollars, we could enjoy ourselves below deck. Would you like that, Roger?" She nuzzled his cheek with her upturned nose.

"Lead the way, beautiful," Hirsch said as he slipped an arm around her supple waist. He'd never felt like a bigger creep in his life than standing on this boat deck propositioning a girl young enough to be his daughter. No amount of the Winslows' money could expunge this incident from his memory.

Candy kissed him on the cheek, then guided him towards a companionway leading below deck.

"Where you from, Candy?" Hirsch asked as they walked together.

"Wherever you want me to be from, baby."

Great, this is how it's going to be, Hirsch thought. "Well, are you a Michigan girl?"

"No. . . ." She placed her index finger over his lips to discourage further questions.

Candy led Hirsch down a narrow flight of stairs that terminated in a passageway with four doors on either side. An enormous hulk of a man, nearly six and a half feet tall guarded the path. He wore a red silk button-up shirt untucked over black slacks that strained against his massive thighs. His dark, curly hair sprang in all directions, and rivulets of sweat dribbled down the sides of his head. He ogled Candy as they squeezed past his mass towards an open cabin door at the hall's end.

"You take good care of our guest, Candy. I don't wanna hear any complaints like last time," the ogre said, depositing a sharp slap on her taunt ass as they passed by. Candy glared at him but snapped her gum in response. She grabbed Hirsch's arm with both hands and hurried their pace towards the open door.

Sounds of coital pleasure emanated from behind the varnished cabin doors they passed. The lurid panting of a fellow passenger filled Hirsch with added revulsion for the entire class of men with high disposable incomes who felt this was a normal, healthy way to entertain themselves. He blanched at the realization that Alexandra Winslow could be onboard.

The Dykmans had outfitted the cabin for one purpose. A white-sheeted, full-sized bed bracketed by a pair of nightstands occupied most of the space. A half-open sliding door led to a small bathroom. Candy shut the door behind him, muffling the sex sounds from the other room. She untied her scarlet handkerchief and dropped it on the bed, then undid the buttons on her blouse, slipped it off, and draped the blouse over a chair.

Candy wore a hot-pink bra that cupped a pair of perky breasts. Her ribs stuck out, and her waist was so slender Hirsch could almost encircle it with his hands. She unzipped the navy skirt, revealing a matching hot-pink thong. She walked alongside the bed towards the nightstand and opened the drawer, leaning over to give Hirsch an unobstructed view of her rear and firm legs. He gulped at the sight but quickly looked away.

"Want a bump?" she asked after turning to face him. Candy held forth a narrow silver spoon piled high with white powder she'd dipped from a small glass vial.

While he had little desire to mess up his concentration with drugs, he worried she'd think he was a narc if he declined. Hirsch leaned forward, pinched one nostril shut, and snorted the cocaine. He reared back and coughed as the powder seared his nasal passages and throat. Intense pleasure nonetheless washed over him in an instant.

"Another?" she asked, coke spoon in hand.

"I'm good," Hirsch replied and sniffled. The last thing he needed was to be royally blitzed the entire evening. He'd already be screwed if the gas company drug tested him.

"Suit yourself." Candy shrugged as she lifted a lump to her nose and inhaled the entire pile in one go. She shook her head and huffed through her mouth several times. When her eyes refocused, she looked at him. "Like I said, it's a thousand cash—up front. Make yourself comfortable." The cocaine had sharpened her previously laconic speech.

He counted off ten hundred-dollar bills with trembling fingers and extended the wad to her. "Sit down," he said while indicating the edge of the bed in front of him.

Candy bit her lower lip as she smiled and lowered herself onto the bed. "So this is how you want it," she said as she stroked him through his trousers and began undoing his belt.

"No, wait," Hirsch said as he brushed her hands aside and stepped back. Confusion clouded Candy's face, and Hirsch rushed to extract another thousand dollars from his wallet. He held the folded stack of bills aloft. "This is for you—but I want you to talk to me, that's all."

"Talk . . . what the fuck about?" she said as she dropped her hands into her lap and glared at him. "Look, mister, I don't care what weird shit you're into, but if I don't show you a good time, Damien out there will take it out on me. The bruises on my butt just healed from last time."

"I want to know how you got into all this."

Candy moved away, drawing her legs onto the bed.

"Are you a fucking cop?" she hissed while her eyes cut towards the door that Hirsch blocked. "I could scream, you know. They'd kill you if they found out."

"I'm not a cop," he whispered. "But I know what goes on here, and I want to help."

"Help . . . how?" she asked with her arms folded across her chest.

"Help you escape and keep other girls from doing the same. Here," he said as he added another stack of bills to the thousand already in his hand, "take this. Hide it wherever you can." Hirsch proffered the pile of hundreds and twenties to the girl. She reluctantly reached a hand forward and gripped it tight in her tiny palm, avoiding his eyes. Hirsch sat alongside her on the bed.

"Tell me how you got here," he said.

"I was in my second semester at Western Michigan. My roommate, Mallory, convinced me to go to this house party in East Lansing. Her boyfriend went to Michigan State and invited us to the party. We had, like, a couple drinks apiece and were having a good time. There were lots of cute boys there. Around, I don't know, midnight, I guess, this woman came up and started chatting me up. She was a little older than us, but I figured she was a grad student or something."

"What'd she look like?"

Candy shrugged. "Long blonde hair, high cheekbones, and tall . . . real tall. She had on a Michigan State sweatshirt and seemed cool. Anyway, she said she worked for this charity summer camp. They needed students who wanted to earn some money next summer by working with disabled kids. My younger sister has Down's syndrome, so this chick definitely had my attention. She texted me her number. I ended up hooking up with this guy that night and forgot all about it for a couple days, but I texted her the next week and said I was interested. She gave me an address in Grand Rapids and told me to go there the next weekend for an orientation.

"Well, I showed up—it was in a strip mall—and there

were, like, five other girls. It all seemed pretty chill. We chatted a bit. Most were college students like me. Not bad looking, either. Sounded like they got the same pitch as I did."

"Do you remember the name of the place?" Hirsch asked.

"I, um . . ." Candy wagged her head and cast her eyes in thought. "It was some Dutch name on a red sign over the door. Pretty normal office, I guess. Not very helpful, I know."

"Dykman?" Hirsch offered.

"Yeah, could be. Anyway, so we were stand—"

The rap of knuckles on the cabin door interrupted her story. "Everything okay in there? Everyone having a good time?" Damien called out.

"Yeah, man, we're good," Hirsch said. "Just getting acquainted and all."

"All right, boss. Just making sure she's taking good care of you. Come to me if she gives you any trouble." Damien's footsteps faded into the distance as he moved down the passageway.

"We need to get going or he'll get suspicious," Candy hissed.

"Here, I'll put on some music." Hirsch pulled out the Winslows' loaner phone and hit play on a streaming music app. "Okay. Then what happened?" he asked as the room filled with soft R&B beats.

"Okay, well, the girl from the party wasn't around, but there was this guy with a creeper mustache there—a colossal dweeb, we all thought—he told us more about this camp on an island in Lake Michigan they were opening for summer. They planned to bring a bunch of disabled kids from all over the state and give them a place to just be themselves. Bobby, the dweeb with the pedo stache, was super convincing, and we all thought the camp sounded pretty cool. So, like, part of the deal was we could check it out that weekend, spend the night, and see if we liked it. If we did, they'd bring us back for the summer as employees. I had a couple friends in high school who worked as summer camp counselors, so it didn't seem like a big deal.

"Anyway, Bobby had this van parked outside. We piled inside and he drove. One girl didn't go—she had some sorority thing that weekend and went back to Ann Arbor. The rest of us got to know each other on the drive up. Bobby bought us lunch and even snuck us each a beer while we waited for the ferry. Everything was chill until we got to Beaver Island and drove into the camp."

"Did you see the sign at the entrance?"

"The creepy Manitou sign? You know about that?"

"Yeah."

"Nah, the sign came later. All they had when we got there was a metal gate that was, like, spraypainted bright orange. Bobby unlocked the gate and drove us inside. That's when we knew something was wrong."

"Wrong how?"

"I mean, the place wasn't like any summer camp I'd ever seen, that's for sure. There were other people around, most of them our age, but they were dressed kinda strange and there were these, I don't know, weird religious symbols all over the place. Bobby could tell we were all a little freaked out and told us it was a former church camp just to get us out of the van. That's when that chick from the party walked in along with a guy named Clint. The woman—her name was Lisa—told Bobby she'd take it from here, and he drove off."

"Did you ever see him again?"

"Nah, from then on it was just Lisa and that asshole Clint."

"So then what happened?" Hirsch asked. He remembered from his days as a trial attorney that whenever you have a witness who's talking, it's best to keep your damn mouth shut.

"Lisa told us we worked for her now. She said we were in the kingdom of God under the authority of his divine whatever on earth, King Strang the Second. I didn't understand much of what she was talking about. Boy, did I find out soon enough. One girl had heard enough and took off running towards the road, but Clint caught up with her. He dragged her back and smacked the shit out of her in front of us. None of us knew what to do after seeing her curled up on the ground crying. I think we were all in shock.

"Lisa made us call or text our parents and friends to tell them we'd found God and wouldn't be able to come home or visit anytime soon. Then she took our phones away. We, like, had to attend a bunch of sermons by the prophet and sit in circles and listen to his crappy songs. At first I was like, great, we've been kidnapped by some cult and have to listen to this shit all day, every day. I wish that was all there was to it. . . ."

Candy fell silent and stared at the floor with a vacant expression on her face before continuing. "We weren't really allowed to chat with the others, but I found out a few of them were there by choice. Like, they actually wanted to be there and were into this weird religious crap. They had a *much* different experience than we did."

"How so?"

"I mean, they spent most of their time just building stuff and growing vegetables and shit out in the garden. It was weird. Like, *none* of us wanted to be there, but these hippie kids were all into the prophet and growing their own food."

"You ever meet a girl named Alex? About your age and height; nose ring."

"Yeah, sure. I mean, you could tell she was this spoiled rich bitch, but she was all about gardening and going back to nature. I think she wanted to fuck him, honestly."

Hirsch nodded. "What then?"

"The girls—I mean the five of us Bobby brought up plus

a few more who joined later—we were put to work doing laundry and cleaning the place. That wasn't the worst, though. They fed us drugs not long after we got there. I'd smoked a little weed and done molly a couple times in college, but they had us doing meth, and, before long, they were shooting us up with oxy or heroin. I won't lie, it felt pretty damn sweet at first, but once they got us hooked on that shit, we'd do any-thing—and I mean *anything*—to get our next fix.

"That's when the sex started. Clint was the first, but before long they had us sleeping with the other guys. Lisa sprouted some religious nonsense to justify it all and said it was our obligation to service the elders, blah, blah, blah. What it meant was having Lisa wake us up in the middle of the night, feed us a little meth, and send us into one of the guys' rooms. Thank God I was so bombed out of my head most nights that I blacked out and can't remember much.

"After a couple months of this crap, Lisa told me my training was over and it was time to raise some money for the cause. Told me if I didn't, they'd cut me off the candy. That's what they called the drugs there—candy, just like me. They'd cut it off once before just to teach me a lesson. I damn near puked my guts out and died in that nasty shed they locked me in for a couple days. At first, I didn't know what she wanted, but once I saw the clothes she laid out for me, I figured it out. They flew me in a floatplane and shoved me in the back seat next to lardass Damien. We flew to, well, here, I guess. It was nighttime, and Damien whisked me out of the plane and onto this boat before I knew what was happening. He told me he'd snap my neck and toss me in the water if I screamed. Wasn't like there was anyone around that late at night to hear anyway.

"And now here I am," she said as she raised a hand and let it fall into her lap, "screwing entitled douchebags on this stupid yacht five days a week. I guess I'm lucky, in a way. They made me shoot porn first for some sick website they run. At least this isn't being videotaped."

"I'm sorry—a porn site?"

"Yeah. I . . . I'd rather not talk about it."

"What about your family? Didn't they try looking for you after you left college?"

Candy snorted. "That stupid cult gave them the perfect cover. They'd tell anyone who asked that I'd found God and was devoting my life in service of King Strang. I mean, who could prove otherwise?"

"Did you ever, you know, try to escape?"

Candy snorted. "One girl tried . . . she didn't make it."

"What other girl? When?"

"BreAnn," she whispered. "The one who tried to run."

"Tell me what happened to her."

"Never mind—I've already said too much."

She fell silent. With her shoulders hunched and hands folded in her lap, she looked like a scared, fragile child.

"What about Prophet Teller?" Hirsch asked softly. "What was he like?"

"Jonathan? I guess he was some professor who, like, decided he was God's messenger and quit his job to go to that stupid island. He'd check in on us, make sure we had enough to eat. He never tried anything like Clint and some of the other guys did."

Damien's off-key whistling in the passageway reached their ears, and Candy's eyes widened in fear. "Look, mister, I've told you everything I can. These guys are going to royally mess me up if they think we didn't fuck."

Hirsch rubbed his temples and said, "Okay, well, act like you're having a good time so you won't get hurt."

Candy began moaning and grew louder as Hirsch joined her with his own imitation of passion. Her performance was convincing, and Hirsch flushed with shame, feeling like a total perv for being in this situation in the first place. After a couple minutes, Candy unleashed a convincing fake orgasm before falling silent and draping herself motionless across the bed.

"Was that good, Roger?" she asked loud enough for Damien to hear.

"God, let's hope so," Hirsch mumbled as he stood.

Candy jumped off the bed and faced him. "Here," she said as she ruffled his hair with her fingers and rumpled the fabric of his shirt and trousers to make him look more like a man who'd just had a roll in the hay. She finished with a long kiss on his lips, dragging his lower lip between hers to smear some of her pink lipstick onto him. "That should help."

"Is Candy really your name?"

"It's Morgan," she replied as she zipped up her skirt and slipped her arms into the blouse. "I grew up on a dairy farm outside Elkhart, Indiana." She finished dressing and put her hand on the chrome-plated door handle before pausing. She shot Hirsch a look of tenderness mixed with pity. "This is a mistake, you know."

"What's a mistake?"

"Messing with these creeps. I meant it when I said they'd kill you. Just like they did with BreAnn." Hirsch opened his mouth to reply, but Morgan placed a finger over his lips. "Now smile and look like you had a good time." She grabbed Hirsch by the hand and escorted him into the passageway.

"You have a nice time in there, sir?" Damien asked with raised eyebrows and a leering smile as they approached the companionway.

"More than you can imagine." Hirsch wrapped an arm around Morgan's hips and squeezed her close to him.

"I'm glad to hear that, sir. Sounds like Candy's finally learning."

"You don't have to worry about this one," Hirsch said as

they brushed past Damien. He reeked of sweat and a cloyingly sweet cologne. Hirsch slipped a couple hundred-dollar bills into the pocket of Damien's silk shirt to keep him happy.

"You come back anytime," Damien called out as they walked up the stairs and into the open air. Twilight had overtaken the Michigan evening, and a pleasant breeze cleared Hirsch's nostrils of the carnal funk below deck.

On deck, Hirsch pulled Morgan close to him. "Just try to make it through the next week or two," he whispered in her ear. "I'll do everything I can to get you and the others out of this mess, okay?"

"Yeah, whatever, dude. Just don't get me killed. Look, we've got an hour left on this cruise; if I don't bring in another trick, Damien will clobber the shit out of me. Now if anyone asks, tell them Candy gave you the best night of your life."

Morgan kissed Hirsch on the cheek, then turned and strutted away. Her white high-heeled shoes clicked along the teak deck planking. Hirsch returned to the bar in a daze as the coke wore off and left his head fuzzy. Jerry glanced up from a blender of margaritas when Hirsch approached.

"What's the verdict, friend?"

"You came through for me, man," Hirsch said as he slid four twenties across the bar with two fingers. He'd burned through more money in a couple hours than he normally spent in a month.

"Another club soda and lime?" Jerry asked, pocketing the cash.

"Nah, better make it a double Jameson this time. Neat," Hirsch said. Nothing would erase the evening's sleaze fest from his memory, but a stiff drink wouldn't hurt.

Jerry gave Hirsch a generous pour and set it down in front of him with an arm tanned to a golden brown. Hirsch wanted nothing more than to seize the arm and knock out Jerry's teeth with his free hand. He restrained himself and accepted the drink with a nod before walking around the party boat.

He understood what he had to do. While the authorities might overlook a bunch of runaway college girls, there was no way they could ignore a murder—no matter how wealthy or well-connected the family behind it. Find the dead girl, jail Prophet Teller and his henchmen, and return Alex and the others to their families. The true believers would just have to deal with it.

The rest of the cruise passed in a blur. Hirsch polished off his double Jameson and ordered a second from a waiter. He migrated to the upper deck for a better view of the shoreline lit by twinkling lights spreading across the low rise of the Leelanau Peninsula. His heart sank when he caught Morgan's eye for a split-second as she escorted a bro below deck. The man looked like he'd just stepped off the golf course in khaki trousers and an untucked lime-green polo shirt. She'd found her second trick—one who would no doubt take full advantage of her situation. Hirsch collapsed into an easy chair on the upper deck to wait out the rest of the trip and shut his eyes.

"Sir, we're back in port. I'm afraid you'll have to disembark," a waiter said while gently shaking Hirsch's shoulder.

He'd fallen asleep for who knows how long. The upper deck was near deserted. Hirsch massaged his face several times with his hands until he felt alive enough to stand. The whiskey's soporific effect had worn off, leaving him dehydrated with a pounding headache and raw sinuses. He stumbled towards the gangway, palming twenty-dollar bills off on the waiter and the hostess who'd greeted him when he first arrived. Against his better judgment, he fired up the Dodge Charger and drove it the handful of blocks to the downtown hotel where Winston had reserved him a room for the night. His remaining minutes of consciousness were a blur as he collapsed on the bed fully clothed and fell into the dreamless void well known to those who anesthetized themselves with booze and pharmaceuticals to blot out the world's horrors.

Chapter 9

A RAY OF SUNLIGHT PIERCING the gap between the hotel-room blackout curtains awoke Hirsch the following morning. He glanced at the alarm clock glowing on the nightstand—7:15 A.M. His nasal passages ached like someone had run sandpaper up his nostrils, and he moaned in agony as a booze-fueled headache walloped him. He buried his face in his arms to block out the light, then remembered his scheduled rendezvous with Chris at 8:30. With the information he'd gathered the previous night, Hirsch's work here was unfinished. He fumbled for his phone and dialed Winston.

"Mr. Hirsch, is anything the matter? Chris should be on her way."

"Can you call her off? I need to stick around a day or two and run down a couple leads."

"She won't like it, but yes, I can call her. No bother with keeping the car an extra day or two, either. Any info I can take back to the Winslows?" Winston asked.

"The Dykmans are way deep in some serious shit. Worse than we thought."

"As we've long suspected. Do you have anything first-hand we can use?"

"Only enough to nail some small-time players. But there's a chance I can blow this open and take down one or more of the Dykmans—and bring Alex home for good."

"Very well, please proceed. Tell me you at least have *some* money left over from last night," Winston said.

"Yeah, yeah, I should be good," Hirsch said, although the thick wad of bills he'd started with yesterday evening was greatly diminished. "It'll get me to Grand Rapids and back."

"That's fine, Ben. Call when you're finished. We'll arrange a time and place to drop the car and have Chris pick you up. Be careful, though; you're entering a lion's den. If they catch you and trace this back to the Winslows, all of us could be in danger. It's one thing for them to think you're a PI hunting for a missing child. It's another matter entirely if you're out to nail them on criminal charges."

"I'll be careful."

"Good. Catherine and Herb have put a great deal of trust in you. Don't disappoint them."

Hirsch ended the call, rolled to the edge of the bed, and planted his feet on the floor. He washed a handful of Excedrin down with a seven-dollar bottle of carbonated water raided from the minibar. A twenty-minute hot shower somewhat restored his mind and spirits, and by the time he dressed and packed his meager travel kit, he felt almost human.

He spent the next hour on his phone researching possible locations for the Dykmans' storefront operation in Grand Rapids. Over two dozen businesses in the region had "Dykman" in the business name, but he eliminated those housed in standalone buildings or office towers that didn't fit Morgan's description. Within an hour, he'd winnowed his list to three locations in strip malls with red signs bearing the Dykman name. One was a daycare and seemed highly unsuited for a crime ring front, while two other businesses—an office supply store and an insurance sales office—emerged as the strongest candidates.

Hirsch checked out of the hotel and threw his bag into the trunk of the Dodge Charger. Over the two-hour drive south to Grand Rapids, he fought to keep the vehicle under eighty—the eight-cylinder engine wanted nothing more than to open the throttle and blast past the motorhomes and semi-trucks clogging the road. While he questioned the need for such an opulent ride, he admittedly relished the raw power under the hood. If he had Lauren next to him, they could cruise all the way to Southern California in style.

The first business on his list—Dykman Office and Stationery Supply—anchored a strip mall on the north side of town near the Alpine shopping center. Hirsch parked where he could keep an eye on the storefront. He killed the engine and spent the next hour watching customers come and go while nursing his lingering hangover with a bottle of 7UP purchased from a Reed City convenience store.

Not a single staff member fit Morgan's description of Bobby. The only moment of interest was a woman in a pencil skirt and heels whose ass wagged invitingly as she departed the store clutching reams of printer paper. Hirsch got a full view of her skirt-clad thighs when she popped the trunk of her car and leaned over to deposit the paper. Close to 11:30, he gave up and drove south across the Grand River on Interstate 196 into midtown Grand Rapids. Exiting the freeway, he located the second strip mall on his list. The bright-red sign above the storefront read "Dykman Family Insurance" with "Auto, Life, Home, Fire" stenciled in white letters on the floor-to-ceiling window to the right of the doorway. Hirsch backed the Charger into a parking spot opposite the entrance and waited. He snapped photos of the storefront and a white passenger van parked out front.

Five minutes after noon, a scrawny man with wispy side-burns extending past his ears and a thin blonde mustache emerged through the front door. The man wore a powder-blue windbreaker over a button-up dress shirt with baggy black trousers that needed to be taken in at the seat. He fit Morgan's description of Bobby to a T. The man flipped over a sign on the door bearing the word "away" with an image of a clock indicating he'd return at 12:30. He entered an early 2010s beige Chevy Impala. As the Impala backed out, Hirsch resisted the urge to follow. If the man returned within a half hour, Hirsch could confront him inside the office.

He slunk down in the driver's seat with his shades perched high on his nose to avoid drawing the attention of any passersby, then clicked on the radio and listened to grim news on NPR until growing depressed and turning it off. Sure enough, the Impala returned five minutes before 12:30. The dweeb exited the vehicle, brushing the remnants of his Taco Bell lunch from his windbreaker. He entered the office and flipped over the sign. Hirsch waited five minutes before popping the Charger's door and approaching the storefront. An electronic bell jangled as he opened the aluminum-framed glass door and stepped inside.

"Be with you in a sec," Bobby called out over the sounds of a copy machine scanning and spitting out duplicates. He had his back to Hirsch and was engrossed in grabbing stacks of collated and stapled documents from the outfeed tray. Hirsch took the opportunity to throw the lock on the door and flip the "away" sign. A set of venetian blinds covered the floor-to-ceiling windows. He spun the plastic wand to twist them shut—cutting the office off from view of the outside world. He headed for the copy machine.

"I said I'd be out in a minute, sir," Bobby said as he turned and glared at Hirsch through thick, gold-rimmed aviator glasses. "If you'd just wait—"

Bobby had no chance to finish his sentence. Hirsch wrapped his fingers around the back of Bobby's head and slammed his forehead into the open copy machine. A spider-web of lines crackled across the green-tinted glass.

"Jesus, what the actual fuck, man," Bobby screamed as Hirsch jerked his head away from the machine. One lens of Bobby's glasses had completely shattered, and thin trickles of blood seeped from a crisscross of cuts on his forehead.

"What's your name, asshole?"

"B—B—Bobby."

"Bobby what?"

"Bobby Devall. Now what—"

"Tell me who you work for," Hirsch said.

"I . . . I work here. Now—"

"Don't give me that shit. I know about the girls, I know about Manitou. Now tell me where I can find your boss."

"Look, man, I don't know what the fuck you're talking about . . . I'm just an insurance agent here," Bobby blubbered between lips smeared with blood.

Hirsch slammed Bobby's head back down onto the copy machine and, with his right hand, bashed the machine's lid over Bobby's skull until the entire tray separated from its hinges and clattered to the ground. Hirsch jammed the man's neck firmly against the glass.

"Okay, okay, stop!" Bobby cried out as he extended a trembling hand towards Hirsch while staring through wide, scared eyes.

"You ready to start talking or what?" Hirsch asked. "You work with Lisa Dykman, don't you? Your employers have put me through enough shit these past few weeks. I have zero patience for this nonsense right now."

"Yeah, all right, I work for the Dykmans. So what? I swear I never touched any of the girls, okay. You've got to believe me on that. My job was just to feed them some bull-shit about a summer camp for cripples and deliver them to Beaver Island. That's it."

"Where they'd be addicted to drugs and forced into prostitution. What happened to the girl?" Hirsch interrupted. "The one you people killed on Beaver Island—BreAnn."

"What girl, killed—what the hell are you talking about?"

Hirsch squeezed harder on the back of Bobby's neck and ground his face deeper into the shattered copy-machine screen.

"You gotta believe me, no one said a word about anyone getting killed," said Bobby. "Do I look like I could murder someone?"

The trembling, weasel-faced dipshit with his face pancaked against a copy machine likely couldn't hurt a mouse, let alone murder a healthy young woman.

"Then deliver me someone who could," Hirsch replied.

"Man, what the fuck do you want from me, anyway?" Bobby said between gritted teeth. "You're not going to get away with this, you know. These guys will find you and fuck you up bad. If I were you, I'd run as far away as you can and hide."

"Which is why you're not going to breathe a word of any of this to anyone unless you want me coming back here. Besides, I doubt the authorities would look kindly on someone involved in organized procurement and corruption of young women. You ever pick up any in Indiana or Ohio, by chance?"

"Huh? I mean, what difference does it make?" Bobby asked.

"'Cause you're looking at federal charges and a long stint in the federal pen with no parole. So tell me—where can I find your boss?"

Bobby hesitated and Hirsch kneed him in the stomach. Bobby doubled over, heaving, before recovering his breath.

"Okay, okay. Lisa and her parents are in charge, but I've only ever dealt with her husband, Braden. Well, and that asshole employee of theirs, Clint, but he's probably on the island right now."

"Braden what?" Hirsch said.

"Braden Van Raalte."

"Where can I find this Braden Van Raalte?"

"Like, how should I know? It's not like I hang out with the guy. He can barely stand to look at me." Bobby's noncommittal response earned him added pressure on the shattered glass. Bobby winced. "He stops by the office every couple weeks. Most times, he's either coming or going from the country club on the west side of town. He drives a lime-green Ford Mustang GT350 with black racing stripes. It's so obnoxious you can't miss the thing."

"Think I'll find him there today?"

"I mean, maybe. Braden's a night owl, so he probably doesn't roll in until early afternoon anyway. He wouldn't miss an opportunity to get a round in before the snow flies. Especially on a day like this."

Hirsch relaxed his grip on Bobby's neck, and the broken man slowly rose to full height. His shattered glasses had fallen from his face, and he raised a quaking hand towards the side of his head. Hirsch tossed him a yellow microfiber towel used to clean the copier screen. Bobby dabbed at the blood trickling from his face and dripping onto his ruined dress shirt.

"How am I supposed to explain all this?" Bobby asked, gesturing at the blood-spattered disaster of a copy area.

"Tell them it jammed and you got angry. I don't care, Bobby. You told those girls some pretty good stories. I'm sure you won't have any trouble coming up with another one."

"Who are you, anyway?"

"None of your damn business. If I were you, I'd take your own advice and get as far away as possible. All the money in the world isn't worth it. The Dykmans are going down, and I guarantee they'll throw you under the bus. Now don't do anything stupid like calling the cops, either. They won't have a shred of sympathy once they hear what you've been up to."

Hirsch backed out of the copy room, leaving Bobby wiping his lacerated face.

Returning to the front office, Hirsch unbolted the door but left the sign on the door indicating the staff was out. As a parting gesture, he flipped the switch powering the LED "open" sign on the window, killing the display.

Hirsch drove twenty minutes across Grand Rapids and reached the west-side country club. He had limited interest in golf. Most of his experience stemmed from hours spent at the driving range in a futile effort to avoid embarrassing himself while entertaining clients. Fortunately, his former law partner, scratch golfer Greg Felton, compensated for Hirsch's blundering around the course.

Hirsch crawled through the expansive parking lot filled with BMWs, Teslas, Range Rovers, Mercedes, and other high-end vehicles. He could have driven one as well had he not fumbled his career and life away. As he rounded the corner of one row, a car's unmistakable lime-green paint job jumped out. Sure enough, it was a Mustang GT350—a loud and brassy vehicle that announced its presence like a bullhorn to all those in its vicinity. Hirsch rolled down his window and snapped pictures of the arrogant vehicle. Confident he had his man within his grasp, he commandeered a nearby empty spot and killed the engine.

Hirsch exited his vehicle and sauntered through the parking lot towards a stucco-clad archway bisecting the pro shop and the driving range. He unfastened the top button of his shirt. The fall day had grown warm, and the thick humidity raised beads of sweat on his brow. The driving range offered a handful of loaner clubs for use by visitors, and Hirsch selected a battered but serviceable 7 iron before purchasing a bucket of balls from an automated dispenser near the driving bays. As the balls clattered into a plastic basket, he surveyed the range. A row of bays fanned out in a semi-arc towards an astroturf field littered with hundreds of white range balls. A ball-collection tractor crawled back and forth across the range, scooping up balls to feed back into the system. Most of the golfers on the range were singletons—a handful working on their form with club pros—but a gaggle of four men in their twenties and thirties sharing a pair of bays at one end of the range caught Hirsch's eye. He walked past them and set up at an adjacent bay within earshot.

"You hit like that during the tournament this weekend and I guarantee you'll lose the fucking thing for us," a tall man with dark-blond hair said as he watched one of his friends hook a drive wide left into the driving-range net. The man wore gray slacks, a burgundy polo shirt, and spikeless golf shoes. Wraparound Oakley sunglasses concealed his eyes.

"Here, like this," he continued as he settled into his stance. He swung his driver, delivering a punishing follow-through that smashed the ball off the tee and sent it careening into the depths of the range. The two other members of the group rested their arms on upturned drivers and nodded in admiration as they awaited their turns.

"I'll have my shit together by then, don't you worry. I screwed up my wrist playing pickleball with my old man last weekend," the second man said as he teed up another ball, swung, and again hooked the shot. Squat and stocky, he had muscular legs that strained against his dark shorts. A thick head of dark red hair culminated in a low brow only a couple inches above his eyebrows. He spat at the ground and cussed at the piss-poor state of his game.

"Jesus, you're such a pussy, Mitch. Pickleball? Next you'll be telling me you pricked your finger at your grandma's knitting circle."

"I just need to chillax, man. Speaking of which—any chance I can get out on the family boat before the tourney?" Mitch asked.

"Don't call it 'the family boat,' dipshit. Your family wouldn't have the brains to steer it out of port even if you could afford it."

"I know, I know, Braden. All I'm saying is if you want me relaxed before the tournament, an hour or two with Serena wouldn't hurt."

"Fuck, man, next you'll be asking me to blow you myself out behind the clubhouse before our tee time."

Hirsch picked that moment to tee up a range ball with the toe of his shoe. He addressed the ball and swung the 7 iron. The club caught the ball on the hosel. It spit out at a forty-five-degree angle, clanging into the perforated metal divider separating Hirsch from his neighbors' driving bay. Braden spun around, his face contorted by fury.

"You mind watching it, asshole! Get off the fucking range or hire one of the pros if you don't know how to hit the damn thing."

"Sorry, man, I'm a little rusty," Hirsch said as he flushed scarlet and cursed under his breath. Braden Van Raalte had him marked as a complete doofus before Hirsch had a chance to talk with him.

"Then do me a favor and move down there," Braden said as he pointed to an empty bay at the end of the row. "Now— before I have a word with the rangemaster," he continued, seeing Hirsch's failure to move.

Hirsch grabbed his remaining bucket of balls and slunk towards the vacant bay with his 7 iron. He remained close enough to eavesdrop on the douchebag gaggle. His next swing—while off-kilter and a low trajectory—at least cleared one hundred twenty yards.

"Is Serena that flat-chested cokehead with the sleeve tattoo?" Braden asked Mitch.

"Yeah, man, that's her."

"I don't know what you're thinking, bro. Candy's a much better lay in my opinion."

"You're telling me Candy and the others aren't sniffing snow?" Mitch said.

"Of course they are, fuckhead, but Serena's like a vacuum cleaner with it. Probably snorts more than she brings in," Braden said as he completed another drive before extending the club back towards one of their colleagues. "Hand me my 6 iron. It's pretty clear Pickleball Wrists here won't do shit this weekend." Braden set up for his iron shot.

"So . . . what about it?" Mitch said after Braden dropped a ball within three feet of the one-hundred-sixty-yard marker.

"You are unrelenting, you know that, Mitch? I see why Lisa's old man hired you despite your being one ugly, obnoxious motherfucker. Yeah, there's a cruise going out this Friday. You know the drill. But I'm warning you—if you miss our tee time Saturday morning and we're DQed from the tournament, I will beat the living shit out of you and tiny-tit Serena myself."

"Braden, you know me. I can party all night, do a couple lines for breakfast, and I'll be out here like the fucking Energizer Bunny all morning."

"That's more like it," Braden said as he vacated the driving mat and set his driver on a rack. "Keegan, take my place for a little while; I gotta hit the can. Should've known better than to order Mexican food from a clubhouse."

"Bryce," Braden said to the fourth member of their quartet—a pale, goateed man in his mid-twenties wearing earbuds and an Ed Hardy shirt—"get us another round of Michelobs while I'm in the shitter." Braden held forth a wad of money.

Bryce accepted the money and headed towards the driving range bar, where a bleach-blonde girl in pigtails and a skin-tight orange crop top waited to take the order. Keegan began striping balls with a 3 wood while Braden walked towards the restrooms opposite the pro shop.

Hirsch hit another ball before following Braden at a distance. He carried his borrowed 7 iron at his hip. He entered the men's room moments after his nemesis and listened as a stall door slammed shut and Braden unzipped and lowered his trousers. Another golfer stood at a urinal, and Hirsch set the 7 iron in a corner against the wall opposite the door. He relieved himself while the other man finished, rinsed his hands, and exited the men's room, leaving Hirsch and Braden as the sole occupants. Hirsch quickly zipped up, retrieved his club, and bolted the restroom door before anyone else had the chance to enter.

Kicking in a bathroom stall door was uncharted territory, but after paying off a sex worker for information, clobbering a dweeb with a copy machine, and tracking a dangerous bro on his home turf, this was no ordinary twenty-four hours in Hirsch's life. He approached Braden's stall, braced himself, and slammed the sole of his boot against the hollow steel door.

The metal latch offered greater resistance than Hirsch expected. A stabbing pain tore through his right leg and up his sciatic nerve, but the door gave way. Hirsch stumbled into the stall, nearly tumbling into Braden's naked lap. Braden gasped at Hirsch, wide-eyed in shock with his phone in one hand.

"Holy fucking shit! What the hell are you doing?" Braden screamed as he twisted away from the figure hunched over him. "Wait—you're that asshole who nearly shanked a ball into my head."

"Keep your fucking voice down," Hirsch hissed as he raised the 7 iron above his head with both hands. "I'm going to make this quick—what happened to the girl you murdered on Beaver Island?"

Braden's outraged scowl melted into a gaze of confusion as he narrowed his eyes at Hirsch. Braden remained silent.

"Don't make me use this thing!" Hirsch said while tightening his grip on the club. He reared back to bring it down over Braden's dark-blond head. "I know her name—BreAnn. Talk."

"Buddy, you don't have a clue what a world of shit you're in for."

"Let me worry about that. I know you killed her. Well, you and that sidekick of yours, Clint. Maybe your wife had a hand in it too. What'd the three of you do with her?"

"I can tell you're not a cop, man. Even the cops around here wouldn't do something that stupid. Who hired you? Detroit? Milwaukee? Don't tell me Chicago sent someone this dumb."

Hirsch brought the heel of his boot down hard on Braden's foot. The thin canvas golf shoe offered little protection, and Braden emitted a howl of pain that rattled the walls of the bathroom stall.

"I'm asking the questions around here, dipshit. You got that?" Hirsch said.

Braden growled through gritted teeth. "I don't know the answer to your question, dickhead. The nice thing about being in charge is I don't have to clean up a mess. And for your information, I've never killed anyone in my life. You are so fucking dead, asshole, you know that?"

Hirsch ignored Braden's threat. "Who killed her, then?"

"I just told you, I don't know shit about any dead girl. Why you busting my balls, man?"

Hirsch tried a different tack. "Tell me about Clint. What's his last name?"

Braden hesitated, and Hirsch jabbed him in the shin with the 7 iron.

"It's Lewisohn, asshole. You'd better think twice about

going after him. He'd dismantle a clown like you."

"How'd Clint wind up working for you?"

"Huh? Ellis handles all that shit. He knew Clint from the Army or something. Like I have time to mess around with personnel. Fuck, man, what's your deal, anyway?"

"Who's Ellis?"

"Man, you really don't know shit, do you? Whoever you're working for must be desperate."

Hirsch had limited time and decided to move on. "What about the porn videos, Braden? You wanna explain those to me?"

"Uh, no, I don't," Braden replied, earning himself a crack across the jaw from Hirsch's right fist.

"Who and where," Hirsch said.

"Look, man," Braden said while rubbing his jaw, "I'm telling you—I don't deal with all that shit."

"Then who does?"

"It's all Ellis's gig. We pay him well, and he produces content for the website. It's one-hundred percent legal, dude. We have it papered and everything."

"What website?"

"It's called Great Lakes Girls," Braden hissed.

Hirsch had passing familiarity with GreatLakesGirls.com, a popular site purportedly featuring "amateur" college girls and young women from the Midwest. It catered to viewers seeking a façade of reality from the young women undoubtedly coerced into participating or desperate for cash. From its ubiquity on the seamier side of the internet, Hirsch had little doubt the website's *cinema-verité* aesthetics generated ample revenue for the Dykmans.

"Listen, I know you're not alone in this, Van Raatle. Tell me who—"

Hirsch never had a chance to finish his question. The locked restroom door rattled, followed by a firm hand pounding on it.

"You okay in there, Braden?" Mitch's muffled voice called from outside.

Hirsch snapped his head towards the door. Distracted by the interruption, he never saw Braden's fist coming as it slammed square into his solar plexus, knocking the wind out of him. Hirsch gasped for air as he collapsed. His lungs screamed for oxygen as he struggled to breathe. Braden shoved Hirsch aside and scrambled to stand, pulling up his pants. He kicked at Hirsch, who had fallen to the floor and lay in a crumpled ball with his head wedged against the base of the toilet. The unflushed toilet's stench left Hirsch on the verge of vomiting. He had the wherewithal to clutch the 7 iron tight to his chest lest Braden retrieve it and beat him to death.

Braden ceased kicking Hirsch's prostrate figure and rushed towards the restroom door, where he unlocked it and allowed Mitch to enter.

"That dipshit from the driving range is a fucking spy or something," Braden said as he led Mitch towards the stall. "He busted in asking a bunch of questions. I nailed him good when you pounded on the door."

The two approached the open stall. They towered over Hirsch as he gasped for air and waited for the sheer agony radiating through his gut to subside.

"Pull the little bitch to his feet," Braden said to Mitch.

Mitch entered the stall, grabbed Hirsch by the shoulders, and yanked him out. Mitch shoved him hard against the restroom's tiled wall.

"Who the fuck are you?" Braden shouted as his fist smashed into Hirsch's jaw. The class ring on Braden's hand caught Hirsch's chin, ripping open a gash and splashing a ribbon of blood over his light-blue dress shirt.

"I'm nobody, that's who," Hirsch responded.

"Oh, this little dipshit thinks he's funny too. Thinks he can wander into *my* golf course, ask me a bunch of stupid questions, and fuck up my foot. You'd better pray I can still play in this weekend's tournament." Braden reared back to aim another punch at Hirsch's blood-smeared jaw.

The entrance of a pair of golfers saved Hirsch from further disfigurement. Two gentlemen in their fifties ceased their conversation and came to a dead stop at the sight of the country club's two most obnoxious bros holding a bleeding man hostage against the wall.

"Just what the hell is going on in here?" asked one of the men. He had gray hair clipped close to his balding skull and rhythmically worked a wad of chewing gum in his mouth. His thick, well-tanned forearms extended from beneath the sleeves of his pink golf shirt.

His colleague, the older of the two and sporting a neat gray mustache, stepped forward. "Mr. Van Raalte, I wanted you out of this club after you slapped that cart girl's ass last month. I warned you any more of this nonsense and you'd be finished here. I don't give a damn how much money your wife's family has."

"Let him go, Mitch," the balding man said as he stepped towards the trio and separated Hirsch from his captor with a sweep of his arms.

"This little perv busted into my stall while I was on the toilet, Gene," Braden said to the mustachioed man. "I—I thought he wanted to rape me or something."

"I somehow doubt that," Gene said, side-eyeing Hirsch. "In any case, you didn't need to beat him. Good Lord, you got blood all over the damn wall, Braden." Hirsch glanced behind him. A distinct spatter of blood from his chin stained the white tile.

"Jesus, someone flush the damn toilet in here," the balding man said, scrunching his nose. "I'll hold it until the ninth hole, Gene." He exited the restroom, shaking his head in disgust.

"And just who are you?" Gene said to Hirsch after his companion left. He glared at Hirsch's blood-stained shirt as though Hirsch had dropped his trousers and defecated on the eighteenth green. "I haven't seen you around before. Are you a member's guest?"

"I'm Roger Sampson," Hirsch said with the base of his palm wedged firm against his chin to staunch the flow of blood. "I wanted to get some practice in on the range. These two clowns jumped me while I was in the restroom."

"This is a members-only private club. It's trespassing unless you're an invited guest. Now, I don't know what you did to piss off these two, but I'm asking you to leave."

"Hold on—you mean to tell me you're letting this asshole walk out of here?" Braden said while stepping closer to Gene and laying three fingers on Gene's polo shirt embroidered with the country club's logo. Gene held his ground, defiant against Braden's hyperventilating figure looming over him.

"Take your hand off me right this minute or I'll have all three of you arrested and thrown out of this club for good. I doubt your wife's family would welcome that attention."

Braden glared at Gene but stepped back and let his hands fall to his sides.

"That's more like it. Here's what's going to happen. Mr. Sampson," Gene said while collecting a handful of paper towels and passing the wad to Hirsch, "take these, leave this establishment at once, and don't come back. We run a respectable club and don't need this sort of element in here. As for you two," he continued, turning to Braden and Mitch, "clean this mess up, then clear out for the day."

"Man, I just paid for another round of beers. Are you serious, Gene?"

"Do you and this meathead want to play in this weekend's

invitational?"

Braden only grunted in response.

"Then get to work and go. Why are you still standing here?" Gene said, pivoting to Hirsch.

"Leaving now," Hirsch murmured through the wad of paper towels turning red from the ample blood continuing to flow from his chin. He made haste to exit.

As the restroom door slammed closed behind him, Hirsch walked towards the parking lot under the stares of patrons and employees beholding the spectacle of a wounded man. He reached the Dodge Charger as the shock wore off. Searing pain radiated along his jaw and danced through the roots of his teeth. With a free hand, he popped the car's trunk with the key fob and extracted a cotton undershirt from his travel bag. He tossed the blood-soaked wad of paper towels into a nearby median, where it came to rest beneath an immaculate row of boxwoods trimmed to an exacting square. Hirsch shut the trunk and lowered himself onto the scorching-hot leather of the driver's seat.

He needed to get the hell out before Braden or one of his asshole friends came after him. He removed the balled-up undershirt from his chin and looked into the rearview mirror. The cut was deep and undoubtedly needed stitches if he wanted to avoid a gnarly scar. Any hospital or clinic worth its salt would ask questions, and the last thing he needed was the cops busting him with a fake ID. He pressed the shirt over his chin and fished his cellphone out of his pocket. He dialed the number from memory. Allison answered after a pair of rings.

"Allie, this is Ben. Say, are you free right now?"

"What is it? I'm at work."

"I need your help bad."

Chapter 10

Allison answered her door to find her ex-husband with a blood-soaked undershirt pressed to his chin and his dress shirt spattered with dark-brown dried blood.

"You're lucky I wasn't in surgery all afternoon," she said while glancing from head to toe at Hirsch's pathetic spectacle. "Follow me," she continued and led Hirsch inside to the kitchen. Allison wore her auburn mane of hair in a ponytail that bounced against the collar of her teal surgical scrubs.

"Looks like the place hasn't changed much," Hirsch said as he examined what had been his home until the previous year.

"Like I have time to redecorate. Sit." Allison gestured at one of the barstools at the counter. She set a suture kit on the countertop and sat facing Hirsch on another barstool. "Let's see what we're dealing with here."

Allison lifted the ruined undershirt from Hirsch's chin. The bleeding had largely ceased, but a ragged tear ran from just under his lip diagonally to the base of his chin.

"Gracious, Ben, were you in a car accident?"

"Nah, a guy wearing a ring caught me good across the face."

"No, seriously, what happened?"

"I wish I were joking," Hirsch replied.

"Since when did you take up brawling? This isn't like you."

"It wasn't a fight, Allie. I was working, and this guy . . . in the country club restroom . . . I don't even know where to start."

"Fine, whatever. Just calm down, okay. I need to clean this before I can stitch you up. This is going to hurt—a lot. You want me to numb it with an anesthetic?"

"Let's get it over with."

Allison irrigated the wound and swabbed his chin with stinging disinfectant. Hirsch flinched as the caustic fluid seeped into his flesh, and he soon regretted not accepting her offer. The one consolation was the raw burn masked the piercing sting as she threaded a row of neat stitches across his chin.

"Remember practicing your sutures in medical school those long nights at our apartment?" Hirsch asked.

"About as fondly as I recall you cursing over your 1L torts casebook."

"You wanted to play piano so bad afterwards but fell asleep most nights on the couch."

"Not much has changed. I have to wipe the dust off the bench most times," Allison said.

"You always hoped we'd have a child you could teach to play."

"Yeah, well, life's full of disappointments, isn't it?" Allison finished the stitches and covered the entire mess with a sterile strip and bandage.

"There," she said, smoothing the bandage over his chin with her delicate, ivory-hued hands. Her nails were bitten to the quick, a habit she'd retained as long as Hirsch had known her. "This bandage will help, but try to keep the stitches dry for at least forty-eight hours. You'll have a little scar, but it'd be worse without them. You headed back to the U.P.?"

"Yeah, why?"

"Then give it two weeks and find someone to remove the stitches. Here," she said, walking over to a cabinet and grabbing a pill bottle from within. She removed the lid, shook two capsules into her hand, then filled a glass from the water dispenser on the fridge with her free hand. "Take these. It'll keep the pain down for a few hours. At least nothing feels broken; otherwise, you'd need X-rays."

Hirsch accepted the pills and swallowed them while guzzling the cool water. He was dying of thirst after a day spent hunting down members of the Dykman crime family and hadn't had a moment to rehydrate. Allison stripped off her green nitrile gloves and tossed them into a nearby trashcan. Hirsch choked on the water as the glint of an impressive diamond ring set in a white-gold band caught his attention.

"What on earth's that?" Hirsch said, staring at the ring and coughing to clear his windpipe.

Allison followed Hirsch's eyes to her hand. "It's an engagement ring, Ben."

"I know, but . . . who? When?"

"He's an oncologist from the hospital. He proposed last month. I accepted."

"It just seems so soon. I mean, already, Allie?"

"Ben, we've been divorced a year now—separated even longer. I needed to move on with my life; I'd hoped you had as well. Are you telling me you aren't seeing anyone now?"

"Well, yeah, but we're not, like, engaged or anything. We don't even live together."

"I don't live with Stephen either. I'm moving in with him after the wedding next spring."

Hirsch looked around. "What'll you do with the house?"

"Christ, Ben, I don't know. I haven't given it much

thought. Maybe we'll sell it, maybe we'll rent it out. It's none of your concern either way."

"I know, I know," Hirsch said. "It's just, this was our house and all. I can't imagine anyone one else living here."

Allison didn't respond. She focused on the glass French doors leading to their back porch and well-manicured lawn. Hirsch glanced out as well. A mature larch tree shaded most of the south-facing yard from the intense sun while, closer to the porch, garden beds festooned with zinnia, lantana, and orchids bracketed a stone path winding towards a grove of beech and ash trees separating the property from the neighbors. Their leaves shimmered and danced in the afternoon sun.

Allison's bright green eyes shifted to the clock on the stove. "I need to get back to work. I have a surgery consult and can't miss it. Take off that shirt. I'll find you something clean." She exited the kitchen, the heels of her shoes clicking on the hardwood floor as she rooted around in the bedroom. Hirsch unbuttoned his dress shirt and removed it as Allison returned with a bright-orange T-shirt emblazoned with the New York Mets logo in her hands.

"Better hand over that undershirt too," she said. Blotches of dried blood had stained it as well. He stripped it off and traded her for the clean T-shirt.

"Really? He's a Mets' fan?" Hirsch said as he held the shirt in front of him.

"Do you want to drive back to Manistique shirtless? Put the damn thing on and come with me."

Hirsch shut his mouth and slipped the shirt over his head. It was a size too large but would do. Allison led him to the door. She caught sight of the Dodge Charger parked along the curb.

"Is that yours, Ben? It's . . . aggressive."

"It's a loaner. My employer rented it for me. Again, long

story."

"I don't know what you've got yourself into, but you need a new career. I thought moving back to Manistique might help. Now I'm not so sure."

"I *had* another career, Allie. I'm doing everything I can to get by. Look, the truth is, the less you know about this whole mess the better."

Allison gave him a hug, enveloping Hirsch in an aroma of honeysuckle. "I know, Ben. You take care of yourself now, okay? We're divorced—but I still care about you."

"I will, honey. And thank you—for this, for putting up with everything."

"Don't mention it. Next time, don't show up bleeding at my front door. Besides, I'll be in Europe the next three weeks for a much-needed vacation."

"With Stephen, I suppose," Hirsch said.

"You're lucky I still like you."

With grave reluctance, Hirsch walked down the footpath towards the Charger parked at Allison's curb. The dull ache in his jaw grew stronger in the absence of conversation. He awaited the moment Allison's pain pills would kick in and work their magic.

After getting back into the car and firing up the engine, he recognized he'd hit a dead end for the time being. Bobby had nothing useful left to offer him, and Braden Van Raatle would undoubtedly beat him to death if he so much as showed his face. He had two angles to work—Great Lakes Girls and the man seemingly at the intersection of the Dykmans' evil—Clint. He'd delegate the latter to Winston.

Hirsch grabbed his cellphone.

"Has this frolic of yours paid off, Mr. Hirsch?" Winston asked without further pleasantries.

"Clint's full name is Clint Lewison or Lewiston, something like that. All I know is he's ex-Army and the Dykmans hired him. Will you see what you can find on him?"

"Let me run his name by a few of my contacts and we'll go from there," Winston said.

"Good, okay. Look, we need to talk—in person. This shit's too weird to hash out over the phone. Can Chris pick me up?"

"I'll find out. Where are you now?"

"East Lansing."

"East Lansing? Wait, I thought you were in Grand Rapids. What gives?" Winston asked.

Hirsch sighed. "It's a long story. I'm here now, though. Can Chris make it work?"

"Give me an hour or so and I'll set it up. You might as well head to the airport. I'll text you where to return the car."

"This whole mess is getting crazier by the hour. You wouldn't believe what I've lived through today."

"Then it sounds like you'll have plenty to share. Safe travels, Hirsch."

CAPITAL REGION INTERNATIONAL AIRPORT WAS night and day compared to Hirsch's experience at the short-runway Manistique and Beaver Island airfields. While he'd flown in and out of Lansing many times as a commercial airline passenger, this was his first experience with the general aviation side of the airport. Following Winston's instructions, he parked the Charger at a fixed-base operator who provided ground services to pilots. The gruff attendant sized Hirsch up in one glance, realized he wasn't a pilot, and grudgingly allowed him to wait in the lounge. Over the course of the next two hours, multiple pilots and charter passengers dropped in to rest and drink a coffee or cold soda while waiting to refuel.

Morgan and Braden Van Raatle's revelation of the porn site troubled Hirsch. After a family of five vacated the lounge, Hirsch had the place to himself and pulled out his phone.

Glancing around to make sure the coast was clear, he opened the browser and typed in the URL for the Great Lakes Girls website. Seconds later, a splash page emblazoned with the website's name in large pink letters across the top and dotted with pictures of scantily clad, fresh-faced young women filled his phone screen. The green "Enter" button towards the bottom took him to another page showing those same girls nude—some naked from the waist up, others on all fours and contorted on display for the camera. He quickly navigated to a link captioned "Models" and scrolled through it. Sure enough, after a couple dozen entries, a picture of Morgan appeared with the moniker "Candy" superimposed over her photo. The smiling woman looked young and carefree in the thumbnail, with her hair worn loose around her shoulders and a coy grin etched on her face. Only the hint of an unfocused glaze in her eyes suggested something might be amiss. Morgan was but one of many featured girls, and Hirsch had little doubt others had passed through the gates of Manitou on their journey to drug addiction and exploitation.

He clicked Morgan's image, which took him to a preview page. A series of pictures with Morgan in increasing stages of undress appeared followed by a text block featuring her measurements and a short "biography." With apprehension, Hirsch clicked on a minute-long sample video. After a five-second theme song played over the words "Great Lakes Girls," the video faded in on Morgan sitting atop a bed wearing a lavender-and-black dress, with her long, smooth legs sprawled sideways across the mattress. A handheld camera focused on her face and different aspects of her physique, then cut to a montage of Morgan stripping and engaging in sex with a man visible from the waist down.

The lounge door burst open. Hirsch scrambled to close his browser and kill the audio. An older pilot wearing a bomber jacket and yellow-tinted aviators entered the room. He shot

Hirsch a sly grin, having undoubtedly heard the audio. The man plopped down in a chair opposite him, cracked open a Dr Pepper, and noticed Hirsch's bright-orange shirt.

"Never thought I'd run into another Mets fan here," the pilot said.

"Tigers fan, actually." Hirsch wished he'd stopped at a Target on the way to the airport and swapped the shirt for something nondescript.

The man's face dropped. "Then what's with that shirt, son?"

"My ex-wife gave it to me. I had blood all over my other shirt. You know how it is," Hirsch replied.

"She do that to your face too?"

"In a manner of speaking."

"At least she had the decency to toss you a new shirt. My ex wouldn't piss on me if I were on fire. Sounds like you let a good one get away."

"You have no idea."

The pilot's phone rang, and he excused himself, exiting the lounge to take the call. He never returned, and Hirsch assumed his plane was ready for the next leg of his journey—or that his ex-wife had finally caught up with him.

Allison's pain pills had begun to wear off. The laceration on his skin stung with his every movement. For lack of anything better, he swallowed two tablets from his aunt Margie's diminishing bottle of clonazepam.

As dusk settled across lower Michigan, Hirsch's eyes grew heavy with sleep and benzodiazepine. He wanted nothing more than to stretch out on one of the black leather couches adorning the lounge and catch a few minutes of rest. That opportunity vanished when the distinct presence of Chris's yellow-and-orange Cessna approached. Hirsch leapt to his feet and headed for the plane, but Chris was already halfway to the door when he stepped outside.

"You think I'm running an air taxi service here? That I'm sitting around the hangar on pins and needles waiting for your call?"

"Sorry, Chris. Winston said you'd be free. I'd have waited until tomorrow morning if I'd known better."

"If the Winslows summon me, I can't say no. They pay me way too much to refuse. But most of their clients show a shred of respect before calling. Here I had a hot date lined up for the supper club in Negaunee this evening. Ten-to-one he took that skank from the marina instead."

"Do I need to take you instead?"

"Don't get cute, Hirsch. Besides, I wouldn't be seen in public with a face like yours. Looks like someone finally had enough of your shit. Throw your bag in the luggage hold and get in. If we hurry, I might make it back in time for pizza and an Old Fashioned at Vango's."

Hirsch stowed his bag and climbed into the passenger seat. Like an old hand, he strapped himself in and fitted the headset over his ears as Chris cranked the engine and taxied towards the runway. The two-hundred-mile flight took them northwest across central and northern Michigan. At an altitude of five thousand feet, the evolving display of farms, small towns, and lengthy stands of hardwood forests mesmerized Hirsch. Despite his initial terror, he now wished he'd taken flight lessons when he had more disposable income. Such a thought was a pipe dream given his financial straits.

They passed Traverse City as the final embers of dusk highlighted the harbor below. Hirsch craned his neck to see if he could spot the *Wanderlust*, but the scene was all too dim to make out anything definitive. He wondered whether Morgan and her hard-luck companions were on the lake below, doing their best to survive one more night of hell as prisoners of the Dykmans. Twilight arrived as they crossed the Leelanau Peninsula and overtook the wide expanse of Lake Michigan.

The light of a slender crescent moon cast a pallid glow across the dark sheet of water. Even at this hour, the shore was but a faint outline.

"Is it safe to fly over the lake at night?" Hirsch asked over the intercom.

"No problem on a clear night like this. Besides, I'm instrument rated. We could fly through the clouds, if needed."

"I could get used to this life," Hirsch said as he leaned back in the seat, feeling like an ersatz mogul with his private plane and pilot. "Maybe Catherine and Herb need help in Florida—or Hawaii. How's that sound, Chris?"

"This isn't funny."

"Think about it—we could cruise to New Orleans, dine on oysters and beignets, then work our way down the coast to Key West. Sure, maybe we'd need to bust a head or two, but I'll bet we could squeeze some marlin fish—"

Chris reached forward on the instrument panel and turned off the ignition switch, killing the motor. The propeller sputtered to a dead stop.

"Jesus, what the fuck are you doing?" Hirsch said as he gripped the armrest on the door. The silence was somehow louder than the motor's roar. Panic seized him, cutting through the tranquilizer fog.

"Do I have your attention now?"

"Yyyess," Hirsch whined.

"Do you think this is some sort of joke, Hirsch?" Chris asked, staring at him.

"Joke? What the hell are you even talking about?" His eyes widened in terror as the plane's nose dipped below the horizon towards the menacing lake below.

"Relax. So long as we glide, the plane won't stall."

"Okay, but what the fuck is this all about, anyway?"

"You seem to think working for the Winslows is some sort of game. That all this is for your amusement. Oysters?

Key West? You really have no clue."

"Fine, fine, I get it, but what's your point?"

"Much as I hate wasting my evenings chauffeuring you across the lake, I can't let you fuck this up. I was no one before I met the Winslows—no one. I know your type. I can't afford for some bumbling jackass of an ex-lawyer to cost me my job."

"What do you mean?"

"I mean you're not the first cocky sonofabitch to assume he could handle life as the Winslows' fixer. You're smart, I get it. But don't let this job go to your head."

The plane shuttered and the right wing dipped with an oncoming stall. Chris pushed the yoke forward, recovering their airspeed but trading precious altitude.

"Whatever you say, Chris. Just restart the goddamn engine before we crash into the lake." Hirsch clamped the fingers of his left hand tight between his teeth.

"Oh, good grief. I practice power-off stalls all the time. But have it your way," she said while priming the engine. She started the ignition, and the motor and propeller roared to life.

Hirsch exhaled as the airspeed increased and they recovered altitude. He'd somehow avoided pissing himself during the ordeal.

"Just don't forget what I said. And you'd better not breathe a word of this to the Winslows or that uptight lackey of theirs, either."

Hirsch could only nod in response. He'd never forget this lesson.

The remaining journey across the lake passed without incident, and it wasn't long before the lights of Manistique appeared on the horizon. They came aground west of the Seul Choix Lighthouse, and Chris reduced the throttle and touched down on the Schoolcraft County airport runway in a perfect three-point landing. She didn't bother to turn off the engine after they'd taxied to the apron.

"Get out," Chris shouted over the engine noise as Hirsch removed his headset and opened the passenger door. "I've got another forty-five minutes' flight home."

As soon as Hirsch grabbed his bag and clicked the baggage door shut, Chris headed for the runway. Her plane was already aloft by the time Hirsch reached his truck.

Chapter 11

Hirsch's jaw throbbed in agony as he drove towards Marquette the next morning. Four capsules of ibuprofen barely made a dent in the pain, and he wished he'd begged Allison for a handful of her special pain pills. He popped open the glove box and extracted a pint of Black Velvet. After passing an oncoming eighteen-wheeler, he took a long pull off the bottle, sealed the cap, and tossed it back in the glove box. Within minutes, the whiskey ameliorated the ache coursing through his jaw and left him feeling halfway normal for his audience with Winston.

Hirsch was dressed in dark-gray tropical wool trousers, black loafers polished to a rich shine, and a light-blue linen sport shirt with his sleeves rolled up above his elbows. He dispensed with a jacket owing to the late-season humidity that hung over the Lake Superior coastline.

Winston answered the door clad in a salmon-hued polo shirt and motioned Hirsch inside. Hirsch followed Winston into his office off the main hallway and sat opposite the Winslows' coordinator-in-chief.

"That information you provided about the Dykmans' henchman proved more valuable than I expected. His full name is Clint Lewisohn—L-E-W-I-S-O-H-N—and it's true he's military. He grew up in Niles, Michigan, and spent three semesters at Grand Valley State University in Grand Rapids before dropping out and enlisting. Clint served four years in the U.S. Army, including a year-long tour of duty in Afghanistan. He was honorably discharged in February but reenlisted in the Army Reserves. Here's where it gets interesting—Clint was stationed at Fort Huachuca in southern Arizona. That mean anything to you, Mr. Hirsch?"

"Nada." Hirsch had never visited the southwest, let alone southern Arizona.

"Fort Huachuca's bread and butter is military intelligence. That tattoo on his arm you described is the Army military intelligence insignia. Ten to one our friend Clint learned a few skills that served him well on Beaver Island."

Winston slid an 8x10 photograph across the desk for Hirsch's inspection. While the uniformed figure in the picture was beardless, the bulging neck, eyeglasses, and haircut all matched Hirsch's tormentor on Beaver Island.

"Yeah, that's him all right," Hirsch said. "How'd an Army soldier get involved with the Dykmans?"

"I think I uncovered the link. The Dykmans' businesses are all family owned, which means they're not subject to the same reporting requirements as publicly traded companies. However, their website lists one Ellis Nygren as head of security. Nygren's from Eveleth, Minnesota, and was an Army captain with counterintelligence training. He did two tours of duty in Iraq and Afghanistan, according to his LinkedIn profile. What he didn't mention was his dishonorable discharge for conduct unbecoming with a female subordinate. He started with the Dykman family soon after. Any guess where he was stationed before his discharge?"

"Fort wherever?"

"Huachuca. Same as Clint Lewisohn. Odds are Nygren

recruited Clint."

"Conduct unbecoming, eh?" Hirsch said, recalling Braden Van Raatle's mention of Nygren in connection with Great Lakes Girls.

"Does that surprise you?"

"Actually, it makes a great deal of sense given everything I've learned the past few days."

"Do tell," Winston said.

"The cruise was everything you thought it was and more. All it took was a generous tip to the bartender and they set me up with a girl below deck. She was coked out of her mind and offered me a bump."

"Did you sleep with her?"

"No, I didn't sleep with her. Good grief, give me a little credit." Hirsch omitted that he *did* take advantage of the coke.

"So what happened?"

"I paid her off and pumped her for information. She was scared like you couldn't believe of the people on the boat— especially this one meathead guarding the hallway—but she came clean about being recruited at college to come work at some kids' camp on Beaver Island. Seems like Lisa herself liked to play sorority queen and target girls at parties. The girl, Morgan, led me to Grand Rapids."

"Go on."

"Morgan told me she went to this storefront insurance company in town to learn more about the job. She was one of several girls that this dweeb named Bobby lured to Beaver Island. What they expected to be a camp for disabled kids turned out to be Prophet Teller's wacko religious cult. They get the girls addicted to drugs and send them to sleep with high-paying clients on the pleasure cruises. It gets worse, though," Hirsch added.

"How much worse?"

"One girl tried to escape. I only know her first name—

BreAnn—but she made a break for it from the camp. Word is she disappeared—murdered."

"And just how did you learn that?"

"Morgan mentioned it. I then got that spineless dipshit Bobby to give up the name of Lisa's husband, this colossal douchebag named Braden Van Raatle. I tracked him down at a country club on the west side of Grand Rapids. It wasn't pretty, but I cornered him alone. Van Raatle denied having anything to do with a dead girl. Honestly, he's dumb enough that I believe him. He did give up the name of Ellis Nygren, though. Braden's how I ended up with this." Hirsch pointed at his bandaged chin.

"He could've killed you," Winston said.

"I know. I thought Van Raatle and one of his buddies might, but two golfers walked in at the last minute and saved my hide. The hooker ring isn't the end of this mess, unfortunately."

"What else is there?"

"Van Raatle spilled the beans that Nygren also dabbles as a pornographer and that he manages a popular porn site—Great Lakes Girls. You heard of it?"

Winston glared at Hirsch. "Mr. Hirsch, I don't have the slightest interest in that garbage, especially straight porn. C'mon."

"I had to ask. Anyway, the Dykmans must be making a small fortune on all this. Thing is, if it wasn't voluntary and these young women were coerced into performing or too drugged out of their minds to know what was going on, we're talking federal felonies here."

"Can we find any direct link between them and the Dykmans?" Winston asked.

"Hard to say. Unless these guys are complete idiots, I'm guessing they've covered their tracks. They're probably using a Grand Rapids business like the insurance office to launder their money. I'd need to dig into the business filings to learn more."

"You think there's a connection between the Beaver Island encampment and the porn site?"

"I'm dead certain there is. I scrolled through this preview page of their models and, sure enough, there was Morgan, under the name 'Candy.' These assholes cycle them through the website and then kick 'em out on the booze cruise. I'm fucking worried what might happen once they're too strung out to even do that."

"What about the prophet? He's tech savvy, right? Think he could have a hand in this mess?" Winston asked.

"Jonathan Teller's no dummy. Could he have the means and know-how to help orchestrate this scheme? It's possible."

Winston leaned back into his burgundy leather chair with a pensive expression on his face. "Now here's the elephant in the room—is Alexandra one of their victims?" he asked.

"I've wondered the same thing myself. I didn't see any pictures on the Great Lakes Girls website that resembled her, but yeah, she could be."

"That's what I'm afraid of, Mr. Hirsch. Excuse me for a minute," Winston said and left the office. Hirsch had several minutes to consider the latest twist in the saga of his involvement with the Winslows. What started as a search for their missing daughter had spiraled into an ugly cocktail of prostitution, drugs, and pornography.

Winston returned with a check in his hands. "As agreed, this is for your recent service to the Winslows. Considering your injury and any inconvenience it's caused you, Catherine insisted on a little extra."

Winston passed the check across the desk—twenty-five thousand dollars instead of the promised twenty. With the money in hand, Hirsch could call Vern Sigurdsson on the way home and have his boiler replaced before winter rendered

Manistique an unrelenting icebox.

"This is . . . generous."

"I trust you recognize such generosity carries an expectation of discretion."

"I wouldn't have it any other way," Hirsch replied as he folded the check and slipped it into his shirt pocket.

"We have one other ask."

"What would that be?" Hirsch said, unsurprised.

"Run down this porn site lead and see what you can find. You were an attorney, a damn good one from everything I've heard. Dig into their business filings and get us some tangible info—especially anything connecting Ellis Nygren and the porn to the Dykmans."

"I'll see what I can do."

"Very good. I'll show you to the door. I expect you have a busy day ahead after your time on the road."

As Winston escorted Hirsch to the front door, Catherine Winslow intercepted him from the salon.

"Mr. Hirsch! Winston tells me you've gone above and beyond the call of duty in tracking down those monsters who brainwashed our daughter. Tell me they didn't hurt you too bad?" Catherine laid a couple fingers on his bandaged chin. Her freshly manicured nails brushed the bandage.

"Nothing an ice pack and a little rest won't heal," Hirsch lied.

"Herb and I want to show our appreciation for all the work you've done on our behalf these past few weeks. Alex isn't home yet, but we know much more than when you started. We're taking the yacht out this Saturday for a few hours on the lake. It may be the last chance of the season. We'd be delighted if you'd join us."

Hirsch hesitated, remembering he'd planned a trip with Edgar the coming weekend to fish the Middle Branch of the Ontonagon River near Watersmeet. "That sounds amazing, but . . . I sort of had plans this weekend with a friend."

"Surely you can reschedule. It's not every day one gets to cruise Lake Superior aboard a catered yacht. We don't scrimp when it comes to food and drink."

Hirsch's resistance weakened. "Any chance there's room aboard for my girlfriend?" Lauren would kill him if he squandered an opportunity to cruise the lake on a gorgeous fall day. Edgar would understand.

"Mr. Hirsch, you never told us you had yourself a lady friend. Yes, I insist you bring her along. Herb and I would be delighted to meet her."

"In that case, count us in."

"Wonderful. Be at the Cinder Pond Marina by 10:00 Saturday morning. Plan for ample sunshine and good times. Come along," she continued, "I'll walk you to the door." Catherine guided Hirsch towards the manor entrance with her fingers on his upper arm. As he stood at the threshold preparing to leave, Catherine paused and looked him in the eye.

"I'll admit I had my doubts about you after that imbroglio with my brothers. I suppose it's only human nature to harbor some resentment. In some ways, I doubt I'll ever forgive you one hundred percent. But you've won us over with your diligence, Ben. I predict a future of great successes for all of us."

"I just appreciate the opportunity to do some real work again. It's been a while since I've done anything this engaging." *Or remunerative*, Hirsch omitted.

"We'll see what else we can find to keep you busy, in that case. Safe travels, Mr. Hirsch. We'll see you and your lady this Saturday."

As Hirsch arrived home late that afternoon, a 3x5 index card tacked to his front door caught his attention. He unpinned the card and read the following message written in a clear hand with a black Sharpie marker:

MEET ME AT INDIAN LAKE AT 9:00 P.M.
OFF DAWSON ROAD
COME ALONE!

Great, more of this shit, Hirsch thought as he ripped the card in half and stuck it in his pocket. *All I wanted was to get my life back on track, and now some crazy wants to meet at night alone.*

From his experience with the Shaw brothers, Hirsch understood that once one of these clowns wanted your attention, they'd get it one way or another. Ignoring the summons to Indian Lake that evening would only mean a visit to his home or workplace at an inopportune time.

He caught three innings of the Tigers-Royals ball game that evening. Around 8:30, he clicked the television off after the Royals scored two runs on a double to centerfield. Hirsch headed to his bedroom and opened the top drawer of his dresser. He extracted his father's Smith & Wesson .38 Special from the drawer. The nickel-plated frame, its metal polished to a mirror finish, reflected a truncated self-portrait back at him. After firing two rounds at Marcus Shaw in the latter's meth lab on Summer Island and witnessing Shaw burn to death before his eyes, Hirsch had dumped the pistol in his dresser and done his best to forget he owned it. Was an anonymous meet-up during the night worth the risk of another shoot-out? Hirsch returned the .38 to the drawer atop a stack of undershirts and pushed the drawer shut. He already had one body on his conscience; he didn't need another. Unarmed, he slipped into a light denim jacket and stepped outside. Night had fallen across the Upper Peninsula, offering a respite from the suffocating humidity that had rolled in off the lake aloft a southernly wind.

Hirsch drove through town along Maple Street and across the Manistique River via Deer Street. He passed the historic water tower on his right, its red-brick cladding illuminated by a series of flood lights. While most storefronts were shuttered for the remainder of the evening, a handful of taverns did brisk business. Hirsch followed State Highway 94 towards the Hiawatha National Forest but turned left on Dawson Road. The darkened fourteenth hole of the Indian Lake Golf Course loomed through the trees, and Hirsch soon came to the end of the paved road as it dead-ended into a narrow gravel drive leading down to the lakeshore. Wedged between two private residences, the driveway offered kayakers and canoeists access to Indian Lake's tranquil waters. Hirsch parked halfway down the drive but left his lights on to illuminate his path to the waterfront.

Gentle waves lapped at the pebble-strewn shore. A ring of birch, maple, and beech trees surrounded the lake. Hirsch faced the water as a hidden great-horned owl hooted in the distance and marked its dominion over the area. The sharp click of a pistol hammer cocking froze Hirsch in his place.

"Put your hands up and hold them where I can see them," a muffled voice called out. Hirsch inched his hands out from his jacket pockets and raised them overhead with fingers spread.

"Now turn nice and slow," the voice continued. Hirsch obliged. A rangy figure clad in a dark ski mask stood ten feet down shore from Hirsch. His gloved hands clutched a jet-black Beretta M9 semi-automatic pistol. A tactical flashlight affixed to a rail on the underside of the pistol snapped on, blinding Hirsch with a beam of high-intensity white light. He moved to cover his eyes but caught himself and squeezed them shut instead.

"Look, Hirsch, I don't know what the hell you want, but you need to mind your own business and leave well enough alone." The figure spoke with a Minnesota accent and coughed several times as though a bone were stuck in his throat.

"I'm not looking for any trouble."

"So why the hell are you poking around Grand Rapids and Beaver Island asking questions, then? I'm guessing you weren't there to find God."

"You think those girls came to find God?"

The man shuffled several feet closer and shook the Beretta at Hirsch's face. "Are you trying to get cute with me, asshole? Who's the one staring down the barrel of a gun? Look, I didn't come here to have a discussion with you. I have one message—stay away from Manitou and the Dykmans; hell, make it all of the Lower Peninsula while you're at it."

The man continued to mouth breathe as Hirsch's eyes adjusted to the blinding light. The man wore a pair of lace-up combat boots matching those worn by Clint.

"You're Ellis Nygren, the Dykmans' enforcer," Hirsch said. "How'd you find me?"

"Who I am, who I work for, or what I do is none of your goddamn concern. It's my job to find people. With you, it wasn't hard. Do you have any clue what you're messing with here?"

"Well, I—"

"Don't think for a minute I couldn't take you down if I wanted. I know where you live. Besides, we're all alone here. You think you're the first person I've killed? The only reason you're still alive is the Dykmans don't want any further attention."

"Okay, okay. Just lower the piece down, man," Hirsch said.

"You don't call the shots here, I do. Now, I'm going to leave you with a warning, bud—if I catch wind that you're poking your nose where it doesn't belong one more time, I won't hesitate to take you out. I have a throw-down piece on me. I can make it look like a suicide. Do I have your attention?"

Hirsch nodded. The barrel of a gun in his face for the third time this year diluted any bravado engendered by his work for the Winslows.

"That's more like it. Be a good boy, Hirsch," Ellis said as he backed away and extinguished the Beretta's flashlight. As Ellis retreated, the night swallowed his figure until he melded with the lakeshore and looming trees into a mélange of darkness. Hirsch stood panting with his hands still held high over his head until his antagonist's footsteps segued into silence. The stillness of the summer night reclaimed the atmosphere.

Hirsch shuffled up the narrow gravel drive to his truck and fumbled for the keys. Despite his hands quaking from fear, he managed to insert the key into his truck's ignition. His eyes ached from the tactical flashlight's intense beam, and he squinted in pain at the passing headlights of each car he encountered. Coupled with his throbbing jaw, his head screamed for relief. He drove into town, found a vacant space along the west side of Cedar Street in front of the bank, and walked a block south to a tavern. It wasn't much to look at, but the neighborhood dive would do the trick. The faux-wood-paneled establishment looked little changed from the 1970s, and it had welcomed several generations of locals over the years. This included Murray Hirsch and his co-workers from the mill, who often dropped by after their shift for a beer and swapped tales before heading home. Hirsch did his best to calm his shaking hands by clasping them together atop the bar.

"You look like you've seen a ghost," the gray-haired woman wearing a Green Bay Packers sweater behind the bar said to him. "What can I get you?"

"Miller Lite," Hirsch mumbled.

The server popped the cap off the bottle and set it in front of him. Hirsch put the bottle to his parched lips and tipped it back, glugging its amber-hued contents in a series of gulps. He set it in the well and waited for the booze to dull the pounding in his head.

"You need another?" the woman asked, eyeing him from behind the cash register.

"Yeah, please. No, you know what—make it a Seven and soda. A double."

The server indulged him with a strong pour, and Hirsch stirred the drink with its red plastic straw, then drank the concoction straight from the plastic cup. This time, the liquor did what the beer could not, and he breathed a sigh of relief as his nerves dulled and the racket bouncing around the crowded bar mellowed into a fuzzy haze.

Three Seven and sodas diminished the white-hot ball of terror clawing at Hirsch's chest. Utter exhaustion soon blanketed his mind and body. He stumbled off the stool, drawing wayward glances from the server and a handful of patrons clustered around an adjacent table celebrating a league softball win. He found the front door and paused out front to catch his bearings. His truck waited nearby, but even Hirsch knew better than to attempt to drive the handful of blocks home in his inebriated state. He staggered down Cedar Street past the handful of dormant businesses before turning left on Oak Street. The lights from Saint Francis de Sales Catholic Church illuminated a segment of his journey, and by the time he reached Steuben, the darkened mass of his decaying childhood home beckoned. He summoned his remaining wherewithal to brush his teeth and shed his clothes across the bedroom floor before collapsing into bed.

AROUND 2:00 A.M., HIRSCH AWOKE to the creaking of his bedroom door as it opened. The warm body sliding into bed alongside him doused his fleeting moment of terror. The aroma of Lauren's vanilla-scented perfume cut through the veneer of cigarette smoke and stale beer that clung to anyone who set foot in Lily's. She'd taken to staying over at Hirsch's house a couple nights per week after her shift. While it made for a longer drive to her job teaching math to highschoolers in Gladstone, the extra hours together was worth the inconvenience. Lauren had slipped out of her work clothes and wore only a pair of silk boy shorts and a thin gray sleeveless T-shirt that hugged the contours of her breasts.

"Long night?" Hirsch said as he sleepily kissed her while draping a hand along her waist.

"Yeah, regular bunch of assholes we had to kick out towards close. None of that matters now. You smell like you've had a couple yourself," she replied, scrunching up her nose at the lingering booze fumes emanating from his flesh.

"Let's just say it was one helluva day. We have plans for the weekend, though. I'll fill you in tomorrow. We should get some sleep," Hirsch said as he cupped Lauren's ass with one hand and drew her closer. Her breasts through her T-shirt pressed against him warmed his chest. They kissed and explored each other's bodies with hungry caresses before shedding their respective underwear. Hirsch climbed between Lauren's legs, and she lowered a hand to guide him inside her. They made gentle love as Hirsch cradled the back of Lauren's head in one hand while she sucked the thumb of his other. He finished first with a shudder, and she wrapped her strong legs around him and soon joined him in her own flood of ecstasy. For that moment, their worldly concerns were forgotten, and they basked in a trance of unity before falling into an exhausted sleep.

Chapter 12

Life aboard the Winslows' thirty-five-foot yacht was a world of difference from the battered Lund crafts of Hirsch's youth. While smaller than the *Wanderlust*, the *C. F. Winslow* surpassed the Dykmans' party boat in comfort and elegance. The ship dwarfed the other pleasure boats and fishing crafts as it cut through the waters of Lake Superior a mile off the coast of Marquette. It was the final weeks before frigid winds would rip out of Canada and freeze over for the winter months. Below deck, twin diesel engines propelled the vessel eastward for a cruise along the storied Pictured Rocks northeast of Munising. Only an ore freighter out of Duluth rivaled the *C. F. Winslow*. The freighter lumbered along the water's horizon on a voyage destined for the Soo Locks and south to the steel mills of Ohio and Pennsylvania.

Hirsch felt a pang of guilt as he recalled his conversation with Edgar days earlier. The excitement in Edgar's voice had been palpable as he answered Hirsch's call before their planned excursion to fish Middle Branch of the Ontonagon River. It would have been Edgar's first fishing outing since his shoulder had healed from Marcus Shaw's gunshot wound.

"Edgar—look, I'm really sorry, but something's come up

and I need to cancel this weekend."

"Is everything all right with you, Ben?" he asked. "If it's money you're worried about, I can pay for gas and bring lunch. There's a pile of sliced liverwurst in my fridge with your name on it."

"No, it's not that. My girlfriend and I have this thing we can't miss, unfortunately. It may be our last chance this year to be out on the lake."

Edgar was silent for a moment. "It's the Winslows, eh?"

"We can totally make it up next weekend, okay? You name the time and place and I'll be there."

"I think I have something going on that weekend, Ben. It's fine, really. I needed to clean out my storage shed anyway now that my arm's better."

"I'll call you as soon as this weekend's over and we'll make plans. Something even bigger and better than the Ontonagon."

"Sure, sure, that'll be fine. Look, I gotta get going now. Ned and Tom are waiting on me at the coffee shop downtown. See ya," Edgar said and hung up without waiting for Hirsch's response.

Days later, Hirsch and Lauren stood opposite Herb and Catherine on the *C.F. Winslow*'s stern. All four enjoyed ice-cold gin and tonics. The cut-crystal glass sweated in the afternoon humidity, and Hirsch periodically swapped the beverage from one hand to the other to wipe the accumulated moisture along his khaki shorts.

"You should have seen Winston's face when I invited the two of you aboard this weekend," Catherine said. She wore a pair of reflective round sunglasses and had her dark-blonde hair tucked over her ears and beneath a red cashmere ballcap. Despite his weeks of service for the Winslows, it was Hirsch's first time meeting Herb in person. Herb was a slight man who wore high-waisted corduroy trousers and a flannel shirt with its sleeves rolled over his elbows. He sported a neat mustache and covered his head with a felt trilby adorned with a smattering of hand-tied trout flies. He looked like the stereotypical wealthy fisherman that Hirsch had encountered time and again throughout his life in the U.P.

"Do you normally sail alone?" Hirsch asked.

"Oh, we have plenty of guests, but it's rare to have an employee out with us. In fact, you might be the first, Ben," Catherine replied.

"At least she makes me look good or you might regret that decision," Hirsch said while drawing Lauren closer to him with his arm around her midsection.

Two crewmen worked the deck. Both wore white trousers and button-up, short-sleeved shirts with navy-blue piping around the cuffs. The younger man, Luis, saw to it that a table laden with snacks for the Winslows and their guests remained refreshed. All took advantage of the tray of smoked whitefish paired with an assortment of water crackers, crudités, and Wisconsin cheeses. The second server, Thanh, was in his fifties with streaks of gray in his dark head of hair. He kept a close eye on his guests and ensured that the quartet's beverages never ran dry. Lauren's smile and flushed cheeks suggested she was relishing the afternoon of luxury so removed from the social abyss of Lily's Tavern. Her glance at him while licking a dollop of whitefish dip off a carrot stick made him wish they could disappear below deck for a quick rendezvous.

"I caught this whitefish a few miles off our lake house on the Keweenaw Peninsula," Herb explained as Hirsch slathered a cracker with the rich, pale flesh. "Most commercial fishermen use gill nets or trap nets, but I like to take our boat out myself and catch them on a fly line. They fight like hell, and I've lost more flies than I can count trying to land them, but it's a hell of a rush to haul one in."

"Wait—you have another place on the lake?" Lauren said.

"It's Herb's great-grandfather's old lodge," Catherine replied. "I find the musty place a bit gloomy myself, but Herb insists we fly over for a long weekend every few weeks. I suppose we're due one more visit before the snow flies."

"Don't sound so disappointed. You keep yourself plenty busy with work whenever we're there," Herb said.

"Well, I have to do *something*, dear. If you're not out on the lake, I have to send a groundskeeper down to the creek at dinnertime when it's getting dark out," Catherine said.

"And I nearly always come back with a creel full of lake trout, sweetheart."

"Did you say you fly there?" Hirsch interrupted.

"That's right. One of the perks of having a pilot on retainer is Chris can land at a grass strip near the house. Guests love it too since she can pick them up and fly them directly there for a fishing retreat," Herb said.

"Sounds like a wonderful time," Lauren said.

"Are you a fisherwoman, Lauren?" Herb asked.

"Um, not so much. I did some with my dad and brothers when I was a kid, but it's not really my thing."

Herb scoffed. "You sound like Catherine. I try to get her to come out with me, even just on the streams, but she'd prefer to work instead."

"One of us has to keep this business afloat so we can enjoy afternoons like this," Catherine said, gesturing with her gin and tonic at the surroundings. The sun washed across the white surf breaking around the ship's wake.

"Let me bring you another of those, sir," Thanh said as he relieved Hirsch of his near-empty gin and tonic. Within a couple minutes, the bartender reappeared with a fresh drink. Hirsch accepted it, squeezed a stream of juice from the lime slice wedged across the rim, and dropped the wedge into the glass. The drink's crisp and tart fizz made him gasp.

"This may be the best G&T I've ever had," Hirsch said.

"Thanh knows what he's doing. He's been the head bartender at the Pioneer Club in Marquette for twenty-plus years now. We pay him dearly to help out on weekend excursions like this, but it's money well spent," Herb said. "Say, Ben, you interested in tossing a couple lines in the water and trying our luck?"

"Sounds fun, but I didn't bring my fishing license," Hirsch said.

Herb dismissed Hirsch's concerns with a wave of his hand. "The Coast Guard has bigger things to worry about than a pair of gentlemen fishing. Come with me."

"Lauren, why don't you join me for some sunbathing and girl talk on the bow while Ben and Herb forage for our supper," Catherine said.

"Enjoy," Hirsch said as Lauren looked at him before wrapping a stark-white towel around her shoulders. Drink in hand, she followed Catherine towards the bow. Hirsch observed the two women settle down along the yacht's honey-hued teak decking. Lauren pulled her ruffled cover-up over her head. She wore a bright red bikini that Hirsch had never seen before. Her breasts bounced beneath the thin fabric as she arranged her dark-blonde hair in a bun. Lauren settled beside Catherine along the towel laid out on the deck. They faced each other slightly elevated on their elbows and engaged in a low murmur of chatter that Hirsch strained to hear but couldn't make out. He gulped as Lauren rolled onto her stomach, giving the men an unobstructed view of her pert rear on display in her cheeky bikini bottoms. If Herb noticed, he was too much of a gentleman to comment.

Herb led Hirsch aft down a narrow walkway over the transom that terminated in a platform suspended above the propeller screws. Two light-tackle fishing rods were at the ready in a pair of swiveling rod holders. All they had to do was loosen the lures tucked into hook keepers, wind up, and cast deep into the ice-blue lake waters beyond. They settled into a pair of seats bolted against the transom and let the lures play in the current.

"Do you and Alex spend much time on the lake?" Hirsch said.

Herb sighed. "I'm afraid fishing is the last way Alex prefers to spend her day."

"Not a fan?"

"She never thought much of fishing, or anything involving death for that matter. Even catch-and-release bothered the hell out of her."

"I take it she never helped clean the fish?"

"You should've seen the looks she gave me. Not disgust, just sorrow," Herb said as he hoisted his fishing rod over his shoulder and cast his line out into the lake.

"Honestly, she sounds like a decent kid."

"She is—and that's what terrifies me about her being around those creeps. She's always been idealistic, but I never imagined her joining a utopian cult."

"Sir, can I ask you something I hope doesn't come off as impertinent?"

"Go ahead," Herb replied and smoothed down his trim mustache with his fingers.

"Do you struggle with being out here knowing what Alex might be going through at Manitou? I mean, what with the drugs and, well, you know what else."

Herb sat silent for half a minute. "Yes, I'm aware—Winston told us. Much as I question Alexandra's life choices, Cathy and I taught her to be strong; to look out for herself. It's the only way to make it in this life. She'll hang in there until we shut that nasty operation down."

"What do you think happened?" Hirsch asked. "With Alex and the prophet's movement, I mean."

Herb sighed. "How much time do you have? Look, Alex has always been impressionable. You'd think growing up a scion of some rich, established family would give her ample confidence. Wrong, big time. She was painfully shy as a child. Not to say she isn't smart. She's bright enough and hardly had to lift a finger to get good grades. We tried sending her to a few schools back east when she was younger—Dana Hall, Miss Porter's, even my *alma mater*, Groton. Every time, she'd call within a matter of weeks sobbing and begging us to bring her home. Seems the other students bullied her mercilessly for coming from a rural part of the country. The final straw was when she slashed her wrists one evening—not serious enough to put her life in danger, but boy did it get the school's attention. Alex spent a week holed up at a hospital in New Haven before we flew her home. Lo and behold, after trying her out at all those exclusive schools, she spends the rest of high school right here at Marquette Senior High School. She came into her own and graduated near the top of her class."

"What changed when she went off to college?" Hirsch asked.

"Well, truth be told, that's where we screwed up. We thought Alex would've been fine attending Ann Arbor or Northern right here on the peninsula where she was most comfortable. Stanford threw us for a loop. She had her mind set on California. We were concerned after all her trouble back east but thrilled she was finally showing some initiative, so we naturally agreed. I can see now what a mistake that was."

Herb reeled in his line and made another long cast into the lake.

"How'd Alex meet this Jonathan Teller and his crew if she was such an introvert?" Hirsch asked.

"Now that's how I know these clowns are up to no good. I think this creep knew which kids were vulnerable and might be ripe pickings for his sort of scam. Seems like his organization, the New Strangites or whatever they call themselves, understood lonely kids were the gateway. Professor Teller had Alex and others like her in class. It gave the so-called prophet and his disciples a chance to talk up the movement they're trying to build on Beaver Island."

"Why not just recruit from a church or something? Seems like the obvious source for new converts."

Herb took his time replying. "I wondered about that too, at first. Then it hit me—this isn't a traditional church or cult. Teller's trying to build something he sees as original. He wants to fulfill King Strang's vision of a new utopia on earth. Old Strang did it his way according to the methods of the 1800s, and Teller's doing the same. He needs smart people—computer science types and engineers—if he wants to make his vision a reality. Now, don't think for a minute that I believe this shit. It's all an enormous con job like any other cult."

"So Teller saw something in your daughter?" Hirsch asked.

"Far as we know. Mind you, this is secondhand and what Winston could glean from interviewing Alex's roommate. Seems our girl quit attending class mid-semester to follow the prophet to Beaver Island."

"Mind if I ask you one more question, Mr. Winslow?"

"Shoot."

"You have a good life, a couple fancy degrees on the wall, and plenty of money—why stay in Marquette when you can live anywhere you want?"

Herb looked at Hirsch. "I've seen enough of the world to last me a lifetime, Ben. There's no place I'd rather live than here. I mean, look around you," Herb said, gesturing with his free hand at the expanse of blue water surrounding them. "Looks like you've got one on the line," he added as the tip of Hirsch's fishing rod jiggled.

Hirsch felt the tug in the line, and he yanked back on the rod to set the hook. The fish took off, and he let it play with the line. Hirsch stood and moved towards the transom's edge as he worked the fish closer, cranking the reel and bringing in the catch inch by inch. Fifty feet from the vessel, the whitefish broke the water, its silvery belly shimmering in the sun amidst the crash of the surf. Herb had placed his rod in a holder and stood by with a hand-held fishing net, ready to assist Hirsch in bringing it aboard. Fearful of losing it in the home stretch, Hirsch took his time landing the worn-out fish until he brought it alongside the boat and lifted it clear of the water. Herb leaned over and ensnared the struggling whitefish in his net.

"Looks around five pounds, I'd say," Herb said. "That's a fine catch."

"Beginner's luck," Hirsch replied, nonetheless proud he'd landed the fish in front of one of the Upper Peninsula's wealthiest men. He reached into the net and snagged the whitefish under its gill with his index finger while wiggling the hook loose with his other. The whitefish was indeed a beauty, and one Hirsch wished his father were here to witness.

"Luis!" Herb hollered over the drone of the engines.

Moments later, Luis scrambled down the stairs. "Yes, sir."

"Will you clean Mr. Hirsch's fish and put it on ice? We'll see if we can't catch a few more to send home with him and his lovely lady."

Luis removed the fish from Hirsch's index finger without comment and returned up the stairs. Hirsch normally fished catch and release. Having another person clean and prepare his catch was a new experience.

"You'll have the best-tasting fish you've ever had for tonight's dinner. Let's get a couple more," Herb said as they settled into the seats and cast their lines out into the water.

They fished for another half-hour and added a pair of

whitefish and a nine-pound lake trout to their earlier catch. Deciding four was enough for one day, they reeled in their lines. By the end of their outing, all four fish would be fileted, individually wrapped in saranwrap, and encased in a Styrofoam container packed with crushed ice to keep them fresh for the journey home.

"I'm headed below deck to check on the motor. You care to join me?" Herb asked.

Hirsch didn't know the first thing about boat motors beyond how to start the pullcord variety. He figured he'd just get in Herb's way. "I'll check on my girlfriend and see if she needs anything," he said.

"A real gentleman," Herb replied. "I can see why Catherine took a shine to you." He clapped Hirsch on the shoulder and passed below deck through the hatch. Hirsch approached the bow.

Lauren was sunbathing beneath the cloudless sky that provided no cover from the September sun radiating across the bathing beauty. She lay supine across a towel spread out on the deck, her skin beginning to turn golden. Her crimson bikini left little to the imagination as it hugged the curves of her hips. She smiled as Hirsch approached and rolled onto her stomach. He sat alongside her and traced his fingers from the base of her neck down her spine.

"Where'd Catherine go?" Hirsch asked.

"She had to make a call."

"I couldn't do her job—managing the Winslows' empire, I mean," Hirsch said as he continued to run his fingers along her back.

"You might be in charge yourself, the way things are going. You mind putting on a little more of that sunscreen while you're at it?"

Hirsch obliged, squeezing a liberal amount of lotion into his hands and beginning to work it deep into her back. Her skin was warm to the touch.

"Untie my top for me," she said.

He pulled a string of the knot holding the delicate garment together and undid her top, spreading the two strands to each side of her before resuming his caresses on her back. She groaned in pleasure as the heels of his palms dug into the muscles of her lower back.

"You seem to be enjoying yourself."

"Mmmm," she murmured with the flash of a smile beneath her oversized sunglasses. "When we met, you never told me you had friends with a yacht. I might've jumped your bones right then and there if I knew."

"When we met, I *didn't* have friends with a yacht."

"Seems like this job's been good for you."

"Other than getting beaten up last weekend, I suppose it is," Hirsch said, fingering the wound on his chin. He'd removed the larger dressing Allison had originally applied and replaced it with a less conspicuous bandage.

"You still haven't told me what happened, you know. Catherine filled me in on their missing daughter, Alex. That she went missing at some religious wacko's place on Beaver Island, and that you're tracking down the people behind this. Can you even imagine?"

"Imagine what?"

"What it must be like to have your child vanish like that. I mean, she's an adult and all, but still. It makes me sick to my stomach to think about having a son or daughter and no way of getting in touch with them. I'm shocked they can keep it together as well as they are. A little higher," she added, then gasped as Hirsch worked his hands up her midback and massaged the stress out of her shoulders. "Jesus, if every teacher at my school could have a weekend like this, we'd all be better instructors."

"I take it the Gladstone School District doesn't have the

budget for a yacht?"

Lauren snorted. "They don't have the budget for school supplies and another math teacher, let alone a damn boat. Anyway, it's sweet what you're doing for them, Ben. Parts of it sound dangerous and all, but if you bring these nice people's daughter home, they'll never forget it."

"Bringing her home is the least of the troubles on that damn island." Lauren cocked her head at him. "Never mind," he added, "it's just I've seen some nasty shit these past few weeks. I mean, you know it exists and all, but until you experience it up close and personal, it's hard to understand."

"Well, we can't solve all the world's problems right away, now can we? Let's enjoy ourselves while we're here."

Catherine approached the pair with a bottle of champagne and three champagne flutes entwined in her right hand. Lauren moved towards Hirsch and whispered, "If we were alone right now, I'd lay you on your back and screw you silly. As it is, I'm going to take good care of you when we get back to my place." She kissed him on the cheek as Catherine sat next to them.

"I thought you lovebirds might enjoy a cold glass of champagne," she said.

She popped the cork, firing it over the side of the yacht. A wall of foam slid down the bottle, and Hirsch resisted the urge to lean over and lick it with his tongue.

"Cheers!"

AFTER FIVE HOURS ON THE LAKE, the *C. F. Winslow* returned to port. Hirsch and Lauren bid farewell to their hosts and drove back to Gladstone in Lauren's Nissan Rogue. Both were exhausted from the sun's vigor and a day spent frolicking on the lake, and nothing sounded better than an afternoon snooze in Lauren's bed. Halfway to her place, a distinct itch and prickling pain spreading across Hirsch's torso heralded the beginning of a killer sunburn. By the time they reached her house, he all but leapt out of the car, eager for relief. He had the wherewithal to grab the Styrofoam cooler stuffed full of fresh fish and wedge it into Lauren's refrigerator for later. He proceeded to strip off his scratchy T-shirt and lay face down against the soft cotton sheets while Lauren changed out of her swimsuit and showered to rinse off the day's accumulation of sweat and lotion.

"You should've put on some sunscreen like I did," Lauren said as she entered the bedroom with a damp washcloth and a squeeze bottle of lotion. She wore a lightweight, pale-blue sundress that fell just above her knees. She dabbed at Hirsch's inflamed back with the cloth soaked in diluted vinegar. Once it quelled the worst of the sting, she switched to the soothing lotion that perfumed the room with an aroma of lavender.

"I'm not used to that much sun. Normally, I'm pretty well covered when I walk the lines."

"I did say I'd take good care of you when we got home."

"This wasn't exactly what I had in mind," Hirsch replied, wincing at the renewed sting.

"You know, this might become a regular thing for us. Catherine and Herb seem to think a great deal of you."

"I'm useful to them. They're not like us, though. We could work our asses off the rest of our lives and they'd never accept us into their world."

"At least let a girl dream," she said. "Besides, this may be the break you needed. You might even get your license back if they put in a good word for you with the bar."

"If anyone could do it, the Winslows could."

"Now roll over and I'll take care of the rest of you."

He complied, and Lauren straddled him and squirted a line of lotion onto her palm. She rubbed her hands together, then transferred the cream to his chest, working it into his pecs and down his stomach. Her sundress bunched around her mid-thighs, revealing a thin pair of striped cotton underwear. He stiffened as her manicured nails traced up and down his chest, and he reached up and cupped the back of her head to draw her closer to him for a long kiss. Her lips tasted of strawberry lip balm and parted as her tongue found his. She guided him inside her, drawing her panties to one side before settling down onto him. Lauren rocked her hips in gentle circles. The release came sooner than he expected as she tightened around him with a sharp cry.

"Stay like this," she commanded. Hirsch was happy to oblige, savoring the warm security of her sex enveloping him in post-coital bliss. She wore her hair up, and he traced his fingers along the sides of her scalp, brushing his fingertips against the delicate curves of her ears. After several minutes enjoying the sensation of their coupling, Lauren snuggled alongside him for a much-needed nap.

After an hourlong snooze, Hirsch unsealed the Styrofoam container of whitefish and lake trout. He diced a handful of garlic cloves and whisked it in a saucepan with melted butter, fresh parsley, and lemon juice while pan searing the fish filets in olive oil. He cooked both sides until they reached a golden brown, then plated and slathered the filets with the garlic-lemon butter sauce. Lauren added generous helpings of a vinegar-based potato salad she'd made earlier in the day along with florets of broccoli steamed with a dash of chopped garlic. Despite the ample snacks aboard the yacht, they cleaned their plates and went back for seconds. They gulped down a pitcher of iced tea to combat the dehydration induced by the hours of sun and multiple drinks consumed aboard the *C. F. Winslow*, then cuddled on the couch and watched half of a Packers-Bears game. Around 8:00 P.M., Lauren had the misfortune of being called into work by her uncle Steve. Another server working the evening shift at Lily's had gone done with what he claimed was a stomach bug. Cursing their bad luck, both dressed and then parted at her front door with a promise to reunite later in the week.

THE LONG NAP AND PITCHER of iced tea left Hirsch brimming with energy by the time he returned home. While it was too late in the evening to make any progress on his derelict yard, Hirsch settled into his couch with a can of Diet Coke, flicked on a baseball game for background noise, and opened his laptop. With a legal pad and ballpoint pen beside him, Hirsch was ready to make good on Winston's request to follow-up on the Dykmans' porn site. He typed "GreatLakesGirls.com" into his web browser, and the now-familiar homepage popped up. Hirsch reached behind him to close his blinds, then commenced his investigation.

A common factor in all the preview pages was the same setting—a large room decorated with contemporary furniture including a king-sized bed and jumbo sofa, a hard-surfaced floor painted bright white, and a ribbon of windows overlooking a garden patio area filled with well-trimmed trees and flowering shrubs. The location was unclear, but the aesthetic and plant life argued against it being Beaver Island.

Federal law gave him a leg up in tracking down the records by mandating that every website producing and hosting adult content include a compliance notice identifying the custodian for the records. Sure enough, a link at the bottom of the webpage designated one "Excalibur Unlimited Entertainment LLC" as the custodian of record for Great Lakes Girls, with a Kalamazoo address. Hirsch opened another browser tab and navigated to the Michigan Secretary of State's business entity lookup. He typed "Excalibur Unlimited Entertainment" into the search box. Sure enough, the organization came up as a limited liability company headquartered in Holland, Michigan. The registered agent of service was a well-known agency office in Dearborn, but digging into the articles of organization revealed Excalibur's sole owner was another LLC going by the name of "Western Tulip Endeavors"—quite possibly the stupidest business name he'd heard in some time. Western Tulip utilized the same agent of service in Dearborn, and its physical address traced back to a UPS Store in St. Joseph.

Damn, these guys covered their tracks, Hirsch realized as he scrolled through the filings. It was the old shell game of one company cloaking itself in the guise of another holding company and using anonymous agents of service. Then he caught a lucky break—Western Tulip Endeavors was registered as wholly owned by 3D Michigan, Inc.

"Bingo," Hirsch said as he clicked on the detail page for 3D Michigan. While the Dearborn-based agent of service mirrored the other entities, 3D Michigan had a Grand Rapids business address. Hirsch copied the address into Google Maps and hit enter. A familiar image surfaced—the Dykman Family Insurance storefront.

"Bobby, Bobby, Bobby," Hirsch muttered as he sank back in his couch and smiled at his good fortune. That little twerp was either more daring than he appeared or incredibly gullible.

Hirsch navigated back to Great Lakes Girls, intending to take a screenshot of the compliance notice for his research file. A second link caught his attention—"Interested in Modeling?" it read. Hirsch clicked the link, bringing up a page inviting prospective models to submit their names and contact information, along with a link to upload photos. He grabbed his phone.

"Hey, sweetie. You wanna help me fight crime?"

Chapter 13

"I GUESS THIS IS HOW IT STARTS," Lauren said as Hirsch stood in front of her. He had his phone in hand, striving to find the optimal angles for their photoshoot. Lauren lay sideways facing him on her bed.

"How what starts?" Hirsch asked.

"A girl's life in porn. One minute her boyfriend's taking some fun and flirty pictures, the next she's getting railed by two dudes on camera."

"Well, in your case, pretend you're an undercover cop—which you sort of are."

"Hmm, I'm sure that's what they all say. 'It's just for art, baby,' or 'We're taking down a clandestine crime ring.'"

"Yeah, yeah, I know. Now turn and look over your shoulder for me," Hirsch said. Lauren scooted around so her rear faced the camera. She had her hair in soft curls, and she tossed it over her left shoulder while gazing at the camera with her mouth agape in a seductive O. Lauren's makeup was altogether too much for Hirsch, but he had to admit the blue eyeshadow and black eyeliner looked good on her.

"You know, you could probably do this for real—I mean, if you wanted," Hirsch said as he snapped a couple pictures.

"Don't make me come over there, asshole! I'm warning you now, if these pictures ever get out, I *will* find a way to murder you. I'd lose my job if my students or co-workers saw these."

"Don't worry. If we do this right, no one but us and the creeps running Great Lakes Girls will see these."

"You'd better pray that's the case, mister. I had a friend in college whose boyfriend uploaded a vid of her giving him a blowjob onto some porn site. That shit really messed up her life."

"I guess that's why they have revenge porn laws and all that."

"They sure as hell didn't back then. Not a damn thing happened to him."

"Say, how come you never dress like this when I'm around?" Hirsch asked. Lauren wore a knit crop top above black denim low-rise shorts that together exposed an ample section of her bare midriff. She went shoeless but had her toenails and fingernails painted a bright scarlet that complemented her fire-engine-red lipstick.

"You're kidding me, right? I went out and bought this crap after you called me about the job. I felt like a total skank just trying them on in the dressing room."

"I mean, you could just wear them around the house once in a while."

"Seriously, I'm warning you, buddy. And don't you have enough pictures for this application yet? I doubt they want an entire photoshoot," Lauren said.

"One more. Take off your top and face me."

"There's no way in hell I'm showing my face and boobs at the same time."

"Just cover them with your hands, then," Hirsch said.

"Okay, fine." Lauren stripped off the knit top and tossed it alongside the bed. She cupped her breasts in her hands and arched her eyebrows as Hirsch snapped a couple more photos.

"I think that should do it."

"Thank God," she said, leaping off the bed. She slipped into a flannel shirt, leaving the top two buttons undone, and traded the slut shorts for a pair of drawstring sweatpants. She joined Hirsch at the foot of the bed as he thumbed through the pictures.

"You think they'll buy I'm twenty-two?" Lauren asked.

"Totally. I mean, look at that ass."

"And you're sure your guy can make me a fake ID?"

"Easy. You should see the one he made for me." Hirsch omitted the details of his cavorting with hookers on a yacht.

"Too bad he wasn't around when I was in college."

"Which reminds me—we need a headshot for your fake."

"Give me a minute so I can look a little more . . . normal, okay?"

Lauren walked into the bathroom. Hirsch could hear water running as she scrubbed at the makeup caked on her face. He favorited a handful of the pictures from the photoshoot until she returned with her hair in a ponytail and looking much more like the young professional she was.

"Where should we do this?" she asked.

"Hmm, stand there," Hirsch said, indicating a spot in front of her neutral-toned wall. He approached, set the image to a square, and snapped a headshot suitable for an ID.

"Maybe I should use that for my next passport photo," Lauren said, inspecting the results.

"I'll forward it to you. Want any of the others?"

"God, no. I'd like to forget this ever happened. So what's next?" Lauren asked. She hopped onto her bed with her leg hanging over the edge.

"I'll pick the best of these and send them off to Great Lakes Girls. Then we wait for the call. I'll get you a burner phone, and you can use that to communicate with them. If all goes according to plan, they'll invite you to their studio for a photoshoot. We'll hit the place and learn what we can about the girls and the drugs."

"This all sounds so hush-hush," she said. "I've never done anything like this before."

"I've done a lot of things lately I never thought I would."

"Isn't it dangerous?"

Hirsch paused. In the past year he'd been beaten up, torched a clandestine meth lab, assaulted a man with a copy machine, and menaced another with a golf club. It disturbed him to realize just how normal raiding a porno studio felt.

"Sweetheart, I couldn't even tell you what dangerous is anymore," he said at last.

"Just don't get killed, okay? And you'd sure as shit better not let these creeps lay a finger on me."

"I'll clobber them with my bare hands if need be before that happens. One other question—what do you want your porn star name to be?"

"Trixie Rae," Lauren replied without missing a beat.

"Sounds like you've already given this some thought."

"Hey, I'm allowed to fantasize too, right?"

"So what does nympho Trixie Rae enjoy?" Hirsch asked.

Lauren smiled. "Why don't you come over here and I'll show you," she said, grabbing his belt and drawing Hirsch closer.

"When you promised to take me away for a weekend, this wasn't exactly what I had in mind."

"Oh, c'mon," Hirsch said, glancing at Lauren in the driver's seat of her Nissan Rogue. For her appointment with the producers at Great Lakes Girls, she wore a skintight ribbed tube-top and a hot-pink miniskirt that fell a few inches below her crotch. Across her lap she'd draped a Wisconsin Badgers sweatshirt, depriving Hirsch of the occasional peek at the purple G-string beneath her skirt. Silver-sequined stiletto heels with ankle straps graced her feet. "You mean to tell me you never wanted to visit Grand Rapids in September?"

"Not dressed like an absolute slut and on my way to see a couple creeps who want to fuck me and videotape it." She wore her hair loose and augmented with a set of silver hoop earrings that dangled from her earlobes. A silver bangle encircling her right wrist clinked against the steering wheel as she navigated Highway 131 through the city's outskirts.

"Well, when you put it like that," Hirsch said.

"Where is this place, anyway? We must be getting close."

"Take the second exit and head west on Leonard Street. There's a gas station on the right about a mile down the road. You can drop me off there and head to the studio."

The producers at Great Lakes Girls had bought Hirsch and Lauren's pitch hook, line, and sinker. After he submitted her application with a curated selection of five photos from their shoot, it wasn't two hours before twenty-two-year-old college student and part-time barista "McKinzie Rae Sawyer" (a.k.a. Trixie Rae) of Grayling, Michigan, received an email from none other than Bobby Devall praising her pictures and exclaiming that she was exactly the type of fresh-faced college girl that fans of Great Lakes Girls would love. A twenty-minute phone call the next day between Bobby and Lauren on her new burner sealed the deal. She agreed to a photo and video shoot the following Saturday, when Bobby would introduce her to the male "talent" and go to work.

"So let me make sure I understand all this," Lauren said as they crossed the Grand River. "I'm supposed to show up at the studio address they gave me, go through the preliminaries for this shoot, and you'll come along in fifteen minutes and crash the party. Do I have that right?"

"That's the plan."

"Remind me what you hope to find there?"

"We need solid intel connecting this operation to the Dykman family."

"And if these creeps are armed?"

"I am too," Hirsch said, patting his left shoulder, where his .38 hung in a leather holster he'd purchased earlier in the week from an Escanaba sporting goods store.

"Jesus, we're all going to die."

"Relax. This isn't my first rodeo, remember? At least these guys aren't psychotic meth heads—I hope."

"That doesn't make me feel any better," Lauren said as she pulled into a gas station parking lot off Leonard Street. "Here you go. I still can't believe I'm doing this for you."

"We're doing this to take down a bunch of assholes who kidnap, drug, and force girls into sex work. Just keep that in mind. If anything gets ugly in there or you get cold feet, call me on the burner and get the hell out." Hirsch popped the door and exited, then looked inside at Lauren.

"I . . ." she began, then faltered.

"I know, me too," Hirsch said. "Let's get through this and we'll have plenty of time afterwards."

Hirsch shut the door and Lauren pulled away for the half-mile drive west to the studio. He spent five minutes perusing the convenience store attached to the gas station. The clerk glared at him with suspicion from behind the counter—whether because he spotted the piece beneath Hirsch's jacket or sized him up as a potential thief, he couldn't tell. Hirsch grabbed a bottle of water, tossed the clerk a couple dollars, and headed out.

Light overcast skies and a gentle easterly breeze made for a pleasant ten-minute walk. Hirsch had studied pictures of the studio from multiple angles on Google Streetscape. The Kent County property tax records revealed the building belonged to an organization known as Sanderson Productions,

Limited—yet another shell company whose ownership was well-concealed beneath layers of organizational obfuscation.

The studio itself was bland to the point of being conspicuous. The single-story building sat amidst a light-industrial sector of town that had seen better days, judging by the absence of activity. The building comprised light-gray stucco walls, a flat roof, a metal front door painted black with a deadbolt, and a courtyard on the structure's northside surrounded by an eight-foot-tall wooden fence. The fence featured a gate to the courtyard protected by a keypad-enabled doorknob. Hirsch had seen enough Great Lakes Girls material to discern a handful of scenes were filmed outdoors in what he presumed to be this very courtyard. Lauren's Nissan sat in a gravel parking strip running alongside the privacy fence. Parked next to it was an orange Chevrolet Camaro with black accents and Bobby's beige Impala from the insurance office.

Who knew that little creep had it in him to run a porno shoot, Hirsch thought as he snapped pictures of the two vehicles.

Hirsch approached the courtyard gate and tried the aluminum knob. As expected, it didn't budge. The fence was too high for him to jump from the ground, but the row of vehicles parked alongside it offered a leg up. It was an easy choice—he hopped onto the Camaro's gleaming hood, coating it with a fine patina of dust and grime as he maneuvered to find his best footing. He backed up towards the windshield facing the courtyard, then took off, flinging himself towards the fence boards. He managed to grasp the top of the slats and clung by his fingertips as his body smacked against the fence. At that moment, Hirsch desperately wished he'd spent the last month doing a set of pushups every morning. He summoned all his strength and forced himself upwards until he could swing his right leg over the fence.

Dropping into the courtyard, he crashed into a row of neatly trimmed boxwoods that crumbled and snapped beneath his weight. He stumbled to his feet and brushed off clinging vegetation. The coast was clear, but the murmur of voices and thudding bass from inside the building reached his ears. The scene before him mirrored the setting of the photographs and video on Morgan's preview page. To the left, a stucco wall terminated in a passageway lined with arbor vitae shrubs and flowering plants. Hirsch flattened himself against the stucco wall, inching his way down the passageway towards the door. He stood alongside the ajar door and listened.

"So what's your favorite position, Trixie?" Bobby's nasal voice inquired.

"Umm, doggy, I'd have to say," Lauren responded with fake enthusiasm.

"I knew you'd say that," Bobby said. Lauren laughed and Bobby continued, "When'd you lose your virginity?"

"I was sixteen."

"Where?" Bobby followed up.

"In my boyfriend's car after the football game." Lauren giggled.

"Were you a cheerleader, Trixie?"

"Color guard."

"Oh, so you waved the flags around?"

Lauren nodded. "I wasn't cute enough for the cheer squad."

"Oh, I don't believe that for a second," Bobby said, punctuated by a staccato laugh. "So, how many guys have you been with?"

"Um, like five. I'm not a wild girl."

"I guess we'll see about that. How about we get you out of those clothes so our viewers can see what you look like naked? Then we'll see what you and Harley here can do."

"Great, I'm excited."

"Okay, good. Let's stand up and start with your top."

It was now or never, Hirsch realized as Lauren's five-inch

heels clicked against the floor and she stood to disrobe. He reached beneath his jacket and unholstered his pistol. With it clenched in his right hand, he charged into the studio.

"Hands up, motherfuckers," Hirsch shouted as he burst inside. Smooth R&B played from a ribbon of speakers built into the ceiling, and an odor of men's body spray and Pink Sugar Body Mist clogged the air. Hirsch coughed as the stale funk filled his lungs. Genuine surprise clouded Lauren's face, and she stood frozen with fistfuls of tube top gripped in her hands, prepared to pull it over her head.

Bobby squealed and shied away, raising his hands over his head to reveal perspiration-soaked pit stains on his teal polo shirt. He squinted at Hirsch behind his thick glasses. A rectangular bandage covered part of his forehead near his hairline—undoubtedly from where Hirsch had clobbered him with the photocopier. Shock blended with abject fear contorted his face as he recognized the man behind the gun. Standing alongside Bobby was a ripped douchebag over six foot tall with blond hair and frosted tips. He stood with hands raised.

"Ah, fuck, not you again, man. What now?" Bobby whined.

"Shut it, Bobby. I'm asking the questions around here," Hirsch said. "Trixie, over here."

"What is this, anyway?" Bobby continued as Lauren smoothed her tube top along her torso and trotted across the room to join Hirsch.

"The fuck did I just say, asshole?" Hirsch cocked the hammer on his .38. "You keep records on this operation?"

"R-r-records?" Bobby stammered.

"Yeah, you know, like paperwork."

"Sure . . . in the office."

"Where's the office?"

With his hands still raised, Bobby tilted his head sideways, indicating a frosted-glass door to their left. "Over there," he said.

"Who owns this operation?"

"Excalibur Entertainment."

"Don't make me use this," Hirsch said, shaking the pistol at Bobby. "I mean *who* as in which of your creep employers."

"Lisa Dykman and her husband, Braden."

"Does Lisa come here often?"

"Lisa? You gotta be kidding me. I never deal with her directly," Bobby replied.

"Okay, who's her go-between, then?"

"A guy named Clint."

"Clint Lewisohn?"

"Yeah, him. But, man, you can't breathe a word to anyone that I told you. He'll have my balls—"

"Stuff it," Hirsch said, cutting him off. "Does Clint come here often?"

"Nah, man, that dude's way too much of a pussy hound. Lisa ordered him to stay away so we could get actual work done around here," Bobby said.

"So where do you and Clint meet?"

"If Clint's not on the island, he's at this club outside Charlevoix—Northwoods Fantasy."

"A strip club?" Hirsch asked. "You been there?"

"Yeah. Trashy as hell, but Clint digs it."

"You—what's your name?" Hirsch asked, swiveling his gun towards Bobby's blond accomplice. He wore a skin-tight black muscle shirt and gray jockey shorts that accentuated his ample package. Hirsch recognized his physique from the Great Lakes Girls website as the male talent who interacted with the girls.

"Harley Steele," the man replied.

"Don't fuck with me, bro."

"It's Herman."

"Herman what?"

"Herman Winkel."

"Jesus, I see why you picked a stage name. Okay, you all got a storage closet around here?"

"There's a janitor's closet next to the office, but why—" Bobby said. Hirsch glanced across the room. The closet door featured a locking knob and deadbolt across the top.

"You got keys for this place?"

"Um, yeah."

"Toss them my way—now."

Bobby reached one hand towards his pocket, digging inside before emerging with a set of keys on a chain. He glanced at them with reluctance before executing a weak toss towards Hirsch. They landed at his feet with a jangle against the painted concrete floor.

"Trixie, baby, be a doll and pick those up for me," Hirsch said. Lauren raised her hand as if to cuff him across the head, but she squatted down and grabbed the keys. Hirsch held out his left hand and she deposited them in his palm.

"Bobby, Herman, here's the deal—you're both going to get in that closet and keep quiet. I know about the drugs; I know about Beaver Island and the girls. You call the cops and you're going down on federal sex trafficking and criminal fraud charges. So unless you both want a long stint at the Federal Pen in Milan, I suggest you keep your mouths shut. Now toss your phones on the ground." Bobby complied, and his iPhone clattered to the floor.

"Uh, dude . . ."

"What, *Herman*?"

"Mine's over there . . . in my pants." Herman turned his face towards a pair of designer jeans draped over an easy chair.

"Fine. Now get in the closet. You first," Hirsch said, pointing the barrel towards Bobby. With trembling legs,

Bobby paced across the room, followed by Herman, into the closet. Bobby stumbled over a mop and bucket on the floor inside but caught his balance. The two men huddled towards the closet's rear with hands raised. Hirsch got a good look inside. Only a few feet deep, the closet featured a row of shelves lined with chemicals and cleaning supplies in neat rows. Hirsch shuddered to think about the filth and germs undoubtedly smeared across the room after a shoot. He wanted to bathe in disinfectant as soon as he got home.

"Now remember what I said," Hirsch said as he slammed the closet door shut and locked it. The deadbolt was one-way, and he figured it would buy them adequate time to finish the investigation. Hirsch raced to snatch Bobby's phone off the floor and Herman's out of his pants and slipped them both into a trouser pocket. He shoved the .38 into the back of his waistband as well.

"Now what?" Lauren asked.

"The office. Let's hurry."

Hirsch and Lauren entered the office and looked around. A computer with dual monitors sat atop a desk next to a tan-colored four-drawer file cabinet. Along the opposite wall, a folding table was stacked high with unopened vibrators and other assorted sex toys.

"Help yourself," he said to Lauren. "You've earned something from this whole adventure."

"Thanks . . . I'll pass."

"You know these retail for over a hundred dollars, right?" Hirsch said while picking up a purple rabbit-style vibrator enclosed in a clamshell plastic case.

"Ben!"

"I'm just messing with you," he said, tossing it back onto the table.

"Besides, I already have one."

"Oh, really?" Hirsch said, pausing. "Am I not getting the

job done or what?"

"Focus, Ben. We've got to get a move on this."

"Fine, fine. Let's see what's in here," Hirsch said while approaching the file cabinet. He tried to open the top drawer. It rattled but held firm.

"Fuck, it's locked," he said.

"Try the keys," Lauren suggested.

"Worth a shot," Hirsch replied as he parsed through Bobby's collection of keys and tried a selection. Not one matched the file cabinet, however. "I'll have to shoot out the lock. Plug your ears, okay?"

Lauren turned around with her fingers clamped tight over her ears. Hirsch yanked the .38 from his waistband, stood three feet back from the file cabinet, took aim at the cylinder lock embedded in the cabinet's frame, and squeezed the trigger. He screamed in pain as a deafening roar filled the office. A high-pitched screech rang in his ears, and he shook his head trying to clear the agonizing throb pulsating through his skull. The hollow-point slug had found its mark and pulverized the file cabinet's steel frame, leaving the cylinder lock little more than a twisted ingot on the floor. Hirsch turned to look over his shoulder.

"You okay there?"

Lauren was huddled in a ball with her trembling hands clamped over her ears and head stuck between her knees.

"What the actual fuck? Was that necessary?" Her voice came across as but an echo amidst the hollow ringing plaguing Hirsch's ears.

"I'm sorry, sweetie. I didn't have time to pick the lock—not that I'd know how anyway."

"I didn't think it'd be that loud," Lauren said. She stood and stretched her jaw.

"Tell me about it. Let's see what's inside."

Hirsch yanked the handle of the top drawer. It stuck on

the twisted railing, but an extra effort freed it. A collection of folders hung inside.

"Banking records, insurance documents, supply invoices, blah, blah, blah," Hirsch said as he thumbed through the contents. He had to hand it to Bobby for keeping meticulous records. "Bingo."

"What is it?" Lauren asked.

"Excalibur Entertainment's payment records. Let's see who's on the take," Hirsch said as he extracted the folder and flipped it open.

"Five thousand to our buddy Herman Winkel, fifty K to Ellis Nygren for security services—whoa—one hundred thousand dollars to Lisa Dykman-Van Raatle and the same to her husband, Braden. What are the chances they're reporting all this as legitimate income?"

"Is it good?"

"Good? This is everything we need to tie these clowns to the Beaver Island sex-trafficking operation. It's evidence Lisa and Braden are deriving direct profit from the scheme. This is only the tip of the iceberg. You mind lending me a hand?"

"Sure, what can I do?" Lauren asked.

"Hold your arms out and I'll stack these files. We're taking it all."

Hirsch heaved the entire collection of files out of the drawer and piled them atop Lauren's outstretched arms. "Let's see what's in the other drawers, then get the hell out of here."

The second drawer was empty while the third contained a smaller stack of hanging files. Hirsch's heart leapt—the files were documentation on each of the women who posed for Great Lakes Girls, complete with signed releases (undoubtedly under coercion), photocopies of identification, and details of each shoot including filming and release dates. He scooped them up and passed them to Lauren. The fourth drawer, at the bottom of the file cabinet, held two padded manila envelopes. Hirsch grabbed them and turned to Lauren.

"We'll take the computer as well. These guys will be royally screwed without all of this."

Hirsch unplugged the laptop attached to a docking station and gripped it in his left hand.

"Let's get the hell out of here," he said and nodded towards the door.

With her arms piled high with folders, Lauren followed Hirsch into the main studio room. She froze before the high-definition digital camera mounted atop a tripod in front of the bed. A second handheld camera sat on a bedside table.

"Ben."

"Yeah?"

"They were filming me. I can't have those videos out there."

"Let me see what I can do."

Hirsch popped the memory cards out of both cameras and pocketed them. As a final salvo he detached the camera from the tripod and flung it against the wall where it shattered into a dozen fragments and clattered against the floor.

"Don't fuck with the equipment, man," Bobby's muffled voice squealed from behind the storage closet door.

"Too late," Hirsch said as he grabbed the handheld camera and spiked it against the ground, eliciting a series of fist pounds against the closet door.

"Good enough?" Hirsch asked Lauren. She nodded. "Okay, let's move."

He made for the courtyard entrance with Lauren clipping behind him.

"Slow down for me," she said. "You try walking in five-inch heels."

"Sorry, babe," he replied as they crossed the courtyard. He opened the fence gate, and they stepped outside. "Keys?"

"In my purse," Lauren said with her arms straining under

the weight of the purloined files. Hirsch unzipped the small pink purse dangling from her arm and plucked her set of keys from within. He unlocked her Nissan and opened the rear passenger door, tossing the laptop on the floorboard before unburdening Lauren of the files. She shook her arms to relieve the strain.

"I'll drive," Hirsch said. He stripped off his jacket and threw it in the back seat before climbing behind the wheel.

Once seated, Lauren undid the straps of her shoes and slipped them off. "I'd better never have to wear these damn things again," she said, rubbing her feet.

"Hopefully not under these circumstances," Hirsch said as he engaged the ignition and backed away from the parking strip.

"Did we just . . . ?" Lauren said.

"Burglarize a porn studio?"

"Yeah."

"Yes, that's exactly what we did," Hirsch said as he pulled the car into the roadway to make a left turn onto the cross street.

"Couldn't they have us arrested?"

"Maybe, but we have a mountain of evidence behind us tying them to a host of crimes—state and federal. There's no fucking way the Dykmans will let them come forward with all this evidence missing. I wouldn't want to be Bobby, though."

"And what if *they* come after us?"

A shotgun blast obliterated the rear window of Lauren's Rogue, showering the cabin with pulverized fragments of glass. Lauren screamed and pitched forward, hitting her forehead on the dash. Standing behind them in the parking lot, Herman Winkel clutched a sawed-off shotgun. He ejected the empty shell and raised the gun to his shoulder, taking aim again. Hirsch gunned the accelerator, propelling the vehicle forward into traffic.

An oncoming Honda Accord squealed its brakes and blared its horn, swerving right to avoid a collision. The sedan hopped the curb as Hirsch pulled hard left, fishtailing the Rogue in the middle of the road before regaining control. A second shotgun blast peppered the rear driver's side quarter panel with a mosaic of dimples but left the tires unscathed. Hirsch jammed the gas, blasting them over forty-five on the residential street and out of the neighborhood. He made for the highway onramp and glanced at the passenger seat.

Lauren reclined against the seat, pale and trembling.

"You okay?" he asked.

"Yeah," she nodded, white-faced. "But you're not." Hirsch followed her eyes to his upper arm. Droplets of blood oozed through his button-up shirt.

Hirsch pulled to the roadside and traced the fingers of his left hand along his wounded flesh. Firm, round pellets were embedded within two entry wounds. Stinging pain erupted at the sensation of his fingertips brushing over the punctures.

"We need to get you to a hospital," Lauren said.

"We can't—they'll call the police and there's no way to explain this."

"Then what—you bleed to death? C'mon, Ben."

"Just wrap it with that scarf and we'll figure something out."

Lauren scooped up the Green Bay Packers scarf curled on the floorboard near her feet. Hirsch gingerly raised his arm while she wound the scarf around it. He gritted his teeth against the searing pain boiling forth as the shock wore off. He was tempted to burn rubber towards East Lansing, but remembered Allison was in Europe with her fiancé.

"We need to get the hell out of here before Herman comes after us," Hirsch said as he caught the Highway 131 northbound on-ramp. "Here," he continued, drawing Bobby and Herman's phones out of his pocket. A white-hot pain flashed through his entire body. "Toss these over the side of the road."

"Right here?" Lauren asked as she rolled down the passenger-side window.

"It's as good here as anywhere. We don't need them, and it'll take those two a while to track them down."

Lauren flung each cellphone out the window one at a time. They disappeared into the overgrown brush coating the highway embankment.

"Fuck," Hirsch said as he tried to lean back in his seat. Any contact along his upper arm felt like course-grit sandpaper soaked in sulfuric acid. He hunched forward over the steering wheel. Rivulets of sweat trickled down his forehead, and Hirsch blinked his eyes to clear the salty drops from his field of vision.

"Can you make it to Reed City?" Lauren asked as they passed the Whitecaps' ballpark on the way out of the city.

"Probably . . . why?"

"I know someone who can help."

PART III

Chapter 14

Hirsch and Lauren made the seventy-mile drive from Grand Rapids to Reed City in under an hour. The nausea and pain shooting along his right arm threatened to overwhelm him, and he fought the urge to pass out. They exited the freeway at Reed City, and he slowed as they approached a roadside motel. A sign advertising the Lazy-Day Getaway Motel glowed in red neon.

"What about here?" Hirsch asked. Painted dark brown with orange trim along the eves and door casings, the low-budget motel had seen better days. An office adjacent to the road anchored a narrow rectangular box comprising ten identical motel rooms. Each featured a single door and a sliding-glass window above a rusted air-conditioner condenser. White plastic chairs yellowed with age sat outside each room. Rust-stained water from the leaking gutter system pooled in depressions along the sidewalk abutting the rooms. It reminded Hirsch of the countless cheap motels from childhood family vacations with his parents and sister. He'd fit right in, though he lamented inflicting the experience on his girlfriend.

Lauren sighed. "It's as good as anywhere. Pull in and I'll see about getting a room."

"Shift it to park for me," Hirsch said as he slowed to a stop outside the otherwise abandoned motel. Lauren reached over and maneuvered the gear shift until the transmission clicked into park.

"Hang in there for me, okay? I'll be right back," Lauren said as she popped the passenger door. She'd switched from her five-inch heels to a pair of flip-flops and pulled her baggy Green Bay Packers sweatshirt over her crop top. She nonetheless stuck out like a sore thumb in the rural community in her pleated miniskirt.

Hirsch drew ragged breaths as he focused on a motel-room doorknob opposite the car. Deep breathing helped calm his panicked brain. Barring infection, the shot-pellet wounds to his upper arm wouldn't be fatal. That knowledge did little to mitigate the sheer panic the pain and caked blood spawned in his mind. It was the longest ten minutes of his life until Lauren exited the motel office and returned with a key attached to a forest-green plastic tag dangling from the fingers of her right hand. Hirsch rolled down the driver's side window.

"Room 4. Let's get you inside," Lauren said.

"Grab my jacket on the back seat. If the clerk sees me bleeding out, I guarantee he'll call the cops."

"I'm pretty damn sure he thinks I'm a prostitute, so we already have that going for us," Lauren replied as she fetched Hirsch's navy-blue polar-fleece jacket from the back seat and draped it over his shoulders. "I told him my boyfriend wasn't feeling well. He waived the early check-in fee."

"Ouch, dammit," Hirsch said as the jacket grazed his pockmarked upper arm.

"I know, it sucks. It'll do to get you inside. You need help getting out?"

"If you can open the room door, I should be okay."

Hirsch stepped outside the vehicle, dropping his feet

on the ground one at a time before applying his full weight and standing. Trembling with skin clammy and pale, he summoned his remaining energy to shut the car door and make baby steps towards the motel room. Lauren waited there, ready to usher him inside. He entered the pitch-black room. Lauren shut the door and fumbled for a light switch beneath the blackout curtains.

He took in the surroundings: a full-sized mattress topped with ratty comforter, twin nightstands constructed of fiberboard laminated to resemble oak, a dark-beige carpet dotted with irregular stains of uncertain origin, and a cathode-ray tube television perched atop a four-drawer dresser opposite the bed, the television's remote bolted to one of the nightstands. The room reeked of mildew and bathroom cleaner mixed with undertones of cigarette smoke saturating the walls and upholstery.

"Jeez, all it's missing are the vibrating beds, right?" Hirsch said as Lauren tossed her purse onto a Formica table next to the window.

"Don't tell me you're thinking about that right now."

"No, I'm just saying—what happened to all the vibrating beds?"

"You've clearly stayed in some classy joints, my friend. Come on, let's get that shirt off you."

Hirsch lowered his arms as Lauren removed his jacket and unbuttoned his green-blue-and-white checked shirt, then slipped it off along his arms. The tattered right sleeve of his crew-neck undershirt was soaked with blood, turning a dark reddish-brown as it dried.

"That undershirt needs to come off too, or it's going to glue to your skin with all that blood. This will hurt—a lot," she said. Hirsch nodded and elevated his hands over his head.

He had to suppress a scream as the sticky fabric caught and momentarily clung to his upper arm before peeling free.

Lauren wadded up the ruined shirt and shoved it into a trash-can. Hirsch stood bare-chested, his vision blurred by the searing pain. He shuffled across the room towards a scratched and chipped mirror screwed into the wall. He turned his back towards the mirror and glanced over his right shoulder to assess the damage. His entire upper arm was a mass of blood-streaked, bruised flesh highlighted by two puncture wounds where twin steel pellets lay embedded inside. While his arm remained mercifully unbroken, the raw pain that alternated between a fiery burn and knifelike stabbings made him long for a hacksaw to shear the whole thing off.

"You said you know someone who could help," Hirsch said as Lauren soaked a hand towel with cold water from the bathroom sink.

"I'll call her right now," Lauren said while returning with the towel. "Here, hold this on your arm if you can." Hirsch accepted the rolled-up towel and inched it towards his upper arm. At first, pain exploded like a supernova through his brain, but before long, the chilled water offered a modicum of relief from his suffering. Lauren sat on the edge of the bed with her phone raised to her ear.

"Hey, Kristy! Long time no chat, right? How's life, girl-friend? . . . Yeah, I'm still stuck in Gladstone teaching high schoolers. . . . Seriously, who would've thought. I'm actually right here at a motel in Reed City. . . . Yeah, I know, small world! Say, I've got a really sick puppy here with me. Think you might have time to come over and look at him? . . . You do, great. We're at the Lazy-Day Getaway Motel, Room 4. . . . Mmhmm, we'll be here. Looking forward to catching up too, babe. . . . Love you, hun." Lauren ended the call.

"Umm . . . who was that?" Hirsch asked.

"A friend from college—Kristy Young. We and two other girls shared an apartment in Madison our junior year."

"And she's a doctor?"

"Totally. I mean, technically, she's a veterinarian—but she's awesome at it from everything I've heard."

"And she knows I'm not a dog, right?"

Lauren remained silent.

"Right?"

"Look, Ben, I'm doing everything I can here. Unless you want me to dig those pellets out of your arm myself with a pair of tweezers, I suggest you just roll with it, okay?"

Hirsch nodded. Lauren's plan was the best they had to work with under the circumstances. "I'm going to lie down until she gets here."

"Good idea," Lauren said as she headed towards the door. "I'll get our bags. I have a feeling we're not going anywhere until tomorrow morning."

As Lauren stepped outside, Hirsch crawled onto the bed and settled onto his stomach with his right arm hooked out at an angle in the least uncomfortable position for his macerated flesh. He didn't realize the extent of his fatigue, and he fell asleep before Lauren returned from the car. His dreams were a swirl of roadside trees, shotgun blasts, and low-budget pornography all playing in a ragged loop.

THE RAP OF KNUCKLES ON THE motel-room door awoke him with a start. His eyes flew open as Lauren alighted from a chair at the Formica table and went to answer the door. While he slept, she'd swapped her pleated miniskirt for a pair of yoga pants.

"Kristy!" Lauren said as she embraced her friend and squealed with excitement. "Oh my God, what's it been— three years already?"

"At least since that college meetup in Green Bay. Remember that?"

"No . . . not really. I think I was hungover for a week solid."

Kristy stood around five foot six, with dark-brown hair gathered in a French braid that draped down the back of her white coat, which was emblazoned with the logo of her veterinary clinic and her name in scarlet cursive embroidery. A pair of clear-frame glasses framed her hazel eyes.

Lauren's eyes widened and she grinned at the sight of the distinct swell of Kristy's stomach beneath her coat.

"Oh my God! I had no idea. How far along are you?" Lauren asked.

"Twenty-eight weeks this Friday. I'm due mid-December with a boy."

"You should've told me. We need to do a shower or something. Come on in." Lauren stood aside so her friend could enter.

Kristy's face crumbled into confusion as she encountered Hirsch's shirtless figure prostrate on the bed.

"Umm, Lauren, where's the dog?" she said, her voice trailing off.

"Okay, okay, I lied . . . there is no dog. This is my boyfriend, Ben. We're in a world of hurt, and you're the *only* person I could think of who could help."

"Your boyfriend, wh—what's wrong with him?"

"We had an accident. He took a couple shotgun pellets to his upper arm. The less you know about it, the better. Just pretend he's a horse, okay?"

"Lauren, what on earth? He's not a fucking horse. I'm a veterinarian; I can't treat people. I could lose my license for this . . . or go to jail. Seriously, take him to a damn hospital—now."

"We can't—I mean, we could, but they'd ask way too many questions. *Please*, you've got to help us here," Lauren said with her hands folded together in supplication.

"What have you got yourself into? Wait—are you back into drugs again?" Kristy asked with suspicion pasted across her face.

"No, I swear I haven't touched anything in years. And this has nothing to do with drugs. Ben works as an investigator for a rich family in the U.P. He got hurt trying to stop some really evil people. I was helping."

"I suppose that explains what happened to your car out there," Kristy said.

"Yeah, exactly. Now, will you help us or are you going to let him die right here in a cheap motel?"

"Don't fucking put this on me, bitch! Yeah, I'll help him. But both of you sure as hell better never breathe a word of this to anyone. I can't believe you used me like this."

"Thank you, thank you, thank you," Lauren murmured as she sank to her knees in front of her friend.

"Enough. Just move and let me look at him."

Lauren shifted out of the way and Kristy approached the bed, where Hirsch lay prone. She lifted the blood-soaked towel from his upper arm.

"Gracious. Sure looks like shotgun-pellet entry wounds. I don't treat many gunshot injuries, fortunately, but it's not unheard of for people to take shots at livestock or pets. I can try to remove the pellets, but it might be more helpful just to staunch the bleeding and stitch the wounds closed. Let me get my bag from the car. I still can't believe I'm doing this."

Hirsch murmured in assent as he regarded Kristy through glassy eyes. She left the room for a moment and returned with a rectangular black bag that she placed on the nightstand next to the bed. She unzipped the bag and snapped on a pair of nitrile gloves one hand at a time.

"Bring me one of those chairs," she commanded Lauren, who obliged by placing one of the steel-tube chairs beside Kristy. The latter sat and drew fluid into a syringe from a small plastic vial.

"I'm going to give you a local anesthetic. It's the best I

can do under the circumstances." She slipped the needle into the inflamed flesh of Hirsch's upper arm. He yelped at the needle's bite into the aggravated tissue, but soon felt relief from the throbbing pain. A layer of sweat coated his skin like cooled grease on a frying pan. Kristy's belly pointed at him, but he resisted the urge to rub it under the circumstances.

She selected a pair of long-nosed forceps and probed the first of the two puncture wounds. Hirsch felt nothing owing to the anesthetic, but Lauren looked upon the process with bated breath and her hands at her mouth as the doctor focused on the task at hand.

"Bingo," Kristy said as she slid the instrument out of the wound and held it aloft in the light of the nightstand lamp. A blood-smeared No. 2 buckshot steel pellet a quarter inch in diameter was impaled between the forceps' twin jaws. She dropped the projectile into a plastic trashcan beside the bed and rinsed the forceps with a sterilizing solution.

"One down, one to go," Kristy said as she headed for the second of Hirsch's two entry wounds. This pellet lay deeper than the first, and the local anesthetic failed to mask the sharp pain that radiated through his arm and upper chest as the steel tips of the forceps explored amongst the shredded tissue. Hirsch emitted a groan as Kristy's probing entered its second minute before she withdrew the surgical instrument.

"The second one's in too deep," she said as she set the forceps aside. "Removing it would do more harm than good at this point. I can't be one hundred percent certain, but I don't think it nicked any major arteries or veins. I'm afraid you'll just have to live with a steel pellet in your arm. Have fun going through airport security. I'm going to clean and close the wounds now."

Kristy flushed the two entry wounds with the antibacterial solution, then stitched the small holes shut to prevent any further blood loss. A syringe full of antibiotics followed, and then she applied sterile strips across the wounds and wrapped his entire upper arm in gauze.

"That should about do it. I don't know a damn thing about human medicine, so you'd better pray this is good enough. Here," she said, fishing a white pill bottle out of her medical bag. "This is amoxicillin in a two-hundred-fifty-milligram dose. Take two every morning until they're gone. If you run a fever or develop severe pain or swelling, then see a doctor as soon as possible—a human doctor, I might add."

"Does he need anything for pain?" Lauren asked.

"I don't have anything with me, and I wouldn't give it to you if I did," Kristy said, glaring at her friend. "Give him acetaminophen or ibuprofen every four hours if you want. It's going to hurt like hell for a few days either way. Maybe this will teach you to stay out of whatever trouble you've gotten yourselves into." Kristy hurriedly repacked her tools into her bag and stood to leave.

"Seriously, girlfriend, we cannot thank you enough for this," Lauren said, moving to embrace her friend.

Kristy raised her hand facing outward and brushed past Lauren. "Forget about it. I just hope he lives. Oh, and Lauren?"

"Yeah?"

"Don't bother looking me up next time you're in town. I thought we were friends. You used me here, and it hurts . . . bad."

"What about a baby shower? I thought—"

"I already have one scheduled," Kristy said as she stomped towards the door.

"Kristy, I—" Lauren began, but her friend had already left the motel room and slammed the door shut. Moments later, Kristy's car fired up, and she pulled away from the gravel parking lot and out of their lives. Lauren stared at the motel-room door slack-jawed as the purr of Kristy's vehicle faded in the distance.

"Lauren . . . I'm sorry," Hirsch croaked.

"Don't. It's fine, really," she said as she settled onto the bed alongside him. "Besides, she stole my boyfriend our sophomore year of college. I got over that, she'll get over this."

"I never meant for any of this to happen," Hirsch said and groaned in exhaustion.

"Shh," she said, running her hand through his dark hair and tracing her nails across his scalp. "I signed up for this, and here we are. Get some sleep. We have a long night and day ahead of us to get you home."

Hirsch slept through the afternoon and deep into the night. His dreams were a tormented mix of nightmarish snapshots of his life over the past year—him tied to a chair and pummeled by Lionel Shaw with an auto-repair manual in the basement of Lionel's decaying farmhouse, flames dancing from the body of Marcus Shaw as fire consumed the deranged meth cook; a crippled Lionel with smashed fingers staring up at Hirsch with ferocious eyes blazing as he lay at the base of a cliff in a mangled pickup truck; the reflection in a cracked rearview mirror of Herman Winkel clutching a sawed-off shotgun as Hirsch and Lauren sped away from the Dykmans' clandestine porn studio. He had little doubt if Murray Hirsch were alive and witnessed what had become of his only son, he'd beat his wayward child within half an inch of his life for making such a mockery out of the family name. But Murray was gone, and Hirsch had to make his way alone in the world as best he could.

Pain awoke Hirsch from his restless hallucinations before the light of dawn reached the windows of their derelict motel room. His sharp cry awoke Lauren as well, and she jumped from the bed and paced to the bathroom before returning with a handful of capsules and a plastic cup half-filled with water.

"Take these," she said. He held forth a trembling hand and accepted the pills. He tossed them in his mouth and gulped down the chlorinated water, then dropped the cup on the nightstand and collapsed onto the pillow.

"We can stay another few hours, but we'll need to check out by eleven," Lauren said.

"No. Let's get out of here—now." He swung himself to a seated position on the edge of the bed before planting both feet on the floor and standing. He shuddered with weakness and exhaustion, but his legs held.

"You sure?"

"Yeah. Give me a hand putting on a T-shirt, though."

Lauren helped him with donning his shirt. Hirsch's arm ached like he'd gone ten rounds with Joe Louis, but it wasn't broken, and he moved it through a full range of motion. While Lauren loaded the car and returned the key to the mo- tel office, Hirsch splashed some water on his face with his left hand before staggering outside into a chilly September morning to begin his days of recovery.

The drive north across the Mackinac Bridge and along Highway 2 was a blur, as Hirsch slept most of the journey. They'd stopped at an Ace Hardware in Reed City and pur- chased some plastic sheeting and duct tape to cover the blown-out rear window of her Nissan Rogue. It kept out the worst of the wind but made for a noisy journey. They couldn't do much for the shot-up quarter panel, and the silver paint remained pockmarked with indentations. Hirsch awoke as they passed through Gulliver east of Manistique.

"You want to stay at my place for a few days?" Lauren asked. "I could look after you, fix you soup, that sort of thing."

"No—I mean, yes, I'd love that—but I shouldn't. I need

to comb through that garbage we took from Great Lakes Girls. If I can put it all together, the Dykmans and everyone around them will be finished."

"Don't you think you've done enough the past few days, Ben? You'll kill yourself if you keep this up."

"I know, I know. I just want to clear this horseshit from our lives and move on. I made a goddamn mess of things as it is getting you involved in the first place."

"Suit yourself. But I'm coming by this evening to check on you."

They reached Manistique and traveled the handful of blocks into the Lakeview neighborhood before reaching Hirsch's house. Lauren helped him inside before making two additional trips to gather the assorted files, laptop, and manila envelopes swiped from the porn-studio office.

"You're really going to go through all that?" she asked, staring at the pile of depravity atop his coffee table.

"Someone needs to. If I can tee it up for the Winslows to take to law enforcement, that's less work they need to do on their end."

"Most girls would be hella pissed if they caught their boy-friend looking at this much porn. I just feel sorry for you."

"After the shit I learned about this operation, you should be. One more thing," Hirsch continued as he walked into the kitchen, rummaged through a drawer, and returned with a wad of money in his hand. "Take this. It's all I have left from the Winslows, but you need to get your car fixed."

"Ben, I . . . don't you need that?"

"Sure, but I'll figure out how to make it back some other way. You can't be driving around with a blown-out window and fender full of steel shot. I insist."

Lauren nodded. "Okay, but if you need anything, say the word."

"I'll survive. As soon as this damn arm heals, I'll be back

at work."

"Sounds good, hon. See you tonight," she said before leaving him alone with his pain and porn.

LAUREN DROPPED BY AROUND SIX that evening. Hirsch awoke from a long nap on the couch as she thumped across the creaking boards of his front porch. She let herself in and stopped in front of where he lay on the couch. With her purse dangling from her arm, she clutched a clear Tupperware container of chicken-and-wild-rice soup with both hands.

"Jesus, you don't look good at all," she said, observing his pale flesh and the beads of sweat trickling down his forehead.

"It still hurts like crazy."

"I figured—which is why I brought you these." Lauren took the container of soup to Hirsch's kitchen and returned with a translucent amber bottle of pills from her purse. "Here, take a couple," she said, proffering the container.

"What the hell's this?"

"Hydrocodone. It's the strongest thing I could get my hands on."

"How . . . how'd you get this?" Hirsch asked. He hadn't taken the container from her yet. Lauren's adolescent drug use and tenuous recovery scared the hell out of him. He'd seen too many classmates and relatives get clean only to relapse and destroy the precious gains engendered by sobriety.

"Does it matter?"

"Yeah, a little. Are you—"

"No, Ben, I'm not using again."

"Did these come from Tony?" he asked, referencing Lauren's older boyfriend in high school who got her addicted to methamphetamine and sent her on a path to rehab and an abortion.

"Do you really want to ask me that? I just held up a porn studio with you, my car's been shot to pieces, and I royally used one of my closest friends from college. Now are you going to push me on this, or will you just take the damn pills? There's only a couple dozen. Once they're gone, they're gone."

"Okay, okay, fine. Thank you," he said, swiping the container from her grasp, popping the childproof lid, and swallowing two capsules dry.

"Good. Now no more until tomorrow. It's dark out and I need to drive home and prep for class. You want a hand job or something before I leave?"

Hirsch laughed. "Babe, normally I'd never say no, but as soon as these pills kick in, I doubt I'll be good for much of anything. Can I take a raincheck?"

"Of course," she said, drawing close to him and exchanging a deep kiss. "How about you come by this weekend. I'll make us dinner, and we'll test just how well you've recovered by then." Hirsch groaned as her hand massaged him through his jeans. "Good, that's what I thought. Now rest up so I can have my way with you in a few days." Lauren gave him a quick peck on his cheek.

Hirsch collapsed on the couch and watched as his girlfriend dashed down the front steps and into her car. A mixture of exhaustion and opioids gripped his brain, and he faded into a blissed-out la-la land with a contented sigh.

Hirsch cloistered himself at home for the next couple days. He covered every inch of his dining room table with the contents of their heist. The laptop they'd seized proved to be password protected, but a pair of flash drives in the manila envelope from the file cabinet's bottom drawer contained thousands of high-definition pictures and video clips from the shoots. There were well over a hundred young women and, while Hirsch recognized that several were likely participating of their own free will, another sealed envelope dispelled any notion that Great Lakes Girls was a legit operation. After Hirsch sliced open the envelope and dumped the contents on his table, dozens of driver's licenses, passport cards, college IDs, and other forms of identification with pictures of young women ages eighteen to twenty-three stared back at him. He sifted through the pile. Sure enough, an Indiana driver's license for Morgan Capehart and a University of Michigan student ID for one BreAnn Elise Fisher were included. The realization settled in that each of these girls had been kidnapped and was being sex trafficked.

The pills dramatically relieved Hirsch's pain but left him woozy and unable to concentrate with his normal degree of precision. Documents he could have skimmed through in seconds took full minutes, while typing his report required a labored focus he hadn't experienced since his first semester of law school. Nonetheless, he buckled down and, sentence by sentence, developed his first substantive document since his disbarment a half-year earlier.

The summary he produced totaled fifteen pages and provided a comprehensive overview of how Prophet Teller and the Dykmans recruited young women to Beaver Island under false pretenses, got them addicted to drugs, and handed them off to Bobby and Herman in Grand Rapids for adult video shoots before farming them out to the pleasure-cruise operation as high-priced escorts. The summary detailed how they obtained consent to the shoots under duress and held their identification hostage. The report's final section set forth the complex business structure behind Great Lakes Girls and demonstrated how the Dykmans and others in their orbit received regular payments from the company. An appendix of scanned invoices, canceled checks, and receipts provided the paper trail he needed to support his assertions.

While Hirsch found the whole Dykman crew reprehensible, Clint Lewisohn held a special place of contempt. The utter lack of details on BreAnn's disappearance troubled Hirsch. If he could find the missing girl, he felt confident he could nail Clint on murder charges. The blanks left to fill in begged for Clint's input, and Hirsch realized he had little option but to confront the man on his own turf. He'd had enough sleaze in the last several weeks to last a lifetime, but a visit to the Northwoods Fantasy Gentlemen's Club was in his cards.

Around 9:00 P.M., Hirsch set his computer aside and called it a day. An intense sting from his shirt rubbing against his bandaged flesh served as a vivid reminder of the past weeks' insanity. He staggered upstairs and fumbled for the bottle of Seagram's buried in his dresser. He poured a couple fingers neat and returned downstairs to catch the last couple innings of the Tigers ball game. He drifted off to sleep on the couch, dreaming of a not-too-distant past when his biggest worries were meeting court deadlines and mowing his lawn—not robbing porn studios and shaking down strippers for information.

Chapter 15

As the sun flowed across the early fall afternoon sky, Hirsch crossed the Mackinac Bridge in his battered Toyota pickup. The straits below shimmered in the golden sunlight, with a gentle breeze rippling the waters flowing from Lake Huron into the widening expanse of Lake Michigan. To the east, a pair of highspeed ferries zipped across the water on their way to Mackinac Island. Crammed full of eager visitors, they would disgorge their load of tourists onto the car-free island to experience a day as close to Eden as one could find in the Upper Midwest.

Hirsch had no time for such diversions. His latest visit to the Lower Peninsula was to piece together the final details of the bizarre mess he'd encountered on Beaver Island. What troubled him was how the Dykmans and their cronies could flout every norm of basic decency, not to mention the law, with unfettered impunity. Even an unrepentant criminal like Marcus Shaw felt the law's firm grasp on a regular basis. If Clint and Prophet Teller were accessories to murder, Hirsch had an obligation to go the extra step and uncover the details, no matter how sordid and heartbreaking they may be.

Hirsch reached the bridge landing at Mackinaw City and

passed between the reconstructed Fort Michilimackinac and the spire of the Old Mackinac Point Lighthouse. His arm still hurt like hell, but a combination of the hydrocodone and half a tablet of clonazepam kept the worst of the pain at bay. He exited I-75 at Mackinaw City and drove across the heavily wooded northern tip of the Lower Peninsula before snaking south on US Highway 31 through Petoskey and into the lakeside community of Charlevoix. A chill hung in the air on the Lake Michigan side of the peninsula. As he skirted the edge of Little Traverse Bay, the clouds and gray skies streaking the horizon previewed the coming winter months.

Hirsch couldn't imagine a more depressing place than a strip club during the day, so he killed time exploring the exhibits at the town's Historical Society Museum. He peered into a glass case to examine the marriage license memorializing the nuptials of Ernest Hemingway and his first wife, Hadley Richardson. The writer's distinct signature stood out in a confident hand. Hirsch then ambled along the shoreline southeast from the South Pier Lighthouse to the boat launch abutting the cement plant. He retraced his steps, then enjoyed a mess of fresh lake trout with a microbrew for supper. As evening fell across the coast, Hirsch strolled Charlevoix's tidy streets, passing a handful of cottages designed by eccentric Michigan architect Earl Young. With their thatched roofs, native stone walls, and curved walls that seemed to bubble up from the surrounding landscape, the homes looked as though they'd been transplanted from an alternate-reality English village. By the time Hirsch returned to his truck, it was nearly 9:00 P.M. and dark save for the streetlights and twinkling beacons of the marina.

Northwoods Fantasy was three miles south of town in a largely rural area populated by farmhouses, open fields interspersed with stands of hardwood timber, and narrow roads jutting off the highway. The club stood at a crossing of two county roads. An expansive dirt-and-gravel parking lot dotted with a handful of battered pickup trucks and SUVs terminated in a square single-story building decorated to resemble a backwoods hunting lodge. Vertical slats painted chocolate brown clad the four walls beneath a low-pitched gabled roof. The rectangular sign emblazoned with the establishment's name was lit up in a lurid purple shade endemic to gentlemen's clubs across the country. A pair of moose antlers hung above the steel front door. A tall bouncer with a shaved head and wearing a dark-green, knee-length coat stood outside the door beneath a yellow light that attracted a cloud of insects to its glow. The bouncer made liberal use of a vape box clutched in his right hand. He ejected long plumes of smoke that mingled with the insects in the overhead light.

Another day at the office, Hirsch thought as he pulled into the strip-club parking lot and headed towards the entrance. He barely merited a glance from the bouncer as he approached.

"Busy night?" Hirsch asked.

"Nah, man. Weeknights are always like this. Lucky if we get a couple dozen vehicles."

"What about weekends?"

"Much better. And when there's some kind of conference at one of the resorts. Now *those* are crazy nights. Let me tell you, corporate employees know how to party."

"I can only imagine," Hirsch said as the bouncer opened the door for him. He palmed a twenty off on the man as he went inside.

"Thanks, bro. Have fun tonight."

A bored hostess with hair dyed bright orange and wearing a black lace-up corset occupied a stool behind the counter and stared at her phone.

"It's a five-dollar cover," she said without glancing up. Her long fingernails clicked away as she composed a text message.

"Any drink specials tonight?"

"Nope," she said, still ignoring him. "It's, like, the usual stuff."

Hirsch paid the five-dollar cover but spurned the near-empty tip jar. He turned a corner into the main dance area. Slow-beating dance music throbbed throughout the club, the pulsating base palpable. The snap of the snare drum ricocheted off the walls like the crack of a rifle shot. It took Hirsch's eyes several seconds to adjust to the dim light and take in his surroundings. The room itself was as sparsely populated as the parking lot. The handful of men occupying the chairs surrounding the main stage were predominantly middle-aged and working class. Clad in jeans, work boots, and hoodies emblazoned with auto-racing logos, they sipped from longnecked bottles of beer and ogled the topless young woman with bleach-blonde hair on stage who moved her body against the pole in time with the music's churning thud. As usual, Hirsch looked out of place in his dark trousers and button-up shirt. In addition to the dancer, four women clad in bikinis stood in the shadows near the bar chatting amongst themselves.

Hirsch bought a Miller Lite from the bar and sat near a small table at the room's edge. Like a fly on shit, it wasn't thirty seconds before a raven-haired woman wearing a violet bikini dropped her purse next to his chair, settled into his lap, and draped her legs across the edge of the seat. Intricately tattooed across her torso from her collarbone to her hips, she wrapped her arms around Hirsch's neck with her head close enough to Hirsch's face that he could smell the mint on her breath from a Tic Tac wedged under her tongue.

"Mind if I sit with you?" she asked.

"Go right ahead, darling," he replied, resting one hand against the small of her back with the other along her lower leg below her knee. "What's your name?"

"Rilee. Yours?"

"Roger," Hirsch said, resurrecting his alter ego from the *Wanderlust* excursion. Roger Sampson was shaping up to be a colossal douchebag.

"Where you from, Mr. Roger?" Rilee traced her fingers through Hirsch's hair. A silver hoop encircling her lower lip glinted in the club's faint light.

"Dearborn Heights outside Detroit. Came up this week to do some fishing. Figured I'd check out the local talent."

"You came to the right place, babe. You been here before?"

"Nah, first time."

"Well, here's how it works. Lap dances here on the floor are ten dollars per song. It's all air dancing, though. I can't touch you and you can't touch me. Private dances are twenty-five per song and *much* more worth it. I don't mean to brag, but I'm a pretty good dancer. No pressure, but, if you want, we can go back and make that happen." Rilee leaned over and nuzzled Hirsch's neck.

Hirsch smiled. "Lead the way, beautiful."

Rilee hopped off his lap, grabbed her purse, and took Hirsch by the hand, guiding him out of the main dance room, down a short hallway, and into a smaller room lined with plush maroon easy chairs. Another patron occupied one of the chairs, obscured by a topless dancer straddling the man with her chest in his face.

"It's twenty-five up front," she said. Hirsch fished out his wallet and handed her a twenty and a five. "Sit and make yourself comfortable," she continued.

Hirsch sunk deep into the crushed-velvet chair while Rilee undid the string holding her bikini top together and removed it. Her breasts were pale and free from the tattoos covering the rest of her torso. She straddled Hirsch with her nipples gliding against his face before rotating to drape the backside of her body across his. Her dense tattoos resembled a reptile's skin moving across him beneath the dim glow of the room's mood lighting. The stench of stripper spray tinged with sweat hung thick in the air.

"Can I ask you something?" Hirsch asked.

"Mmm, sure, baby," Rilee said while grinding her rear against his crotch. Despite Hirsch's keen sense of purpose in this visit, he struggled to concentrate.

"You know a guy named Clint who comes in here?"

A perceptible pause interrupted Rilee's gyrations. "Maybe. Lots of guys come here. Some use a fake name."

"You'd know if you saw him. Short but built like a brick shithouse. Dark beard, no mustache. Head like a bowling ball. He has this Army tattoo on his arm right here," Hirsch said, tracing his fingers over Rilee's upper-left arm to indicate the position of Clint's tattoo.

"Could be one of our regulars, but . . . I couldn't say."

"Will this help jog your memory?" Hirsch said as he fished a couple twenties out of his shirt pocket and waved them in front of Rilee's face.

She reached up with fingernails polished with a jet-black lacquer and snatched the bills from Hirsch's hand. "That helps, but I just don't know."

Hirsch couldn't fight the hustle. He had two twenties left and needed one for gas money to get home. He selected one and added it to the two gripped in her hand. "Here—this is all I have left."

"Okay, baby. I think I remember him now. Give me a minute, and I'll see if I can help."

The song had ended, and Rilee leapt from Hirsch's lap and stood. She preened her raven hair and trotted out of the private room, leaving Hirsch alone in the chair. She returned a minute later with the bouncer in tow. The bouncer crossed the room, grabbed fistfuls of Hirsch's shirt, and hauled him out of the chair. The stench of mentholated vape fumes filled Hirsch's nostrils as the bouncer yanked Hirsch close to his face.

"Why the hell are you coming in here and asking about one of our VIP customers?" the bouncer demanded.

"Hey, man, I thought we were friends," Hirsch said, recalling the twenty he'd palmed off at the door.

"You picked the wrong night to fuck with me," the bouncer said as he grasped Hirsch by his belt and shirt collar and dragged him out of the VIP room and through the lobby. Hirsch stumbled along to keep from falling, and his head banged against the heavy steel door as they burst outside into the cool autumn night. The bouncer released him but delivered a powerful jab to his solar plexus. Hirsch doubled over in pain and collapsed onto the damp ground of the parking lot as the punch's force extinguished the breath from his chest. He lay writhing in agony as the bouncer and Rilee hovered over him.

"You're lucky Clint's in Arizona hunting along the border for illegals or he'd snap your neck," Rilee said.

"Get the fuck back inside, Rilee," the bouncer said, shooing her away. She glared at him but turned and clipped through the door in her heels. "As for you, if I see you come 'round again asking questions, I'll take you out back and beat the shit out of you. Now get lost," he said and ejected a stream of saliva that landed against Hirsch's mud-stained shirt.

Hirsch could hardly breathe, but he summoned his strength to roll over and crawl across the filthy parking lot until he reached his truck. He leaned against a tire for several minutes until recovering sufficient composure to drag himself upright, climb into the driver's seat, and fire up the engine. He'd call Winston first thing in the morning. A visit to the American Southwest awaited.

"You want to go where?"

"Southern Arizona. Look, I know this sounds crazy, but by all accounts, Clint could be there right now training with his Army unit. Say, what's the name of that base where he was stationed?"

"Fort Huachuca," Winston replied. "It's also where Ellis Nygren was stationed before he was court marshaled for being a predator."

"Is it near the border?"

"About twenty miles away."

"Okay, she told me it was right on the border, so that's something, right?"

"And your source is a hillbilly titty bar stripper named Rilee?" Winston said.

"Hey, man, that information cost me near every dime I had on me. I know it's not much to go on, but there's no way in hell I can wander into Prophet Teller's camp again. We've hit a dead end. Nygren's a ghost, and Braden and Lisa Van Raatle will cap me the first opportunity they have. We have the money trail, but if we're going to link them to Prophet Teller or find that missing girl, BreAnn, Clint's our last, best hope."

The line fell silent on Winston's end for several seconds.

"Okay, you'll have two days. I'll book you a ticket departing Marquette tomorrow morning. Get in, see what you can learn, and get out. This better damn pan out or you'll be explaining to Catherine why they sent you on an all-expenses-paid vacation to Arizona."

"Thank you, Winston. I won't let them down—or you."

"One more thing."

"What?"

"You're flying coach, okay?"

"Like I'm used to anything else," Hirsch said and ended the call.

Chapter 16

Hirsch walked through the sliding doors of Tucson International Airport into a hundred-degree blast furnace of bone-dry heat. It was his first venture into the Southwest, and he regretted wearing long pants the minute he stepped outside. Palm fronds swayed in the hot wind, and a smattering of saguaro cacti and green-spined agave plants dotted the airport's unique landscaping. He made for the rental car lot, fumbling for his sunglasses to ward off the white glare radiating off the pavement.

On the connecting flight from Chicago, he'd swallowed the last of Lauren's oxycodone tablets and spent the entire flight near comatose, waking as the wheels hit the ground in Tucson. It was just as well—wedged into a middle seat in the next-to-last row between a pair of stout travelers, an unmedicated three-hour flight would have been intolerable. Although the pain in his right arm resurged as the drugs wore off, Hirsch was determined to tough it out. The discomfort cautioned him against attempting anything foolhardy this time around, he reasoned.

Hirsch checked in at the rental-car desk, obtained the key fob, and located his gray four-door Mitsubishi Mirage hatchback rental—the cheapest option available. He threw his small travel suitcase in the back and wedged himself into the fabric-covered driver's seat for the journey southeast to Fort Huachuca. The heat inside was stifling even in the covered car-rental garage, and rivulets of sweat trickled down both sides of his brow. Hirsch turned the air conditioner on full blast and manipulated the vents to direct the airflow straight at his dripping face.

He exited the airport and found the eastbound Interstate 10 on-ramp towards southeast Arizona and the New Mexico border. The first several miles of freeway featured a bumpy roadway strewn with trash and construction debris along the median. Jacked-up Ford F-150 and Dodge Ram pickup trucks blew on a regular cadence despite his doing ten over the speed limit in the rattling Mirage. He soon transitioned into a desert valley flanked by tall, jagged mountains to the north and south. The unfamiliar flora of the Sonoran Desert delighted him—stands of ocotillo plants with elongated canes decorated by oval green leaves and topped with curving plumes of dark-orange flowers, a variety of gnarled green and purple cholla cacti flecked with thousands of thorns, and yucca and sotol plants whose unique shapes and sprouting appendages called to mind something out of a fantasy or science-fiction film.

The pleasures of the desert made for a swift trip along the interstate. Near the town of Benson, he exited the freeway and headed south on a two-lane state highway leading to Fort Huachuca and the neighboring city of Sierra Vista. The landscape morphed as he climbed higher in elevation. The cactus-strewn vistas of the Sonoran Desert lowlands gave way to sagebrush scrubland interspersed with open areas carpeted with long, honey-toned grasses reminiscent of the pampas of South America's Patagonia region. A gentle breeze rippled the flowing grass, and Hirsch longed to lie amidst it with his face towards the sky.

Traffic increased as Hirsch approached Sierra Vista and the fort itself. Armed guards blockading the entrances subjected any motorists wishing to enter the grounds to inspection. Hirsch wouldn't have the luxury of waltzing on-base and snooping around like he would at a Michigan golf club or backwoods titty bar. His latest operation called for a heightened degree of planning.

It was early afternoon when Hirsch turned left at Fry Boulevard in Sierra Vista. Any military town worth a damn had an ample selection of taverns and dive bars. Sure enough, within a couple blocks a nondescript one-story establishment constructed from mortared concrete blocks painted bright white caught his eye. A faded sign facing the street read "Borderlands Lounge," and a banner hung along the roofline advertised live music on weekends and five-dollar margaritas from three to six every day. Only five vehicles occupied the weed-strewn parking lot. Hirsch parked the Mirage and headed inside.

Compared to the violent sunshine and ninety-degree temperatures outside, the lounge's interior was downright glacial. Filtered light emanated from a handful of glass-block clerestory windows lining one wall while four underpowered incandescent bulbs dangled from the ceiling. Only three other patrons were present. A middle-aged Hispanic man wearing an Arizona Diamondbacks baseball cap and chambray shirt with sleeves rolled above his elbows manned the bar. Hirsch commandeered a barstool. A balding patron in a gray hoodie sat at the far end.

"Miller Lite," Hirsch said to the bartender.

The bartender snorted. "This ain't the Midwest, bud. We don't serve any Miller here."

Hirsch looked over the selection of handles for the beers on tap. "Dos Equis Lager then, I guess."

The bartender grabbed a glass bearing the Dos Equis logo and filled it from the tap. He jammed a wedge of lime on the rim and set it down in front of Hirsch.

"Six dollars," he said.

Hirsch put down a ten and, when he received four singles in change, he pushed them towards the well of the bar. "Can I ask you a question?" he said.

"Sure, man," the bartender said while unloading a tray of clean glasses from the dishwasher and lining them atop a counter opposite the bar.

"It's my brother's birthday. He's stationed at the base and I'm trying to find him. Any idea how I might go about that?"

"Uh, why not just give him a call? Or phone the base and they can get ahold of him."

"Yeah, yeah, I figured I could do that . . . but like I said, it's his birthday. I really want to surprise him. Any suggestions?" Hirsch took a long drink from the chilled glass, savoring the tart lager as it cooled his parched throat.

The bartender shrugged. "Your guess is as good as mine, hombre. We get soldiers in here most weekends, but so does every bar in town. If he's a football fan, there are a couple places on the south end of town people like. You know what unit he's with?"

"Nah, not really. I mean, he's in the reserves and all, so he's only down here to train for a couple weeks. But it's not every day your bro turns thirty." Hirsch had no idea of Clint's actual age.

The bartender paused and stroked his thin mustache. "Well, if he's on his annual drill assignment, I doubt he has much time for R&R."

The balding man wearing the gray hoodie glowering over his mixed drink at the end of the bar opposite Hirsch raised his head. "They train in the hills behind the base most mornings while it's cool out. Some trails are open to the public. If you want to give him a real surprise, that'd be a helluva way to do it."

"Thanks," Hirsch said, raising his beer in acknowledgment. The man grunted in response.

"You'll have to go through security. Better damn well not have any guns or drugs in your car, if you know what I mean," the bartender said.

"Makes sense," Hirsch said. He'd toyed with checking his pistol in his luggage but realized if it came to an armed confrontation with a service member, he'd come out worse for wear. "I'll give that a shot. I wanted to see the desert while I'm down here."

"Good luck—I guess. I'd just call him up if I were you, but it's your life, man. Can I get you another?" he asked, seeing Hirsch had drained the glass of lager due to dehydration.

Hirsch wiped his mouth with the back of his left hand and made to leave. "I'm good. Thank you." He slapped a twenty down on the bar. "You've been more help than you know. And one more round for our friend," he said, adding a ten.

"Where you from, anyway?"

"Michigan. The Upper Peninsula."

"Near sea-level, then. Bring extra water and go slow if you're hiking. You'll be above six-thousand feet most of the way. I guarantee you'll feel like someone's wrapped a metal strap around your chest and cinched it tight otherwise."

"Will do, man." Hirsch pushed open the swinging door and moved from the tavern's air-conditioned comfort into what felt like an oven with the broiler set to high.

Since he'd left his outdoor equipment at home, Hirsch drove to a sporting goods store on the eastern edge of town amidst a cluster of retail stores. Maxing out his credit card, he purchased a high-capacity water bottle, a hiking backpack with reinforced straps, synthetic climbing rope, a topographical map of southern Arizona, emergency rations in the form of protein bars and electrolyte powder, SPF-70 sunscreen, a first-aid kit, and a wide-brimmed hat to shelter him against the fierce sun forecasted to last the coming week. He added a knockoff Ka-bar knife to his shopping basket, knowing he needed some leverage in the absence of his trusty .38 Special. At a significant hit to his wallet, he also purchased a pair of high-top hiking boots and wool socks. He wanted a fighting chance of making his way in and back without blistering his feet.

Leaving the sporting goods store, he spotted a food truck in a Walmart parking lot. Three tacos al pastor dripping with Hatch green chile hot sauce and washed down with a guava-flavored Jarritos soda restored his mind and spirits. He spent the next hour canvassing the foothills west of town, exploring the arroyos that opened into the valley and provided access to the vast network of mountains and canyons of the Coronado National Forest. The black line of the international border wall loomed in the distance—a stark reminder of his whereabouts in the country's geopolitical scheme.

He paid cash for a basic motel room off Buffalo Soldier Trail and spent the evening assembling his pack before spreading his newly purchased map of the Coronado National Forest across the bed. With a red Sharpie marker, he highlighted a trail that ran south along Huachuca Canyon for approximately six miles before taking a sharp turn eastward. The trail then ran northeast another couple miles up a mountainside to its terminus at the crest of Huachuca Ridge at an elevation of near seven-thousand feet. The eight-mile hike would challenge a U.S. Army soldier in their prime, let alone an out-of-shape former attorney in his late thirties whose idea of hiking was a leisurely stroll along Manistique's two-mile lakefront boardwalk.

Too nervous with anticipation to leave his room, he ordered a Domino's pizza and ate the entire sausage-and-mushroom-topped pie while watching the Phoenix Suns battle the Dallas Mavericks in a primetime televised matchup. Before going to bed, he dialed Lauren, thinking she'd be wrapping up a shift at Lily's.

"Hello," she answered, her voice groggy with sleep.

"Sorry to wake you, babe. I figured you'd still be at work."

"No . . . I'm off tonight. I'm giving a midterm tomorrow morning. Where are you?"

"Southern Arizona. I'm reasonably certain Clint is here too. I'm going to track him down and find out what happened with the missing girl."

"What? Why Arizona?"

"Clint's in the Army Reserve. His unit trains here. I'm going to ambush him tomorrow and make him talk."

"Ben—I know you want to help Herb and Catherine, but none of this is worth dying over," Lauren said.

"I know, I just want to talk with him and find out what happened. He's the link between the Dykmans and the prophet. Besides, I—"

"You were shot two weeks ago. I mean, they could've killed you. They could've killed me. Isn't that enough?"

"Babe, I can't quit now. I'm ninety-nine percent sure Clint's behind another girl's murder. I need something solid to put the prophet behind bars, shut Manitou down, and bring Alex home."

"Ben, listen to me—this has gone too far. Pardon my language, but you're too smart to be someone's bitch. I like Catherine and Herb, but they're using you. You told me you had enough to bust the Dykmans. If that doesn't get the Winslows their daughter home, I don't know what will. You're not a cop. You don't have a single person there to back you up if that asshole tries to hurt you. I'm not trying to start a quarrel here, but you've got to listen to me."

"It sure as hell sounds like you are," he replied, conscious it sounded exactly like his arguments with Allison towards the end of their marriage when the two of them, equally head-strong, refused to back down.

"Do we really need to do this now?" Lauren said, her voice heavy with exhaustion.

"No—we don't," he relented. "I'm coming home right after this, okay? Let's talk when I'm back. We'll see what we can figure out."

"Okay . . . just try to come home alive. I'm tired of having to worry about you every goddamn day. It's late, I'm exhausted, let's call it a night and try to sleep. We both have big days tomorrow."

"I'll check in with you as soon as I'm on my way home. Goodnight, babe."

Hirsch ended the call and flopped back on the bed. He stared up at the yellowing popcorn ceiling decorated with blossoming water stains. Sleep came with great difficulty that night, and it wasn't until early morning that he had the sense to quell his mind with a stiff dose of tranquilizers and force himself into a respite of dreamless sleep.

Hirsch awoke to the shrill buzz of the alarm clock on his motel-room nightstand. He slapped at the unfamiliar instrument, but the buzz intensified. He managed to silence it by ripping the cord out of the wall socket. He sat up at the edge of the bed, wincing at the dull ache emanating from his upper arm where scar tissue worked at encircling the quarter-inch steel pellet embedded within. With his supply of narcotics vanquished, he'd rely on other means to quell the pain. He staggered to the window and pulled aside the blackout cur-tain to peer at the predawn landscape. The sun had yet to crest the Mule Mountains to the east, where the storied cop-per mining town of Bisbee lay nestled in their midst. The highway was quiet as well. The headlights of a lone semi-truck rolling by splashed weak light across the motel parking lot and surroundings.

Hirsch rinsed off in the shower, then threw on lightweight hiking pants and a T-shirt. His new hiking boots swaddled his feet in comfort and stability. Their rugged construction made him feel like a bona fide outdoorsman. He used a roll of duct tape to bind the Ka-bar knife to his lower leg like he'd once seen in a movie, slathered his exposed skin in sunscreen, and fitted the wide-brimmed hat over his head before grabbing his backpack and heading for his car. Despite the forecast of near ninety-degree weather later in the day, the pre-dawn desert air was cool and fresh. As he exited the parking lot, he rolled down all four windows to clear the sickeningly sweet air-freshener funk and flood the cabin with fresh mountain air.

The drive to the Fort Huachuca gate took under five minutes. As he approached, an armed attendant leaned out the duty-station window. Hirsch stopped alongside the station.

"Where you headed, sir?" the young, blue-eyed corporal clad in baggy camouflage and matching cap asked as he visually inspected Hirsch and his vehicle.

"I'm hiking the Huachuca Ridge trail. My map said this was the best way to get there." Hirsch jerked his thumb at the map spread across the passenger seat to buttress his credibility.

"It's the only way so far as I know. Driver's license or other government identification," the corporal requested. Hirsch proffered the documentation and the corporal jotted down his information on a sheet. "How long you plan to be on-site today?"

"Probably a half-day. No more than mid-afternoon with the heat."

"Good idea," the soldier said, handing Hirsch back his

Michigan driver's license along with a permit card. "This is your identification pass while on military reserve grounds. Keep it on you, even when you're hiking, in case security asks you to produce it."

"What's the easiest way to get to the canyon trailhead?"

"Follow this main road east as far as you can go," the corporal said while pointing down the main road. "You'll see signs directing you to the cemetery and the canyon beyond. There should be plenty of parking near the trailhead this early. One word of warning—there may be personnel out on the trail. Stand aside and don't interfere with their run."

"I'll keep an eye out for them. Thank you for your time," Hirsch said with a wave as the gate opened, allowing him to pull through and onto the base. He left unsaid precisely why he'd be keeping a close watch.

Hirsch navigated the dinky Mirage hatchback across the historic military installation—the oldest west of the Mississippi and once the Army outpost in the U.S. government's long campaign at the close of the nineteenth century against the Apache Indians and Geronimo in the Apache Wars. As the corporal suggested, the trailhead was nearly abandoned. Only one other vehicle occupied the parking area. Hirsch parked, repacked his map into his backpack, then saddled up to begin the long hike up Huachuca Canyon. The rising sun painted the desert with pink light.

The first four miles made for an easy hike with the elevation rising in a gradual climb along the canyon's graveled basin. The sun, peeking through gaps in the canyon's eastern wall warmed Hirsch as the morning's lingering chill melted into a balmy mid-sixties. The surrounding landscape was a serene montage of high desert bliss. Amidst the far-off dry pop of gunshots echoing through the canyon from the base's shooting range, the shrill ack-ack-ack call of a Gila woodpecker competed with the melodious song of a cactus wren perched along the branches of a mesquite tree. A mile into the hike, Hirsch froze at the sound of rustling in the brush, only for a covey of Gambel's quail to emerge from a patch of brittlebush. Gray-bodied, with plumes of black feathers springing from their foreheads, the male quails were graced with a bright rufous-shaded patch on their heads. They darted across the trail, clucking away as their churning legs sped them into the safety of ground cover.

The hike intensified as he climbed Huachuca Ridge. Hirsch gasped for breath as his unacclimated lungs struggled to keep up with the thin oxygen in the air. He had to stop several times with his hands flat against his knees, fighting to keep from passing out and collapsing on the trail. The vegetation surrounding him had changed as well. Twisted pinyon oak, creosote bushes, and long grasses covered the jagged landscape. In the meadows along ravines separating the mountain rises, tall stands of Mexican pinyon pines, coiled alligator juniper, and Arizona sycamore—its smooth bark illuminated creamy white beneath the morning sunlight—competed with smaller mesquite shrubs, manzanita, and Firecracker penstemon about the periphery.

Hirsch paused on a switchback another couple hundred feet up the trail. He removed his ballcap and wiped a thick sheen of sweat from his head, brushing it dry on his pantleg. There wasn't a soul in sight, but sooner or later, any soldiers out training would have to pass through this area to reach the ridge. On his left, the trail gave way to an unguarded forty-five-degree slope that eased into a heavily wooded ravine bed some fifty feet below. To the trail's right sat a boulder partially obscured by an Arizona pine, twisted and bent by the winds howling through the canyon.

With an eye towards any rattlesnakes nesting in the cracks and crevices surrounding the boulder, Hirsch crawled behind the pine tree. While it was far from comfortable, a narrow gap between the boulder and the hill allowed him to wedge himself inside. His vantage point exposed the uphill portion of the trail headed to the ridge. In addition to the cool stone against his back, the pine offered a modicum of shade against the sun beating down across the ledge. He drank deep from the water bottle. With a gasp of relief, he returned it to his backpack before settling into the makeshift stakeout point.

For the next forty-five minutes, Hirsch waited. A crimson-crested Arizona woodpecker alighted on a pine branch and crab-walked towards the trunk where it tapped its head against the ragged gray bark until the reverberation of an Army cadence and the heavy footfall of boots against the trail scared it away. The soldiers' voices echoed in unison against the canyon walls, making them sound closer than they were. Another handful of minutes passed before the leaders thundered past Hirsch's boulder. The pair had their shirts tied about their waists as glistening sweat streamed in streaks along their tanned backs. Another thirty seconds passed before two more soldiers—a man and a woman with her hair pinned beneath her cap—passed by. They huffed the thin air but nonetheless maintained a steady pace uphill.

After a dozen soldiers passed, a desperately winded man with thick legs dragged himself uphill along the trail at a pace just over a walk. Hirsch had his man in his sights. Clint strode along, red-faced, with sweat soaking the dark-green Army shirt that hugged his belly. He was alone, the runners in front of him having crossed by some thirty seconds earlier, and well out of view of the others. Having come this far, Hirsch wasn't about to waste the opportunity despite the insane risk. He crouched, leaning into the gap towards the uphill view of the trail.

Clint's huffing gasps echoed through the canyon and grew louder as approached the boulder. The moment Clint emerged into Hirsch's field of vision, Hirsch sprung from his hiding spot, thrusting himself through the air towards his target. His face landed square against the side of Clint's sweat-soaked T-shirt. He wrapped his arms around Clint's shoulders as the inertia of his leap carried them both over the trail edge and down the slope.

"What the—" Clint shouted as they crashed with a thud against the slope. Hirsch bearhugged Clint as they rolled *en masse* down the steep grade. Their collective weight flattened a creosote shrub clinging by its roots to the cliffside and outright tore a barrel cactus from its precarious perch. Both howled with pain as a generous smattering of barb-like needles embedded themselves in their legs. A Manzanita tree towards the base of the ravine arrested their descent in a spectacular collision. A cloud of snapped red branches and green leaves rained down on them as both lay wide-eyed with Hirsch atop his captive soldier. Hirsch was cut, bruised, and cactus-pricked, and his right arm throbbed with pain.

Clint howled in agony. "Holy fuck, man. Who—" Hirsch slammed his palm over Clint's mouth to avoid drawing the attention of any passing soldiers on the trail overhead.

"Shut up or I'll smother you right here and now," Hirsch said as he hardened his grip over Clint's nose and mouth. Clint continued to gurgle below Hirsch's palm, and Hirsch slid the long-bladed knife out of the leather sheath he'd strapped to his calf just above his ankle. He raised it to Clint's throat. "You going to be quiet now?"

Wide-eyed with terror, Clint ceased his moaning and nodded at his captor. Hirsch raised his hand off Clint's face and the latter drew greedy lungfuls of desert air. A cut across Clint's lower lip soon coated his chin with a veneer of blood.

"You remember me?" Hirsch asked.

Clint's eyes narrowed. "Wait—you're the guy from Beaver Island. The one we had to kick out for being too nosy."

"No, I'm the guy you waterboarded and shot at as I ran

from that stupid camp."

Clint laughed but grimaced as the pain from his injured ankle sent spasms through his body. "Man, this is one shitty idea."

"Why's that?" The knife trembled in Hirsch's hand.

"Because assaulting a member of the United States armed services is a federal felony. As soon as my squadron mates notice I'm missing, you're done for, asshole."

"Well, I'm the one holding your life in my hands." He pressed the knife closer to Clint's throat. "After the way you fucked me over, I'm not afraid to use this either."

"What the hell do you want, anyway?"

"Look, I know about the girls, the Dykmans' fuck boat, the porn studio, the whole works. The bullshit with the prophet and some spiritual community at Manitou is just a front for this disgusting crime ring. I've got enough on you to put you away for years as it is. What I don't know is this— what happened to the missing girl, BreAnn?"

"Dude, that wasn't me. I'm serious."

"Don't fucking lie to me," Hirsch replied as he jabbed the knife tip into Clint's fleshy throat. The virgin steel drew a bead of blood that trickled down his neck.

"I mean it! I swear to God I didn't kill her."

"But she's dead, right?"

"Yeah . . . she is. What of it?" Clint blubbered as Hirsch increased the pressure on the knife.

"Then who killed her?"

"It was my boss, Ellis. You gotta believe me on this."

"Tell me what happened."

"BreAnn did a shoot for Great Lakes Girls. She'd already tried to escape once before, and we didn't trust her enough to send her to work on the ship. Bobby and that dolt Harley—"

"You mean Herman Winkel?" Hirsch interrupted.

"No way, is that his real name? So Bobby and Harley—

Herman—sent BreAnn back to the island on the floatplane so we could dope her up a little more. We wanted to make sure she wouldn't try anything stupid. She was way smarter than we all thought and, one night, she managed to escape. I got an alert on the perimeter alarm. Me, Lisa, and Ellis took off after her. She made it all the way to the dock. I didn't want to kill her, so I fired a couple times to scare the shit out of her and slow her down. I'm a trained marksman; I could've hit her if I wanted. Ellis grabbed the rifle and shot her dead in the water."

"She might've made it if it weren't for Ellis, then?" Hirsch said.

"Fat chance. Like she could swim all the way to the mainland. Seriously, you gotta believe me that I didn't want to kill her."

"I don't give a shit what you wanted," Hirsch said as he cuffed Clint across the forehead with the butt of the knife. "What'd you do with her body?"

"I fished her out and buried her myself."

"Where?"

"You should know," Clint said.

"What the hell is that supposed to mean?"

"You're the one who dug her grave, dickhead."

"What . . ." Hirsch said, his head swimming with confusion and dread.

"That foundation you dug your first day at Manitou—we needed a deep hole so we could hide the body before anyone noticed."

"You mean—"

"That was your handiwork, pal. The day I chased you out, I threw her in and we poured a concrete foundation on top, three feet thick. No one suspected a thing."

"You and that whole camp are so fucking finished," Hirsch growled. He wanted nothing more than to grab Clint

by the head and bash his skull against the rocks. He needed more, though. "What about the so-called 'prophet'? How
much did he know about all this?"

Clint scoffed. "That dipshit knew as much as we told
him. He knew about the girls and what we were doing with
his camp. We made it clear we'd ruin him and take him down
if he so much as squealed a peep to anyone. And when he
found out about BreAnn, well, you should've seen the look
on his face. All he could do for the other girls was keep his
mouth shut and spread the good gospel of bullshit he'd made
up for this whole group."

"So Teller's not getting a cut?"

"Fuck no, man. We have that stupid little hippie wrapped
around our finger."

A wave of pain contorted Clint's face. "I think you broke
my damn ankle." His ankle was visibly swelling within his
boot. "How do you plan to get us both out of here, man?"

"I'm not getting *us* out of anywhere," Hirsch said as lifted
the blade from Clint's throat. He stood and placed the sole of
his hiking boot on Clint's chest. "Here's what'll happen—I'm
going to run like hell and you're not going to utter a word to
anyone for a good fifteen or twenty minutes. If you're lucky,
one of your Army pals will rescue you. If anyone asks, you
slipped on the trail and fell. You so much as try and rat me out
to them or anyone else, I'll spill the beans to law enforcement
that you murdered BreAnn and tell them where to find the
body. Besides, I have the receipts on all your other activities."

"How the hell do I know you won't do that anyway?"
Clint glared at Hirsch with gritted teeth and pain contorting
his face.

"You don't. But much as I think you're a piece of shit,
Clint, I'm more interested in nabbing Ellis and the whole
Dykman family. You play this right and you could be a coop-
erating witness against them. Quite frankly, you're not worth

my time."

Clint nodded, too enfeebled by the white-hot agony radiating from his ankle to contemplate any smartass response.

"Good—and if I were you, I'd stay here in Arizona and never set foot on Beaver Island again. Hell, re-up to active duty and get a posting overseas. Stay as far away from the Dykmans as you can. I wouldn't put it past them to snuff you out, even from a jail cell."

Hirsch lifted his foot off Clint's chest and stepped back. "One more question for you, bud."

"What?" Clint said, wheezing between breaths.

"Remember what you told me when I first came to Manitou—all that crap about hard work, salvation, and the path to redemption through the prophet's word?"

"I guess—what about it?"

"Did you mean a word of it, or was it all bullshit?"

Clint looked away. "Me, no. But, hey, it's all what you make of it. If you want to believe it, go ahead. Plenty of others there sure did. It's no skin off my ass."

"That's what I figured. The whole thing's a con from start to finish."

"What isn't these days?"

Hirsch shook his head in disgust and took off downhill across the ravine through a grove of sycamore and oak trees. He picked his way through patches of prickly pear cactus and thorny acacia shrubs until the ravine intercepted the trail a mile away at a lower elevation. Propelled by sheer adrenaline, he raced down Huachuca Canyon, passing a pair of fellow hikers but avoiding any soldiers before reaching the Mirage parked at the trailhead. His hands shook as he navigated the winding roads of the base on his way back to the motel.

After a quick shower to rinse off the dust, dried blood, sweat, and stench of his tussle with Clint, Hirsch jammed his clothes and toiletries into his small suitcase, slapped the motel-room key on the TV stand, and hauled ass north on the two-lane and west on the interstate until he reached the Tucson airport.

It was time to pay Prophet Teller a visit, and he didn't have a minute to spare.

Chapter 17

Hirsch arrived at the Charlevoix ferry terminal with minutes to spare. A late afternoon flight from Tucson and connection in Chicago delivered him to Sawyer International Airport south of Marquette close to midnight. He'd spent much of the journey tweezing cactus thorns embedded in his arms and legs. Bleary-eyed from exhaustion, he drove home to Manistique and fell hard asleep in the early morning hours, not waking until near midday. Another three-hour drive across the Mackinac Bridge and along the northeast shore of Lake Michigan delivered him to the ferry terminal just in time for the day's final crossing.

"One way or roundtrip?" the impassive attendant asked.

"Uh, roundtrip, I guess."

"Two hundred dollars. Cash or credit?"

"Jesus. Are you serious?"

"I can get you aboard as a walk-on for thirty, one-way. Better make up your mind quick," she said. A half-dozen vehicles were lined up behind Hirsch's truck. "I have three spots left; I'm sure one of the others would be happy to take your place."

Hirsch sighed. "Just charge me for the roundtrip," he said

as he proffered his credit card. He wanted to save his limited cash for the island; he prayed he had enough available balance on the card for the crossing.

The credit-card machine beeped, and the attendant handed back his card with a receipt. "Pull on ahead now and follow the directions."

An orange-vested young man wearing earplugs and safety glasses directed Hirsch towards the starboard side of the vessel before signaling him to stop. Hirsch set his parking brake and killed the motor. A dozen other vehicles had already boarded. A family in a maroon minivan alighted from their vehicle and headed towards the passenger deck stairs. Two girls in their early teens along with a younger boy around nine or ten years old ran across the deck towards the stairs. They giggled, their excitement palpable as their harried parents hollered for them to slow down. The kids called to Hirsch's mind the girls in Bobby's van. They had no idea what they were getting themselves into when they'd boarded the same ferry months earlier. They'd expected a summer spent working with disabled children when what awaited them was drug-fueled imprisonment and indoctrination as sex workers for the Dykmans' booze-cruise outings.

Hirsch had scant desire to join the tourists above deck. His recent experiences with being chauffeured around Michigan by airplane made the ferry ride to Beaver Island feel like a comedown. He'd had enough of planes, ferries, and pothole-infested highways over the past couple months to last him a lifetime. He uncapped the dwindling bottle of expired clonazepam he'd nicked from Aunt Margie's medicine cabinet, dropped a pair of the light-yellow tablets onto his tongue, and washed down the bitterness with a swig of flat Pepsi. The expired pills nonetheless packed a swift punch. Before long, his head rolled backwards with the sweet relief of oblivion.

The rap of knuckles against Hirsch's window woke him from a dreamless void. It felt as though he'd lowered his eyelids only moments earlier. His head snapped to attention, his bleary eyes struggling to focus on a rotund figure standing with arms akimbo outside the driver's-side door.

"Get a move on it, buddy. You're holding up traffic," the attendant said with a wave of his arm to shoo Hirsch off the ferry.

Hirsch raised two fingers in acknowledgment while wiping away a ribbon of drool trailing down the left side of his chin. The tranquilizers retained their grip on Hirsch's brain, and he fumbled to put the car in gear and head towards the gangway. Behind him, the driver of a silver Prius flailed his hands in exasperation and glared at Hirsch as they made eye contact via the rearview mirror. His reflection startled him. Bloodshot, red-rimmed eyes glared back out of a weathered face lined from insomnia and coated with a day's worth of stubble. He appeared one step away from being another burned-out pillhead haunting the streets. It was long past time he got a grip on his life. He shook his head to clear the cobwebs and drained the remainder of the lukewarm Pepsi.

Hirsch drove into the village and spotted a harborside hotel with rooms available. He parked his truck away from the hotel and paid cash for two nights, paranoid that one of the Dykman crew might come after him in the night. While he'd escaped southern Arizona unscathed, he assumed Clint had apprised Ellis and Lisa of their tussle. Forgoing dinner, he locked the door to his room, slid the chain across the bar, and shoved an armchair against the door for the night. It was the best he could do apart from placing his loaded Smith & Wesson .38 Special on the nightstand beside him. Before going to sleep, Hirsch washed down a handful of Advil with a swig of rye whiskey from a half-pint stashed in his travel bag. He settled atop the threadbare blanket covering the bed and caught the tail end of a Detroit Lions football game before falling asleep.

Upon waking the following morning, Hirsch got out of bed, walked over to the windows, and spread the mildewed curtains to peek outside. The water was near dead calm, and a ribbon of cars waited in line to board the *Emerald Isle* for the morning's return voyage to the mainland. Hirsch rubbed the stubble coating his jaw, wishing he could be like every other tourist visiting this damn island rather than a man on the tail of sex traffickers and religious zealots. After showering, shaving, and donning a clean pair of underwear and socks, he unbarricaded the hotel room door and headed out. He needed to get a message to the prophet; one of his well-intended followers was the best way to go about it.

Manitou's conduit to the outside world was the farmer's market, where they peddled produce from the communal gardens to support their endeavors. The market set up shop every weekend near Hirsch's hotel. He put on sunglasses and pulled his Tigers baseball cap low over his forehead. Hirsch stopped by his parked truck on the way and retrieved a notepad and an old ballpoint pen.

"Meet me tomorrow morning—10:00 A.M.—the beach opposite East Side Drive," he scrawled on a slip of yellow paper. He folded the note and shoved it into his pocket before heading for the market.

Two men dressed in Manitou's denims stood behind a folding table laden with fresh vegetables for sale. One was Brother Liam, the same young blond man Hirsch had encountered during his weekend at the camp. Hirsch waited until the other man was engaged with a customer before approaching the familiar face.

"Whaddaya got today?" Hirsch asked Brother Liam while perusing the assorted produce.

"We got tomatoes, zucchini, carrots, rutabaga, turnips, and a few squashes left. All fresh from our garden, man."

Hirsch nodded. "Okay, I'll take a half-dozen tomatoes, a couple zucchini, a rutabaga, and maybe one of those squashes."

"Cool, man. You got a bag?" Liam asked.

"Nah, sorry. I left it at home."

Liam tsked at Hirsch but said, "No worries, dude. I have a paper sack you can use. Just don't forget it next time, okay? You know, the planet and all." Liam shook the bag open and began loading Hirsch's purchases into the bag.

"No, the big one," Hirsch interrupted when Liam went for a smaller squash.

"Your deal, boss," Liam said as he dropped the largest squash into the bag. "Twenty-four dollars."

Hirsch handed him twenty-five and told him to keep the change. Liam started to hand the bag across the table and Hirsch said, "You mind carrying those to my truck for me? Bad back, you know."

Liam examined Hirsch with skepticism but shrugged and turned to his business partner. "Watch the store for a few while I help this dude with his stuff, Brother Zander."

"I got it," the goateed young man, who had his long hair coiled up into a man-bun atop his head, replied. Liam grabbed the sack and followed Hirsch to the latter's truck.

"Thanks for the hand," Hirsch said as he took the bag from Liam and set it on his passenger seat. "Say, you still living down at Manitou?"

"Uh, yeah, sure am. . . . Do I know you?"

"We've met. I was there myself a month or so ago. Decided it wasn't for me."

"Oh, okay, well . . ." the youth said as he looked down the street past Hirsch, obviously eager to get back to his table at the market.

"Think you could do me a favor?" Hirsch asked.

"Like, what kind of favor?"

"Get this message to the prophet," Hirsch said. He held the folded slip of yellow notepaper aloft between his index and middle fingers.

"Nah, man. I don't know what you want with me, but I really should get going." Liam tried to move past Hirsch.

"Here," Hirsch said and dug in his pocket. He pulled out three of the remaining hundred-dollar bills from the Winslows' fun money. "That make it worth your while?"

"For real, dude?" Liam said, incredulous.

"One hundred percent. Just get him the note. It's for his own good."

"Okay, but I gotta get going or Brother Zander will think this is real suss." Liam walked away from Hirsch.

"Just make sure you give it to Prophet Teller himself. Not Lisa, not anyone else," Hirsch whispered after him.

Liam gave the faintest of nods, then sped down the street with his sandals clipping against the pavement.

The matter was out of Hirsch's hands. All he could do was fritter away the day in his hotel room, show up at the beach the next morning, and hope Teller could do the same. The welfare of every innocent person at Manitou depended on it.

IF A MORE BEAUTIFUL PLACE on earth than northern Michigan in fall existed, Hirsch had yet to find it. A robust mixture of maple, birch, and beech trees lining the shore had begun their annual transformation into the rich medley of colors that drew so many visitors north for a glimpse of their awe-inspiring radiant display. The warmth of mid-September's lingering summer continued, and sunlight glistened over the calm waters of Lake Michigan. The steady pulse of gentle waves lapping on the shore competed with the melody of songbirds enjoying their final weeks of residence before their migration south. Across the water, the mainland appeared as an uneven green line painted on the horizon by an unsteady hand from across the topaz expanse of lake.

Hirsch sat facing the water with his forearms resting atop his knees, clad in corduroy trousers. The slender half-pint bottle of Bulleit rye peeked out of his back pocket. He came unarmed, knowing if Lisa or Ellis intercepted his note to the prophet, he'd be dead before he saw either one of them. He placed his faith in Brother Liam delivering the message and the prophet recognizing the well-intended missive for what it was. A nip of whiskey gave Hirsch the courage he needed to stay put.

Ten o'clock came and went as he sat alone on the shore. A lone mosquito left over from summer bit him. Hirsch slapped at his neck, leaving a smear of blood on his palm that he wiped across the dark fabric of his pants.

Hirsch was about to give up and leave when he heard the brush rustling behind him. Jonathan Teller emerged wearing a loose-fitting pair of cotton trousers and his ridiculous V-neck caftan. His shaggy blond hair was slightly longer than when Hirsch last encountered him, and strands of gray decorated his golden beard. The morning sun reflected off the round lenses of Teller's granny glasses, and he squinted as he approached Hirsch.

"I didn't think you'd make it," Hirsch said and stood as Teller approached.

"I nearly didn't. Two congregants called me in to mediate a squabble. You'd think they'd have better things to do than bother their prophet with who should have first crack at the showers in the morning."

"How'd you get away?"

"I told them I needed time to receive the prophecy and contemplate God's mission for us. I get out for a walk most days that way."

"Don't they get suspicious?"

Teller shrugged. "So long as I'm back within an hour or so, no one's objected. And I've always come back. Is that what I think it is in your pocket?" Teller eyeballed Hirsch's whiskey bottle.

"I shouldn't be surprised a messenger of the Lord needs a drink every now and then," Hirsch said as he handed the bottle to Teller.

"Well, I'm a lousy prophet," Teller said as he undid the cap, raised the bottle to his mouth, and tipped it back. He gasped at the strong booze and ran his tongue over his lips.

"You know who I am?" Hirsch asked.

"I remember you from last time. You pissed off Clint and Lisa something awful. They could've killed you, you know."

"They might wish they had. My name's Ben Hirsch. I used to be an attorney. I came here looking for the missing daughter of my employers in Marquette. I've uncovered something far worse. I know about the girls; I know about BreAnn. What I want to know is what the hell you're doing here, Professor Teller."

Teller's face fell. "Maybe we should take a seat."

Chapter 18

"IT'S TIME YOU HEARD THE full story of how I ended up here," Teller said as he settled onto the shore next to Hirsch. The smooth pebbles coating the beach had absorbed the heat of the morning sun. Their warmth flowed through Hirsch's backside, soothing the lingering ache from his tumble with Clint Lewisohn. He leaned into the gravel and prepared to hear Teller out.

"From the beginning?" Hirsch asked.

"From the beginning." Teller sipped from the pint of rye and drew a deep breath.

"Coming home to this island was my destiny. My great-great-great grandparents, Josiah and Ellen Teller, started all this after answering the call of Prophet Joseph Smith. You know about the early history of the LDS Church, Ben?"

"Very little," Hirsch replied. The topic was only touched on in his American history class at Manistique High.

"I'm not surprised. Most outsiders don't. Here's the deal—this was the 1830s and Smith had left his upstate New York home and headed west to found an American Zion. Smith settled in Ohio for several years, which is where my ancestors encountered him. They were farmers in Lake County—and longtime Baptists. After Smith arrived in Kirtland, they saw the light and became his followers. Josiah and Ellen paid a steep price for their apostasy. Their families and other townsfolk shunned them. Josiah lent Smith a hand building the Kirtland Temple, so in a sense, he was a church founder.

"It wasn't long after they built that first temple that the locals chased Smith and his followers out of Ohio. Josiah, Ellen, and their two young children found themselves on the road to resettlement in Missouri. My ancestors' stroke of luck was that they owned their one-hundred-twenty-acre farm free and clear. They sold it for what it was worth whereas most of Smith's followers had little to nothing. Ellen hid the money for when times got tough. The whole movement didn't last long in Missouri. Several ended up in jail—Smith and Josiah included. They escaped and fled across the river to Illinois, where they founded another community called Nauvoo. It was there that Josiah and Ellen encountered a young man by the name of James Strang."

"King Strang?"

"Yes, my predecessor. Prophet Smith had sent Strang north across the state line to Voree, Wisconsin. The day Joseph Smith died, an angel visited Strang and ordained him as Smith's successor and the new head of the LDS Church. Strang courted my ancestors to join the new colony in Wisconsin. The family up and abandoned a house they'd just built in Nauvoo and journeyed north with Strang. By this time, they had six children, so uprooting them all was no small feat. Josiah helped Strang manage the Voree stake for the next four years.

"There was a leadership tussle after Smith's death, and several apostles were jockeying to assume Smith's role as church leader. Strang ordained women as priests of the Strangite church, Ellen Teller included. He also accepted Black people into the church, something the mainline denomination didn't endorse until the 1970s. This didn't sit too well with the traditionists—folks like Brigham Young and Joseph Smith's children—and Strang found himself on the outs with his fellow apostles, who were busy relocating to Utah. But Strang had the revelation he needed to found a second stake of Zion—right here on Beaver Island all the way north across Lake Michigan," Teller said as he patted the ground between them.

"The crossing from Wisconsin to the island was horrible, and the schooner that carried the family tossed, buckled, and nearly went under. Ellen swore she'd never set foot on another boat as long as she lived. They made it, though, and Strang built a new kingdom of God. It wasn't two years later, in 1850, that they crowned Strang king. Ellen and Josiah stood nearby as a tin crown was lowered onto Strang's head."

"Was he dressed like that?" Hirsch asked, gesturing at Teller's flowing caftan and drawstring trousers.

"He wore a long crimson robe with a white collar flecked with black," Teller said, ignoring Hirsch's sarcasm.

Couldn't any of these zealots dress like normal people? Hirsch wondered. "Go on."

"Not long after they arrived, Josiah and Ellen took what money they had left and bought this three-hundred-acre chunk of land. As usual, the locals resiented the coming of the Strangites. They felt like they were stealing jobs and land right out from under their noses. But my ancestors paid cash and owned this land outright. They had the paperwork to prove it, and there wasn't a judge in the great state of Michigan who could take that away from them—try as hard as some of the locals might.

"Strang made plenty of enemies within a few short years. People spread lurid tales about Beaver Island—most of it half-true. The federal government put him on trial for various high crimes in 1853, but he won acquittal on every charge.

Strang even got himself elected to the state legislature later that year. The merchants here and on nearby Mackinac Island had it out for him, though. See, it was illegal then to sell liquor to Native Americans, but plenty of unscrupulous traders did it anyway. Strang railed against the liquor trade in the legislature and raised a real stink. They'd made a fortune in the illegal booze trade, but Strang shat all over their enterprise in front of anyone who'd listen.

"Strang's own people brought about his demise. He'd excommunicated a pair of followers for bad behavior, and they wanted revenge. He refused to go into hiding or carry any sort of weapon. The pair shot Strang three times in the back, and he died soon afterwards. It wasn't long before the gentiles had their turn. Three weeks after the shooting, a gang of Mackinac Island drunks and lowlifes invaded Beaver Island. Over two thousand men, women, and children were herded onto steamers and forced off their home of the past several years. Most escaped with only the clothes on their backs. The invaders stole the land, livestock, and personal property the Strangites had cobbled together. Almost overnight, nearly every last follower of King Strang was forced off Beaver Island."

"Nearly?" Hirsch said.

"Nearly all—except my ancestors. Many of Strang's followers lived within a couple miles of town. It made for easy pickings when the time came to round them up. Being this far south, Josiah and Ellen's family stood a fighting chance. Not to say the mob didn't try. About thirty rode down on horseback from St. James one night bearing torches and rope, ready to bind and haul off the last of the Strangites. Josiah and three of his sons met the drunken mob with a volley of musket fire over their heads. The gunfire scared the horses witless, and the mob leaders turned tail to ride back to town. Evicting the Teller family wasn't worth the effort. Besides, with King Strang removed from the scene, the liquor trade flourished once again."

"So what happened to the people who shot King Strang?"

"Not a damn thing," Teller said. "No one went to jail, no one suffered a single consequence. And here we are today; nothing's changed."

"How'd your family survive after the others were kicked out?"

"Any way they could. Most of this island was heavily forested, but they cleared a few acres and planted crops. Weather permitting, they caught whitefish and lake trout from a hand-built Mackinaw boat. After a few years, some of the island's animosity towards the Mormons died down. The Tellers sold firewood and fish to the locals. They weren't well-off by any means, but they endured all the same."

"So how'd you end up out west?" Hirsch asked.

"I have my great-grandfather, Lucas Teller, to thank for that. He was born right here on the homestead in 1889. As the eldest grandson, the family expected him to follow in his grandparents' and parents' footsteps and lead the local Strangite church. He had other plans. Lucas was a rebellious child and an even more ornery young man. More than once his pa took a strap to his backside for sassing his mother or smoking a forbidden cigarette.

"When he was fifteen, Lucas awoke before dawn, scrawled a quick note that he slipped under an oil lamp on the supper table, and took off in the family's boat. He headed for the U.P., where he stood less of a chance of being returned home. Most employers rightly took him for a runaway, but Lucas was big for his age. A two-bit logging camp was so desperate for men that it knew better than to ask too many questions. They put him to work as a choke setter—one of the most dangerous jobs in the entire camp. His job was to wrap metal cables around fallen timber so a team of horses could pull them free and transport them to the nearest saw-mill. The logs could shift or roll in the process, which is why the work was so dangerous. It wasn't uncommon for a choke setter to lose a limb or even his life.

"Lucas survived his season in the camp, and they paid him off. After a few seasons on a two-team sawyer crew near Watersmeet, he scraped together enough to purchase eighty acres of virgin timber in Beltrami County, Minnesota. He set to work, but it wasn't meant to be. Only months after he arrived, the Baudette fire of 1910 wiped out his entire claim. He made it out with the clothes on his back and jumped in the Baudette River to survive the blaze. He was only twenty-one when his future burned to ashes. He had plenty of years left ahead of him, and he did what so many desperate young people did before him—he went west. His parents had made sure he could read and write at an early age, and he had an education comparable to a Michigan high school graduate in those days. His father even saw to it he learned Latin and a smatter of Ancient Greek, in hopes he might follow in his footsteps in the Strangite church leadership. In many western towns, not a damn person had a college degree, and you were lucky if a handful of them could write their own names. He taught in one-room schoolhouses in Wibaux, Montana; Salmon, Idaho; and Baker City, Oregon. Once he'd had enough of freezing cold winters and rising before dawn to tend the schoolhouse stove, Lucas escaped to California.

"Lucas' father—my great-great grandfather—was near death some twenty years later, around the late 1930s, when Lucas was pushing fifty. He hadn't seen or spoken with his parents since running off all those years earlier, but his sister wrote to him of the old man's decline. Lucas decided it was time he made his peace with his folks. Whatever happened in those following weeks must have worked—Lucas and his father reconciled, and when the old man passed away some weeks later, Lucas inherited this whole place as the eldest rightly restored in his father's eyes. Pretty damn unfair to his siblings who stayed and kept the faith all those years, if you ask me, but those were the times.

"By the time my grandfather inherited the property in the mid-sixties, he was an aerospace engineer for the Douglas Aircraft Company in Santa Monica and didn't want anything to do with a crummy old homestead in a backwater part of the country. He held on to the land but let it fall into ruin. It stayed that way until I inherited it a few years back when my parents crashed their motorhome on an icy highway in southern Utah."

"Was that when you decided to return and build Manitou?"

"I didn't *decide*—God spoke to me through my predecessor, King Strang, one morning while I was hiking in the redwood forests west of Palo Alto. He delivered the family land into my hands for me to rebuild the kingdom of God on earth after a hundred-and-fifty-year absence. To tell you the truth, Ben, up until that moment with the sunlight glittering amidst the redwoods, I considered myself a man of science and agnostic, if not an outright atheist. I believed pure mathematics was the pathway to a universal truth. Once I heard Strang's voice murmuring in my ear, pure truth penetrated my core—like a white-hot, unbridled bolt of reality smashing into my head. He opened my eyes. I recognized my entire professional career was nothing but a waste of time, and that I needed to establish Manitou as a refuge from the evil and ills of this world for those with the fortitude to hear the call as well. And I was blessed to have a select group of students willing to leave everything behind."

"And your music—was that part of the calling?" Hirsch asked, recalling the excruciating evening spent as the guest of honor at Prophet Teller's impromptu concert.

"You didn't like my songs?" Teller asked with hurt in his eyes.

"I never said that."

"I can tell. You don't have to lie."

"How many here are part of the Dykmans' operation?" Hirsch asked, changing the subject.

"I'm not entirely sure. Several handle the drugs and report directly to Clint and Lisa. Then you have the girls who were kidnapped. The rest are my followers. Word spread about Manitou, and they answered the call. Young and old, from all ways of life. I couldn't believe what I'd created after showing up here with only a handful of adherents." Teller paused and glanced over his shoulder. "Look, if I don't get back soon, they'll come after me." He drained the remaining half inch from the bottle of rye before wiping his lips and stumbling to his feet.

"You're really going back? You can leave, you know. My truck's parked up the road. There's another way out of this," Hirsch said.

"I'm the only thing standing between these kids and God knows what the Dykmans have planned for them. Every person I can help survive another day is a small victory. Besides, I still believe in what I built here, and I can't abandon my followers."

"And BreAnn . . . was she one of them?"

Teller gazed at the ground and covered his lower face with his hand. "I failed BreAnn. The poor girl was eighteen, Ben. Just a kid. I knew what they had in mind for a pretty girl like her, and I couldn't stomach seeing it happen. I pulled her aside one afternoon and spilled the beans. She was understandably freaked out. It wasn't more than a few nights later that she went missing. At first, I was so grateful she made a break for it and escaped. I later learned what Ellis and Lisa had done. I have to carry that on my conscience the rest of my life."

"Who killed her—Clint or Ellis?"

"Ellis bragged about doing it. He knew I'd planted the seed of escape in BreAnn's mind and wanted to send me a message—to show what would happen if I tried it again."

"What about Alex Winslow? Is she a true believer?"

Teller's face lit up. "Alex was the reason I started this community in the first place. I knew she came from a privileged background like many of my students, but she was passionate about organic gardening and living in a community devoted to a better world. Alex didn't hesitate to drop out and join me the moment I told her about my plans for Manitou. If I had a hundred followers like her, well, I can only imagine what we could accomplish."

"Does she know what goes on here?"

Teller shrugged. "Hard to say. I mean, Lisa, Clint, and Ellis did their best to hide the truth from the congregation, but who knows. If she does, she'd be the first to protect them."

"So no chance she'd leave of her own free will?"

"Zero. Alex will be a priestess of the Strangite Order before long."

"One more question—what happens when the next BreAnn comes along—maybe one even younger than her?"

"That's just what I have to figure out," Teller said as he placed his hand on Hirsch's shoulder. "Go back home, Ben. I know you mean well, but interfering will only make things worse. Not for me, but for the young people here. The Dykmans will find some other way to exploit them and ruin their lives. You might even wind up the next body washed up on shore. I wouldn't put it past these sociopaths. If you want to make a difference, nail some of the guys on the other end of this whole mess."

Hirsch opened his mouth to reply but couldn't gather a response. The Dykmans had Teller's head in a vise either way. Teller nodded, then turned and sauntered into the forest. His footsteps faded into the distance, leaving Hirsch alone to ponder how best to help a man who was damned any which way he turned.

"Winston, it's Hirsch. We need to talk." Hirsch called the Winslows' fixer upon his return from the island. He'd spent a frantic day and night revising his written summary and annotating it with exhibits from the Great Lakes Girls heist. He bundled the evidence and prepared a tidy package for his employers. As a failsafe, he saved scans of everything to an external hard drive and placed it in a little-used basement storage closet where his dad used to hide Playboys.

"You have something Herb and Catherine can use to bring their daughter home?" Winston asked.

"The Dykmans are pure evil, no surprises there. But Teller's innocent in all this. Sure, he's a kook, but he's doing what he can to protect kids like Alex." Hirsch went on to summarize the salient points of his conversation with Teller, how the Dykmans hijacked his community's mission, and the sword of Damocles hanging over Teller's head if he defied their will. "If we go about this wrong," he continued, "the Dykmans will ruin Teller, not to mention other innocent people on that damn island. I know Herb and Catherine want Alex back . . . but this isn't the way to do it."

"So what do you suggest?"

"It all comes back to that strongman of theirs, Ellis Nygren. He's the go-between for the Dykmans and any dirty work that needs to be done. He killed that poor girl, BreAnn. I pulled an all-nighter writing my summary, and I have reams of evidence for you. It's enough to take to the police and arrest them all."

"Clint Lewisohn included?"

"That asshole's probably laid up somewhere in southern

Arizona nursing a broken ankle. There are bigger fish to fry than him, but yeah, he's knee-deep in this mess."

"This is marvelous work, Mr. Hirsch. Bring me everything you have; we'll take it to the state police. Assuming it all checks out, the authorities can arrest as many of the Dykmans as they can, and everyone stuck in that compound can go home to their families—Alex included."

"I'll drive up now."

"Oh, and Ben?"

"Yes?"

"My deepest appreciation on Herb and Catherine's behalf. None of this would've been possible without you. Mark my words, this could be the start of a glorious partnership."

Hirsch ended the call and dialed Lauren.

"Hey, babe, what's up?" she answered.

"It's over."

"What's over?"

"The Dykmans, Ellis Nygren, even that dipshit Clint Lewisohn. They're finished," Hirsch said.

"Wait—were they all arrested or something?" Lauren asked.

"Not yet, but it's only a matter of time. I'm handing over my report to the Winslows along with all that evidence we gathered in Grand Rapids. I guarantee those guys will be in bracelets before long. They've used Jonathan Teller for months as a cover for their operation."

"And does this mean . . . ?"

"All those girls—they're saved. This'll put an end to the call girl ring, the porn site, the camp at Manitou, all of it. Alex Winslow should be home any day now."

"Ben, that's wonderful. I'm so proud of you for, well, everything."

"I couldn't have done it without you, babe. Or should I say Trixie Rae."

"Maybe Trixie Rae needs to show you her appreciation," Lauren purred into the phone.

"Don't make me drive over there right now."

"But seriously, we should celebrate. Maybe, like, dinner this weekend or something."

"I'll make a reservation at the Stonehouse Inn. Who knows, the Winslows could throw a little extra our way once Alex is home."

"I can't wait, but I *am* going to take good care of you next time we get together."

Hirsch ended the call. With his gas line work dried up for the winter months, he'd need another source of revenue soon. His success in unravelling a crime ring couldn't hurt. *Let's see what Winston and the Winslows have in store for me next*, he thought as he poured a couple fingers of Maker's 46 bourbon he'd purchased that morning.

After a twisted road through hell, life was revealing some blessing.

Chapter 19

A TEXT FROM LAUREN REACHED Hirsch the following Saturday morning while he scrubbed at rusty water stains dotting the tilework of his kitchen floor.

"Turn on ur TV," the text read. Hirsch crawled to his feet and entered the living room. He snapped on the television and sat on the couch. The Marquette news station returned from a commercial break and cut to helicopter footage of a lakeshore. Hirsch immediately recognized the images as the beachfront of Teller's Beaver Island property. He cranked up the volume.

At 5:00 A.M. today, a joint task force of officers from the Michigan State Police and the Charlevoix County Sheriff's Office raided a compound on Beaver Island owned and operated by former Stanford professor of mathematics Jonathan Teller, the news anchor narrated. The station superimposed a professional headshot of Teller on the screen. *Teller is believed to be the leader of a secretive religious group that had taken up residency on his property several months ago. Their activities drew the attention of island neighbors. Police arrested Teller on suspicion of aggravated rape, kidnapping, and sexual assault in connection with several young female residents of his compound. Police also suspect Teller's involvement with a drug-trafficking and pros-*

titution ring that resulted in the simultaneous arrest of several Grand Rapids businesspeople this morning. The screen shifted to a pair of sheriff's deputies removing Teller from a police boat at the Charlevoix harbor and escorting him into a white utility van bearing the logo of the Charlevoix County Sheriff's Office. The fringes of Teller's caftan were torn and muddy, and rain had plastered his long hair to the sides of his face. *Authorities transported Professor Teller to the county jail in Charlevoix, and he is expected to be arraigned Monday on multiple charges related to the allegations.* Additional footage depicted a column of adherents walking out through Manitou's front gate with blankets wrapped around their shoulders to protect against the chill of the morning. A line of school buses awaited to shuttle them to town. Several followers attempted to shield their faces from the prying eyes of the news cameras, and Hirsch couldn't discern whether they included Alex Winslow. *A security manager for the unnamed Grand Rapids company affiliated with the compound is reportedly cooperating with law enforcement and blew the whistle on his supervisors and Professor Teller in exchange for immunity from prosecution.*

A sickening wave of nausea washed over Hirsch as the ugly truth became palpable—the unnamed whistleblower could only be Ellis Nygren. Hirsch had spoon-fed the Winslows everything they needed to bring the Dykmans and Nygren to justice. Instead, they'd approached Nygren and orchestrated this entire raid. But he couldn't grasp why they would do so if their goal was to bring their daughter home safe.

"This ur deal, right?" another text from Lauren read.

"Yeah . . . but this isn't what was supposed to happen," he replied.

The television screen displayed written statements from both the county sheriff and a detective from the state police before cutting to a montage of interview footage with local

Beaver Island residents. He recognized one as the man with the truck who gave him a ride to Manitou his first day on the island.

"Well, they always seemed a bit suspicious to me," the bald man said to the cameraman while standing in front of a local café in the village. "I only dealt with them once or twice, but anybody fooling around with that many young people out in the middle of nowhere can't be up to no good." The interview ended and the station returned to the news anchor sitting in the comfort of the studio.

Channel 6 will continue to bring you live coverage of the arrests as this story develops.

Hirsch clicked off the television and called Winston, his hands trembling with anger as he awaited an answer.

"You saw the news, I take it," Winston said.

"What the hell was that? You know as well as I do Jonathan Teller shouldn't be behind bars."

"I know, Ben; I read your report. It's out of our hands now."

"What do you mean 'it's out of our hands'? I gave you everything you needed to nail the Dykmans. And what's this horseshit about Ellis Nygren of all people being a whistleblower? He's a goddamn murderer!"

"Look, I'm sorry about all this. It's not what I wanted either . . . but at least the Dykmans are looking at long stints in jail, and Alexandra and the other poor girls there will go free."

"Put Catherine on right now!" Hirsch screamed into the phone.

"Ben, she's not here and this isn't a good time. I'll have her return your call if you can control yourself."

"I don't give a damn what she's doing. Where is she?" Hirsch asked as he ran his free hand over his unshaven face.

"It's really not your place to be dictating terms, is it? Besides, the Winslows have an offer in mind that you'll appreciate."

Hirsch ignored Winston's entreaties. "If you don't fucking tell me where I can find her, I'll stake out their corporate office and make the absolute biggest stink I can."

Winston sighed. "Have it your way. Herb and Catherine are attending a charity breakfast this morning followed by a reception at the Marquette Pioneer Club. It's an invitation-only event, and I'm afraid—" Hirsch ended the call, cutting Winston off mid-sentence. He scrambled, grabbing his Carhart jacket and slipping on a pair of work boots—the closest footwear he had at hand. He dashed outside into the light drizzle of the September morning and fired up his Toyota. Hirsch did a U-turn onto Michigan Avenue, squealing the truck tires and spraying gravel across the empty street. Dale Cromley stood on the opposite side, slack-jawed, with a cigarette dangling from his lower lip as he watched his neighbor tearing down the road.

Hirsch reached Marquette in record time, traveling north through the Hiawatha National Forest on State Highway 94 to Munising before following the Lake Superior coast on Highway 28. The venerable Marquette Pioneer Club occupied half a downtown city block. Its gray stone façade and solid-oak doors communicated its exclusivity in no uncertain terms to passersby. The members-only policy and rigorous vetting of new applicants excluded most locals from admission—people exactly like Benjamin J. Hirsch and his family. He pulled to the streetside fronting the club and screeched to a stop with one wheel jumping the curb.

Hirsch alighted from the vehicle and entered the club through the heavy wooden door. A maître d' with slicked-back hair and a thin mustache standing alongside an elegant walnut staircase glared at him as though he were streaked from head to toe in dog shit.

"Can I help you, *sir?*" the maître d' asked while glancing

with palpable contempt at Hirsch's unkempt workingman's attire and mud-spattered boots. In contrast, the maître d' wore a tuxedo shirt and bowtie above dress trousers with a sharp crease.

"Catherine and Herbert Winslow—where are they?"

"Sir, this is a private club restricted to members and their invited guests. You can't wander—"

"Just tell me which room they're in, goddammit."

"Sir, I'm asking you to leave right this minute or I'm calling the police," the man continued as he paced towards a telephone affixed to the paneled wall opposite the staircase. Laughter and the murmur of conversation from upstairs reached Hirsch's ear. In a split-second decision, he lunged for the telephone and ripped the phone cord out of the wall before darting up the carpet-covered staircase. His filth-streaked boots deposited muddy footprints on the plush burgundy runner.

"I'm finding another phone and I'll have you arrested, you hear me!" The host's nasal twang echoed into the white-oak-paneled atrium. Hirsch reached the second-floor landing and encountered a pair of mahogany doors with solid brass doorknobs affixed to each. He turned both knobs and flung the doors open.

Conversation instantly ceased as the fifty-plus occupants in the ballroom stared with a mixture of loathing, contempt, and curiosity at the unwelcome interloper. Despite it being a Saturday morning, most of the attendees—skewing towards middle-aged and older—wore business attire while the remainder sported well-tailored slacks and luxurious cashmere sweaters. Their gawking continued as Hirsch trampled into the center of the ballroom. The Winslows stood towards the rear by a picture window that overlooked the ore docks and Lake Superior. Catherine was engaged in conversation with a pair of men Hirsch recognized as local politicians of some repute while Herb stood near an older gentleman who must have shared his passion for fly fishing given that his khaki vest was festooned with a dozen or so flies. Hirsch made a beeline for Catherine.

"What's all this bullshit I'm seeing on TV with Professor Teller being dragged out in handcuffs? I told you he had nothing to do with the Dykmans' operation. My report laid the entire fucking thing out. Ellis Nygren's the one who should be behind bars," Hirsch barked as Catherine stepped away from her politician friends to intercept him.

"Mr. Hirsch, this really is out of your bailiwick, I'm afraid. Jonathan Teller made his choices in life, and now he's reaping the consequences. Besides, you know full well I can't control the police."

"But Teller didn't do anything wrong," Hirsch shouted. "He might be a total crank, but he's not a criminal."

"The authorities beg to differ," Catherine replied. Every set of eyes in the ballroom was glued to the two, witnessing a scene of disruption unparalleled in the club's century-plus history.

"And what's all that nonsense about Nygren cooperating? He's dirtier than anyone in this whole mess. That was you, wasn't it?"

Catherine ignored his question. "It's none of your concern anymore. Herb and I paid you handsomely for your services. I don't see how we owe you anything further—least of all an explanation. I'll have you know, we were planning on offering you a permanent position with the Winslow Group. I can see it was foolish of us to even consider the notion."

"But it's not fucking right! This is sex trafficking and murder we're talking about."

"Who said the first thing about murder, Mr. Hirsch?"

"You know exactly what I'm talking about, Catherine."

"That's quite enough already, Ben," Herb said as he approached and placed a hand on Hirsch's shoulder. Hirsch swatted Herb's hand away.

Catherine leaned towards Hirsch. "I suggest you go back to your little job with the gas company and leave well enough alone. I can make things very unpleasant for you—and those close to you," she hissed.

"What do I have to lose?" Hirsch said as he looked about the room. The haughty disdain emanating from the audience that he'd battled his entire life filled him with shame.

"There he is!" the maître d' squealed while pointing at Hirsch from the ballroom entrance. A pair of uniformed officers from the Marquette Police Department bracketed the man.

"I'm going to expose every goddamn thing you've done, Catherine. Lionel and Marcus were assholes—but they weren't half as evil as you," Hirsch growled, inches away from Catherine's face. "I kept the receipts—the truth will come out."

"I wouldn't make threats," she said as the officers reached Hirsch and grabbed him by his upper arms. "Bother us again and it'll be your face gracing the morning news. Now I suggest you go peaceably with these officers unless you want a long stint in jail."

"Come with us, buddy," the older of the two officers said as they dragged Hirsch away from Catherine. He glanced over his shoulder, where Catherine regarded him with set lips and a steely gaze. The game was up, and resisting would only compound the world of shit he'd already plunged himself into. Thanh the bartender stared at him from behind the bar and shook his head. Hirsch allowed the officers to march him down the staircase with his head hung. A squad car parked directly behind Hirsch's Toyota awaited. The maître d' followed them outside and observed with obvious delight as one officer, reeking of cologne, popped the rear passenger door while the other wrapped Hirsch's wrists in handcuffs behind his back. The cold steel rings cut into his flesh.

"In you go," the officer said as he guided Hirsch's head into the back seat. A stench of vomit mixed with fecal overtones pervaded the cabin, and Hirsch fought back tears and the urge to kick out a window as his frustration boiled over.

He glowered in the back seat as the officers drove him to the local precinct and booked him on charges of aggravated trespassing and malicious destruction of property.

As it was Saturday, no judge was on duty until Monday morning, and he spent the next two days and nights in county lockup. Dressed in a county-regulation orange-and-white striped jumpsuit, Hirsch lay on his bunk with his hands laced behind his head, staring at the graffiti-scrawled ceiling and doing his best to ignore his hick cellmate.

"You get any pussy at least before they threw you in here?" the man asked. Jailed for a drunk driving arrest Friday night, the slurring man glowered at Hirsch. "Fucking prick," he muttered when the latter refused to take the bait.

Sheer embarrassment at his predicament left Hirsch unable to call Lauren, Rachel, or any friend or family member he'd normally reach out to in a crisis. He used his free phone call on Sunday afternoon to dial the one person he could trust in this situation.

"Ben!" Edgar Trehearne answered. "Long time no hear. Look, I'm glad you called. The guys are getting together tomorrow morning for hotcakes at the VFW here in Escanaba. I was think—"

"Edgar," Hirsch interrupted, "I need your help. I'm sitting in lockup at the Marquette County Jail. I need someone to bail me out first thing after arraignment tomorrow morning. Think you could lend a hand?"

"Aww, jeez, Ben, sorry to hear that. Of course I can. Say, don't tell me you went a little wild at the tavern last night. I know I let off some steam a time or two when I was younger, but those were different times, ya know."

"Nah, nothing like that. Honestly, it'd take too goddamn long to explain right now. Meet me at the county courthouse on Baraga and Third around nine tomorrow morning. The hearing shouldn't take long."

"I'll be there, Ben. You can count on me," Edgar said.

"I don't deserve a friend like Edgar," Hirsch muttered as he returned the receiver to the payphone. The armed guard escorted Hirsch to his cell. He stumbled while climbing to his bunk, landing flat on his ass against the concrete floor. His cellmate leered at Hirsch and said, "What's the matter, chief, too much hooch?"

For a split-second, Hirsch lunged at the man, but then restrained himself and resumed his climb. Resigned to another half-day in the pokey, he did his utmost to sleep and make this nightmare pass as quickly as possible.

MONDAY MORNING FOUND HIRSCH standing in his jail-issued jumpsuit before the municipal judge. A court-appointed attorney who looked fresh out of law school with a brush of acne across her chin addressed the judge. She advocated reduced bail for her client considering his clean record and past accomplishments.

"Your honor, Mr. Hirsch is a former attorney and has worked hard after returning home to the U.P. to rebuild his life. This is his first arrest, and he is the definition of a low flight risk," she said.

"I appreciate what you're saying, Miss Wilkinson," the judge said from the dais. "I see in the complaint that Mr. Hirsch is alleged to have illegally remained in a local private club after being asked to leave, damaged club property, and menaced several of the community's upstanding citizens. I also understand the state disbarred Mr. Hirsch for unethical conduct. It hardly seems it's the first time he's bent—if not broken—the law, and I question whether it'll be the last. That said, I don't see much value in holding him without bond. I'm ordering bail set at twenty-five thousand dollars. Entry of plea is in one week's time," the judge concluded and tapped his gavel.

With my luck, the judge probably belongs to the Pioneer Club, Hirsch thought. He glanced towards the gallery, where Edgar sat wearing his usual paint-spattered jeans and ragged T-shirt stretched taut across his ample belly.

"Be back here in one week," Hirsch's attorney said as she leaned towards him. "You know the drill, so I won't give you the usual spiel I give my clients. We'll need to confer at some point on our defense." Attorney Wilkinson had shoulder-length curly brown hair and gave off a sweet fragrance of lilac as they spoke. Hirsch couldn't help but feel a tug of desire despite his predicament. She must have picked up on his interest, as she interrupted her instructions and said, "You listening to me, Mr. Hirsch, or is something bothering you?"

"Loud and clear," he replied, regaining his composure and sitting up straight as a bailiff approached. "I'll be in touch."

"You able to make bail, son, or do I need to put you back inside?" the gruff, heavyset bailiff asked.

"Yeah, my ride's right here," Hirsch said, then turned to the gallery. "Edgar, it's time to roll."

The bailiff removed Hirsch's handcuffs and escorted him and Edgar to a nearby office. Edgar tendered the ten-percent cash bond on Hirsch's behalf. In contrast with Attorney Wilkinson's fresh aroma, Edgar reeked of the hotcakes, fried potatoes, eggs, and sausage he'd gobbled down at the VFW hall before coming to Hirsch's aid.

"Jeepers, Ben, you must be a regular John Dillinger or something the way they talked about you in there. Twenty-five grand ain't pocket change. Guess you'd better show up next week," Edgar said as they exited the Marquette County Jail. The drab, modern structure contrasted markedly with the neighboring historic courthouse, a turn-of-the-century Greek Revival sandstone edifice that was the setting for the quintessential Upper Peninsula film, 1959's *Anatomy of a Murder*.

"I'll pay you back the moment I have the money, Edgar. Seriously, I'm so sorry about all this."

"Oh, I'm not upset about the money . . . it's you I'm worried about. Say, you're not mixed up with those Winslows again, are you?"

Hirsch sighed. "I'll explain it all as soon as I can. Right now, I just need to get my truck, and you can be on your way home. I promise we'll sort all this out over coffee in Escanaba later this week."

Edgar drove Hirsch in his battered Chevy pickup towards the Pioneer Club. Edgar was uncharacteristically quiet.

"Hey, Ed," Hirsch said.

"Yeah, what is it?"

"I need to apologize—I mean, for blowing you off these past couple of months. I did get caught up in business with Catherine and Herb. I pretty much dropped you and everyone else who showed me a lick of kindness after I moved home. You took a bullet for me. I shouldn't have done you this way."

Edgar drove in silence before responding. "You know, Ben, when I was a young man—before joining the gas company and all—I had a job working for an old Scotch forester out of Powers by the name of Marvin McCorkle. We'd spend the day cleaning up cutovers the big logging outfits had left behind and salvaging what scrap timber we could sell to the mills. It was backbreaking, and I'd come home scratched up and stinking of wood smoke. But it was honest work, and Marv paid well enough, all things considered. Maggie and I had a young daughter at the time, and I did a little yardwork on evenings and weekends around town to help make ends meet. One yard I mowed belonged to Henry Stephenson, the owner of the town's papermill.

"Well, Mr. Stephenson, as we always called him, took a shine to me, or so I thought. He promised to pay me double what Marv paid his cutover crew if I came and worked for him as his full-time groundskeeper. I couldn't fathom making that kind of money in those days. With dollar signs in my eyes, I accepted Mr. Stephenson's offer right on the spot with a handshake. I blew off Marv and didn't even give him the courtesy of a phone call to tell him I wouldn't be on the crew come the next day."

"So what happened?"

"Oh, I did mighty well—for a while. Mr. Stephenson had plenty to do around his place, and I became something of a handyman besides clipping his lawn and all. Winter hit, though, and there just wasn't as much for a groundskeeper to do. I'd show up every morning before dawn to shovel his sidewalks and do odd jobs here and there. Around December, as I was replacing one of his storm windows that had come loose in a gale blowing off the bay, Mr. Stephenson stepped outside and called me over. He handed me two weeks' pay in cash and told me my services were no longer required. Seems he didn't need anyone full-time anymore and could just as easily hire some neighbor kid to shovel his walk after it snowed. Later I come to find out he pulled this crap with some poor fool near every year—hired them when there was plenty to do with promises of a big job, then let 'em go midwinter. Been doing it for years.

"Well, I was rightfully out on my ass. Me and the family had some mighty lean months until springtime came and I caught on with the gas company, walking the lines like you've done this past summer. The thing is, months later I ran into Marv McCorkle at this greasy spoon outside Powers. I had on this blue shirt embroidered with the gas-company logo, and Marv sized me up the minute he walked through the door. He was with a couple of the guys I worked with on his crew. I went up to their booth and started to apologize. Marv was an old-school Scotsman and all he did was raise a hand to cut me off and said, 'Trehearne, save it for these lads who worked past nightfall to cover for you. Maybe you'd best join your friends, the Stephensons, if you're looking for a friendly ear.' I had nothing to say to that, and I turned around red-faced and walked right out of the café, my lunch uneaten on the counter.

"My point is, I learned the hard way that the rich and powerful will take any advantage of you they can and toss you aside when you're no longer of use. It sounds like you learned the same hard lesson. I know the feeling, and I'll spare you the shame Marv nailed me with that day in Powers."

"What happened to Mr. Stephenson? Did he ever . . . ?"

"Get his comeuppance?"

"Yeah."

Edgar laughed. "About ten years later, Mr. Stephenson unloaded the mill to a group out of Pontiac. They laid off half the workers and replaced all the well-paid local managers with their own people from downstate. He sold his fancy house and moved with the missus to Florida. I imagine he had a real fine life in the sun and surf. Now, let's see if we can't find that truck of yours."

Edgar drove twice up and down Front Street as they searched for any sign of a battered Toyota Tundra. Hirsch's heart sank—his truck was nowhere to be found.

"Pull over here, Ed," Hirsch said. Edgar slowed at the curb and Hirsch hopped out with his phone in hand. He googled the contact information for the local traffic authority and dialed the number.

"Marquette impound," an impatient voice answered after

half a ring.

"My name's Ben Hirsch. Did you tow a 2006 Toyota Tundra from Front Street between Spring and Baraga this weekend by chance?"

"Give me a sec," the man said as he shuffled through paperwork. "Okay, yep, got it right here. We hauled it over on Saturday."

"Okay, great," Hirsch said. "How do I get it back?"

"It'll be a five-hundred-dollar impound fee plus a two-hundred-fifty-dollar charge for a weekend tow. We charge a fifty-dollar administrative fee for each additional day it's in impound. So, all told we're looking at eight-fifty out the door if you pick it up today. Oh, and there's a three-percent surcharge if you pay by credit or debit."

Hirsch covered the receiver with his free hand and let loose a string of profanity as he paced along the sidewalk. He kicked at a parking meter, which responded with a hollow *dong*.

"Give me a little time, will you?" Hirsch said, composing himself and resuming the call.

"Okay, but just remember—it's fifty dollars each day that goes by. If you don't collect your vehicle within sixty days, we have the legal right to assume title and put it up for sale at auction to cover our costs."

Hirsch ended the call, buried his face in his hands, and took a moment to process the utter shitshow he'd made of his life in the past few weeks. His home in Manistique teetered on the verge of collapse, his one source of dependable income had dried up for the season, he faced multiple criminal charges stemming from his own bullheadedness, and now his sole means of transportation sat behind a razor-wire fence with its ransom growing by the day. With no way of getting back and forth to Marquette for his hearings, he had one remaining option. Hirsch returned to Edgar's Chevy and popped the door.

"Well, what's the trouble now?" Edgar asked.

"Edgar, it looks like I'm going to my sister's."

TWO DAYS FRESH OUT OF JAIL, Hirsch sat at Rachel's kitchen table studying the scheduling order issued by the municipal court. He had an appointment with Ms. Wilkinson that afternoon to review their case in advance of his plea hearing next Monday. Hirsch intended to plead not guilty, but he needed time to figure out how best to outline the Winslows' scheme in a way that might convince a jury to excuse his behavior at the Pioneer Club. The challenge was crafting an explanation that didn't make him sound like an insane conspiracy theorist. His ace in the hole was the hidden hard drive with copies of his report and the Great Lakes Girls archive stashed in his basement. Returning to his law-practice habits, he jotted notes on a yellow legal pad. The back door leading to the kitchen burst open, interrupting his ruminations. Rachel ran inside, out of breath and disheveled.

"Ben, have you talked to Mom?"

"No . . . why?"

"She's been trying to call you all morning." Hirsch's phone was plugged into the charger in Rachel's guestroom, and he'd left the ringer on silent as usual.

"Is she okay? What happened?" Hirsch rose from the table and faced Rachel.

"There was a fire at the house. She's worried sick something happened to you."

"Whoa, whoa, whoa—what do you mean there's a fire?"

"As in, like, the house burned down, Ben. Our childhood home. The fire department in Manistique called her early this morning and told her it was in flames. She thought you were inside."

"This is the last fucking thing we need right now." Hirsch

stumbled around the kitchen, shoving his legal papers into a folder and pulling on his shoes. He ran into the guestroom and retrieved his phone—sure enough, there were a dozen missed calls from Justine and half as many voicemails.

"What's this all about, anyway? First you get arrested; now the house burned down. What's next?" Rachel's eyes pleaded for an explanation as she wiped away tears.

"We don't know the house is gone. Maybe they caught the fire in time. I'm going to do my best to find out what the hell is going on. Can you do me a favor?"

"Okay, what?" Rachel said and sniffled.

"Call Mom and tell her I'm fine and that I'll deal with the house. For God's sake, don't mention anything about me being arrested. I'm headed to Manistique to get to the bottom of this." Hirsch slipped on a jacket and turned towards the door.

Rachel stopped him with a hand on his chest. "Ben, please tell me this doesn't have anything to do with those awful people you're involved with."

"I honestly don't know. Mark my words, though, if they had anything to do with this, they'll pay."

Rachel nodded with downcast eyes. "Go. I'll call Mom."

Hirsch gave his sister a quick peck on the cheek and flew out the door. He jumped into his Toyota. He'd borrowed nine hundred dollars from Rachel the previous day to get his truck out of impound, with a promise to reimburse her. He barreled down the highway, passing trucks and motorhomes with reckless alacrity as he sped through the Hiawatha National Forest. His heart sank as he exited Highway 2 on Range Street and turned right onto Michigan Avenue. A cavalry of emergency response vehicles lined either side of the road in front of Hirsch's home, and wisps of smoke drifted skyward past the trees. He stopped at the end of the previous block and approached the intersection of Steuben and Michigan

Avenue to behold the devastation.

Nothing remained of his childhood home but a smoldering pile of charred wood and building material that had collapsed in on itself and caved into the basement. Two firefighters directed a spray of water from a firehose, striving to douse any remaining embers. Yellow barricade tape surrounded the property, and the fire chief intercepted Hirsch as he lifted the plastic tape over his head and stepped inside.

"This area's off-limits until we get the entire blaze under control. Are you the owner?" the fire chief asked.

"Yeah. I mean, my mom owns the place, but I live here. Any idea what happened?" Hirsch asked as a support beam in the basement gave way, sending a cloud of ash and smoke pluming into the sky.

"Best as we can tell, it caught fire around 5:30 this morning. A neighbor was out for a cigarette, saw smoke pouring out of the windows, and called the fire department." Hirsch glanced over the fire chief's shoulder. Dale Cromley stood in his soiled bathrobe with a Winston Light clasped between his lips, savoring every minute of the action. "Unfortunately, it was too late for us to do anything other than keep it from spreading to the neighbors' houses. Most of these old homes are tinder dry and burn up quick once they catch fire." The fire chief looked at the remains of the conflagration and shook his head.

"Any idea what caused it?" Hirsch asked.

The chief sighed. "Hard to say. We won't know for sure until the state inspector out of the Soo takes a look. Ten to one, I'm guessing it was electrical. Either that or kids playing with matches. Do you know if anyone was inside?"

"No, I'm the only occupant. I was in Marquette visiting my sister."

"Sorry this had to happen to you, sir. These calls are never easy. Say, wasn't this Murray and Justine Hirsch's old place?" the chief asked.

"Yeah, they're my parents."

"I knew your mom when she worked at the hospital. We'd bring in patients for smoke inhalation and burn treatment. Give her my sincere condolences, will you?"

"Uh, sure, I can do that," Hirsch said, still in a daze over the loss of his home, his meager possessions, and his sole copy of the exculpatory evidence in the Dykman case.

The fire chief patted Hirsch's arm and headed towards the pit. He stopped and turned around.

"Hey, there is one bit of good news," he said.

"What's that?" Hirsch couldn't see much of any good in this entire mess.

"The garage survived. That's something . . . I guess."

Behind the house, the weathered garage built in the 1900s for horse and buggy remained unscathed by the flame. Within its sliding doors, the contents included a jumble of scrap wood, holiday decorations, broken household appliances, and other detritus with next to no practical or monetary value whatsoever.

Wonderful, I'm blessed, just blessed, Hirsch thought.

"Yeah, that's something, all right. . ." Hirsch muttered as the chief went to speak with the two firefighters extinguishing the remaining blaze.

Hirsch wandered around his yard until he sensed Dale Cromley's eyes boring into the back of his head. With reluctance, he crossed the street to his neighbor's porch.

"Real shame to see it happen, Ben. I'm glad you're alive, though."

"Thanks for calling it in all the same, Mr. Cromley. The chief told me what you did."

"I stepped out for a cig. Saw smoke pouring out of the back porch near the kitchen. By the time I finished talking with the dispatcher, the flames were in the living room. Wish

I could've caught it quicker, son." Cromley fell into a coughing fit, and it took him a good twenty seconds to recover his breath.

"You did what you could," Hirsch said. "At least no one else's place burned down."

"Did you have some electrical work done lately?"

"No . . . why?"

"It's just that yesterday afternoon I saw a guy wearing a tool belt and a blue hard hat walking away from the house. I don't know how long he was there, but he jumped into this metallic-green Land Rover and drove off. I figured he was from the electric company."

"Yeah . . . could be," Hirsch said as red-hot anger coursed through every fiber of his being. His hands trembled and his lips curled over his teeth in an involuntary display of sheer rage.

"What are you going to do now?" Cromley asked.

"Huh?" Hirsch barked, still consumed by a fury that blinded him to all outside input.

"I just wanted to know what you plan on doing now, Ben. I mean, where will you live and all?"

Hirsch snapped out of his trance and shook his head. "I wish I could say. Head back to my sister's for now, I guess. I gotta go; I'll see you around."

He walked away from Cromley's porch towards his Toyota. He took one more look at the smoldering hole where his home used to be before making a U-turn to return to Marquette.

ONCE BACK IN MARQUETTE, his situation went from bad to worse. Rachel blamed him for the loss of their childhood home and resented his presence, despite her tacit permission for him to remain as a houseguest. He cloistered himself in her guestroom and flipped through a paperback copy of poems by the ill-fated Spanish poet Federico Garcia Lorca. Around 10:00 P.M., wide awake with anguish and guilt, he palmed the last of the three pilfered clonazepam tablets and swallowed them dry. The next eight hours were a dreamless void that brought neither rest nor relief from his predicament. Knowing his presence the next morning would only inflame matters for the time being, he donned his boots and left her house soon after dawn. He walked several blocks down the street until he reached a commercial thoroughfare. A near-empty Denny's beckoned where he could sit alone and gather his thoughts.

"What can I get you, hon?" the waitress asked after he slid into a booth.

"Just coffee. Black, please."

"You sure you don't need a little something to eat? You look like you could use it."

"Maybe later. Just the coffee for now."

"Suit yourself," she replied as she filled his cup from the carafe.

Hirsch sipped the acrid brew with trembling hands. A discarded newspaper on a neighboring table caught his attention. Seeing no one around to claim it, he walked over, picked it up, and drew the front page closer to his eyes.

"Winslow Corporation to Purchase Three-Hundred Acre Parcel for Future Beaver Island Resort," the *Mining Journal* headline read. Three paragraphs down, the article noted: "The Winslows intend to give Teller-compound whistleblower Ellis Nygren a role in managing operations in recognition of his efforts in unraveling recent criminal activities at the compound."

Hirsch flung a five-dollar bill on his table before bolting from the Denny's. He ran the dozen blocks back to Rachel's house. Muffled strains of Mendelsohn's violin concerto emanated from behind the door of Rachel's bedroom. Out of breath, he walked down the hall and tapped on the closed door.

"What now, Ben?" Rachel asked, her voice muffled by a pillow.

"Hey, sis, I need to borrow your car for a day."

Chapter 20

An eerie calm reigned over Sawyer International Airport as Hirsch waited outside the airport's general aviation gate. His sister's ice-blue Subaru Forester made for an innocuous cover given the all-purpose vehicle's ubiquity in the region. Hirsch wore sunglasses and sipped from a Styrofoam cup of gas-station coffee as he profiled each passing vehicle. Near 7:00 A.M., a flame-red Dodge Ram 1500 truck approached the airport's gate. His former and future pilot sat behind the wheel. Hirsch waited five minutes before engaging the Subaru's ignition. When a windowless white Econoline van turned into the side road to the airport's entrance, Hirsch pulled out and made to follow the van.

Despite the placard admonishing drivers against tailgating entering vehicles, Hirsch trailed the van through the gate and entered the airport. He parked the Subaru at the end of the row of pale-blue T hangars. Chris's Dodge Ram was parked midway down the row, and Hirsch crept along the facades towards her hangar. The door stood ajar, and the sound of Chris pre-flighting the Cessna reached his ears. He peeked inside. Chris stood with her back to him, tinkering with an end wrench on the six-cylinder engine. Hirsch stepped through the door and slammed it shut behind him. At the clang of the steel door rattling in the frame, Chris jerked away from the engine and spun around. Hirsch held his .38 Special pointed at Chris's midsection.

"Make one noise and I'll shoot. Drop the wrench," Hirsch said. Chris obliged and the wrench fell to the ground, where it clattered against the painted concrete and came to rest. "Take me to the Winslows," he continued.

"What do you need me for? You know where they live," she said with a strained expression of confusion on her face.

"Cut the shit, Chris. I know about their lodge on the Keweenaw Peninsula. Herb wouldn't miss one last chance to fish the creek before the weather turns to crap."

"You think you're going to waltz right in and ambush them? Catherine told me to call the cops if I saw you."

"That's exactly what's going to happen," Hirsch said, shaking the pistol for emphasis. "You're going to give me a ride; the rest is none of your damn business."

"I'm flying a pair of guests to the Winslows' lodge in an hour. What'll they think if I'm not here to meet them?"

"I guess they'll just have to wait for another time. You have your phone on you?"

"Yeah . . . why?"

"Reach into your pocket real slow and toss it to me."

Chris kept her eyes fixated on Hirsch but inched her right arm down to her back pocket and extracted an Android phone. Her mouth was a thin line of rage and scorn as she tossed the device across the void between them. Hirsch ducked forward to catch it with his left hand. He bobbled and nearly dropped it before securing it in his grasp. He popped out the SIM card, tossed the phone into a corner of the hangar, and snapped the SIM card in two. The card's now-useless fragments fell to the ground, and Hirsch wiped his fingers against the leg of his pants.

"This thing have fuel?" he asked, gesturing at the Cessna with his .38.

"I topped it off yesterday evening."

"Good. I'm going to open the hangar. Don't so much as twitch a muscle or I'll shoot."

Hirsch inched backwards towards the forty-foot-wide by twelve-foot-high folding door that ran nearly the entire length of the hangar. He flipped a steel bar at the center that locked the door in place, then paced to the side where a series of buttons controlled the door's operations. He pushed the green "start" button, and with a whirr of the motor, a metal cable wound and raised the door. Daylight flooded inside the previously dim hangar as the door rose inch by inch. Hirsch fixed his eyes on Chris the entire time with his gun trained on the center of her chest. Once the door reached sufficient height to let the Cessna pass through, he hit the red "stop" button and approached the pilot. On his way, he swiped a spool of duct tape from an open toolbox.

"Get in and strap yourself in," Hirsch ordered.

He waited until she had buckled herself into the left-hand front seat before walking around the plane's nose and popping the passenger door. He folded the co-pilot's seat forward and crawled into the two-person back seat in one fluid motion. Confidence had vanquished his timid movements from his first flight weeks earlier. He slid across the Naugahyde-covered seat and took his place directly behind her.

"What now?" she asked while glaring straight ahead out the cockpit window.

"Take me to Herb and Catherine's. And no funny business with the radio. If you so much as touch the transponder, I'll fire a round through the back of the seat."

"You know hijacking's a federal crime, right?"

"Let me worry about the legal niceties, okay? Now start the goddamn plane and let's get moving. And I'm warning you, if you pull any shit with the engine midflight again, we're both going down because you won't have a chance to start her up."

Hirsch grabbed a headset and slipped it over his ears as Chris primed the engine, turned the ignition key, and brought the six-cylinder, 260-horsepower Continental O-470 motor roaring to life. Hirsch kept the pistol well below the windows, camouflaging it from view of any outsiders. After testing the flight controls, Chris advanced the throttle and the Cessna crawled out from inside the hangar and onto the tarmac.

"How far is it to their airstrip?" Hirsch asked over the intercom.

"About eighty miles. Why?"

"Run it hot."

"I need to contact ground control," Chris said as they reached the end of the row of hangars.

"Go ahead. But I have the gun pressed against the back of the seat. One wrong word and I squeeze the trigger. The Winslows have fucked me and everyone I love so bad I have nothing to lose."

Chris radioed ground control for permission to taxi to the runway. While her voice was uneven, she got the job done. They soon cleared the taxiway and were positioned on the runway facing west for takeoff.

"This is your last chance to call this off," Chris said. "I know Catherine. She won't let you get away."

"Let's do this," Hirsch said.

Chris opened the throttle. The plane initiated its takeoff roll and, in under a thousand feet, the wheels left the ground. Hirsch kept an eye on the instrument panel and her every movement.

"More power," he commanded over the intercom after Chris reduced the throttle upon reaching an altitude of five thousand feet.

"It's bad for the engine to run it that long in the yellow."

"You have a gun to your back and you're worried about the engine?"

Chris's sigh crackled over the microphone, but she reached forward and advanced the throttle to three-quarters of maximum power. The engine responded with a hearty roar, and the airspeed indicator moved from 150 miles per hour to a punishing 185 miles per hour towards the upper limit of the airspeed indicator's yellow zone.

With his purloined chariot clipping across Marquette County at a steady pace, Hirsch reclined into the passenger seat and allowed himself a final moment of relaxation before confronting the Winslows. He almost laughed at the absurdity of the situation. It was as though he were a small-time drug kingpin, pistol in hand, off to challenge the authority of a rival syndicate. A year ago, he'd occupied a nondescript office in Lansing, drafting legal pleadings and doing his utmost to pry money loose from various insurance companies on behalf of his clients. If his old self could see him now, he wouldn't believe the transition.

The forests below were a mélange of oranges, reds, and yellows, as the trees were fully in the grip of their fall transformation. The plane crossed L'Anse Bay and the territory of the L'Anse Indian Reservation inhabited by Hirsch's Lake Superior Chippewa cousins to the west. He had a couple minutes to gaze at the broad expanse of Keweenaw Bay flowing north into greater Lake Superior before the Baraga State Forest swallowed up the view. From there, it was but another dozen minutes before Lake Superior's western shore emerged ahead.

"We're a few minutes out," Chris said over the intercom. "I'm going to begin our descent."

They headed towards what looked to Hirsch like a solid forest wall of tall conifers mixed with hardwood trees. It was only when Chris reduced the power and turned north that a narrow clearing materialized and a ribbon of bright-green grass runway unfurled before them. The landing was rougher than Hirsch's previous experience on the hardtop runways. The aircraft bounced twice before the nosewheel made contact. The airstrip's only structure was a small cabin constructed of logs painted a warm brown with an asphalt shingle roof. A navy-blue golf cart was parked next to the cabin, beneath an awning.

"Pull over there and kill the engine," Hirsch directed, pointing at the cabin.

They stopped in a tie-down area near the cabin. Chris turned off the engine and set the parking brakes. An irregular ticking of the cooling engine replaced the motor's roar. Hirsch stripped the headset off his head and tossed it on the seat.

"Keep your hands on the controls," he said as he popped the passenger door and hopped out. The morning remained cool, and dew clinging to the grass soaked Hirsch's shoes and wetted his pant legs as he walked around the plane's tail. He stuck his .38 in his back pocket and opened the left-hand door. He loosened a fresh strip of duct tape from the roll he'd snatched at the hangar and began wrapping it around Chris's wrists. Methodically, he weaved it through the yoke, fastening her to the controls.

"I hope you're prepared for a long stint in prison, Hirsch," Chris said as he crouched to duct tape each of her ankles to the brackets securing the seat to the cabin floor. He unwound the roll several times around each leg before biting off the tape.

"I'm sorry about this. You got in bed with the wrong people when you went to work for Herb and Catherine. I don't hold it against you—I made the same mistake. The only difference is I knew when to get out."

"Do you even have a plan?" she asked.

"I'll know soon enough. Keep your mouth shut and I won't tape it over. If I hear you hollering, I'll come back. Once this is over, I'll make sure you get home. Now, which way is it to the Winslows' place?"

Chris pointed her nose at a crushed-rock path leading from the airstrip into the forest. "It's a quarter mile down that path," she said. The route was wide enough to accommodate the golf cart, but Hirsch would hoof it on foot.

"Wish me luck," Hirsch said as he shut the door. With the cool weather, he wasn't worried about Chris overheating, but he cracked open the pilot-side window for her comfort. Chris watched him through the 182's green-tinted windshield and shook her head. Whether in dismay or disgust, Hirsch couldn't tell.

Turning his back on the plane, Hirsch walked alongside the gravel-covered path, doing his utmost to minimize the sound of his footfalls against the leaf and pine straw coating the ground. A thousand feet into his walk, the gentle babble of a stream reached his ears. He froze. Crouching, he pointed his pistol at a forty-five-degree angle to the ground as he inched through the heavy brush towards the stream. Amidst the water's delicate song and a chorus of songbirds chattering in the warming morning, the distinct clacking of Herb Winslow's Orvis click-and-pawl fly reel announced his presence on the water. Hirsch fell to his stomach and eased himself forward beneath the brush. He surveyed the scene.

A stand of pine trees shrouded the thin creek from the Winslows' retreat. Crystal-clear water gurgled as it flowed over the river stones. Herb stood alone, calf-deep in the roiling water ten feet ahead, with his back to Hirsch. Rising to his feet, Hirsch approached one pace at a time towards his target, keeping the pistol's iron sight pointed squarely at Herb's back. Herb cradled his split-bamboo fly rod and executed a smooth cast into the shimmering waters in pursuit of brown trout. A wicker creel hung from a strap at Herb's side. A pair of rubbered knee-high waders protected his legs from the creek's chill. He teased the line, making the fly dance across the water's surface as he tugged the slack towards him for another cast.

Hirsch cocked the hammer of his .38 Special. The click rang out even above the steady drone of the water. Herb froze. He held his expensive fly rod in his right hand with a length of line entwined in his left. The rod's quivering tip pointed skyward as Herb abandoned his next cast. He turned his head slightly towards Hirsch and licked his upper lip with a trembling tongue.

"Run or make a fucking noise and I'll blow a hole through your chest," Hirsch said. "Drop the rod."

"It's a six-thousand-dollar handmade bamboo rod, Ben. C'mon, now."

"Do you really want to drown with it?"

Herb sighed and dropped the rod. It splashed into the river. The current carried it downriver before it vanished below the surface. A grimace of agony contorted Herb's face as his eyes followed the loss.

"Now walk backwards towards me with your hands raised."

Herb Winslow did as Hirsch directed, nearly stumbling over the slick stones before exiting the water and backing up towards Hirsch on dry land. Beads of water trickled down Herb's dark-green waders.

"You could've just knocked at the front door, you know."

"Yeah, so one of your goons could rub me out as an intruder. Now shut the fuck up and do as I say."

Hirsch grasped the back of Herb's handstitched leather belt and yanked the man close to him. He jammed the pistol's muzzle into the base of Herb's skull.

"Walk," he commanded. Herb's shuddering sent quivers through the pistol's heavy steel. They made their way through the forest grove and across the lawn towards the towering lodge constructed of thick pine logs stained golden brown.

"Open it," Hirsch commanded as they approached a side entrance to the lodge. The solid-core white-oak door swung open without a sound.

"Lead me to Catherine," Hirsch said after they stepped inside. He shut the door behind them.

They walked down a hallway clad from floor to ceiling in aged, expensive hardwood. Lining the walls on both sides were black-and-white photographs of the Winslows of yesteryear. While most depicted bucolic scenes of upper-class leisure and sport, one oversized image captured the Winslow patriarch, C. F. Winslow, clad in a three-piece tweed suit and glowering in front of the half-constructed retreat in which they now stood. C. F.'s eyes seemed to follow them, as if expressing stern disapprobation over Hirsch's actions.

The hallway terminated into a cavernous sitting room at the center of the lodge. High wooden crossbeams a solid foot in diameter soared above them, and a bank of tall picture windows and French doors looked out over the windward stretch of the Keweenaw Peninsula onto Lake Superior. A steady wind raised whitecaps on the water's surface. As they entered the sitting room, Catherine Winslow looked up from where she sat in an overstuffed leather chair reading a slim volume cradled in her hands. She dropped the book to the floor upon seeing her husband with a gun pressed to the back of his head. It landed with a thud against a priceless Baluchi rug.

"Herb!" she exclaimed as she rose halfway to her feet.

"Sit," Hirsch ordered Catherine as he jammed the muzzle deeper into the base of her husband's skull for emphasis.

"This is thoroughly out of line, Mr. Hirsch," she said but

nonetheless followed Hirsch's command and sank into the leather chair.

"It was out of line when you had Professor Teller arrested. It was out of line when you burned down my house. This is justice."

"How'd you even get here?"

"Chris flew me in. She's back at the airstrip but won't be going anywhere."

A movement to Hirsch's left caught his attention. Alexandra Winslow sat in a corner opposite Catherine wearing yoga pants and a hooded Stanford sweatshirt. She held a smartphone and had wireless earbuds jammed into both ears. She bobbed her head to a tune unheard by the other three. Alex tapped away at the phone, oblivious to the insanity playing out around her.

"Well, at least you got your daughter back," Hirsch said.

"Mr. Hirsch, this is all rather unnecessary," Catherine replied. "Put the gun down, let my husband go, and we can talk it over."

"Forget it," Hirsch said as he tightened his grip on Herb's belt and trousers, drawing a wince from the trembling man. "And tell Alex to take her goddamn headphones out."

Catherine glowered but waved in Alex's direction to get her attention. "Alex, dear, turn that off for a minute, will you?"

Alex looked up, surprised to see her father held at gunpoint. A tinny sound of rhythmic Techno music played from her earbuds after she plucked them out.

"Dad, what the hell?" Alex said, then shifted her eyes to Hirsch. "Wait—I remember you . . . from Manitou. Wha . . . what are you doing here?"

"Your parents got Prophet Teller arrested, Alex. They tricked me and everyone involved. I've had enough of their bullshit."

"Don't listen to this man, honey," Catherine said to her daughter. "He's a disgruntled former employee who's very dangerous. He's obviously lost his mind."

"All you wanted was Teller's property. Sure, you may have wanted your daughter back in the beginning, but once you found out the Dykmans were involved, you couldn't pass up the opportunity to screw over Teller and steal his land," Hirsch said.

"Hold on—what? You got Jonathan arrested, Mom!? How could you do this to us?" Alex said, her face contorted with hurt and rage.

"That horrible man took advantage of you, dear. Your Dad and I have always wanted what's best for you." Turning to Hirsch, Catherine continued, "Jonathan Teller signed a buy-sell agreement on his three hundred acres last week. Seems his dalliance with the Dykmans left him in desperate need of legal fees. We were only happy to step in and help under the circumstances."

"But why? Don't you have enough land as it is right here?" Hirsch asked, gesturing with the barrel of his gun around the lodge's great room.

"Those three hundred acres will form the core of our latest business initiative—an all-inclusive deluxe resort catering to high-end travelers from across the country. We've even filed a permit for direct ferry service from the mainland. Oh, and a private runway for our executive guests. Just imagine it—a twenty-four-hour spa, mini-golf for the kids, kayak and canoe rentals so guests can paddle around that lovely little lake right in the middle of it all. Of course, I can't imagine *you*'ll be able to afford staying there anytime soon."

The thought of Teller's pastoral spread of forestland and lakeshore despoiled by roving hordes of tourists and vulgar rich made Hirsch's blood boil. Alex moaned with her face in her hands as the scope of her parents' betrayal became clear.

"What about Ellis Nygren? He was the muscle behind the Dykmans' operation; he killed that girl. Why isn't he sitting in shackles instead of Teller?" Hirsch asked.

"Wait—killed? What girl?" Alex said, raising her tear-streaked face from her hands.

"Not now, Alex," Catherine replied.

"I really do think now is the time to explain," Hirsch said.

Catherine sighed. "After we perused your well-written summary, we approached Captain Nygren and offered him a deal. Either he turn state's witness and help take down both Teller and his employers, or we'd ensure he spent the rest of his life behind bars in Jackson State Prison for murder and sex trafficking. We were so impressed with his eagerness to work with us and how he'd kept that entire camp in line for months, we offered to keep him on as an employee at the Manitou Spirit Resort and Suites. In fact, he's here now onboarding as our new chief of security."

"The Manitou Spirit—" Hirsch was too angry to even finish repeating the name.

"Catchy, isn't it?" Herb said, earning him a stiff jab in the carotid with the muzzle of Hirsch's pistol.

"You fucking lied to me," Hirsch said to Catherine. "Both of you," he continued and jammed the .38 muzzle deeper into Herb's neck.

"You killed my brother," Catherine replied.

"So, what, we're even now?"

"In a manner of speaking. Shame you won't live to see it all come to be."

"Which one of us has the gun?"

"Don't be daft, Hirsch. You really think we don't have cameras all over this place? Captain Nygren will be here any minute. Yes, the death of a burglar and extortionist will make the news, I suppose, but I doubt anyone's going to give a rat's ass that a disbarred and broke former attorney is dead."

"What about your husband?"

"Yeah, honey, what about me?" Herb asked, glancing from his pistol-wielding captor to his wife, who sat across the room with a placid expression.

"Herb, please tell me you wore that bullet-proof vest I gave you last week?"

"No . . . not right now. You know how heavy that damn thing is when I'm out on the water?" Sweat poured off Herb's brow and trickled down his face, dripping onto Hirsch's hand and the .38 gripped within.

"Oh, Herb," Catherine replied. She picked up a saucer and teacup from an end table beside her chair and sipped from it with her eyes still on her crestfallen husband. The sliver of ice in Catherine's heart outstripped the malevolence of her late brother Marc's psychopathy.

Their opportunity for further dialogue vanished when a tall, rangy man with sandy hair and wearing a black turtleneck over charcoal trousers entered the great room from a side passageway. Hirsch recognized him as Ellis Nygren from his physique and bearing alone. Ellis leveled a Glock 19 9mm semi-automatic pistol at Hirsch and his captive.

"Captain Nygren, just in time," Catherine said.

"Let Mr. Winslow go and drop the piece, buddy," Ellis commanded in a sonorous baritone as he locked eyes with Hirsch.

"Fuck you," Hirsch retorted. He backed towards the hallway with Herb Winslow in tow.

"I'm warning you, I'll put a round through your head if you don't give this up," Ellis continued, racking a cartridge into the chamber for emphasis.

"At least I'm a grown-ass man you're aiming at this time, not some scared college girl."

"What are your orders, ma'am?" Ellis asked Catherine without breaking his steady gaze at Hirsch.

"Take him out," she replied.

"What about your husband?"

"Aim well!"

Ellis Nygren's face flushed red with adrenaline and concentration as he steadied his weapon and took aim.

"Don't shoot him!" Alex screamed as she bolted from her seat and dove across the room. She crashed into Ellis as he squeezed the trigger.

A deafening pop echoed throughout the cavernous room as Ellis and Alex tumbled to the ground. The 9mm hollow-point round caught Herbert Winslow square in his head. His skull exploded, sending a shower of viscera and bone fragments all over Hirsch, the wall behind him, and the parquet hardwood floor beneath. An earsplitting scream erupted from Alex Winslow as she clobbered Ellis about his head with closed fists. The sound of the gunshot reverberated against the wooden ceiling. Hirsch added to the chorus of screams as he flung Herb's body away from him. The stench of cordite and an indescribable odor that Hirsch intuitively knew was Herb's blood nearly made him retch. Across the room, Ellis escaped from Alex's clutches and struggled to his feet. "You fucking bastard," Alex hissed between sobs. Hirsch turned to run down the hall towards the exit that offered his only chance at escape.

Herbert Winslow had saved Hirsch's life. He slipped on the slick hallway floor and fell. Sharp fragments of bone cut into his bare forearms as he slammed into the ground. Two shots fired in quick succession filled the void where Hirsch had stood a split-second earlier. He crawled along the floor by his elbows. He wiped one eye clean with his free hand and reached back across his body to take a shot at Ellis. With a squeeze of the trigger, the .38 went off with a pop—a higher timbre than the 9mm rounds fired from Ellis's Glock.

The slug found its mark, and Ellis Nygren doubled over

and howled in agony as he grabbed his right knee. A sheet of red oozed over his hand, and the disgraced ex-Army officer collapsed to the floor when his leg folded beneath him. Hirsch seized the opportunity to stumble to his feet and zigzag down the remaining hallway until he burst out the door into the sunlight of the late September day.

Hirsch ran at full speed away from the Winslows' cabin towards the shore of Lake Superior. While fully awaiting pursuit by one or more of Catherine's heavies, he reached the water's edge unmolested. He paused and glanced back. A maimed Ellis Nygren limped out of the lodge, headed for the pathway leading to the airstrip. Blood flowing from his wounded knee darkened the lower leg of his trousers. Hirsch continued north along the shoreline, running for his life with what energy he could summon. Struggling for breath, he collapsed on his knees into the stone and pebble-strewn beach. A bewildered fisherman took one glance at Hirsch's bloody, viscera-streaked face, screamed, and dropped his fishing tackle before bolting in a dead run down the beach towards a nearby resort. Hirsch gripped his father's .38 Special tight in his right hand, the muzzle still warm from the fired shot. While the polished-nickel instrument had once enchanted him, the sight of it now engendered only revulsion as he examined its blood-flecked frame. Once Hirsch recovered his breath, he stood, reared back, and flung the pistol with all his might into the churning waves of the lake. It cartwheeled end over end before disappearing into the water with a splash of foam. Two men had died at his hands since that gun came into his possession; he had no desire to increase that toll.

Hirsch crawled to the water's edge and immersed his entire head into the lapping waves, doing his best to wash the mess away as he splashed water on his neck and over his arms. Rising to his feet, Hirsch made his way to the resort a half mile up-shore and dialed the Ontonagon County Sheriff's Office.

"Sheriff's Office. How may I direct your call?"

"My name's Ben Hirsch. I'm at the Aspen Tree Resort. I've got a story you have to hear to believe."

Epilogue

Winter arrived as Hirsch rolled through Raco along Highway 28 towards the Soo. His Toyota Tacoma shuddered in the wind as a gale off Whitefish Bay plunged the temperature into the mid-thirties. A band of precipitation moving across Lake Superior out of Ontario sent snow flurries swirling across the road. A passing westbound semi-truck sent up a whirlwind that momentarily obscured Hirsch's view. He cranked his heater and grasped the wheel with both hands to steady it along the narrow two-lane highway. The wind and slick road surface resurrected all the challenges of winter driving and heralded a preview of the coming six months. Nonetheless, the white-knuckle drive from Marquette to the Soo gave him ample opportunity to rehash the aftermath of his entanglement with the Winslows.

The days following his ambush of their Keweenaw Peninsula lodge were a blur of exhaustion, conversations with state and local officials, and fitful attempts at sleep only to be jerked awake by apparitions of Herbert Winslow's exploding head replaying in his brain. Following Hirsch's initial interview with the Ontonagon sheriff that afternoon, an investigator took pity on him and gave Hirsch a ride back to Marquette. He crashed at his sister's house and slept for an unsettled twenty hours. The following weeks witnessed him mired in additional law enforcement interviews and formal hearings. While the sheriff and representatives from the Michigan State Police initially viewed Hirsch's story with great skepticism, two unlikely allies emerged to corroborate it—Winston Maki and Alexandra Winslow.

Alex couldn't forgive her parents for their behavior towards her beloved Prophet Teller. She put the blame for her father's death squarely on her mother and Ellis Nygren. In the end, the Ontonagon County Attorney declined to charge Hirsch for taking Herb Winslow hostage. While Ellis now faced indictment for Herb's and BreAnn's deaths, the disgraced Army captain was nowhere to be found. Also missing in the aftermath was Chris and her Cessna. Air traffic control records indicated the plane had departed the Winslows' airstrip shortly after Hirsch reached the Aspen Tree Resort but disappeared from radar over Lake Superior. Hirsch could only speculate that Nygren had hobbled to the airstrip, freed Chris, and offered her a sweetheart deal to fly them to Canada where they could vanish into new lives.

After learning of Herb's death, Winston shed his remaining loyalty to the Winslows and offered up Hirsch's bonanza of evidence exonerating Prophet Teller. The findings freed Jonathan Teller from the Charlevoix County Jail, where he'd been held pending trial, but his legal fees nonetheless compelled him to put his Beaver Island land up for sale again after the agreement with the Winslows collapsed. A group of investors from Battle Creek won the bidding war, and the islanders were rife with speculation on the group's plans for the three-hundred-acre parcel. Hirsch had little doubt some variation on the Manitou Spirit Resort lay in store.

It wasn't all bad news for Prophet Teller. With the ample money inherited from her father's estate, Alex purchased a two-thousand-acre ranch in northwest New Mexico. At last report, High Priestess Alexandra and the new King Strang were in the process of once again rebuilding the kingdom of heaven on earth—this time in an isolated corner of the American Southwest.

Dogged coverage of the proceedings by local journalists led to a series of articles in Marquette's *Mining Journal* chronicling the sordid mess from top to bottom. A front-page article featured an image of Hirsch clad in suit and tie, testifying before the Marquette County circuit court regarding the Winslows' scheme from start to finish. The result left Catherine Winslow's reputation in tatters. While county prosecutors were undecided about filing criminal charges related to her machinations, her disgrace compelled her to issue a terse resignation from the university board of trustees. Claiming to be overcome by grief, she departed Marquette for the family condominium in Fort Myers, Florida, and declined all inquiries from the media.

Hirsch did have to pay his debt to society for his altercation at the Pioneer Club. Attorney Wilkinson convinced him to plead guilty to one misdemeanor count of disturbing the peace. In atonement for his transgressions, Hirsch spent eighty hours clad in an orange vest collecting trash along Highway 41 with a group of fellow lawbreakers.

After reaching the Interstate 75 interchange, Hirsch made the short drive up the freeway, exited at 3 Mile Road, and headed for the Sugar Island ferry. The trees lining the shore had shed their leaves, and the north wind churned the waters of the St Marys River into menacing whitecaps. The ferry ride from the mainland to Sugar Island was mercifully short. Hirsch paid twenty dollars for passage, drove aboard the blue-hulled watercraft, and parked atop the deck. Only a handful of other motorists joined him this morning, and with a blow of the whistle, they were underway for the fleeting crossing.

Upon reaching the Sugar Island terminal, Hirsch alighted onto 1-1/2 Mile Road and drove to Uncle Henry's rambling house midway across the island. Henry's nephews, nieces, and a handful of neighbor children ran about the yard, kicking a soccer ball back and forth towards two makeshift goals. All were bundled up in bright-colored winter coats against the chill of the November day. Their game ground to a halt, and they watched Hirsch with curiosity as he pulled into the gravel driveway and parked alongside Uncle Henry's Buick LeSabre. Uncle Henry stepped out onto the porch as Hirsch exited his vehicle and waved to the gaggle of children. Henry wore his blue jeans and well-worn tweed jacket, and he grinned from ear to ear at his nephew's arrival.

"Welcome back, Ben!" Uncle Henry said as he clomped down the weathered front-porch steps and embraced his nephew in a bear hug. "Tell me you're here to stay for a while this time."

"Well, is your offer still open?"

"You're just in time. Trouble's rolled in from downstate. They're putting the squeeze on our casinos. The tribe needs a hand like you wouldn't believe."

"That seems to be my specialty as of late," Hirsch said.

Uncle Henry laughed. "Come inside, nephew. We don't have a moment to lose."

Henry wrapped his long arm around Hirsch's shoulders and escorted him inside the house. His career as the Michilimackinac Tribe's fixer awaited.

About the Author

Nathan Shore is an attorney and labor relations professional. He lives in Saint Paul, Minnesota, with his wife and Siamese cat. He is the author of *The Blue Flame*.